The Barred Window

ANDREW TAYLOR

PENGUIN BOOKS

Pe
Penguin C   1P 2Y3

Penguin Group (Australia), 250 Camberwell Road, Camberwell, Victoria 3124, Australia
(a division of Pearson Australia Group Pty Ltd)
Penguin Books India Pvt Ltd, 11 Community Centre, Panchsheel Park, New Delhi – 110 017, India
Penguin Group (NZ), 67 Apollo Drive, Rosedale, North Shore 0632, New Zealand
(a division of Pearson New Zealand Ltd)
Penguin Books (South Africa) (Pty) Ltd, 24 Sturdee Avenue, Rosebank, Johannesburg 2196, South Africa

Penguin Books Ltd, Registered Offices: 80 Strand, London WC2R 0RL, England

www.penguin.com

Published by Sinclair Stevenson 1993
Published in Penguin Books 2007

3

Copyright © Andrew Taylor, 1993
All rights reserved

The moral right of the author has been asserted

Set in 11.75/14 pt Monotype Garamond
Typeset by Rowland Phototypesetting Ltd, Bury St Edmunds, Suffolk
Printed in England by Clays Ltd, St Ives plc

ISBN: 978-0-141-02766-1

www.greenpenguin.co.uk

PENGUIN BOOKS

The Barred Window

'Taylor is a major talent' *Time Out*

'The most underrated crime writer in Britain today'
Val McDermid

'The master of small lives write large' Frances Fyfield

'An excellent writer' *The Times*

'Andrew Taylor is a master storyteller' *Daily Telegraph*

'A sophisticated writer with a high degree of literary
expertise' *New York Times*

'As Andrew Taylor triumphantly proves . . . there is still
room for excellence' *Irish Times*

'Like Hitchcock, Taylor pitches extreme and gothic
events within a hair's breadth of normality'
The Times Literary Supplement

'What's rare and admirable in Taylor's fiction is his painterly
and poetic skill in transforming the humdrum into something
emblematic and important' *Literary Review*

For Diana

One

'Do you believe in magic?' Esmond once asked me.

Assumptions are a sort of magic: spells to make sense of life or at least to make it tolerable. For example, I assumed that after my mother's death and the return of Esmond I should live happily ever after like a prince in a fairy tale. One man's magic is another's rational assumption and a third man's wishful thinking.

I lived happily ever after from my mother's funeral in May, when Esmond came back, until the end of September when I had my first intimation that something might be going wrong. At the time I was listening to Esmond and Bronwen, who were talking in the sitting room.

When eavesdropping, I always took the precaution of putting something on the floor. On the afternoon in question I lifted my book, a selection of Lorca's poems, from the seat of the chair and laid it on the carpet. No one had ever come in while I was on my knees but one day someone might; you couldn't be too careful, not where my cousin Esmond was concerned.

'I've just dropped my book,' I would say. Or my glasses or my pencil. 'Silly old me.'

The chair was a barrier between me and the door. There was a twinge of pain in my left knee and I felt very dizzy. I remember thinking that I was getting too old for crawling around on floors. I was forty-eight, which I know isn't really old. Most people would call it middle age. But I think that there was a moment in 1967 when I leapfrogged from being a young man to being an old one. I am as old as I feel.

I rolled back the corner of the carpet to expose a triangular section of broad oak floorboards. Part of a floorboard had been replaced by a fifteen-inch length of unvarnished pine. The carpenter hadn't bothered to nail it on to the joists beneath.

I levered out the rectangle of wood with my fingertips. A spider sprinted away from the light. The bottom of the hole beneath was lined with wood-shavings and fragments of plaster. Tendrils of dust stirred like the grey seaweed in Blackberry Water. The hole was my private place. No one else knew about it. I kept private things there. Also, of course, I used it for listening.

I had not imagined the murmur of voices below: the other two really were in the sitting room. As a general rule they used this room only in the evenings. Still on my knees, I bent forwards with my head to one side so that my right ear was in the gap between the joists. The draught brushed my cheek.

'Has Rumpy had his walk?' my cousin Esmond asked.

'Oh, for God's sake stop trying to change the subject,' Bronwen said.

'You're making too much of this. Trust me.'

A spoon clinked and scraped on china. I guessed that Bronwen was stirring sugar into her coffee. It was entirely typical that she used the spoon as a pestle and the cup as a mortar.

'Had you any idea this was going to happen?' she said. 'You must have done.'

'It was always a remote possibility. No more than that.'

'You should have warned me.'

'Why? What good would it have done?'

'I like to know what I'm getting into, that's why.' When Bronwen was really angry, as opposed to merely tetchy, her voice grated like a grindstone on the blade of a knife. 'If you really want to know, I think you've been bloody stupid.'

'Calm down. We've got plenty of options.'

'If you ask me, it's time for us to –'

'Oh, I wouldn't do anything rash,' Esmond interrupted. 'Not if I were you. Is there any more coffee?'

'What do you mean?'

'Oh, you know. Thomas and I used to have a motto when we were children.' Esmond raised his voice and chanted: '*All* for *one*, and *one* for *all*. United we *stand*, divided we *fall*.'

'You bastard.'

I smiled.

After a moment Esmond went on: 'As a matter of fact, I think we've been rather lucky.'

'Are you insane?'

'Think of it like this,' Esmond said patiently. 'It's not so much a problem as an opportunity. But you haven't answered my question. Has Rumpy had his walk?'

'It goes on and bloody on.'

Esmond ignored this. 'I fed him this morning,' he said. 'He's got a good appetite for his age, hasn't he? But he also needs exercise. It's good for him.'

'Woof,' Bronwen said. 'Woof bloody woof. He can't enjoy life, can he? We should have him put down.'

3

'Rumpy? Oh no . . . it wouldn't be the same without Rumpy. You know that as well as I do.'

'He won't last for ever,' returned Bronwen. 'In my opinion, he's getting senile practically by the minute.'

'Aren't we all?'

'And sometimes he smells.'

'Nobody's perfect, dearest,' Esmond said.

I replaced the board over the hole and the carpet over the board. A moment later I was sitting on the window-seat with the book open on my lap. The sky was lined with banks of grey cloud; but between the banks were shreds of pale blue. Perhaps the weather was clearing. There were two cats in the garden.

The first of them was a regular visitor to Finisterre – an old black-and-white tom with a torn ear and a limp. The second was a new one; she was a young tabby, about half the size of the tom and far more cautious. And she was beautiful. I hated her more than the tom because in the nature of things she had longer to live.

I rapped on the window. If the tom heard the sound, he ignored it. Like all old cats he had long since come to the conclusion that he was invincibly superior to the rest of animate creation. The tabby had the grace to stop and glance round; but when she failed to identify the source of the rapping, she too decided that it was safe to ignore it.

I stayed on the window-seat for nearly an hour. The cats made cautious forays across the lawn. As far as I could tell their base was in the shrubbery; they were ignorant of what lay beneath them. If there was one thing I missed from my old life, it was my ability to deal with the cats.

The sun came out for the first time in three days. It streamed across the sea and up the garden. The stepping stones across Blackberry Water gleamed like tiny metal studs. The blues and greens were so vivid that they hurt the eyes. The sun threw the shadows of the window bars across the carpet.

I counted the shadows. There were six bars and therefore six shadows, just as there had always been for as long as I could remember.

At four-thirty, Bronwen came into my room empty-handed. I was expecting my cup of tea. She never knocked; but she never took me by surprise either, because she made so much noise as she approached.

I coughed and looked at her in what I hoped was a meaningful way. 'Oh, I thought it was teatime.'

'Esmond says you're to have it with him today,' Bronwen said. 'He wants you in the study.'

I blinked at her. She was a big woman with coarse, dark hair and firm, almost conical breasts. The hair came down to her shoulders and smelled faintly musty. She favoured tight jerseys and short skirts. In Welsh, Bronwen means 'white breast'; but I imagine hers were sallow-skinned and perhaps hairy round the nipples.

'In – in the study?'

'That's right. Come on, I haven't got all day.'

As usual, surprise made me dither and dithering made me panic. I couldn't remember where I had left my jacket; Bronwen found it on the back of the door. I wanted to comb my hair but my hand shook so much that I had to give up the unequal struggle to produce a straight parting. When I mentioned my need for a clean handkerchief, she grabbed my left arm just above the elbow and pulled me to the door.

'For Christ's sake,' she said. 'It's only Esmond.'

She led me across the landing and down the stairs. Her thumb and first two fingers dug into my skin between the muscle and bone of my upper arm. In the hall, there were Michaelmas daisies in white vases. At the foot of the stairs, Bronwen released my arm and prodded me gently on the shoulder, as though urging forward a reluctant child. Her capacity for unexpected gentleness always disconcerted me.

I crossed the hall slowly – almost with pleasure. The sunlight poured slantwise through the fanlight above the front door. Esmond had had the floorboards stripped and returned to their natural colour, and he had brought a pair of Turkish rugs from London. Together with the glaring white of the vases and the pinks and purples of the Michaelmas daisies, the place was full of colour. *Mine eyes dazzle*, I thought. An irritatingly familiar quotation from somewhere: for the moment I could not remember the rest of it, but suddenly I was no longer happy. I knocked on the study door, and Esmond told me to come in.

He was standing by the window. With the light behind him he looked half his age. He was tall, with broad shoulders and slim hips. His hair was as thick as when I had first met him, and the few grey streaks seemed a sign of distinction rather than age. When I was with Esmond I felt smaller, older and uglier than usual: he always had the power to make me feel that I belonged to an inferior species. As a boy, I had never

6

minded. I think I was flattered that Esmond should condescend to associate with me.

'I want you to write a letter,' he said. 'Sit down. We'll have tea afterwards.'

He nodded towards the desk. I sat down behind it in the green leather armchair. The seat was warm from his body. A sheet of writing paper lay on the blotter. I uncapped my fountain pen, which by a lucky chance was in my jacket pocket, and tried it surreptitiously on the blotter. It still had ink in it. I glanced at Esmond to see if he had noticed.

His hands in his pockets, he was staring out of the window. I waited, rolling the pen between my thumb and forefinger. The paper had once been white but had yellowed with age particularly around the edges. I remembered my mother ordering a ream of this letter-head from a printer in Kinghampton. *Finisterre, Ulvercombe, North Cornwall.* No telephone number of course – the telephone had been one of Esmond's innovations.

At first I had no objection to waiting. I liked being with Esmond and I liked being in the study. It was a well-proportioned room and it was pleasant to see it freshly decorated and the furniture gleaming with polish. In the old days, before my mother stopped using the study, she did the household accounts once a month sitting in this chair at this desk.

I waited for so long that I began to wonder if Esmond had forgotten me. That was when I really did stop enjoying myself. When I was young I used to have nightmares about Esmond's forgetting me; I still did, though less often. There were several variations on the theme. Sometimes, in the dream, I would walk into a familiar room – the nursery, perhaps, or our classroom at Bicknor College – and he would be there. My heart would jump at the sight of him – an unpleasantly physical sensation, as though the heart were literally trying to tear itself out of my chest. But Esmond's face wouldn't light up with pleasure at the sight of me, or even with recognition. He would look puzzled and irritated by the interruption: that was all. It was as if I were a perfect stranger who had no right to be there.

Sometimes in the dream he wouldn't even notice me coming in. Sometimes he would be with someone else, a friend. He would laugh at me, as we children laughed at cripples and anyone with a physical disability. All the different versions amounted to the same thing. The point was that Esmond had forgotten that we were cousins and friends: that he saw me objectively, with the cool and unbiased eyes of a stranger.

'It's the 30th September,' he said.

I wrote down the date. Esmond turned away from the window. He wandered across the room to the cupboard that filled the lower half of the alcove on the left of the fireplace. There was a row of directories on the cupboard. He ran an index finger along their tops and examined the fingertip as if checking for dust.

'My dear Alice,' he went on, still staring at his finger.

I waited, pen poised. '*Alice?*'

'Yes.'

'*Our* Alice?' Somehow I could not bring myself to say 'my'.

He nodded. 'Trust me.'

I wrote.

'Thank you for your letter. I was sorry to hear about your marriage. Of course I'm not upset by your suggestion that we meet.'

'Could you slow down, please?' I asked. The nib scratched on the paper and my fingers ached.

'New paragraph,' he said after a decent pause. 'However, I am not in the best of health.' I glanced sharply at Esmond, who still wasn't looking at me. 'I live very quietly down here with my cousin Esmond and his wife Bronwen. My doctor advises me to avoid travel – and indeed any excitement. So, in the circumstances, I must decline your kind invitation to come up to London.'

After 'excitement', I stopped writing and murmured, '"Decline your kind invitation . . . ?"'

'What's wrong with it?'

'Would I say that? It's a bit formal, isn't it? A bit pompous.'

'What do you suggest?'

'How about, "So I'm afraid my coming up to London is out of the question"?'

'All right. Well done.' He waited while I wrote the amended sentence, and then continued with the letter: 'But it would give me great pleasure if you could come here for a few days. It would give us all a chance to get to know each other.'

'No,' I said. 'Please, Esmond – I don't think I could bear it.'

He frowned at me. I wrote down what he had said.

'Esmond or I will phone you,' he went on, 'in a day or two. With best wishes . . .' He paused. 'Yours truly, Thomas Penmarsh. That's all. You'll find an envelope in the second drawer down on the right.'

I opened the drawer. 'I don't understand.'

'You don't need to understand.' Esmond strolled to the desk. He picked up the letter and glanced through its contents. 'Trust me, eh?'

I took out an envelope. Before I shut the drawer, I noticed a bunch of small keys, some with rust-streaked labels. Almost certainly the cupboard key would be among them. Esmond dictated the name and address – a private hotel in Earls Court.

'Not an address that inspires confidence,' he said as he sealed the envelope. 'Come on. We'll have our tea in the sitting room.'

I felt myself flushing. I was embarrassed, and a little angry. 'Do you think I might read her letter?'

'Better not. Leave it to me. I don't want you to worry about it.'

'She might not like what we've done here. Shouldn't we have asked her permission?'

Esmond squeezed my shoulder. 'You mustn't worry so much. I'll take care of everything. That's why I'm here, remember?'

He dropped the letter into a drawer and moved towards the door. I stood up. In my haste to follow, I jarred my thigh against the corner of the desk.

'If you must know,' Esmond said, 'I think she's a bit strapped for cash. She's not looking for love, she's looking for a nice fat cheque.'

'Did she actually –?'

'You could read it between the lines.' He opened the door and glanced over his shoulder. 'It's a hard world out there. Lucky you've got me to look after you.'

The sitting room was a large room with windows to

the south-west and the north-west. The tea tray was waiting for us on the table behind the sofa. I noticed with pleasure that there was a big plate of biscuits; I have a sweet tooth. We used the Crown Derby service. Only two cups had been put out, which suited me very well. It was quite a treat for me to have Esmond to myself – almost like old times.

He was no longer in a talkative mood. Having poured the tea, he sat in the big wing-armchair and stared at the fire. The new central-heating system at Finisterre was very efficient; but it wasn't cold enough to use it during the day, and in any case Esmond liked a proper fire.

I wondered if I had offended my cousin. I bolted down three Bourbon biscuits and drank the first cup of tea while it was too hot. The changes in routine had unsettled me. That and the news of Alice.

'A penny for them,' Esmond said.

'What? Oh, nothing.'

'Tell me.'

I scratched my bald patch. I had always found it difficult to lie to Esmond. 'I – I was wondering what she was like,' I said.

'Alice? We know she's mercenary. That's all that matters.'

'Yes, of course. I do see that. It's just that I'm naturally curious about her.'

'Naturally?'

'She's my daughter.'

'You're not the only one who's curious,' he said. 'No doubt it runs in the family. If you must know, she asked a few questions in her letter.'

I noticed that there was a tiny chip on the rim of my cup. My mother would have been furious. I heard the distant whine of the chain saw: Bronwen was busy – sawing seemed to give her pleasure. Someone nasty in the woodshed. My head began to throb and hum. I wished Alice were dead, like all the others.

'Questions? What about?'

Esmond took his time over lighting a cigarette. 'She wanted to know all about her mother, her real mother, that is. I think she may have heard something.'

I put down my cup, and stared at the sleeve of my jacket. I had lost a button from the cuff. In places the tweed was shiny with age and grease. My headache was much worse.

'Don't worry so much,' Esmond said, and his voice sounded far away but full of irritation. 'I'll look after you. You're quite safe.'

I shrugged.

'What you need is a bit of fresh air to blow those blues away.' He smiled and clicked his tongue twice against the roof of his mouth. 'Come on, Rumpy,' he said to me. 'Walkies.'

Two

Sometimes I dream of Alice lying on her bed at Finisterre. I see just her head and shoulders. She lies face up. Her eyes are open. They are nothing like her mother's. (How strange to think of Lilian being a mother. How strange to think of her growing old as I grow old.) Alice's eyes are smaller than Lilian's. They are pale brown, but in some lights they seem hazel or even greeny blue. Too small for beauty, perhaps, but to my mind they fit neatly in her face.

Nothing moves in the dream. The white of the pillow is blinding. Then I realize that I am looking not at Alice but at Lilian, and I cannot understand how on earth I could have confused the daughter with the mother.

I am having second thoughts about where I should begin. It's too late now, of course – I *have* begun: with the arrival of Alice's letter. But the ghosts of the dead moved invisibly among the four of us who were then alive – Esmond and me, Alice and Bronwen.

I am always having second thoughts, about anything and everything. Esmond used to laugh at me. 'For God's sake, make up your mind, Rumpy,' he'd say. 'It's not *that* difficult.'

Oh, but it is.

Finisterre stood in a valley running westward to the Atlantic. The valley was steep-sided and very narrow –

there was barely room for our house, the garden, the stream and the unmetalled lane that led to Blackberry Water and Ulvercombe Mouth.

The house was about half a mile inland. The village of Ulvercombe was further inland still and nearly a mile away from us. Finisterre wasn't much to look at – a self-effacing stone box with a slate roof. The outside woodwork was painted dark green. There was nearly an acre of garden. For some reason the house reminded me of a toad squatting on its haunches. I quite like toads. I also liked the name 'Finisterre'. It had a pleasing air of finality about it: thus far and no further.

The place had been built in the 1880s for a prosperous grocer from Budstow. I believe he designed the house himself. He built carefully but without ostentation, less for himself than for the generations that were to come after him. He retired to Finisterre and died within six months; his wife soon followed him; and by 1939 only one daughter survived of their five children. She was unmarried. There were no grandchildren. She sold the house to my father soon after the outbreak of war.

When I first heard the story of the Sleeping Beauty, I thought the enchanted palace, hidden from the world by brambles, must have been like Finisterre.

'Is there a spell on this place?' I remember asking my mother. This was long before I met Esmond. I was about six years old.

'Oh, don't be so stupid, Thomas,' she snapped. 'Magic isn't real.'

You couldn't see the house from the lane, which was bordered by thick, high hawthorn hedges and was in any case considerably lower than our garden. Besides, there was no proper car park at Ulvercombe Mouth and because the lane was unmetalled, very few motorists used it even in the height of summer. As for the walkers, they usually stayed on the coastal path and rarely ventured inland from Blackberry Water.

The house was further sheltered by two windbreaks planted in the 1930s. The windbreaks were dark, ugly places. The trees – all conifers – grew close together. Their dense shade had long since killed everything else except some ivy and a few holly trees. Even the pines seemed to be dying from the ground up, slowly destroying themselves by blocking out the light.

The windbreaks were ugly but useful. The prevailing winds blew from the west and often they were gales. In our part of the world, the tops of all the trees and bushes were bent inland, and normally their growth was stunted on the seaward side.

'This is a cruel coast,' Lilian used to say. She was fascinated by tales of the wreckers whose false lights lured the big ships on to the rocks of Ulvercombe Mouth.

After Mr Jodson's first stroke, in 1977, both house and garden decayed. (Mr and Mrs Jodson lived in the village. They worked for us, on and off, for over thirty years.) There were other reasons, too – around the same time my mother's sight grew worse, and her income was badly affected by inflation. I observed with both interest and mild regret the windows that wouldn't open; the bindweed that smothered the hydrangea; the slates one found on the gravel after stormy nights. The dilapidation spread like a cancer a little further each day.

I suppose I could have done something about it. Mrs Jodson wasn't getting any younger, and in the end she stopped coming too. Occasionally my mother wanted me to get someone in to clean the house. Such a bother; as well as finding a cleaner in the first place, I had to get a taxi to bring her out and take her back. Once they reached the house, the cleaners invariably spent most of their time drinking tea, complaining about the dirt and telling me about their families and their ailments. And they always disturbed things, however often I told them to be careful. Once or twice I was forced to get a handyman to come over — for example when the pipes burst. It was such an effort. Really, it wasn't worth it. In the end I decided it was much simpler to muddle along by myself.

All this changed when Esmond returned. Esmond — Esmond Arthur Chard. I used to think it was the most romantic name in the world. Esmond looked after me.

'Esmond will look after Thomas,' Aunt Imogen had said, all those years ago. It was an order.

Aunt Imogen was Esmond's mother. She and my mother were sisters. You could tell they were sisters by looking at them. Both of them had small chins, large noses and plump cheeks. Both had prominent front teeth. Esmond used to say they had rabbit faces. I had known, even then, that rabbits could be cruel and powerful. The Jodsons' son had a big buck rabbit who, it was said, had once killed a puppy.

Aunt Imogen issued her decree in the summer of 1954. At the time I had just passed my eleventh birthday; Esmond was approaching his, and Lizzy, Esmond's sister, was scarcely more than a month old. Despite the fact that Esmond and I were cousins, we had not met before. He had been born and brought up in Ireland. Lizzy, I gathered from overhearing my mother discussing the matter, was a 'mistake' – a description which puzzled me greatly. I assumed that the arrival of babies was governed by God, and I had been led to understand that God was incapable of making mistakes.

On that first occasion, my mother and I drove from Finisterre to Barnstaple where the Chards were then living. I was wearing my new Bicknor College uniform: perhaps my mother wanted me to get used to it gradually, or perhaps it was a way of showing off in front of her sister. It was a warm day in late July and I was uncomfortably hot; but my mother refused to have the windows open on the grounds that the dust and the draught would ruin her hair.

Not only were my grey suit and shirt too warm for the day, but their newness made me want to scratch. The shirt collar was irritating my neck. Car journeys were always difficult because of the danger of travel-sickness. Worse than this was the prospect of meeting unknown people.

My mother glanced at me. 'If you're going to be sick,' she said, 'mind you give us plenty of warning.' She added with that air of omniscience I used to find so terrifying: 'Esmond is never sick in cars.'

The nausea came closer.

On the other hand, I found comfort in the possibility that I might be able to show myself to advantage at Barnstaple. After all, Esmond was younger than I, and he had grown up in Ireland; everyone knew that Ireland was a primitive place that had foolishly decided to reject the manifold advantages of being British. And I had gathered from overhearing my mother's conversation that the Chards were to be pitied. This was partly because they did not have much money; but there was more to it than that.

'Poor Imogen,' my mother had said when discussing the proposed visit with Aunt Ada, who was her confidante, not a relation. 'If only she had known.'

The house in Barnstaple was one of a terrace that crawled up the side of a long hill. An identical terrace stood opposite. Each house was separated from the road by a low wall and a front garden that was perhaps four feet deep. The Chards' front garden was almost entirely occupied by two dusty laurel bushes.

'Oh dear,' my mother said. She turned off the engine and peered up at the façade of the Chards' house with a satisfied expression on her face. 'Oh dear.'

She pursed her lips, and her face became a network of powder-lined wrinkles. In a rustle of silk she swept out of the car, across the pavement and through the open gate. As she surged up the path, Aunt Imogen opened the front door. A foot apart, the two women stopped.

'Fiona.'

'Imogen.'

Each inclined her head towards the other's right shoulder. For an instant, as if by accident, lips brushed cheeks. Both women straightened.

'And this,' said Aunt Imogen, 'must be little Thomas.'

'Come and shake hands with your aunt.'

I crept up the path.

'Stand up straight.'

Aunt Imogen gripped my hand. 'He's small for his age, isn't he?'

Somewhere indoors the baby was crying. Aunt Imogen ushered us into a small, dark room at the front of the house. A black upright piano and a brown sofa with a high back filled most of the space. The floor-length velvet curtains were partly drawn across the window. There was also a net curtain, stained irregularly with damp, which had been doubled over to afford extra protection from the curiosity of passers-by.

'Arthur is so sorry he can't join us,' Aunt Imogen said. 'He has a business engagement.'

The two women exchanged glances. At the time I sensed that Uncle Arthur, Esmond's father, was a source of strain; but I did not understand why until much later.

'What a pity,' my mother said with patent insincerity. 'I was so looking forward to seeing him again.'

'But Esmond is here.' Aunt Imogen put her head in the hall and called him. The baby's wails increased in volume. 'And Lizzy, of course. She's a little unhappy, I'm afraid. It's probably wind.'

'Oh dear,' said my mother. 'How trying.'

Footsteps clattered on the stairs.

'Quietly, please,' Aunt Imogen said. She turned back to her sister. 'Do not distress yourself, Fiona. Wind is quite normal, even desirable.'

Esmond was at least two inches taller than me. He walked straight up to my mother and held out his hand. 'How do you do, Aunt Fiona?' he said. He did indeed have a slight accent but to me it sounded not so much Irish as interestingly different.

'And this is Cousin Thomas,' explained Aunt Imogen. 'Perhaps you would like to show him the garden.'

I stared at my feet, which were pigeon-toed. My mother stirred beside me, and I prayed for her to intervene, to save me from the unfamiliar.

'Oh – you have a garden?' she said. 'How delightful.'

'Esmond will look after Thomas,' Aunt Imogen said. 'Run along, children. Don't get dirty.'

Esmond glanced at me and led the way out of the room. We walked in silence down the narrow hall, into a kitchen and through another door to the garden. But it was not what I had been brought up to call a garden.

The yard was bounded by the house on one side and high brick walls on the others. There were two dustbins, an outside lavatory, a coalhouse, a washing line and, in the far corner, a square of earth covered with weeds. The opposite wall was divided in two by a gate. Above it you could see the roofs and windows of another terrace of houses.

Everything was grey or brown with the exception of the blue sky overhead and the weeds. Many of these were in flower, and their colours were unnatural here: the cream of cow parsley, the rich purple of rosebay willowherb and the yellow sunbursts of dandelions.

Esmond stuck his hands in the pockets of his short trousers. His hair was a very dark brown with a hint of copper; it clung to his head like a cap. His face and the way he stood reminded me of a picture I had in the nursery at home: the coloured frontispiece of *The Adventures of Robin Hood*.

'See this?' Esmond held out the palm of his hand. On it was a sixpence. 'Guess how I got it.'

'I don't know,' I said. I stared at the coin because it gave me an excuse not to look at Esmond's face.

'There's a boy next door – he's twelve – I'm not meant to play with him, of course. Anyway, we bet each other sixpence we couldn't hop along the top of that wall. Not just the wall – the gate as well: that's the really difficult bit. If he fell off he had to pay me, and if I fell off I had to pay him. Understand?'

'It's a long way to fall,' I said.

'The ground's hard, too. Unless you fall in the weeds. Then the nettles get you.'

'What happened?'

'He fell. I didn't. It was just as well because I didn't have sixpence to give him.' Esmond pocketed the coin and added casually: 'He got cut. The doctor had to sew him up.'

We were silent.

'Have you got any money?' Esmond said.

I knew it would be wiser to say no. In my pocket was a little leather purse containing a new half-crown; Aunt Ada had given it to me on my last birthday. But I had been told – by my mother, by Aunt Ada (who, as the vicar's wife, was also my Sunday School teacher), and by others who might be expected to have privileged information on the subject – that to lie was to sin; and that God would be well within His rights if He struck the liar dead at the very instant that the lie was uttered. I also wanted to impress my cousin. I took out my purse and showed Esmond the half-crown.

'Tell you what,' he said. 'If you can hop along the wall without falling off, I'll give you the sixpence.'

'And if I fall?'

'You give me sixpence.'

'I haven't got a sixpence. Only the half-crown.'

'I'll change it for you at the shop.'

I looked back at the house. 'But won't they mind?'

'They won't know.' Esmond pointed at the gate. 'We'll go the back way.'

'They might come looking for us.'

He shrugged.

I began to tremble. At the time it seemed to me that I was perfectly still and the whole world, including Esmond, was pulsing with the fear I felt.

'I don't think I could get up there,' I said.

'It's easy. You can climb up the back of the gate. Anyway I'll help you.'

'But –' To my dismay, I felt warm, wet tears trickling down my cheeks.

'Oh. Oh, I see.' Esmond frowned and took a step backwards. 'Well, never mind. Suppose I do it instead? And if I don't fall, you give me sixpence.'

'Yes. Yes, please.'

'All right. If that's what you want.' Esmond smiled at me, and I felt overwhelmed with gratitude. His kindness seemed superhuman. 'Come on. You can give me a hand getting up there.'

We ran down to the gate. It consisted of six vertical tongue-and-grooved planks tied together by three horizontal bars. Climbing it was more difficult than Esmond had led me to expect. He had to use my body as a ladder. The heels of his shoes dug into my shoulder.

'You see?' Esmond said when at last he was balancing on top of the wall. 'It's easy.' He flung out his arms and grinned down at me. 'Now. I'll walk to the corner. Then I start hopping.'

As I watched, I knew with the fatalistic certainty of the young that if he fell off he would be killed, and that everyone would say it was my fault. Terrible though this prospect was, it would have been even worse if I had been the one on the wall. Whistling, Esmond marched to the corner of the yard. He turned to me. Then he hopped towards the gate.

The width of the wall was the length of a brick – nine inches. But the top of the gate was much narrower. When he reached the first gatepost, Esmond paused, frowning with concentration. I shut my eyes. When I opened them again, Esmond was beyond the gate and hopping along the other stretch of wall. He stopped at the end and looked down at me.

'I changed legs at the gate,' he said. 'It's allowed, you know. It's in the rules.'

I nodded. Esmond returned to the gate and allowed me to help him down. I took out my purse and gave him the half-crown.

He examined it carefully. 'It's an old one. That means it should be solid silver.' He bit it. 'You can't be too careful. That's what my father says.'

He opened the gate and we went into the alley. It ran between the backyards of the Chards' terrace and those of the terrace behind. There was barely room for the two of us to walk side by side. The alley smelled of urine and coal dust. Even on a hot summer day, it was muddy underfoot.

We came to a street with a shop, a small general

store. Two boys were standing outside; their knees and mouths were dirty. They were rough, dangerous and what my mother would have called 'vulgar'. They pointed – not at Esmond but at me – and one of them said, 'Who's a little darling, then? Looking for your mummy?'

Esmond ignored them. He marched into the shop with me scuttling behind, and asked for two penny bars of chocolate. The woman behind the counter refused to serve him until she had seen the half-crown.

When he had the change, Esmond gave me two shillings and pocketed the remaining four pennies. He held out one of the bars of chocolate. My mother did not allow me to have sweets.

'It's for me?' I said. Once again, tears prickled against my eyelids. I did not deserve such generosity.

'Go on. Take it.'

To my relief, the rough boys were no longer in sight. Esmond peeled off the wrapper, threw it on the ground and began to eat the chocolate. I looked around to see if anyone was watching. A few seconds later, I followed Esmond's example. We strolled back to the alleyway. By the time we reached the gate, the bars were finished.

'Have you got a handkerchief?'

'Yes.' I always had a handkerchief.

'You'd better wipe your mouth. You've got chocolate all over it.'

At that moment I realized how dirty I was. It wasn't just the chocolate: my shoes were muddy and so were the shoulders and arms of my new school suit. Esmond, by contrast, was spotless, apart from the soles of his shoes.

'What's wrong?'

I explained.

'Don't worry,' Esmond said. 'I'll look after you.'

We went into the yard. Esmond found a ball in the outside lavatory. We had kicked it between us no more than twice when Aunt Imogen opened the window and told us that tea was ready. Had she been a minute earlier, she would have discovered our absence. Esmond was almost always lucky.

My mother was in the kitchen with baby Lizzy, Esmond's sister, clamped to her shoulder. Lizzy was like a little pink-and-white monkey: too small to be properly human. My mother's lips parted, exposing the teeth, when she saw me. I wanted to run away.

'What *have* you been doing?'

Esmond marched up to her. 'It's all my fault, Aunt Fiona.' He stood there, very tall and straight, with his hands clasped behind his back. 'I slipped in the yard, you see, and Thomas was helping me up. But he sort of tripped over me and fell in the flowerbed.'

My mother smiled. The smile faded as she glanced at me. The colour rose in her cheeks. She looked across the table to Aunt Imogen and said of Esmond, 'He's quite a manly little fellow, isn't he?' She took a breath as if about to say something else, but an instant later her mouth snapped shut.

'Very like Arthur at that age,' Aunt Imogen said, and now it was her turn to show her teeth. 'As I dare say you've noticed.'

There is documentary evidence to show that I did not meet Esmond's father, Arthur Chard, until the end of the summer. (For example, the private investigator's report puts it as September 1954.) In memory, however, it seems as though I met him the day after I first met Esmond. When looking back at childhood, I find time has a tendency to telescope. In a way, it is curious that I have any memory of Uncle Arthur at all.

During the summer we saw a good deal of Aunt Imogen, Esmond and Lizzy. Usually they came to Finisterre. No doubt my mother made the most of the disparity between our material circumstances and theirs. I remember formal picnics at Ulvercombe Mouth; I remember crying behind a rock because the shingle on the little beach hurt my bare feet; I remember Aunt Ada screaming when she was stung by a jellyfish; and I remember the first time I saw Esmond swimming, and how I wondered if there were such things as merboys.

At the time, I saw nothing odd in Uncle Arthur's absence from these family parties; children are such self-centred little brutes. I suppose I must have assumed he was engaged in some mysterious masculine pursuit which took precedence over visiting relations and other summer relaxations. As an adult, I attributed his absence to pride and to my mother's obvious dislike of him. Now, of course, I know that there were other and more powerful reasons.

Towards the end of the summer, however, Uncle Arthur paid his first and last visit to Finisterre. The Chards had been invited to lunch and tea. My mother could not spare the time to fetch them from Kinghampton so Mr Jodson went instead. I hid in the shrubbery that lined our little drive and waited for what seemed like eternity for the car to come back. The bushes were dusty and made me sneeze so much that I had to go indoors. By this time I knew Esmond much better, and I was very excited at the prospect of seeing him again. It would be inaccurate to say we were friends. Friendship implies equality.

When the car arrived I was in my room fetching a clean handkerchief. I peeped over the windowsill, gradually raising myself until I could peer down at the foreshortened figures below. I already envied Esmond the possession of a father, and my envy increased when I saw that Arthur Chard was big, black-haired and broad-shouldered.

I forced myself to go downstairs. Uncle Arthur was equipped with a military moustache and was even taller than I had expected. He did not look at me as we shook hands but his grip was so firm it made me squeal. Like Esmond, he struck me as a heroic figure. I imagined him, Sten gun in hand, wiping out a German machine-gun nest or nonchalantly leading his platoon through a heavily mined no-man's-land. I later discovered that living in Eire had enabled him to avoid the war altogether.

Uncle Arthur chain-smoked untipped cigarettes, which he kept in a worn silver-plated case. It was exceptional to see anyone smoking in our house. I was too scared to look much at his face. I remember his hands. They were brown, with the backs thickly covered with dark hairs; and above all they were restless, like little animals trying to escape.

During lunch he opened his mouth only to put food in it. He ate a great deal. Afterwards he said he was going out to buy some cigarettes. My mother and Aunt

Imogen exchanged glances, and my mother wrinkled her face as though an unpleasant smell had reached her nostrils.

She said, 'I believe they sell them in The Forley Arms.'

No one else said anything. Esmond was staring at his plate, frowning slightly as if he were working out a sum in his head. Uncle Arthur pushed back his chair and left the room.

At the time my mother's remark puzzled me. I knew you could buy cigarettes at Atkinsons, the one shop in Ulvercombe. Atkinsons was on the Finisterre side of the village whereas the pub was a couple of hundred yards further on, near the church and the vicarage.

'Fiona – ?' Aunt Imogen swallowed.

'What is it?'

'Nothing, dear.'

'When do you imagine Arthur will be back?' my mother asked.

'He shouldn't be more than half an hour,' Aunt Imogen said.

My mother smiled at her, showing her teeth. 'You know best.'

Three

The nursery used to puzzle me. The grocer's children must have been far too old to need a nursery when Finisterre was built in the 1880s. And as far as I know none of them had any children: at least, not ones they cared to acknowledge. So whom was the nursery for? The six vertical bars looked as if they had been there as long as the window frame, as long as the house itself. The only possible answer was that the grocer must have provided a nursery for the grandchildren he never had. The room was a monument to the folly of trying to arrange your descendants' lives.

Still, it was useful to us if not to our predecessors. Unlike the death room across the landing, it was rarely empty during the fifty-odd years that the house was owned by the Penmarshes. For most of my life the nursery was my bedroom. I slept there until my marriage, and when that ended my mother suggested I move back to my old room.

'Fewer unhappy memories,' she said. 'I've already made up the bed and moved your clothes.'

I was never very good at arguing with my mother – particularly at that point in my life. She may have meant well; I am not sure, which is a galling admission to have to make. (It is often difficult to distinguish between stupidity and insensitivity on the one hand, and active malevolence on the other.) Once I was back in the nursery, it was simpler to stay put. A year later, I didn't want to move.

'I always associated you with this room,' Esmond said when he came back to Finisterre after my mother's death. 'But I never thought you'd still be using it.'

'Why not?'

'Well – I suppose it seems like a child's room. What with the bars and everything. Don't you find it a bit claustrophobic?'

'Not really. I don't notice the bars.'

'So you might as well stay here,' Esmond said.

In the months between my mother's death and Alice's arrival at Finisterre, I spent most of my waking hours in the nursery. It was not that I was a prisoner. I liked routine. I liked living quietly. For most of that time the house was full of builders and decorators, and Esmond pointed out that I would find it less disturbing if I kept to my room; also, I wouldn't get in the way.

Of course I didn't spend every moment cooped up in the nursery. Esmond thought that daily walks were good for my health. 'Rumpy's constitutionals', he called them, and he and Bronwen took it in turns to take me. Moreover he liked me to have occasional changes of scene, partly for variety and partly because it was sensible to show my face around the neighbourhood. He called it 'showing the flag', which made me feel like a gunboat with the White Ensign fluttering at the stern.

Sometimes we would go shopping in Kinghampton or further afield to Budstow or Bideford. Very occasionally we went out to lunch at a restaurant. I was glad of his and Bronwen's company. I had never liked being by myself in crowds. Esmond diverted me by making a game of our being in public. He would be very solicitous, and treat me as though I were infinitely fragile.

'You must be in the draught, Thomas,' he would say in a rather louder voice than usual. 'Waiter, we shall need a different table. Mr Penmarsh is too near the door.'

'So kind,' I would murmur. 'So thoughtful.'

When I had been settled at another table, and when the waiter had gone, Esmond would look at me with the laughter in his eyes; and I would be hard put not to giggle. Esmond had a way of making us conspirators. I think Bronwen was jealous.

Before Alice came, the three of us had achieved a sort of equilibrium. As I have already hinted, it wasn't just a case of the two of them ganging up on me. Often it was Esmond and I in one camp, and Bronwen in the other. Sometimes Bronwen became so furious with Esmond that she wanted to talk to me about him – or rather to complain. And Esmond soon slipped back into his old habit of coming to confide in good old Rumpy up in the nursery. In many ways it wasn't such a bad life. I wasn't lonely. I was safe. I was living happily ever after.

Then Alice came and spoiled it all. My darling Alice.

My mind keeps leaping forward – to Alice, to those last few days at Finisterre. This won't do. 'You'm putting the cart before the horse again,' as Mr Jodson used to tell me. Effects can only be explained if their causes are described first. And causes only really make sense if presented in chronological order. Which brings me back to that Saturday in September 1954: the day the four Chards were together at Finisterre for the first and last time.

Uncle Arthur set off for the village ostensibly in search of cigarettes. Esmond and I spent the afternoon playing in the garden. We were not allowed to go to the beach by ourselves. Heat and rich, fatty foods had made us lethargic. Our mothers and baby Lizzy stayed in the sitting room. (At this time Esmond's sister must have been about three or four months old.)

At teatime I noticed that there was what we used to call 'an atmosphere' between my mother and her sister. Aunt Imogen made the best of a bad job by saying that Uncle Arthur must have been delayed.

'I'd rather gathered that, dear,' my mother said.

Perhaps, Aunt Imogen suggested, he had met an acquaintance. He would not have been able to let us know because unfortunately Finisterre was not on the telephone. (This remark was an arrow aimed at my mother, who, Aunt Imogen affected to believe, was absurdly conservative in her tastes.)

'I didn't know that Arthur knew anyone in Ulvercombe,' my mother said. 'Anyone but us, I mean. What a tease he is.'

No doubt, Aunt Imogen said, Arthur would wait for our car to pass him in the village if he did not have time to return to the house.

'Outside The Forley Arms, perhaps?' my mother suggested.

Aunt Imogen rallied. 'Why on earth should he wait there, Fiona?'

'Because the forecourt is the only place one can

pull over in the car. You know how narrow the road is.'

When the time came we all piled into the car. It was a fine evening. The atmosphere persisted as we drove up to the village. My mother made it worse by wondering aloud when The Forley Arms reopened for the evening. Aunt Imogen, who was holding baby Lizzy in her arms, responded by pretending to be frightened by my mother's inadequacies as a driver. Esmond and I sat in the back. We did not speak.

Uncle Arthur was not waiting for us outside The Forley Arms or anywhere else in Ulvercombe. My mother drove on to the forecourt. The pub was still shut for the afternoon. Aunt Imogen said she would enquire in Atkinsons.

'Cooee!' Aunt Ada leaned over the wall of the vicarage garden and waved a pair of shears at us. 'Fiona! Imogen! Cooee!'

My mother rolled down her window. 'Ada? Have you by any chance –?'

'Seen Mr Chard? Yes, indeed. And I have a message here for Imogen.'

All of us got out of the car. The vicarage was opposite The Forley Arms. Aunt Ada, a big, pale woman whose floral dress made her look like an overstuffed sofa, met us in the drive. She produced a white but earth-stained envelope from beneath the trowel and fork in her trug. My real aunt had met my honorary one several times during the summer.

'It was a little before three, I think,' Aunt Ada said. 'Mr Chard popped his head over the wall and asked if he might borrow an envelope. Or rather have one. You know what I mean. I knew who he was – I saw him in the car this morning. He said he'd just telephoned a colleague from The Forley Arms . . .'

My mother and Aunt Imogen ignored her. Inside the envelope was a small sheet of lined paper – perhaps a page torn from a loose-leafed memorandum book. Aunt Imogen passed Lizzy to my mother. She half turned from us. It cannot have been a long note but it took her what seemed a very long time to read it.

'. . . an urgent appointment,' Aunt Ada was saying. 'I said, could we run him into Kinghampton? And he said he couldn't possibly put us to so much trouble and anyway the bus would be almost as quick. So I said I could drive down to Finisterre with his note if it was urgent but he said there was no need, and that Mrs Chard was half expecting it –'

'Were you, Imogen?' said my mother.

'Eh?' Aunt Imogen looked up. 'Oh yes. Didn't I say?'

'Anyway . . .' Aunt Ada blinked as she realized that the contents of the letter were not as expected as Arthur Chard had led her to believe. 'I – I hope it's not bad news?'

'No,' my mother said, automatically closing ranks. 'Of course not, Ada. Whatever gave you that idea?'

I felt very excited. Even at the time, I sensed that something catastrophic had happened, or was about to. As a child, I was an emotional barometer: the glass was falling rapidly.

'Thank you so much,' Aunt Imogen said to Aunt Ada. 'Goodbye.'

She walked unsteadily towards the car. The rest of us followed her across the road.

'Is there anything I can do?' Aunt Ada called out.

'No, thank you, Ada,' my mother said. 'We'll see you tomorrow, won't we?'

We climbed into the car. Frowning, my mother started the engine and drove half a mile down the Kinghampton road. She parked across a gateway into a field.

'Well, Imogen,' she said. Her voice sounded breathless. 'What does the note say?'

'It's just as I thought, just as Ada said. Arthur had to make a business telephone-call, and he's been called away.'

'At the weekend?'

'Time and tide wait for no man, Fiona.'

'But surely people don't transact business at the weekend? Even in this day and age.'

Aunt Imogen and my mother had turned to face each other. I think they had forgotten that Esmond and I were in the back of the car; or, if they had not forgotten us, then they had decided to discount us. That was what I found most disturbing. It also increased my excitement.

'Meetings,' Aunt Imogen said, her colour rising and her teeth showing, 'discussions, preliminaries and so forth. So much of that sort of thing can be done informally –'

'In a hotel, perhaps?' my mother put in, unmasking her own teeth. 'Or a golf club?'

'– and indeed more efficiently when possible clients are away from their offices.'

I saw my mother's face in profile. An eyebrow rose, a semicircle of disbelief. Her eye looked like a wet marble.

'But my dear, he's only an insurance agent.'

'I don't think you quite understand the sort of work Arthur does, or the responsibilities he has to shoulder. Of course he confides very fully in me, which is natural enough; but he has to be discreet even when –'

'I'm sure it must be fascinating. What it is to be the – ah – helpmate of a man of affairs.'

'Yes, indeed.' Aunt Imogen returned the note to its envelope and put it in her handbag.

'But don't these sudden comings and goings make it rather difficult to maintain a domestic routine?'

'I'm glad to say we manage, Fiona.' Aunt Imogen smiled, and that was the first time I realized that smiles could be cruel and triumphant. 'Of course there are compensations.'

My mother sucked in her breath as if Aunt Imogen had stuck a pin in her. The sisters glared at each other. My mother started the engine and drove jerkily and noisily to Kinghampton.

After my mother's death, I sorted through the desk in the study. In her prime she had been a tidy woman. Every key had a label. The bills were paid, receipted and filed. Each letter was endorsed with the date of her reply and a précis of its contents.

Her photographs were usually dated on the back, and sometimes the names of people and places were added. 'Blackberry Water August 1951' or 'Thomas aged eighteen months'. Most of the photographs had been taken before 1960, and most of them were from her side of the family. Perhaps the Penmarshes did not like exposing themselves to the camera. Or, more likely, my mother had no wish to keep mementoes of them.

There were photographs of herself and Aunt Imogen when they were girls in Ireland. Their father, my maternal grandfather, owned a general store, and the family lived above it. My mother used to make the shop sound like Harrods. 'Everyone who could afford it came to Bradleys. It wasn't cheap, mind you, but you could buy anything you wanted there. And it was all good quality.'

There were photographs of the Chards, too. My mother, Aunt Imogen and Arthur Chard had played together as children. Arthur was the younger son of the people who kept a hotel in the same town. The Chards and the Bradleys worshipped in the Church of Ireland church. Grandfather Bradley lies in the churchyard, behind the east window. I have seen a photograph of his gravestone. *Not dead but gone before.*

Among my mother's photographs was one of Esmond and me in the garden at Finisterre. Probably Aunt Ada had taken it; the vicar was a keen photographer, and Aunt Ada liked to enter into her husband's interests. In the photograph Esmond towers over me. I know it must have been taken not long after we first met because half of baby Lizzy's pram is in the picture. Esmond has his chin in the air and his lips curl up at the corners. He looks like a *Boy's Own* hero, a natural leader. I am not looking at the camera but up at Esmond's face. I am smiling smugly, perhaps because Aunt Ada has promised me a print of the photograph; or perhaps just because I am with Esmond.

In the centre drawer of my mother's desk there was a so-called 'secret' compartment. I found it after her death. Inside was a sealed brown envelope. When I opened it, I found the private investigator's report and also a photograph of Arthur Chard as a young man. It was a postcard-size photograph with the stamp of a studio in Dublin. Arthur wears a double-breasted pin-stripe suit; his hair is slicked back from his forehead and gleams with grease. He smokes a cigarette in a black holder. His face is unlined and smiling.

Fiona, he'd written on the back, *forever yours, Arthur.*

I burned the photograph – for Esmond's sake.

Four

My father looked not unlike Dr Crippen. The photographs show a mild little man with a receding hairline, an unobtrusive chin, small, metal-rimmed glasses and a bushy, even luxuriant moustache. I never knew him. He died of pneumonia at Finisterre in August 1943, two months after my birth, and he is buried in Ulvercombe churchyard.

'He hated the sound of your crying,' my mother once said.

I know nothing else about his feelings for me. My mother also said he was a fine amateur flautist; and she made such a fuss about this achievement that I often wondered whether my father had no other distinguishing characteristics worth remembering. I imagine she liked my father's money as much as my father; but I may be doing her an injustice. His family came from Birmingham, where they owned a firm that made wooden seats for lavatories. This was not a fact that my mother liked to have generally known. The firm was sold before the war and my father invested his share of the proceeds, which gave him, and later us, enough to live on. My mother had been his secretary: that was how they'd met. They bought Finisterre because they expected that the bombs would rain on Birmingham.

It is possible that Fiona Bradley married George Penmarsh for money. It is probable that her sister

Imogen married Arthur Chard for love. The Chards got married first – in January 1940. My parents were married four months later after what Aunt Imogen once described to Aunt Ada – in my mother's presence and, I think, with the intention of hurting – as 'a whirlwind courtship'.

'So romantic,' she said. 'Arthur and I were delighted.'

On the face of it, however, my mother got the better deal. She might not have loved my father but at least he had the grace to remove himself from her life promptly and in a socially acceptable manner. Thanks to him, she inherited Finisterre and enough money to live there; and she had the pleasure of being able to lord it over her relations from Ireland.

Aunt Imogen, on the other hand, got her heart's desire, which I have noticed often leads to unhappiness. It is hard to be sure but I think that Arthur Chard was little more than a confidence trickster – and not even a successful one. For some years during and after the war he worked for a bank in Wexford: there was some sort of scandal, my mother always hinted, and he was forced to leave. He found it difficult to find work in Ireland so he had to come to England. He and Imogen gravitated towards their rich relation.

Poor Aunt Imogen. There she was with two young children, no money, a feckless husband – and a wealthy sister who was determined to make the most out of the difference in their circumstances.

Then why wasn't my mother happier?

As I have said, my mother died suddenly. The absence of warning meant that she did not have time to go through her papers. I have also already mentioned the photograph of Arthur Chard. I don't imagine she would have wanted me to find either that or the report from the enquiry agent.

Arthur was traced to a liner that made the Atlantic crossing in October 1954, about five weeks after he'd abandoned his family. He travelled steerage. The agent offered to pass the case to an associate in New York. My mother had scrawled 'NO', underlined twice, across the bottom of the report. It was just possible that my mother had hired the enquiry agent on Aunt Imogen's behalf. Possible but unlikely.

Sometimes I thought of Arthur Chard in America. I wondered if his hands were still hairy and restless, like little furry animals trying to find the way out. For years and years my mother never mentioned his name. Esmond might have been the miraculous product of a virgin birth. ('Esmond's a proper little Bradley,' she used to say with pride. 'Thomas takes after the Penmarshes.') A few months before she died, however, my mother suddenly asked me if I thought Arthur Chard might still be alive.

'Arthur?' I was flustered. 'Er – how old was he when he . . . when he left?'

'He would have been forty in November,' she said. 'November 1954.'

'So he'd be in his late seventies now. He might be alive, I suppose.'

'He always smoked and drank too much,' she said. 'I never thought he'd make old bones.'

'You can never tell.'

Suddenly she banged the tip of her stick on the floor.

The noise frightened me. I dropped my book on the floor.

'Don't be stupid, Thomas. Use your head. If Arthur was alive he'd have tried to borrow more money from me.'

I cannot remember a time when I was not afraid of something or someone. The object of my fear has varied; and sometimes I have felt afraid and scarcely been able to know what was frightening me. As far as I am concerned, fear – like guilt – is best considered as a condition not a consequence. The causes of some conditions are so deeply buried that they might as well not exist.

When I think of fear I think of my first proper school – and of Esmond, of course, always Esmond. The school had the grandiose title of 'Bicknor College', and I went there in September 1954, just after Arthur Chard disappeared; previously I had attended the little village school in Ulvercombe.

Bicknor College was a small preparatory school for boys aged from seven to thirteen. It occupied a detached and ramshackle eighteenth-century house in Kinghampton. The rooms smelled strongly of polish, disinfectant, damp wool and decaying vegetable matter – despite the fact that it was school policy for windows to be open at all times. There were a few boarders, but most of us were dayboys. The headmaster was a Mr Broadbent-Brown – Bee-Bee: known behind his back as 'Buzzer'. His assistant was Mr Maulet, pronounced 'Morley': a man notable for his artificial leg, his inability to remember most of his pupils' names, and his tendency to flush dark purple when angry. The older boys affected to believe that Mr Maulet nursed a torrid passion for Mr Broadbent-Brown's unmarried sister. She acted as her brother's housekeeper, taught art, music and geography, and was supposed to lend a touch of femininity to the establishment. She did not have a nickname.

I was afraid of Miss Broadbent-Brown for an entire year. The words inadequately express the sheer terror she aroused in me, especially during my first term at the school. Nowadays people would say that she was a repressed spinster who took out her sexual and emotional frustrations on the little boys in her charge. 'Tosh and balderdash,' as Mr Maulet used to say. I have known plenty of repressed people, myself included, and almost all of us have managed to avoid being sadists. The only convincing explanation is that the biological fairy-godmother gave Miss Broadbent-Brown a special gift at her christening: the ability to enjoy inflicting cruelty.

Mr Maulet could be cruel, too; but his was an unthinking and usually physical cruelty – a clip round the ear, a stinging blow with a twelve-inch ruler. It sounds absurd, but there was no malice in it. Miss Broadbent-Brown, however, rarely laid a finger on us. She didn't have to. She had subtler methods of maintaining discipline.

Once we were having an art lesson with her and I was bursting to use the lavatory. I know my need must have been urgent, or I would have waited. As it was, desperation overwhelmed my shyness and I put up my hand.

At first Miss Broadbent-Brown ignored me. I squirmed in my seat. In our culture the fear of wetting oneself goes mysteriously deep. Such a loss of control is considered quite beyond the pale, particularly by children.

Miss Broadbent-Brown must have seen my waving hand. That woman saw everything. Like Argus, she had a hundred eyes. She pretended to be absorbed in telling someone how to mix blue and yellow paint to make green.

'Please, Miss,' I squeaked. 'Please, Miss.'

The fact that I dared to speak without permission showed how my desperation had increased.

Miss Broadbent-Brown looked up. Her gaze travelled in a leisurely way around the room. She looked at everybody's face in turn. Finally her eyes came to rest on me. She was a tall, thin women with a long face whose features gave the impression of having been twisted out of shape by some powerful external agency.

'Penmarsh,' she said. 'Have you something you want to share with us? A piercing artistic insight, perhaps?'

'Please, Miss. May I go to the toilet?'

'No.'

She turned her back and strolled between the two rows of trestle tables to her desk, which stood on a dais. I could not understand. I knew that Miss Broadbent-Brown allowed children to go to the lavatory during lessons. Still with my hand in the air, I stood up.

'Please, Miss. Please may I be excused?'

She actually smiled at me. 'No, Penmarsh, you may not be excused. In a sense one might call you inexcusable.'

Some boys tittered.

'Sit down.'

I sat down. 'But Miss –'

'I want you to draw an apple,' Miss Broadbent-Brown announced to the class. 'A green apple, with a stalk, standing on a plate. Try and make it look edible. Do you think any of you can possibly manage that?'

Heads bent. My brush rattled in its jam-jar. The pain was bad; the knowledge of impending shame was worse. I gave a sob which must have been audible on the dais. Tears ran down my cheeks.

'Say *lavatory*,' someone whispered behind me.

'Troon,' Miss Broadbent-Brown said, without raising her eyes from the novel she was reading. 'You know I do not permit talking in my class. Go and stand in the hall. You will see me afterwards.'

Troon — a lonely, red-faced boy who had never before shown me any sign of friendliness and never, to the best of my knowledge, did so in the future — stumbled out of the room, his boots scraping on the bare boards of the artroom floor. I realize now that he must have had something heroic about him. By trying to help me he was defying not only the tyranny of Miss Broadbent-Brown, but also the mood of the class; little boys are sycophants who side with the strong against the weak.

I raised my hand. 'Please, Miss,' I gabbled, 'may I go to the lavatory? Please?'

Miss Broadbent-Brown slowly raised her head. By now I was standing, ready to dart towards the door.

'Who said you might stand up, Penmarsh?'

'Sorry, Miss.' I sat down again.

'You want to go to the lavatory?'

'Yes. Yes please, Miss.'

'Then why on earth didn't you say so before?'

45

'Sorry, Miss.'

At home, at the village school and in any other situation I knew of, it was considered acceptable to ask to be excused or to go to the toilet. Here, apparently, it was not. At Bicknor College, as in life, ignorance was never a defence that succeeded.

Miss Broadbent-Brown's eyes returned to her book. A few seconds crawled by. They might just as well have been centuries. She yawned, covering her mouth with her hand.

'Very well, Penmarsh,' she said. 'Off you go.'

I bolted for the door. But it was too late. I felt a warm and shameful wetness between my legs.

'Aunt Imogen and your cousins will have Christmas with us,' my mother told me in December. 'Won't that be fun?'

Fun? The stupid woman! I knew that it would be a time of marvels and terrors and joys. The one thing it would not be was 'fun'.

My mother went through the motions of keeping up appearances in front of me, but she made no real effort to prevent me from overhearing her conversations with Aunt Ada. I heard words and fragments of sentences delivered in a rapid monotone with hissing sibilants; the hisses were caused (I think) by my mother's ill-fitting false teeth, and they made her most ordinary remarks sound sinister.

'Yes, dear, the police. At least three dishonoured cheques. What Mother will say . . . Well, when all's said and done, they're flesh and blood. It's the children I feel sorry for. Flesh and blood . . .'

'You're a true saint, Fiona,' Aunt Ada said, not once but many times for she was that sort of friend. 'A *true saint.*'

'What will happen in the long run, I just don't know. But it's Christmas, isn't it? It's a time for the little ones. Practically dressed in rags, I gather.'

'It doesn't seem fair, dear.'

I sat on the hard chair at the table behind the sofa. I was doing a jigsaw, I remember: it showed the railway networks of England and Wales before they were nationalized.

'But what will happen afterwards?' Aunt Ada said. 'You really can't be expected to . . .'

'They'll have to go back to Ireland. Since my father died . . . It's not a large house, but they live quite well in a modest sort of way. Much more sensible . . . And Esmond will be able to . . . Still, flesh and blood . . .'

Esmond going to Ireland? For ever and ever?

'It just shows,' Aunt Ada said, without going on to specify either what 'it' was or what 'it' showed. 'Well, Fiona – I always say blood's thicker than water.'

My mother nodded. 'I warned her, you know. If I said it once, I said it a hundred times. Arthur was always –' She stopped and glanced over her shoulder at me. 'Go and wash your hands, Thomas,' she said. 'It's almost time for tea.'

I knew that Christmas 1954 would be the most wonderful Christmas there ever was. And I was right.

Esmond came the week before – with Aunt Imogen and baby Lizzy, of course – and he was due to stay until the second week of the New Year.

Finisterre had five bedrooms, not counting the attics which we used for storage. My mother and I each had a bedroom, mine being the nursery with the barred window. I should have liked Esmond to sleep in my room, but my mother refused on the grounds that we would keep each other awake. Esmond slept in the third bedroom – the smallest one; it was partly over the porch and faced inland. And Aunt Imogen slept in the fourth bedroom with baby Lizzy in a cot at the end of her bed. The fifth and largest bedroom was left unoccupied.

'Couldn't I put Lizzy in there?' Aunt Imogen asked on the afternoon they arrived. 'She tends to wake very easily when we share a room.'

'I'd rather not, dear. We may need that room, you see.'

'You're expecting guests?'

'Quite possibly,' my mother said vaguely.

The room had been my father's. My mother kept in it a state of constant readiness for a guest that never came. By my teens I realized her behaviour was, to put it kindly, eccentric, but until then I'd accepted it as an unalterable and unremarkable part of the fabric of life. The bed was stripped and remade once a week. The hand towel and the bath towel were changed. But on the rare occasions when people came to stay, they always slept in other rooms.

My father had died there, and I think that is why my mother would never use the room. It was not that she cherished his penultimate resting-place for sentimental reasons. Rather, like many stupid but strong-willed people, she was profoundly superstitious: she was afraid of offending his ghost, afraid he would reach out and embrace her from the grave. Sometimes I would open the door and peep at the big, high bed with the dark, carved headboard: my father's body had lain there. I knew that for certain because the Jodsons had told their son, the boy with the killer rabbit, and he had told me. The fifth bedroom belonged to the dead.

When I say it was a wonderful Christmas, I do not mean to imply that I was happy the whole time. I lived in a continuous state of excitement. Often I was very frightened. Esmond made me do things that terrified me. It was as if he had devised a series of tests for me, like the trials a medieval hero has to face, in order to find out if I was worthy of his friendship.

Once he made me steal some sweets from Atkinsons. On another occasion he took me up to the attic floor, where there were two boxrooms, one on either side of an uncarpeted landing. He made me follow him through a skylight on to the roof, which was steeply pitched with grey slates.

I could see into the garden; and, seen from such a height, it was transformed into an unfamiliar and frightening place. A wind that felt like a Force Ten gale was blowing up from the grey sea. I imagined being lifted up on a moving bed of air. My fingernails would scrabble vainly on the slates for a handhold, and then a sudden gust would cast me far inland, to Kinghampton or beyond.

I saw Aunt Ada coming round the corner of the house. She was the size of a doll. There was a lull in the wind, as though the gale were drawing breath. Now the ground seemed to be pulling me towards it. I whimpered. Esmond grabbed my belt and hauled me back towards the skylight.

'I saved your life,' he said when we were back in the safety of the boxroom. 'If it hadn't been for me, you'd be dead.'

Gratitude welled up inside me, and I thanked him. How irrational we are. I knew very well that without Esmond my life would not have been at risk in the first place. Yet my gratitude was genuine. I think I was grateful because he took the trouble to notice me.

Baby Lizzy cried and cried. In my memory she spent whole days, nights and weeks crying away.

'She's never normally like this,' Aunt Imogen said, showing her teeth. This was at breakfast on Christmas Eve. 'It's most unlike her. I wonder what's upsetting her.'

'Yes, I heard her in the night,' my mother said. 'It must have been nearly five before she dropped off.'

'I hope she didn't keep you awake, Fiona.'

'Oh don't worry about *me*. It's Lizzy we must think of. The poor little thing. If you ask me she looks a bit peaky.'

'It might be the unfamiliar surroundings. Or perhaps she can hear me breathing. She's not used to sharing a room.'

'She can hardly hear your breathing when you're downstairs. Who knows what is going on in their minds?'

'I usually have a tolerably good idea. One does, you know. Especially with a second child.'

Such exchanges look so innocent when written down. My mother and her sister had conversations like that which seemed to last for hours. The malice spurted to and fro between them. By the subtlest of hints they accused each other of enormities: of being a bad mother; of forcing Arthur Chard to run away; of being materialistic; of being unchristian; of being sluttish; of producing unhealthy children; of being the next best thing to barren. Perhaps it was meaningless – a hangover from childhood squabbles: a matter of language rather than feeling, of form rather than content. But I don't think so. My mother and Aunt Imogen were rivals first and sisters second.

On New Year's Eve, Esmond and I were playing Commandos under the dining-room table. When the table was not laid for meals it was covered with a blue-green chenille cloth which hung down almost to the floor. Children were not allowed in the dining room by themselves because there were sharp knives and delicate china. Then we heard footsteps.

'I don't know if I can bear it much longer,' my mother murmured. 'It's more than flesh and blood can stand.'

One of the sideboard doors opened. Glasses chinked together. Esmond's shoulder was touching mine.

'I know it can't be easy, dear,' Aunt Ada said.

'She's always trying to upset me. It's jealousy, pure and simple jealousy. She was always like that.'

'You must try to rise above it.'

'And the baby – the *endless* crying. You've no idea. Heaven knows what Imogen does to her. And she's a nasty little thing; Lizzy, I mean. You can tell; there's something about the eyes.'

'It's strange how personalities show themselves even in very young children. I remember my –'

'And Imogen's upsetting the Jodsons, too. Half the

time she treats them like dirt, and then she encourages them to be overfamiliar.'

'Oh dear,' Aunt Ada said, abandoning her attempt to play anything more than a supporting role in the conversation.

'Jodson came to me only this morning. Did I really want the yard swept? he said, because in this windy weather there's really very little point. Of course not, I said. And he said, did I know that Mrs Chard had told him to do it? I was never so embarrassed in my life.'

'You shouldn't have to put up with it.'

'I could do without it, Ada, I don't mind telling you.'

'At least you –'

'I don't mind the boy, mark you. He's a nice little chap, and he's very good for Thomas. He's the spitting image of his father as a boy. Outwardly, that is. Not in character, thank heavens.'

'Well, at least you won't have to put up with it for much longer.'

My mother snorted, spurning comfort. 'This time next week they'll be in Ireland, but –'

Aunt Ada coughed. 'Is that someone on the stairs?'

It must have been Aunt Imogen coming down from her bedroom. We heard retreating footsteps and the closing of the door. Esmond lifted the edge of the tablecloth. Light flooded across the carpet.

'I've just radioed headquarters,' Esmond said as if there had been no interruption in our game, 'and you've been out scouting. And you've just come back to tell me there's a Jerry staff officer driving across the –'

'Shouldn't we go somewhere else?' I urged. 'They might come back.'

'Don't worry so much,' Esmond said. 'I'll look after you.'

One evening early in January 1955, two days before the Chards were due to catch the boat train to Ireland, my mother and Aunt Imogen had a quarrel. In a sense the whole visit had been one long quarrel. But this was the first time that the sisters did not trouble to conceal their anger.

Lizzy's crying was the spark that started the blaze. No doubt there would have been something else if she hadn't been crying. It started before Esmond and I went to bed, which was earlier than usual because Aunt Ada and the vicar were coming to dinner. He was always the vicar in our household, never an honorary uncle and my mother liked him to see both her and her surroundings at their best. Therefore the crying upset her even more than usual.

'I wish she'd shut up,' Esmond said as we went upstairs.

'So do I.'

'If this goes on, your mother's never going to invite us here again.'

'She will. I'm sure she will.'

'I don't know.'

'I'll make her,' I said.

Esmond smiled at me. 'Bloody Lizzy,' he said sweetly. 'I could kill her.'

Soon we were in our beds. Lizzy was in her cot, in Aunt Imogen's room. She was still crying. Aunt Imogen and my mother came upstairs to change. That was when the quarrel really got under way. They stood on the landing and hissed at each other.

'I'm going to put her in the spare room,' Aunt Imogen said. 'Can't you see that's the root of the problem? She's not used to sharing with me.'

'But you're not with her now, you –'

'Yes, but she knows it's my room. Perhaps you can't remember, perhaps you never noticed, but babies of that age are really quite –'

'Are you implying –?'

'If the cap fits, dear. You said it, not me.'

'Said what?'

'Well, dear, I can't help noticing that you obviously feel guilty about giving poor Thomas so little of your time.'

'I've never heard such rubbish in my whole life! When I think of –'

The doorbell rang. The vicar and Aunt Ada had arrived. The quarrel had to be abandoned. I heard my mother's heavy tread on the stairs, voices in the hall and the creak of the sitting-room door.

Aunt Imogen stayed. She must have gone to see Lizzy because the baby's cries suddenly slackened and became whimpers. A moment later I heard a scraping sound. There were thuds and bangs.

I got out of bed. I remember the cold even now, the draughts that swirled around my ankles. My door was always left ajar and the landing light was on. I peeped through the crack. I saw Aunt Imogen on the landing. She had baby Lizzy, still whinging, on her hip. With her free hand she was pulling the cot through the doorway of her room. The teeth were poking out of her mouth and her cheeks were pink with temper and physical effort. Aunt Imogen was not a large woman and it was a heavy wooden cot. But she was very determined.

She pulled the cot across the landing to the door of my father's room. She glanced in the direction of Esmond's door and then at mine, as if sensing someone was watching her. I retreated on tiptoe towards the bed. I heard clicks, and thuds and scrapes. There was a moment's complete silence. Aunt Imogen's footsteps moved briskly across the landing to the stairs. Her heels clacked on the tiles in the hall. The sitting-room door creaked. Baby Lizzy started crying again, but this time it was different – her voice sounded louder and oddly surprised; and I knew that she was in my father's room with my father's ghost.

At one point my mother came upstairs, ostensibly to go to the lavatory. Afterwards she went into my father's room. Lizzy cried even more. My mother muttered like the madwoman we sometimes saw in Kinghampton. She did not try to move the cot. Nor did she come and see me. She thundered down the stairs.

Lizzy was still howling when they went into dinner. The crying went on and on. I was increasingly worried, finally to the point of despair. My thoughts were lurid; all children see their lives as melodramas with themselves as heroes or victims, or both. Once the vicar and Aunt Ada were out of the way, my mother would throw the Chards out of the house. I should never see Esmond again, and all because of a baby's crying. My unhappiness made it hard to breathe. I felt as though someone had strapped a belt around my diaphragm and they were gradually tightening it, notch by notch. Somehow the crying had found a way inside my head, where it made an unearthly noise like the wind sighing and singing through telegraph wires.

In a while the crying stopped. I felt so relieved. It was a blissful absence, like the disappearance of a toothache. Relaxation seeped into me. I realized that my feet were cold. I climbed into bed and made a nest from my blankets. My mind was quiet and empty. I listened. After a few minutes I heard the grown-ups going from the dining room to the sitting room. The vicar said something and my mother laughed. And I fell asleep.

When I woke up it could have been any time in the night. I had been sleeping very deeply. I woke suddenly with the sense of rushing movement, like a swimmer rising swiftly through dark water to the surface.

The sound I heard was like nothing I had ever heard before. Someone was screaming and sobbing at the same time.

And I heard my mother say, in a high, breathy voice I barely recognized, a voice that was more like a bird's squawk than anything else: 'Immy! Immy, what is it?'

Five

'Extraordinary,' my mother said to Aunt Ada. 'It's as if she thinks it was our fault.'

In January 1955, a week before the beginning of the Lent Term at Bicknor College, Aunt Imogen gave up trying to cope with her financial troubles, her husband's desertion and her bereavement. She went into Kinghampton Cottage Hospital and, a week after that, to a private nursing home in Budstow; my mother paid the bills. I now realize that Aunt Imogen had some sort of nervous breakdown after Lizzy's death. She did not want to visit Finisterre. She refused to see my mother, me or even Esmond. She wanted the company of strangers.

'Quite extraordinary,' my mother said of her sister's behaviour; not once but many times.

Esmond stayed at Finisterre when his mother went into hospital. It was intended to be a temporary measure. When Aunt Imogen recovered, she would take Esmond back to Ireland. Nevertheless my mother decided that Esmond might as well go to Bicknor College with me while he was with us. When I heard the news, I threw my arms around my mother and hugged her, which is something I do not remember doing at any other time. I don't think I have ever been so happy. At the time it did not occur to me that her readiness to pay for the nursing home and to assume responsibility for Esmond might be a way of trying to expiate guilt.

I had already told Esmond about Miss Broadbent-Brown. '*Now* you'll see,' he said when we heard that he was to join me at Bicknor College. On the same day, the carrier brought his trunk to Finisterre, which seemed a delicious sign of permanence. We were walking upstairs to my bedroom and had just passed the trunk in the hall. 'Now you'll see. I'll sort the old cow out.'

'Hush,' I said.

'The old cow,' Esmond repeated, a little more loudly than before. 'That's all she is, you know. A cow.'

We went into the nursery. I shut the door.

'Moo!' he said.

'Be careful. They'll hear.'

'No they won't. Don't worry so much.'

'But what will you do?'

'To the cow? Wait and see.' Esmond shook the bars of the window as though trying to bend or break them. 'Don't worry. I'll look after you. Why do you have these here? They're babyish.'

'My mother says it would cost too much to have them taken out.'

On my bookcase was a money-box in the shape of a china house. It was almost full; I did not have much opportunity to spend the contents. I knew that some of the coins it contained were silver. I picked it up and put it in Esmond's hands. 'For you.'

'No. Someone might notice.' Esmond was always sensible, always practical. 'Tell you what, I'll just help myself to a little bit every now and then. All right?'

For the first term at Bicknor College, all my fears had been concentrated on the person of Miss Broadbent-

Brown. Some teachers are emotionally sane; others cannot help choosing favourites; and a few, like Miss Broadbent-Brown, choose victims. Miss Broadbent-Brown chose me to be her victim, and she used me to entertain herself and the rest of the class.

In her way she was an artist. She tortured not with the thumbscrews but with the superior force of her personality allied to superior knowledge. Once I said 'can' when I should have said 'may', and she spent an entire lesson, forty-five minutes, extracting the greatest possible pleasure from this elementary confusion. I see now that this must have been a virtuoso performance. At the time, however, I had nightmares about Miss Broadbent-Brown. I begged my mother to take me away from the school; I dared not tell her the truth because I feared that Miss Broadbent-Brown would find out – I was so terrified of her that I dared not rule out the possibility that she possessed supernatural powers.

Esmond changed all that when he set to work on Miss Broadbent-Brown. The labourer was worthy of his hire. His tactics were cruel. Unlike most people he had the will to be ruthless, which was one of his greatest strengths. He was not sadistic – cruelty gave him no pleasure for its own sake – but he was implacable until his purpose had been achieved.

For example, I remember an episode involving cat's excrement on her chair; it occurred on an afternoon when the parents of potential new pupils were visiting the school, and the excrement transferred itself to the seat of her skirt. On another occasion he experimented with insects in her desk. Here he was lucky: her fear of spiders was quite pathological. Her authority over the class was never quite the same after that. By instinct he was psychologically shrewd. His tactics made his victim look foolish, which on many occasions must have prevented her from appealing to her brother and Mr Maulet. She was a strong, proud woman – in some respects not unlike my mother. What Esmond showed me was that strengths could be weaknesses.

Miss Broadbent-Brown tried without success to find out who was responsible for her persecution. She punished the entire class. She interrogated everyone individually and in private. Only I knew that Esmond was behind the campaign. But I was worried that I might inadvertently betray him. Miss Broadbent-Brown had the power to make me feel transparent. Once again, however, her strength was her weakness: when she began to question me, I was so overwrought that I burst into tears.

'You disgusting little cry-baby,' she said, and dismissed me without bothering to wait for my answers.

Esmond was very clever: many of his most spectacular achievements might plausibly have been the work of fate rather than of a malign individual. The cook, for example, owned an elderly cat which sometimes roamed through our part of the house and which might have left the excrement on the teacher's chair in our classroom. Once – by removing a dead mouse after Miss Broadbent-Brown had discovered it in her handbag but before she had returned with help – Esmond managed to suggest to her brother and Mr Maulet that she was imagining things. The more he humiliated her, the less capable she was of finding out who was responsible.

Simultaneously, Esmond managed to deflect some of her wrath from me in class, often by asking innocent questions about prosody, which was Miss Broadbent-Brown's great passion. He became one of her favourites – she liked manly little boys who feigned an interest in iambic pentameters. Esmond made sure that my tie was properly knotted and my shoes were shined. Also he helped me with my homework. Miss Broadbent-Brown had so demoralized me that I found it difficult even to prepare for her lessons. After Esmond came to the school, my place in the form order rose, and she found fewer grounds on which she could attack me. I remained afraid of her, but my fear was so diluted that I barely recognized it as such.

I still had nightmares, but now they concerned Esmond and my fear of losing him: he would be unmasked and expelled from school; my mother would send him back to Aunt Imogen and our grandmother Bradley in Ireland; alternatively, he would get bored with me and find another friend, with whom he would laugh at me.

Esmond always laughed at me. I did not mind that. I was his fool, his creature. I did not mind his laughing at me as long as he did it by himself. His laughter pleased me – I could interpret it as a symptom of our intimacy. I desperately wanted him to like me. The Rumpy incident illustrated that all too clearly.

It was typical of Bicknor College that physical training should be in the hands of Mr Maulet – the oldest member of staff and the only one who could not by any stretch of the imagination be labelled 'able-bodied'. Looking back, I suspect that Mr Maulet had a particularly ill-fitting prosthesis. We used to joke about his leg needing oiling, and I am sure that it was more than a joke – that the prosthesis did in fact squeak. He walked as though he were tramping along the deck of a ship at a thirty-degree angle in the middle of a gale. He stamped along with his body tilted to the left and his mouth clenched with effort. He had fleshy lips, tobacco-stained teeth and a slow, rasping voice. When he moved or talked, you could almost feel what this cost him in physical effort; it was as if every word he said and every pace he took represented a few seconds lopped off his lifespan.

Physical training took place in a big room at the side of the house; this was not only the gym, but also our dining room and our assembly hall. Twice a week we would change into white shorts and singlets. Mr Maulet would lean on the single radiator. We would line up before him in rows, our places determined by the alpha-betical positions of our surnames. Mr Maulet would grind out commands: 'Touch your toes'; 'Attention'; 'At ease'. And occasionally he would comment on our performance – 'You, boy. Stand up straight.' He addressed each of us as 'You, boy', which gave one a not unpleasant sense of anonymity.

On this occasion the Buzzer, Mr Broadbent-Brown, paid us a visit. Every now and then he made a tour of inspection through the school, and at first I assumed this was the reason for his being here. As always he was dressed in a blazer with brass buttons and a shield in the front pocket; his grey trousers were sharply creased; and his black hair gleamed, which gave him a lacquered appearance.

'Carry on, Mr Maulet,' he said. For a moment or two

the Buzzer watched as we contorted our bodies in accordance with Mr Maulet's instructions. His eyes moved methodically from left to right along each row of boys, beginning with those at the front. He examined us individually. This was a departure from his usual practice. Still staring at us, he walked slowly round the room, his heels clicking on the bare boards.

'That boy's slacking, Mr Maulet,' he said, stretching and bending his vowels as though they too needed exercise. He took an actor's pleasure in the sound of his own voice. 'Wouldn't you agree?'

'Which one, Headmaster?' Mr Maulet said.

The Buzzer completed the circuit and rejoined Mr Maulet. He waved a languid arm. 'That one.' Unlike his sister he was not particularly malicious, but he liked to make his presence felt.

'You, boy,' snarled Mr Maulet. 'Come here. At the double.'

At least six of us looked at one another. But no one moved.

'The one behind Chard, Headmaster?' It was typical that Maulet knew Esmond's surname if no one else's, despite the fact that Esmond had been at the school for less than a term.

'No, no. The one on the right of the one behind Chard.' The Buzzer raised his arm and waggled his index finger up and down, up and down. He was pointing at me. Embarrassment flooded over me. I wanted to shrink, to vanish. I wanted to die.

'You, boy!' Mr Maulet said.

The Buzzer nodded. 'The boy with the plump rump.'

The 'r' rolled; each 'p' exploded like a hand grenade;

each 'u' was perfectly rounded. For an instant the room was silent.

'Rumpy,' someone whispered.

He might just as well have shouted. A nervous snigger, instantly suppressed, ran through the ranks of boys. Though I was the object of the joke, I managed to express my solidarity with a little snort of my own, albeit a few seconds after everyone else. The form acted with a sense of common purpose it rarely managed to achieve in physical training.

'Who said that?' the Buzzer demanded. 'Step forward, that boy.'

No one replied.

'Rumpy,' Mr Maulet said. 'Rumpy?'

He began to emit a loud and wordless sound rather in the manner of one gargling. It was as though invisible hands were strangling him. Simultaneously his face changed colour from pink to red to purple. I noticed the intense blue of his eyes.

'What is it, man?' the Buzzer said, his voice rising.

I knew the answer before he asked the question. Mr Maulet was laughing.

'Nothing, Headmaster.' Mr Maulet's complexion began to return to normal. 'Crumb in my throat.'

The Buzzer nodded impatiently. 'Quite so, quite so.' Then he abandoned the pretence that his was a routine inspection. 'Now, I am afraid I must interrupt the lesson.' He leaned towards Mr Maulet, inclining at the waist as though hinged there, and murmured a few words in his ear.

Still shaking, Mr Maulet leant unobtrusively against the wall. The headmaster turned to face us. Everyone seemed to have forgotten my slacking. I think the whole episode must have been the Buzzer's way of nerving himself to say what had to be said.

'I have something very terrible to tell you,' he announced.

From his tone I imagined that the Queen had died or, at the very least, that the Russians had dropped a bomb on Kinghampton, causing immense loss of life.

'Someone has stolen a ten-shilling note from Miss Broadbent-Brown's purse.'

'Tosh and balderdash, boy,' Mr Maulet said as he watched us getting changed. 'Be quiet.'

He and the Buzzer stood at opposite ends of the changing room. One boy had just asked him if a burglar could have broken into the school and stolen the money. I was conscious that a great shadow lay over us all. This was absurd. Somehow the theft had become the responsibility of everyone. We shared the shame of it without a second thought. We accepted that at Bickner College ignorance was no excuse. One of us, of course, was not ignorant. *All for one*, as Esmond and I used to say, *and one for all*.

I have forgotten some of the details. The Buzzer's preliminary investigation had indicated that the money must have been stolen by a boy in our form. He had already searched our classroom and the clothes we had left in the changing room. He had found several illicit objects – sweets, a few pence, a comic or two – but not the ten-shilling note. He reasoned that the thief must therefore have the money concealed about his person.

The two men studied us as we changed. When we

were dressed in our normal clothes we had to line up along one wall with our PT kit ready for inspection. Everyone knew that the ten-shilling note must be concealed somewhere in the folds of a singlet or tucked into the toe of a plimsoll. There could be no other explanation.

Mr Broadbent-Brown waited a long moment. The nervous strain was considerable. Three boys were crying. I was trembling and on the verge of tears myself. Then he moved down the line, shaking out the clothes and poking his forefinger into each of the shoes.

As he moved on to each boy, he said in a voice like overripe cheese: 'Look at me. Can you look me in the eye and *promise* me that you know nothing about this theft?'

All of us knew that promises were sacred things that invoked the sanctity and the authority of God, the Queen and our mothers. When my turn came, the tears began to flow and I mumbled and snivelled and sniffed my way through the brief formula the Buzzer demanded. Even Esmond seemed affected by the gravity of the occasion.

The money was not found. The Buzzer did not lose his temper. He decided that we were all guilty by association and proceeded to punish the whole school. (This may have been a ploy to encourage tale-bearers. If so, it failed to work. At Bicknor College there was the usual, ridiculous taboo against sneaking.) There were no games for a week. Every boy in the school was given extra homework. And every boy in our form was beaten.

I didn't have an opportunity to talk privately to

Esmond until we were at home that evening. After tea, with my mother presiding over the table, we went up to the nursery. Esmond sat – gingerly, because he was still sore – in his favourite place, the window-seat.

'Are you all right?' he said.

I burst into tears.

'Oh Christ,' he said. 'Don't worry. It's all over.'

Finally I wiped my eyes, blew my nose and rolled down my left sock. The ten-shilling note was tucked under the black elastic garter that held up the sock. Esmond frowned at me. Once unfolded, flattened and dried, the note turned out to be as good as new. When I handed it to him, it was still a little damp.

'For God's sake,' he said. 'Do you mean it was you?' And to my amazement he started to laugh.

'I thought you'd be cross – because of the beating and the homework.'

'*You?*' He turned the note over in his hand and held it up to the light. 'Where did you hide it?'

'It was in my plimsoll. And . . . and in the changing room I put it in my mouth.'

He snapped questions at me. Between sobs – because I thought he must really be cross – I told him about passing the open door of the Broadbent-Browns' sitting room and seeing the purse on the table, with the corner of the note sticking out. I had acted desperately and on impulse: after a quick glance up and down the hall, the note was in my pocket and I was hurrying away almost before I knew what was happening. It was as if for a few, crucial seconds, someone else had taken over my body. Someone who wasn't timid, law-abiding and indecisive. In fact someone rather like Esmond.

'But why did you do it? It was so risky.'

'I did it for you.'

He said nothing. The setting sun was behind him. His face was dark. By a trick of the light it looked as though he were behind the bars of the window, not in front of them; as though the bars divided us. I waited, with my head bowed, for his verdict.

'Silly old Rumpy,' he said.

That was the first time he used the name for me, and I knew at once that it was going to be special, a sign of our friendship.

'You see there's not much money left in my money-box,' I said. 'And I was afraid . . .'

'Afraid I'd stop sorting out the old bitch for you?' His voice thickened. 'Don't worry. I'm after teaching her a lesson she won't forget. The bloody old bag.'

No – I hadn't been afraid of that. I had been afraid of losing Esmond.

'Where will you hide the money?' I asked.

'Don't worry yourself about that.'

I found fresh reasons to be afraid. I imagined police-men searching our house. I imagined Mr Broadbent-Brown telling my mother what I had done. 'Suppose someone saw me? Suppose . . . ?'

Esmond ignored me. As he walked across the room, he rolled the ten-shilling note into a cylinder and squashed it flat. He fed it into the slot of my money-box.

'There you are,' he said. 'That is the one place where no one will ever look.'

Six

'What a pretty little girl,' Aunt Imogen said when she saw the silver-framed photograph of me as a two-year-old which my mother kept on her desk. It is immaterial whether Aunt Imogen was making a mistake or making mischief. I *did* look like a girl: that was the point.

In early photographs my hair is long, and my clothing is on the feminine side of androgynous. In those days I had large eyes and delicate features. It wasn't that my mother didn't like boys – she certainly liked Esmond. Perhaps it was more personal than that: she wanted me, Thomas, her only child, to be a dutiful daughter. To be, in fact, what she herself had spectacularly failed to be; my Irish grandmother was never invited to visit Finisterre.

The deeper I pry into motives, whether my own or anyone else's, the more confused I become. But if I had to guess what was the keynote of my mother's character, the one feature that gave sense and shape to all her actions, I would say it was that she was terrified of strangers and terrified of solitude. She did not want to live alone. But she feared to go among strangers. My father's sudden death in 1943 must have come as a terrible shock to her, almost a betrayal. There she was, in a large and lonely house which was isolated still further by the circumstances of war, with only a ghost and a wailing baby for company. No wonder she wanted me to stay with her for ever and ever.

I tried to explain this to Esmond, just after we wrote the letter to my unknown daughter Alice. He and I were walking down the lane to Blackberry Water and the beach. The slanting evening sunshine made my eyes water.

'That's nonsense, of course,' Esmond said. 'If your mother had really wanted company, she could have got Granny to come and live here. She'd have come like a shot.'

'It wouldn't have worked. Because she couldn't boss Granny around. Granny was her mother. And besides . . .'

'What?'

'Granny was older. She was going to die first.'

'OK. Then why didn't your mother get married again? If she was that worried about being alone.'

'But who to? She didn't know anyone around here. Not properly. Only Aunt Ada and the vicar. She didn't *want* to meet new people.'

'I don't see what this has got to do with her wanting a girl.'

'Girls stay at home,' I said. 'Or they used to when my mother was young.'

'In the nineteen-twenties?'

'All right, perhaps they didn't stay at home in the nineteen-twenties. Not in reality, I mean. But they did in some Irish never-never land.'

'Some corner of County Cork,' Esmond said, swinging his stick at a clump of nettles, 'on which the sun never set.'

'Girls didn't need jobs or money. They didn't even need husbands. When they grew up, the first and most

70

important thing they had to do was look after their parents. That's what my mother thought, deep down. Not thought – *felt*. That's why she wanted me to be a girl.'

Esmond grunted and fumbled for his cigarettes. He increased his pace slightly so we were no longer walking abreast. He didn't want to talk to me any more. I listened to our footsteps and to the irregular whine of the chain saw; Bronwen was still in her woodshed. The sound of the motor was louder here than it had been in the house. Our little valley, broadening as it neared Ulvercombe Mouth, acted as a gigantic megaphone.

The mud beneath my feet was hard after the long summer. The sea came into view: an improbably blue inverted triangle framed by the horizon above and cliffs on either side. The lane, which had been running steadily but gently downhill, suddenly dropped into a steeper gradient.

On our right I heard the rustle of the stream that ran past our garden. Ahead, to the west, the cliffs rose like the rim of a plate. The lane, still descending, made a leisurely 180-degree turn to the southern shore of Blackberry Water. Blackberry Water was a shallow pool, roughly egg-shaped, with its wider end on the seaward side. It was fed from the east by the stream, which re-emerged at the western end of the pool and slipped almost invisibly through the shingle to the sea. Sometimes – particularly when gales coincided with spring tides – the waves crashed up the beach, through the opening in the cliffs and into Blackberry Water itself. This was where the pure water from the stream met the salt water from the sea. And near the landward end of the pool, the round stepping stones marched from south to north like buttons up a waistcoat. The turf around Blackberry Water was always neat and green. A farmer from Ulvercombe grazed his sheep there. There were blackberry bushes in the lane but none near the pool.

When we were children, we sometimes had our picnics by the pool rather than on the beach of Ulvercombe Mouth. On the bank near the southern end of the stepping stones there was a level rectangle about the size of a croquet lawn. My mother would spread the red-and-white checked tablecloth on the coarse, close-cropped grass among the thistles and sheep turds. Nearer the sea, where the water was deeper, Esmond taught me with infinite patience to swim a few strokes.

I glanced upstream through the green cleft between the hills. Our conifer windbreaks were dark green smudges, almost black. The sunshine had made the windows of Finisterre blank and golden. *Mine eyes dazzle*, I thought; and once more I felt a shadow passing over me.

Esmond lit another cigarette from the stub of the last. He squinted through the smoke towards the house. 'That place'll be a bloody goldmine come the spring,' he said. 'Just you wait and see.'

I smiled. 'I'll wait. I'm not going anywhere.'

'I hope not.'

'But what do you mean?'

He sucked in a mouthful of smoke and turned away. 'The girl could complicate things.'

'But you wouldn't go away?' I said, panicking. I remember what I'd heard Bronwen saying when I'd eaves-

7 2

dropped on their conversation in the drawing room earlier in the afternoon. 'You wouldn't, would you? Whatever happened.'

'Don't worry. I'll look after you. But I may need your help.'

'Anything,' I said. 'I'll do anything.'

There were times when I was jealous of Esmond, which was only to be expected. It is harder to believe that he was occasionally jealous of me.

In the Easter holiday of 1955, Mr Maulet gave our form a holiday task. Each of us had to write an essay entitled 'His Future Life'. Mr Maulet wanted us to describe how we saw both our careers and our private lives developing. We had to pretend we were our own biographers, that we were looking at ourselves from the outside. We had to pretend that our subjects – ourselves – were dead.

'I want to know everything about you,' Mr Maulet said. He stamped slowly round the classroom firing each clause above our heads: 'Where you lived; what you did; whether you were married; what your children were like; how you died.' He grunted, either with pain or with amusement. 'Remember. You're writing about the most fascinating person in the world.'

Each biographical essay had to include the words, 'So-and-So attended Bicknor College, Kinghampton, an experience which did much to form his character.' The length had to be four or five pages of our English exercise books. The only rule was that the contents should remain within the realm of reasonable possibility. It would be acceptable, for example, to have oneself become prime minister, but not to make oneself emperor of the universe.

Esmond and I left our essays until the last day of the holidays. This turned out to be one of those wonderful April days which are like the best of summer but without the nasty bits like wasps and tourists and excessive heat. At breakfast we ate our Corn Flakes and boiled eggs in the dining room.

'We'll have a picnic today,' my mother said. 'Won't that be nice, boys?'

'Lovely,' Esmond said.

'Where?' I said. 'Picnic' was an ominous word in the vocabulary of my childhood. And I knew that Esmond preferred cafés, ice-creams and man-made amusements.

'Blackberry Water, I think. It's perfect at this time of year. We'll be nice and private.'

'But Mummy –' I knew my mother liked it when I called her 'Mummy'. '– we haven't done our holiday essay yet. Couldn't we go into Budstow this afternoon instead?'

There was an amusement arcade in Budstow with air rifles and automata, and primitive viewing booths which showed you what the butler had seen.

'It'll be terribly crowded, darling,' my mother said. 'Especially on a day like this.'

'It won't take long to do the essays,' Esmond said.

'There you are,' my mother cried, bestowing a smile on Esmond. 'You do your work, and Mrs Jodson and I will see to lunch. And when you've finished we can go.'

'Can we swim?' he asked.

'I don't see why not. Mind you, it'll be very cold.'

'Oh – I've just remembered: I haven't got any swimming trunks. Not here, I mean.'

For an instant my mother's mouth hung open. I knew with the intuition that is inspired by love that Esmond didn't have any swimming trunks at all. Esmond was poor.

'Now don't you worry about that,' she said. 'I'm sure we can find you something to wear.'

'Thank you, Aunt Fiona.'

That earned him another smile.

After breakfast Esmond and I went into what my mother called the 'schoolroom'. This was a little room between the study and the sitting room. It faced east and perhaps had once been used as a breakfast or morning room. When Esmond came to stay with us and joined me at Bicknor College, my mother decided that we needed somewhere to do our homework. We also played here when we weren't outside or upstairs in the nursery. (Esmond's bedroom was too small for playing in.)

It took me about an hour to write my essay. I did not concentrate very hard on it. My mind was occupied by other things. Esmond appeared to be able to make my mother do anything he wanted, and this made me angry with both of them (but especially with my mother). I was also irritated by being cooped up inside. Finally, over everything hung the doom-laden knowledge that this was the last day of the holidays. Tomorrow, life would become far more hateful than it was today. Tomorrow I should see Miss Broadbent-Brown unless a merciful fate had struck her dead since last term.

I wrote about how I saw my life developing. When you are a child all adult activities seem equally remote. No eleven-year-old really believes he will grow up. You can visualize being a field marshal as easily as you can visualize being a dustman: since both goals seem unattainable, the practical differences between them are insignificant.

At the age of thirteen (in my biographical fiction) I went to Rosington, the minor public school where my father had been educated; this, I had always understood, was what my mother planned for me. At Rosington I swiftly rose to be Captain of the First XI and Head of School. I won a scholarship to Oxford, where I studied architecture and wrote poetry. At the age of twenty I left Oxford and went to London. My first commission was to design the exhibition centre for a new Festival of Britain. My design was so successful that a flood of important commissions swept in from all over the world. The President of the United States wanted a new capital city, so I built him New Washington in the Californian desert. The Russians offered me a fortune to design an experimental space station in Kamchatka but I was otherwise engaged on remodelling Buckingham Palace. The Queen was so pleased she made me a viscount as well as appointing me Poet Laureate. I married – a blonde American film star, though I was too coy to mention this in my essay – and fathered four sons. I built a great house by the sea, where I lived with my family, pets and friends. I died aged eighty-nine, laden with honours and surrounded by my sorrowing family.

When I had finished I turned to see what Esmond

was doing. He had finished too, and was staring out of the window.

'Can I read yours?' I asked.

'If you want.'

He pushed his exercise book across the table and picked up mine. This is what he had written. *The life of E. A. Chard. Chard attended Bicknor College, Kinghampton, an experience which did much to form his character. Afterwards he lived and then he died.* At first I thought that Esmond was playing a joke on me, and that he had written his essay on other pages or in a different exercise book.

'You can't hand in this,' I said. 'Maulet will kill you.'

Esmond did not reply. He turned over the page. Frowning, he read the rest of my essay.

'Please tell me,' I said. 'Why didn't you write a proper essay?'

He slammed both his hands, palms-down, on the table. 'Because I haven't got a proper life, have I?' he shouted.

'But Esmond –'

He swept my exercise book away from him. Pages fluttered like white wings. It fell on the floor. The impact wrenched the cover from the staples that held the pages together: a beatable offence at Bicknor College.

'All this stuff – going to Rosington and Oxford; being an architect, being a poet – you could *do* that.'

'So could you.'

'Oh yes. Where do you think we're living? In a fairy tale?'

I stared at him.

77

'Don't you realize it all costs money? Not that it matters to you.' By now Esmond was on his feet. 'You've got money, haven't you?'

He ran out of the room and slammed the door behind him.

My mother made a cult of the seaside picnic.

In her more expansive moments she liked to talk about the picnics of her childhood and adolescence: those epic trips to Timoleague and Inchydoney Island, to Courtmacsherry and Kinsale, formed part of the folklore of my childhood. For her, each had been a little adventure lapped in comfort and security. The sun shone interminably upon huge and perfectly sandy beaches where no one else came. The sea was warm, blue and somehow more distinguished than any other sea. The lobsters were always larger than anyone had seen before, the cream thicker, the ham tastier. Passing peasants – Catholics, naturally – were infallibly deferential. Cousin Harry was so droll he kept everyone in stitches. Cousin Fanny was trapped by the tide and had to be rescued by Mr Alfred Chard, who owned the Royal Hotel and was Esmond's grandfather. Arthur Chard was never mentioned but I felt his invisible, unstated presence in my mother's stories. Why else should she find the memory of those picnics so exciting? Why else should she describe them time and time again – as if repetition made the magic stronger?

Parents like their children to worship at parental altars rather than to set up altars of their own. My mother was anxious that I, too, should look back on my childhood as a series of idyllic seaside picnics. Hence

78

those tedious trips to Ulvercombe Mouth which so disfigured my childhood.

The beach was tiny. It was a noisy place, what with those wretched Atlantic breakers and the scratchy voices of the sea birds. One had only to take a bite of a sandwich for regiments of wasps to appear. The shingle was so uncomfortable it must have been especially imported. Along the bottom of the cliffs and trailing in double lines out to sea were the rocks: these were razor sharp and crowded with unpleasant surprises – the bones of gulls; rotting seaweed, often treacherously slippery; oil-stained plastic drums and the white froth of chemical pollutants; and, once and most mysteriously, the half-eaten corpse of a Dalmatian dog. The beach smelled of salt and decay.

The wreckers from Ulvercombe village, Lilian told me later, used to put a fire on the headland to the south. The ships hit the rocks to the north, and if the tide was right the wreckage was swept up into Ulvercombe Mouth. There was a parliamentary enquiry about it in 1788. An East Indiaman from Bristol was wrecked, and most of the crew got ashore. But the men from the village were waiting with pitchforks and cudgels.

'By the time the coastguards arrived,' Lilian said, 'the wreckers were gone and all of the crew were dead. And do you know what? None of the sailors had drowned.'

In my mind there was always blood on the beach at Ulvercombe Mouth: blood slipping almost invisibly through the shingle like the overflow from Blackberry Water. No wonder the place smelled of decay.

Quite apart from my general distaste for the location, there were other reasons why our picnic on the last day of the Easter holidays in 1955 was doomed to be a failure; and there was a futher reason, of course, why the whole affair stayed so vividly in my mind, and why this day became a sort of symbol for the entire series of Ulvercombe picnics.

But I anticipate. In those days the lane was muddier than it later became – tractors used it more often and the council laid down hard core only in 1969. At this stage of her life my mother refused to drive the half-mile from the house to Blackberry Water unless the lane was not only dry, but also uncharacteristically free of ruts. She had bought a four-door Standard Eight a year or so earlier and treated it with far more maternal solicitude than she did me. When we were a little older, Esmond made a joke of this: he said it was only natural because the car had cost my mother nearly five hundred pounds, whereas I had cost her nothing.

In consequence we had to walk. This would not have been a problem had my mother been less ambitious in her conception of what a picnic should be. Her idea, which perhaps had some basis in reality in more spacious pre-war days, was startlingly simple: the purpose of a picnic was to recreate in a picturesque outside location your life at home in all its complexity; and the closer you came to realizing this aim, the more successful the picnic deserved to be.

'One might as well be comfortable,' my mother used to say.

The rigid observance of this principle meant that most of our picnics at Ulvercombe were blighted by the necessity of our tramping down the lane, and (worse) up it, laden with a wide selection of household goods.

Before we left Finisterre, my mother would marshal ourselves and our burdens in the garden.

'Just let me check my list,' she'd say. And if she were in a particularly frivolous mood she would sing, 'I've got a little list – I've got a little list.'

The list was a formidably long document, the result of many years of field research in Britain and Ireland. Essential items included a primus stove, methylated spirits, paraffin and matches (if possible these were carried separately for fear of spontaneous combustion during the march); a kettle, fresh water (the stream which fed Blackberry Water was considered to be impure), a teapot, tea, sugar in a tin and milk in a milk bottle (if we had visitors – Aunt Ada, for example – we would also take a sugar bowl and a milk jug); the red-and-white tablecloth, deckchairs for my mother and any other adults, a small folding table which stood by her chair, and an inflatable air cushion made of thick, blue-and-orange striped rubber with an unforgettably sweet and sickly smell; plates, cups, saucers, teaspoons, knives, forks, dessert spoons and napkins; a bowl to wash up in, a scourer and a tea towel; swimming costumes and towels; my mother's substantial handbag whose contents ranged from a purse and a diary to a library book and a roll of lavatory paper; and – almost as an afterthought – food. There were many optional extras; for example a saucepan, a frying pan, more chairs, a larger table, a first-aid kit, a variety of games, raincoats, hats, umbrellas and a contraption made of wood and canvas which was meant to act as a windbreak but invariably blew over.

This picnic in April 1955 seemed particularly bad;

perhaps that is merely because I remember it so vividly. We had to make the journey up and down the lane twice before we had ferried all the items which my mother considered essential to our well-being. Esmond was angry with me – I might almost say he was sulking – and I felt utterly miserable. He walked with my mother. They were in front of me all the way there, all the way back, and all the way there again. They found plenty to talk about. My mother kept smiling down at him. I heard them laughing.

Once my mother turned round. 'Hurry up, Thomas. And *please* stop looking so glum.'

We had no sooner settled ourselves on the beach when the sun went in and the wind freshened. The breakers were large and grey. A cloudy April day is a very different proposition from a sunny one.

'Oh! How tiresome,' my mother said. 'And I do believe the tide's coming in. Perhaps we had better move.'

We shouldered our burdens once more and re-treated through the gap in the cliffs to Blackberry Water. We laid out our lunch in the place by the stepping stones, which my mother gaily referred to as 'our picnic lawn'.

'I expect the pixies feast here at midnight,' my mother remarked. In certain moods she was capable of flights of girlish whimsy. 'Did I ever tell you of the time Aunt Imogen and I tried to catch a leprechaun?'

At this moment I sat down on a sheep dropping. Esmond laughed at me without making a sound. My mother was furious. She made me change into swimming trunks. I sat shivering on the grass.

'Lunchtime,' my mother announced a little later. 'Isn't this splendid?'

While we ate, the seagulls wheeled overhead like vultures. The sandwiches tasted of sand. A cold and slimy section of tomato fell on my bare leg. Believing it to be a bird-dropping, I screamed.

'Oh for heaven's sake, don't be such a baby,' my mother said. 'Use the cloth in the bowl.'

Afterwards Esmond volunteered to get the primus going for my mother's tea. To my surprise she allowed him: such a messy, interesting and potentially dangerous job was usually reserved for an adult. I was set to do the washing up – in cold water, of course, and with the westerly wind skimming through the gap in the cliffs.

'Is that a car?' Esmond said suddenly.

We all listened. All I could hear were the cries of the gulls, the roaring sea and the hissing of the primus' blue flames.

'I don't think –'

My mother stopped. An engine in low gear was revving in the lane.

'How tiresome,' my mother said. 'I hoped we should avoid the trippers at this time of the year. Would anyone like some fruit?'

'No, thank you,' I said.

'It's good for you, Thomas.'

'I think it's Aunt Ada's car,' Esmond said.

A moment later the vicarage's Austin Twelve appeared. It nosed slowly down the last semicircular bend to Blackberry Water.

'Good Lord,' my mother said.

I knew why she was surprised. The vicar was driving; Aunt Ada was beside him in the passenger seat. The vicar rarely had time for picnics, the seaside and the beauties of nature.

The car stopped about ten yards away from us. Its wings were streaked with mud from the lane. Aunt Ada leapt out and ran clumsily towards us, holding up the front hem of her flapping, flowered skirt. When she ran, you thought of liquid slopping about in a container made of some pliable material like rubber.

My mother rose to meet her. 'Ada, I thought you were off to Budstow today.'

Aunt Ada was very pale; and even such a short run had made her gasp for air. She took my mother's arm and drew her away from Esmond and me. Meanwhile the vicar switched off the engine and climbed out of the Austin Twelve. He was smaller than Aunt Ada, and my memories of him are entirely monochromatic: black clerical suit, white dog-collar; white skin and black hair. He strode with very long strides, which were perhaps designed to make him seem taller than he was, towards the women. They muttered together.

Esmond took a massive bite of an apple. The apple was one of last autumn's; we stored them in the loft above the garage at Finisterre, where many of them rotted or were eaten by rats. By this stage of the spring the apples had leathery skins, bright and wrinkled like the complexions of elderly gypsies. You could never quite tell what you would find when you bit into them. If you were lucky, the flesh inside tasted sweet and rich – almost like a dessert wine. Esmond wasn't lucky.

He retched, and spat out what was in his mouth.

It landed in the water. He threw the rest of the apple after it.

The vicar broke away from the two women and came towards us. 'Are you all right, Esmond?'

'Yes, thank you, sir.'

'Would you like this, dear?' Aunt Ada said to my mother. As she spoke, Aunt Ada's features twisted themselves into those of a grotesque stranger – either because of emotion or because she was trying to convey a wordless message – and she held out a large and freshly ironed white handerchief that probably belonged to the vicar.

My mother took it. She nodded her thanks. She took a deep breath and advanced on Esmond and me. I looked at her in astonishment.

'What is it?' I asked. 'What's wrong?'

My mother put her arm around Esmond and squeezed his head against her chest. Taken by surprise, he wriggled. His expression was bemused. For once, what was happening lay outside his experience. With her free hand she held out the handkerchief. She was holding it by one corner. The linen unfolded itself. It masked Esmond's face from me.

'My poor boy,' my mother said. 'I'm your mummy now.'

Seven

'Are you insane?' Bronwen said sharply.

'By your definition anyone you don't understand is insane,' Esmond replied. 'So that covers most of the human race.'

'I could kill you sometimes.'

'Yes, most of the human race. Including yourself, incidentally.'

They were in the sitting room after dinner on the evening of the 2nd October. I was in the nursery – on my knees, with the floorboard up. It wasn't much more than forty-eight hours since I had written the letter to Alice but my life before the letter already seemed to belong to a different person in a different time and place.

'Look, Esmond. She's his *daughter*. She's going to start wondering. She's going to ask questions.'

'Let her. I've got nothing to hide.'

'You *are* insane, aren't you?'

'The house is looking very nice at present. We have done a good job. It will be quite obvious that we've been faithful stewards. With a bit of luck we'll get some good autumn weather.'

'I do not believe this.'

'You don't have to believe it,' Esmond said. 'Just do as I say and everything will be fine. Trust me.'

Bronwen laughed, or rather snorted sarcastically. 'Like Rumpy does? Woof woof?'

'That's the spirit, dear. All for one and one for all. Alice is coming down by train tomorrow afternoon. I said I'd meet her at Exeter.'

'I think you should have talked it over with me before you phoned her.' Bronwen's voice was still louder than most people's would be for an indoor tête-à-tête but it had lost its cutting edge. 'Oh Christ, I'm just not used to this sort of set-up.'

'Why don't you sit down,' he suggested.

'It's not natural, is it? No, come on – be honest for once – it's a bit sick.'

'Life is a sickness: a long and invariably chronic illness that ends in death.'

This was not the sort of remark I expected to hear from Esmond. I wondered if he was quoting Lilian's brother, Stephen Sandwell, who had a weakness for making such pronouncements.

'Cut it out,' Bronwen said. 'You've had too much to drink. What did she sound like?'

'Young. Nervous. Breathless. Maybe shy? Quite a pleasant speaking voice, actually. Can you make up the bed in the death room?'

'I wish you wouldn't call it that.'

'It's a very good name. My sister Lizzy died there, and my uncle George. Among others.'

'You'll have to get Rumpy used to the idea. I'm not doing it. Rumpy's your responsibility.'

'All right. I'll say you suggested it, though.' There was a long silence. Then Esmond said in quite a different voice, 'Come here. No, closer, you stupid woman.'

After a while it became obvious that whatever they were doing it did not include talking. I replaced the floorboard. Naturally I was very upset. I sat on the window-seat. I watched my face reflected in the black glass. Then I leaned my head against the wall of the embrasure and closed my eyes.

Until I had seen my mother's will I had not thought of Alice as being a real person. All I had was a dim memory of something small, pink and constantly hungry; something that cried and slept and sucked; something I had very little to do with. In the absence of any data to go on (my mother had destroyed or hidden the photographs and all the other evidence), I suppose I made up a version of Alice.

If Lilian had had an abortion I should probably have done much the same thing: I should have created a conditional child – the condition in question being 'Had the baby lived'. Alice was still alive, but to all practical purposes – as far as I was concerned – she had died a few months after Lilian, her mother. Every now and then I would think, 'If Alice were here, this would be her twenty-first birthday' or 'She might be thinking about going to university now' or 'She would be old enough to have boyfriends.' Such speculations had hardly any emotional weight to them. They made me feel a little sad and they also gave me a little pleasure. Looking through old photographs produced much the same blend of sensations. Just as one knows that one can never have the past again, so I knew, or thought I knew, that I could never have Alice.

My mother's death began to change all this: it brought Alice closer to reality. But she was still no more than a word or two on a piece of paper; she was still an abstraction. I certainly wasn't cross with Alice about the will. No – I was cross with my mother, who had been very real but now was safely dead, not with Alice.

The one thing I didn't want to do was to meet Alice. I was perfectly accustomed to my pretend version. I didn't want my daughter herself – in the flesh, capable of acting and speaking and thinking independently. The three of us at Finisterre were like a mixture of chemicals which in itself is perfectly stable; but if you added an unknown and probably volatile substance, anything might happen. Esmond couldn't understand that. For once, as it turned out, I was right and he was wrong.

For the last forty-eight hours I had kept my fingers crossed and hoped that Alice would have the wit to refuse the invitation. I assumed that it all depended on how desperate she was for money. I wished Esmond had told me more about her. I wished they had given me more time to prepare myself. If she came, I hoped it would just be for a short visit: perhaps I shouldn't have to see her. Esmond might tell her there was no money, or not until I died, and she would go away.

Perhaps shy, Esmond had said of her. *With quite a pleasant speaking voice.* It wouldn't have mattered if it had been Bronwen's idea to put her in the death room. But Esmond had suggested it. That was what really worried me.

When my mother temporarily changed her mind about the death room it shocked me far more than Aunt Imogen's death. Children have short memories, I suppose; and Aunt Imogen had been out of my sight for nearly four months. The death room, on the other hand, was always with us: its door was directly across the landing from the nursery's.

The adults around us wrapped Aunt Imogen's death in euphemisms. As far as my mother was concerned, she had passed on or over. Aunt Ada said that it was in many ways a merciful release. According to the vicar – who gave us his professional opinion in church on the following Sunday – Aunt Imogen was watching over us from Heaven on the right hand of the Lord. I overheard the Jodson family discussing it. Mrs Jodson said that Mrs Chard was 'pushing up the daisies, poor soul.' On another occasion, young Bill Jodson said she had kicked the bucket; and his father remarked that she had gone for a burton.

At the time I simply wasn't interested in the manner of her death. Bill Jodson knew – I remember some hints he made, and with hindsight can interpret them – but he must have been afraid to tell either Esmond or me. It was not until some years later that I discovered that after breakfast on that fine April morning Aunt Imogen went upstairs to her room at the nursing home. She tore up a sheet and made a rope from it. She tied one end of her rope to a leg of the bed. She made the other end into a noose and placed it round her neck. Then she jumped out of her window. At the inquest, it was decided that she had hanged herself while the balance of her mind was temporarily disturbed follow-ing the death of her baby daughter. Her death was a tragedy, the coroner said, for which neither she, her family nor the nursing-home authorities could reason-ably be blamed.

If Aunt Imogen's death could be considered as a cloud, it had a number of silver linings, one of which I discovered immediately: the picnic was abandoned, and we and our impedimenta had a lift back to Finisterre in the vicar's Austin Twelve. When we got there, the vicar took Esmond away for a walk in the garden. ('He made me kneel down and say a prayer for my ma,' Esmond told me afterwards. 'It was just beyond the compost heap. And then he stroked my neck. Jesus Christ.')

'Oh, the poor darling boy,' Aunt Ada whispered to my mother as the rest of us were getting out of the car. 'Isn't he being brave?'

'She was my sister, you know.'

'Fiona, I'm so sorry. I didn't mean to imply –'

'It doesn't matter,' my mother said with Spartan fortitude. 'Esmond's loss is obviously much greater than mine.' She dabbed her eyes with her handkerchief. As she did so she caught sight of me, and realized I had been listening. She flashed her teeth at me. 'Go into the kitchen and stay with Mrs Jodson,' she said. 'Tell her to put the kettle on.'

The real shock came in the evening after all our visitors had gone. It was after supper, and the three of us were in the sitting room. No one had eaten very much and Esmond was unusually pale. Otherwise things were much as they always were. Everyone, it seemed to me, was pretending to be dreadfully normal. Esmond and I were reading, or pretending to read, on the sofa. Suddenly my mother laid down her knitting on the arm of her chair.

'Boys,' she said. 'I think it's time we had a little chat. A family conference.'

This was a novelty. A family conference was the sort of thing that children were always having in books, along with midnight feasts, holidays in gypsy caravans and adventures involving secret passages, hidden treasure and criminals who invariably dropped their aitches.

'I want you to know, Esmond, that this is just as much your home as it is mine and Thomas's.'

Esmond stared at the carpet. 'Thank you, Aunt Fiona.'

'Of course, if you prefer, you could go to Granny's. To live, I mean. You must be perfectly frank. Would you like to go back to Ireland?'

'Please,' he said, 'I'd like to stay here with you.'

My mother's lower lip trembled. 'I am so glad, dear. We should love you to stay, shouldn't we, Thomas?'

'Oh yes,' I said. 'Yes please. For ever and ever?'

'For ever and ever,' my mother said gravely. 'Amen.'

Esmond looked at me. I knew he was about to burst out laughing. He scrambled off the sofa and ran out of the room.

'Poor boy,' my mother said softly. 'He has had such a lot to bear. We'll leave him to himself for a moment or two.'

A moment later, Esmond came back. He apologized for rushing out of the room. My mother said it was quite all right, she understood perfectly; and Esmond and I didn't look at each other because we both knew if our eyes met the laughter would well up again.

'Now that you're really one of the family,' my mother said, 'we shall have to do something about your bedroom. Your present room is rather small, isn't it?'

'There's room for another bed in my room,' I said.

'I don't think that would be terribly . . .' My mother paused, presumably to run a list of adjectives through her mind. '. . . hygienic.' The word must have pleased her, perhaps because it sounded irrefutably scientific; in any case she repeated it with additional emphasis. '*Hygienic*. And I prefer to keep the spare bedroom free in case we have visitors. One can't really do without a spare bedroom, can one? But there's the *other* spare room, isn't there? We don't really need two.'

'You mean . . .' Esmond swallowed. 'You mean the room . . . ?'

'But Mummy, you can't put him there,' I said – rather more loudly than I'd intended.

'I don't think that I was asking your opinion, Thomas. Correct me if I'm wrong.'

'But no one ever –'

'Please,' Esmond interrupted. 'I think I'd rather stay where I am. If you don't mind.'

My mother was not a subtle person. Like most people, she followed the promptings of her emotions without trying to articulate them to herself, and she was incapable of self-analysis; she lacked both the will and the vocabulary for introspection. To any reasonably intelligent adult it would have been obvious that she wanted to put Esmond into my father's bed. Perhaps the promptings of her emotions had as much to do with superstition as with sexual frustration: she might have been trying to exorcize a ghost. Did Esmond realize all this or sense it without being able to put it into words? Was that why he was so against the idea? Or was it because it was the death room? The room where my father died. And – more to the point where Esmond was concerned – the room where baby Lizzy died.

The strength of my mother's desire had blinded her to this last consideration. But at last the penny dropped.

She bared her teeth at me and desperately tried to retract what she had said without admitting that she had made a mistake. She claimed that all along she had meant Esmond to have the spare room, not my father's room, and that I wilfully or through crass stupidity misunderstood her. I had the wit to apologize to her, which was almost always a sensible policy. Esmond showed a becoming gratitude. It was tacitly agreed that for the time being he would stay where he was.

'I think it might be a good idea if we all went to bed early,' my mother said.

'Will I have to go to school tomorrow?' Esmond asked.

'No, dear. I think not. Would you like Thomas to stay at home and keep you company?'

'Yes, please.'

So there was another silver lining. Aunt Imogen's death had delayed my return to Bicknor College and Miss Broadbent-Brown.

I kissed my mother's cheek. Usually Esmond did the same. On that night my mother turned her head at the last moment and accepted his kiss on the mouth. I saw her own lips move. The kiss disgusted me. I don't think Esmond liked it either. In the hall he wiped his mouth with the back of his hand and wrinkled his nose. He didn't say anything until we were safely upstairs. It was the first time we had been alone together since before the picnic, since our quarrel in the schoolroom.

'The bitch,' he said. 'Can you beat it?'

I was relieved that he seemed to have forgotten our difference of opinion. 'I just can't understand it,' I said. 'She never lets anyone sleep in the death room.'

'I don't mean her, you fool. I mean *my* mother.'

That night I heard Esmond crying quietly in his little room above the porch. It was the first and last time I heard him crying. I did not dare to go in to him because my mother might hear. In any case, I did not know how to comfort him.

The astonishing thing about Aunt Imogen's suicide was how little it affected us. At Finisterre and Bicknor College, everything went on more or less as before. Esmond hadn't seen Aunt Imogen since January, so he had had plenty of time to grow accustomed to her absence. My mother was already acting *in loco parentis*.

I doubt if anyone except us wanted Esmond. His father had shuffled off his family responsibilities. There were no other close relations on the Chard side of the family. Grandmother Bradley was too old, too frail and too poor. In legal terms, I think my mother was Esmond's guardian; she did not formally adopt him. But in all other respects he was treated as another son, indeed as the favourite son. When talking to third parties, she would refer to us with careful ambiguity as 'my boys'. When others referred to us as 'your sons', she was delighted.

At Bicknor College, everyone knew that Esmond's mother had died and that he was now a permanent part of my family. Towards the end of the summer term, a boy in the year above ours asked me how I liked having a cuckoo in my nest. His name was Corby. He was fat and pink like a pig, with a slim, disdainful nose and a head of coarse yellow curls. It was just after lunch, and we were all outside. Corby pinned me against a wall in the playground. He swayed from side to side, preventing my feeble attempts to escape, and chanted 'Cuckoo! Cuckoo!' I pretended not to understand what he meant. I felt his malice like the heat of a fire.

While we were waiting for the first lesson of afternoon school, I told Esmond what had happened. In my desire to demonstrate how despicable I thought our tormentor was, I spoke with uncharacteristic ferocity.

'There must be something we can do to him,' I said. 'I'd like to kill him.' I added a phrase I'd learned from Bill Jodson, 'The bloody bugger.'

Esmond laughed, but he treated what I had said as a serious suggestion: 'There'd be too many questions if we killed him.'

'But we can't just let him get away with it.'

'Who said we were going to? I'll need your help. One for all, Rumpy. And all for one.'

A few days later, after school, Esmond lured Corby into the lavatories. These were known as 'the bogs'. He said he had seen Corby's cap in one of the cubicles – which was true, because Esmond had put it there. Just after school was a good time to choose for our enterprise because the rest of the boys were gone and the staff were having tea in the Broadbent-Browns' sitting room at the other end of the house. I kept watch in the corridor while Esmond knocked out one of Corby's front teeth and gave him a bloody nose. Then Esmond called me in. He and Corby were in the cubicle. I helped him force the boy's head into the bowl of a lavatory; and it was I who pulled the chain.

'Dear God,' Esmond said. 'Here's a bleeding bog-brush. Does the Pope know? It must be a bleeding, bloody miracle.'

The blood on the porcelain mingled with the water. It made streaks like strawberry ripple – the syrup they put in vanilla ice-cream. Its colour varied from a full dark red to a pale pink according to the degree of dilution. For years afterwards, the smell of disinfectant made me think of blood.

'We make a good team,' Esmond said as we slipped out of Bicknor College by the tradesmen's entrance. 'Now if he sneaks, we just deny it. They can't prove anything.'

The next day, and the next, Corby avoided us in the playground. My ferocity gradually gave way to fear: I returned to my natural condition at Bicknor College. But nothing happened to us. I began to hope we would escape retribution.

On the third day, however, I had a nasty surprise. Mr Maulet was making us recite French irregular verbs in chorus. *Nous allons, vous allez, ils vont.* It was near the end of the afternoon on a hot July day and everyone was behaving like a zombie. I was staring out of the window and noticed a small black car turning into the drive. It looked familiar. A few seconds later – for I was thinking very sluggishly – I realized that I had seen my mother's Standard Eight. She was not in the habit of ferrying us to and from Bicknor College. We caught the bus or we had a lift with one of the two other Ulvercombe boys at the school.

The bell rang for the end of school. Mr Maulet dismissed us. I told Esmond what I had seen. I saw the alarm in his eyes. Our victim had sneaked. Parents were always summoned when a boy was going to be expelled.

Despair settled over me. In the hall, as I had expected, the duty monitor summoned us with an imperious wave modelled on a gesture used by Mr Broadbent-Brown. He ordered us to wait outside the Buzzer's study. In his accusing face I read confirmation of my worst fears.

'And no talking,' he ordered. 'Or you'll regret it.'

'Aren't you going home?' Esmond said.

'Of course I'm bloody going home. Don't be –'

'Then you won't know whether we talk or not, will you?'

'Don't be cheeky,' the monitor said.

'Jesus,' Esmond said. 'You know what happens to turds, don't you? They get flushed away.'

He walked away with me running after him. I expected the monitor to swoop after us – to shower us with lines, to threaten to report us to authority. But when I glanced back he had gone. Esmond stopped outside Mr Broadbent-Brown's study and leaned against the wall.

I whispered, 'Do you think he's heard what we did to –'

'Of course he's heard,' Esmond said in his normal voice. 'That was half the point of doing it.'

'But what shall we do?'

'Don't do anything, Rumpy. Leave the talking to me.'

He grinned at me, and at that moment the study door opened.

'I need hardly say how sorry we shall be,' Mr Broadbent-Brown was saying. 'We had great hopes of Common Entrance. Even – just possibly, Mr Maulet was telling me – a scholarship.'

My mother appeared in the doorway. She surged into

98

the hall with her handbag clutched to her stomach. Perhaps she thought Mr Broadbent-Brown was planning to steal it.

'Ah, Chard and Penmarsh,' the Buzzer said. 'I have just heard the sad news.' He turned back to my mother. 'Of course, if circumstances change, you must let me know, Mrs Penmarsh. Miss Broadbent-Brown was saying to me only the other day what an asset Esmond is becoming in class discussions.'

My mother bared her teeth at him in what I think was meant to be a gracious smile.

'And – ah – Thomas is doing very well, too, of course. Very well indeed.'

'Yes. Well. Good. Thank you so much for all you've done, Mr Broadbent-Brown. Come along, boys.'

He held out his hand. 'Let us hope, dear lady, this is a case of *Au revoir* rather than *Adieu*.'

'Quite possibly,' my mother said. 'Good afternoon.'

We followed her out into the sunshine. As usual Esmond sat in the front of the car and I sat alone in the back; the arrangement suited everyone. We drove home in silence. My mother was not a confident driver and the heat made her worse. There were great patches of sweat on her dress under her armpits. 'The sad news' – all I could think of was that someone else had died. I was uncertain what this had to do with Mr Broadbent-Brown.

At Finisterre, Esmond leapt out to open the gate. He ran on to open the doors of the garage.

My mother turned round and looked at me. 'Did you really want to go to Rosington?'

'What?'

'To the school your father went to.'

I gaped at her.

'For heaven's sake stop looking so idiotic. Look, Thomas, you're old enough to keep a confidence, I hope? Well, I had a chat with the bank manager today. And the long and short of it is, there just isn't enough money to send you both away to school.'

'I want to stay with Esmond,' I muttered. My mother had never discussed money with me before. I could not believe what I was hearing. 'If – if that's all right.'

She ignored me. 'Two boys are much more expensive than one. Even doubling the Bicknor House fees has been a strain. A proper boarding-school would be impossible. You do understand, don't you?'

'Yes, Mummy.'

'So really there's not much point in your continuing at Bicknor College, is there?'

'No, Mummy.'

Esmond was coming back. He looked puzzled. He was probably wondering why my mother hadn't driven into the garage.

'I've told Mr Broadbent-Brown that this term will be your last. And next term, you and Esmond will go to Kinghampton Grammar School together. You might as well start as soon as possible.'

I nodded.

'And there's another thing, Thomas. Don't tell Esmond. It might upset him, to think that he's costing us lots of money. He's a very unselfish little boy.' She leant out of her open window and put on her jolly, all-chums-together voice. 'Did you think we were never coming?'

*

Of course I told Esmond straightaway. Even at the time we suspected that my mother was lying. After her death, Esmond went through the records, which in those days she kept meticulously. In 1955 she was still quite comfortably off. It was not until the later 1960s and the 1970s that her financial problems began. She could easily have afforded the expense of sending the two of us away to a minor public school.

But she didn't. She used her pretended poverty and the extra expense of Esmond as an excuse to keep us at home. Her actions cannot be explained in any other way. As far as she was concerned, Finisterre was where we belonged. She did not want to be left alone with the ghosts. And perhaps she did not want to be parted from Esmond either.

I think Esmond was more upset than I was. He felt we had been deprived of something valuable – something that was ours by right. To me, however, Finisterre and my mother had the great advantage of familiarity. Rosington would have been a completely alien world, and I knew I would find it hard, perhaps impossible, to come to grips with it.

Perhaps my mother sensed Esmond's disappointment. Or she may even have felt guilty. Be that as it may, she tried to bind Esmond more closely to her by making a special fuss on his birthday, which was a few weeks after the end of term.

Esmond was twelve. There was a party at Finisterre. He had lots of presents, most of them from my mother and many of them far more lavish than I was used to receiving. The most expensive and the most surprising present of all was a .22 BSA air rifle.

Eight

Alice was due to arrive at Finisterre on Thursday 3rd October.

'Won't that be fun?' Esmond said to me. 'A family party.'

She was coming by train from London to Exeter. Esmond had arranged to meet her at the station and bring her home in time for a late dinner. He came up to the nursery and explained this to me after breakfast on Thursday. In other words he postponed telling me officially for as long as he could, which did not come as a surprise.

'All four of us under one roof,' he went on. 'This roof, too. Seems appropriate somehow.'

For as long as I could remember, Esmond had tended to be miserly with information, even when there was no particular reason to be secretive. It was as if at an early age he had sensed instinctively the importance of reserving for himself the maximum possible space for manoeuvre. Reticence was one of Esmond's little habits – a habit which sometimes I found hurtful, and a habit which became more marked as he grew older. Still, I suppose each of us has a few quirks.

'The family reunited at last.' He gasped with laughter, and the gasp turned into a cough. 'Those of us who are still alive. A sort of celebration for the survivors, eh?'

Without my floorboard, I should have been much worse informed. I imagine that Esmond told me about Alice's impending arrival so early in the day only because he and Bronwen were going to spend most of the next twelve hours rushing about the house to get everything ready for our distinguished visitor. He must have felt that even I might notice the divergence from our usual routine.

'You don't mind, Rumpy? Do you?'

'No,' I said. Fortunately I had had time to consider this question in some detail. 'I don't think so. To be honest, I'm not sure what I feel.'

'That's natural enough. It's not a situation that's covered by the book of rules.'

Esmond was sprawling on the window-seat with a cigarette in the corner of his mouth. He had the daylight behind him so it was hard to see his face. I was in my armchair near the floorboard. We were having a cosy little chat. On the other side of the window everything was grey and out of focus. The rain was coming up from the sea.

'Isn't there a fairy tale?' I said. 'About a princess who's lost as a baby and her father the king –'

'Dozens of them, I expect.'

I knew he was in a hurry, that there was something else he wanted to say. So I said, while I still had the opportunity, 'But – I wish I understood: why ask her down here?'

'Trust me.'

'You know I do. But why?'

'She's your mother's residuary legatee. All this belongs to her. You've just got a life interest in it.'

'I know.' It meant, among other things, that I couldn't make a will leaving Finisterre and everything else to Esmond. Nor could we sell the house and go and live elsewhere, or at least not without the trustees' agreement. 'I understand all that.'

'The point is, Alice could make things difficult for us. If she chose to, that is. We've made considerable changes here, for example, and we didn't ask anyone's permission. On the other hand, she could also make things easy. How do you fancy Provence?'

My confusion must have shown in my face.

'Living there, I mean,' Esmond said. 'You, me and Bronwen. Think of it. Think of the food. Think of the days of wine and roses. Fields full of lavender. All the sunshine we could eat. No more gales off the Atlantic. No more damp in every other room.'

'But the trustees wouldn't let us.'

'I've not seen a solicitor yet. But I've a feeling that if Alice agreed with us, there wouldn't be a lot they could do.'

The trustees were my mother's solicitor and her accountant, both of whom had their offices in King-hampton. They were tall, grey men, and I was a little afraid of them.

'Wouldn't they think that Alice was too young to know her own mind?'

'She's well over twenty-one.'

'But surely there'd be legal difficulties?'

'Why? You and she are the only interested parties. All the trustees are doing is looking after an asset for her, and letting you have the use of it till you die. But if you and Alice decide you want to enjoy that asset in a slightly different form – well, they're not going to object, are they? Why should they?'

I shrugged. People were always making objections for what seemed to me to be inadequate reasons.

'It's not as if you'd be proposing to make the asset less valuable. You'd just be converting it into a slightly different form. Might even make a profit.'

When Esmond was enthusiastic, I always found it next to impossible to argue with him. It usually wasn't because I couldn't see the flaws in his idea; it was more that I loved to see him so happy, and I didn't want to be the one to break the spell.

'On the other hand, perhaps you feel that Provence is more or less one of the Home Counties these days.'

'Too many English-speaking voices?'

He nodded. 'Like Tuscany. I wonder. Northern Spain might be worth investigating.'

Castles in Spain, I thought: why in Spain? What I said was, 'In fairy tales, when the princess comes back to her widowed father, that's usually the end of the story. She gets married to the handsome prince who rescued her, and they all live happily ever after.'

Esmond looked sharply at me. He got up and stubbed out his cigarette in the ashtray beside the china-pig money-box on the mantelshelf. I kept the ashtray for him; no one else used it.

'But perhaps the king isn't really delighted,' I expanded. 'He could be just pretending – for the sake of the happy ending.'

For a few seconds neither of us said anything. Then Esmond smiled. 'You do talk a lot of nonsense.'

'Stories always leave out more than they tell. The

king wouldn't have seen the princess since she was in her cradle. Now she's suddenly come back as a grown woman. Perhaps he's got used to not having any women about the place. After all, castles are masculine places. Perhaps he thinks his future son-in-law is an interfering young fool.'

Esmond paused in the doorway, looked back and flashed me another smile. 'It's an interesting theory. But I must be off.'

'Or perhaps the princess embarrasses him in public. She hasn't had a proper royal upbringing, has she? So she might eat peas with her knife at state banquets. Or her husband might turn out not to be a real prince after all. He could be an impostor.'

'Very possibly.'

'Esmond. What was that about Alice's marriage? In the letter, you told me to write that I was sorry to hear about her marriage.'

He shrugged. For a moment I thought that was all the answer I would have. But he came slowly back into the room and stood in front of me.

'Good point, Rumpy. Perhaps I'd better explain about that. But first – how do you think your story would have ended? If it had been in real life.'

'For the princess and her father?' I shrugged. 'I imagine it would have ended in tears. One way or another.'

The first time I saw Lilian Sandwell I thought she looked like a princess. Not just any old princess, but the one whose face was everywhere in the 1950s: Princess Margaret, the Queen's sister.

I remember the exact moment when I thought that. We had just been introduced by Aunt Ada. Lilian didn't linger. She shook hands perfunctorily, first with Esmond, then with me, murmured something about seeing to the food and slipped away from us.

'Poor child,' Aunt Ada said.

I doubt if anyone else saw the resemblance. Princess Margaret was dark, glamorous and grown-up. Lilian was thirteen, almost fourteen. She had fair hair and slanting eyes masked by glasses with pink National Health frames. She and her brother Stephen, and their widowed father, had just moved from London to Kinghampton. That must have been in the autumn of 1959. They took over what used to be the haberdasher's shop in Bay Street and turned it into a bookshop. They lived in the flat above.

We knew all this because our vicar had been a cousin of Lilian's mother, and in consequence Aunt Ada had taken the Sandwells under her capacious wing. Thanks to Aunt Ada, my mother, Esmond and I were invited to the grand opening of the bookshop, which was attended by most of Kinghampton town council, a representative from the local paper and the headmaster of Kinghampton Grammar School. Then, as now, Kinghampton was a dull little place in winter. The townsfolk would never admit it but they missed the tourists. Even the opening of a little bookshop was a welcome break in the out-of-season monotony.

I had three reasons for thinking that Lilian was like Princess Margaret. First, I thought the shapes of their skulls were similar. Second, Lilian had one of those crisp and carrying voices which cinema and radio had taught me to associate with the upper classes in general and with royalty in particular. Third, Lilian, like Princess Margaret, came from London and therefore was tinged with the metropolitan glamour that so completely enveloped the princess.

At the opening party there was orange squash for the children and sherry for the grown-ups. Aunt Ada shepherded Esmond and me towards our host, Mr Sandwell. Ignoring Esmond, he shook my hand and asked with an air of desperation whether I liked reading. He was a skinny man with a nose like a bird's beak and semicircular ears set at right angles to his skull. When he talked, his fingers fluttered in the air at about the level of his thighs as though he were caressing the heads of pets which no one else could see.

'Yes,' I said, 'I like reading.'

'Good, good. Splendid. Now where's Stephen, I wonder?'

Mr Sandwell floated off, his hands stroking and scratching the heads of invisible dogs. For a moment I watched him. He was moving steadily away from Stephen, not towards him. He edged towards the curtain that hung across the stairs leading to the flat above. He glanced round the room. Quickly I looked away. A second later, he was gone. The curtain was swaying.

There was a high-pitched squeal, rather like a horse's neigh, from the direction of the counter. My mother was laughing, a rare phenomenon. I looked across the shop and saw that she was talking to Lilian's brother, Stephen.

Stephen Sandwell was very different from his father. He was plump rather than thin; indeed, he seemed much larger in all directions because he was so full of energy and anger. He was fair like his sister, and they both had small, regular features. A moment later he left my mother and bounced about the little shop, filling glasses, shaking hands and talking. To my horror he made a beeline for us.

'Do you ever buy books?' he asked Esmond.

'Not often.'

'Then by rights I should throw you out.' He waved the jug he was carrying, and the liquid inside slopped dangerously near the brim. 'Waste of good orange squash.'

'But my cousin Thomas does.'

Stephen glanced at me. I felt hot and sweaty. But he wasn't interested in me.

'That doesn't make you any less of a dead loss,' he said to Esmond.

'Oh it does.'

Stephen put his head on one side. 'How do you work that out?'

'If I leave, Thomas will leave too. And we won't be spending any money in your shop. But if I stay, Thomas will stay. And Thomas will buy books from you.'

The oddest thing about the conversation was not what was said, though that was odd enough, but the way in which Stephen and Esmond spoke to each other. An outsider would have thought they were old acquaintances – not friends, perhaps, but sparring partners. And if the outsider had shut his eyes, I think he would have assumed they were the same age, which was perhaps the oddest thing of all. In fact, Esmond and Stephen were respectively sixteen and twenty.

'No time like the present,' Stephen said to me. 'Don't let me stop you browsing.'

Bottle in one hand, jug in the other, he darted towards the woman who ran the Kinghampton public library.

'Do *you* buy books, madam?' I heard him say.

'Isn't he strange?' I said to Esmond.

'Would you like a sandwich?' Lilian said.

She appeared without warning behind us. She must have heard what I said but she gave no sign of it. Instead she thrust a large meat-dish with a chipped rim between Esmond and me. The dish was laden with sandwiches – well-filled triangles of sliced bread piled in two untidy heaps. I pretended an interest I did not feel. The sandwiches had a slapdash air about them, as if they had been flung together by someone whose mind was on other things.

'It depends what they are,' Esmond said.

'The ones on the right are Spam. The others are fish paste and cucumber.'

'No, thank you.'

'You'll have one, won't you?' Lilian pushed the plate at me; it jarred my elbow. 'Someone's got to eat something.'

I took one of the fish-paste sandwiches. A piece of cucumber fell out and landed on the carpet. Simultaneously Lilian and I crouched to pick it up. For a moment we were isolated from the rest of the room. Our faces were less than three feet above the ground and almost touching. I felt her breath on my cheek.

'They're not very nice,' she murmured. 'I think the fish paste was a bit old.'

She held out the plate. I replaced my sandwich on it. She picked up the cucumber and put it on top of the sandwich.

'Have Spam. It's safer.' She lowered her voice still further. 'I had a friend whose cousin died after eating a fish-paste sandwich.'

We stood up. I started to eat my Spam sandwich because I didn't know what else to do with it. The bread was a little old, too, and the meat was pink and rubbery.

'I think making sandwiches was probably a mistake,' Lilian said. 'No one's eating them.'

'Apart from Thomas,' Esmond said.

'You're sure you won't have one?'

'No thanks.'

'I don't blame you.'

Lilian was about to move away. There was a crash. Conversations stopped. For a few seconds no one moved. The crash had come from the stairs behind the curtain. I felt that we were all on the brink of some terrible revelation. One of the lower corners of the curtain twitched. A black cat peered out. It saw us all and withdrew.

The invisible Mr Sandwell groaned. The groans modulated into words.

'Oh, bugger that cat,' he drawled.

'Father?' Stephen called, as he slipped through the crowd towards the curtain. 'Father? Are you all right?'

'Oh, bigger bogger bugger.'

When we met Lilian and Stephen, Esmond and I were in our first term in the sixth form at Kinghampton

Grammar School. It was a small sixth form because Kinghampton was not an academic school; most boys left after the fifth year.

Both of us were studying for three A levels. I had wanted to do courses which would be a suitable preparation for a university degree in architecture. This proved not to be possible. I was informed that there would be insurmountable timetabling problems. Both my mother and the school authorities made me feel that I was being unreasonable. Unlike most of my school fellows I had been permitted to spend an extra two years at school, and I should be grateful for the privilege: instead I was demanding further favours.

'Give you an inch,' my mother said, 'and you'll try and take a mile.'

So, like Esmond and almost everyone else in the sixth form, I studied English literature, history and geography. Our staying on in the sixth form suited my mother very well: it kept Esmond and me at home, and as far as she was concerned things went on as they always had. Neither Esmond nor I worked with any enthusiasm: the teaching at Kinghampton was mediocre, the subjects did not interest us, and our aim was merely to pass. That we learned anything worth knowing was entirely accidental and had nothing to do with the school. During our two tedious years in the sixth form, our real classroom was the bookshop in Bay Street, and our teacher was Stephen Sandwell.

The relationship evolved by accident. Esmond and I needed to buy some books for our A level courses. Quite soon after the grand opening, we visited the bookshop after school. Only Stephen was there. He had his feet up on the counter and a long yellow cigarette in his hand. He was reading a volume of Larkin's poetry.

I had written down a list of the books we needed. He glanced at it.

'Christ,' he said. 'Shakespeare. Don't you have any choice?'

I shook my head. Stephen counted as a grown-up. Grown-ups were not supposed to talk about this. I wished Esmond would help me. But he was tickling the black cat under its chin.

'What about *A Taste of Honey*? Shelagh Delaney.' Stephen grunted. 'This girl from Salford gets pregnant by a black man. Can you imagine?'

'Well, actually, no.'

'What happens?' Esmond asked.

'A homosexual looks after her. No one else cares, you see. The point is, these people exist. These things happen. It's relevant. Girls do get pregnant when they don't mean to. Whereas this crap – Shakespeare, Keats, Jane Austen – well, it's another world, isn't it?'

'Yes.' I made a desperate attempt to change the subject. 'My mother says she spoke to you about opening an account.'

'Ah, money. Of course. Your mother's Mrs Penmarsh, I suppose?'

'Yes.'

'Of Finisterre.' He said the name of our house with a flourish. 'Land's end. The end of the world. The beginning of the sea.'

Esmond stopped stroking the cat. 'We're nearly a mile away from the sea,' he said.

Stephen shrugged. 'Ah well. One can't have everything. Do you really want all these books?'

'Sorry.' I felt this was somehow my fault. 'We don't have any choice.'

'I could suggest far more interesting ones.'

'What sort of books?' Esmond asked.

'Like this.' Stephen pushed the Larkin towards us. 'Oh, for God's sake. Why don't we have a cup of tea?'

I looked at Esmond who said, 'All right.' He went back to stroking the cat, which had a torn ear from which blood was oozing.

'If it's not too much trouble, that is,' I said.

'Would I have asked you if I felt it was too much trouble? Of course I wouldn't. Besides, my motives are purely mercenary. Have you ever been in an oriental bazaar?'

'No.'

'Well, I have. If you just show an interest in something the stall-holder will give you a cup of tea. Sometimes if you don't show an interest. It's a baited hook to catch a buyer, you see. But it doesn't just keep people on the spot while you do your sales patter. Oh no. It's subtler than that. It also puts people under an obligation. Simple psychology. They feel they have to buy something from you just to be quits. You understand?'

'I think so,' I said.

'But we wanted to buy something anyway,' Esmond pointed out.

'Ah.' Stephen blew a cloud of smoke towards him. 'I am looking beyond this one occasion. I want to see you again and again. Not just this year but next year, and the next, and the next – for as long as I'm selling books. I want you to buy a whole *library* from me.'

Esmond glanced at me. Stephen came round the end of the counter and stood at the bottom of the stairs.

'Lil,' he shouted. 'Put the kettle on.'

'How many?' she called back; and she sounded so near that I wondered if she had heard our conversation.

'Four, if you want some.'

'Won't your father mind?' Esmond said.

Stephen lifted himself on his toes and twirled round to face us. 'As it happens, the pater isn't here this afternoon.' He raised his eyebrows. 'And if he were with us, I am sure he would be the first to applaud my commercial acumen.'

He held the pose for a second: standing on tiptoe, with raised eyebrows, his portly little body inclined slightly towards us. For the first time, it occurred to me that there was something not quite human about him. Not necessarily in a pejorative sense, but as a simple matter of biology. Suppose goblins existed in reality as well as fairy tales, as a separate race, humanoid but not human, though capable of interbreeding; one of Stephen Sandwell's grandparents might have been a goblin.

'Let this be a lesson to you,' he said. 'If you ever engage in the retail business, remember that a cup of tea costs very little and it is often extraordinarily effective.' He raised the curtain and stood aside so that we should precede him up the stairs. 'As you will see.'

'You might have a customer,' Esmond said.

'Possible if improbable. And if we do, you'll find that

we have a bell mounted on the shop door to meet just such contingencies.'

The skin on Esmond's face tightened momentarily, which was often a sign that he was on the verge of losing his temper. But he nodded and went upstairs. I followed. As I passed Stephen I smelled an acrid perfume on him – like the incense they sometimes used in Ulverscombe church.

The treads creaked, and some of them moved beneath my weight. The stair carpet was so worn that the pattern had disappeared except along the borders. There were holes in several places.

'A deathtrap,' Stephen said behind me. 'A perfect deathtrap.'

Esmond looked back. 'Did your father trip at the opening party?'

'Yes, indeed. The poor pater. But if he is to be believed, we should not blame the stairs or the carpet, or even himself. No, he says that the real culprit was Grimalkin there.'

As Stephen spoke the black cat was negotiating the stairs.

'The name was the pater's choice, I need hardly say. I don't think Grimalkin likes it, do you, puss? She's always lying in wait for him and trying to trip him up.'

The stairs turned back on themselves and at the top of the second flight was a little landing with three doors opening on to it; all of them were closed. Another flight of stairs continued upwards. Stephen passed us and opened the door directly in front of us. Grimalkin slithered between his legs.

The room beyond was furnished as a kitchen. Lilian, wearing an apron but still in her High School uniform, was standing at the sink scouring a frying pan. Beyond the sink was a window with a view of backyards. She looked over her shoulder.

'He's been at the biscuits again,' she said.

'The pater has so few pleasures,' Stephen said. 'It's hard to begrudge him the –'

'If you want some more,' Lilian cut in, 'you'll have to go out and buy them.'

'I think we can do without.' He turned back to us. 'Come and sit down. We shall feast on the pleasure of Lilian's company.'

'Can you get the milk off the windowsill?' she said to him. Her eyes swung towards Esmond and me.

Stephen raised the sash window and brought in a pint of milk. 'Cheaper than a refrigerator and in this weather just as effective. Lilian, may I introduce – ah – the Messrs Penmarsh.'

'They were at the party,' she said.

Esmond said loudly, 'My name's Chard, Esmond Chard.'

'Oh.' Stephen pantomimed surprise with raised eyebrows and rounded lips. 'I thought Mrs Penmarsh said . . .'

'And this is my cousin, Thomas Penmarsh.'

'Well that seems quite straightforward. Thomas and Esmond – Stephen and Lilian: don't let's be formal. Now do sit down.'

Lilian had abandoned the saucepan in the sink and was making the tea. We sat down at the deal table in the middle of the kitchen. The table top was rough and faintly slimy, as if it had been inadequately wiped with a damp cloth in the recent past. Apart from the oven, the gas rings on top and the Ascot water heater, there appeared to be no source of warmth. The room was very cold. In my ignorance I wondered why it was not as clean and tidy as our kitchen at Finisterre.

'Ah,' Stephen said, rubbing his hands together. 'The cup that cheers. If only it inebriated as well.'

Lilian put the brown teapot on the table. She fetched cups and saucers, which represented a mingling of two main patterns with one or two singletons. One saucer was for Grimalkin's milk, which she drank on the table. The milk remained in the bottle and the sugar in the packet. To me it seemed thrillingly bohemian, a world away from the petty provincial conventions that ruled the tea tables of Ulvercombe.

'Thomas and Esmond are going to buy lots of books from us,' Stephen said. 'Mrs Penmarsh has opened an account for them. Isn't that nice?'

Lilian said nothing but this was not an uncomfortable omission because Stephen did not on that occasion require an answer. She sat down between her brother and me and began to pour the tea. I noticed that she was not wearing glasses. Perhaps she had slipped them off when Stephen called up the stairs. The only sign of them was a pink indentation across the bridge of her nose.

'They need books for school, of course,' he went on. 'But we shall interpret our brief more broadly than that. Our role is not to educate – no one can educate others – it amazes me that this laughable misconception is so widely subscribed to. No, in the final analysis education is a heuristic process. Our role, Lilian, is to provide Thomas and Esmond with the *tools*.'

Esmond and I looked at each other. For us, the word 'tool' had an obscene slang meaning which caused much merriment among our peers at school.

'The *tools*,' Stephen repeated, lingering on the word in a way that suggested he was well aware of what was in our minds. 'As somebody once said, give us the *tools*, and we shall get on with the job. In this case the job of acquiring culture.'

While we drank dark, sweet tea, he talked or rather lectured. He designed the syllabus for a new A level in contemporary culture. I was too excited to take much in on that first occasion. I heard names like Kerouac, MacInnes and Camus for the first time – Miles Davis, Thelonius Monk and Jimmy Yancy, Bergman and Truffaut; and other names which were familiar I heard in unfamiliar contexts – James Dean and Marlon Brando, for example, Elvis Presley and Bill Haley. It was very cold. I warmed my hands first round the teapot and later between my legs.

While Stephen talked, he smoked. He pushed his packet of cigarettes towards us. Lilian appeared not to notice; I shook my head; Esmond, who was already an experienced smoker, took one. And while Stephen talked and smoked I looked as often and as closely as I dared at Lilian.

Like Stephen, she gave the impression of being not entirely human. She had the same delicate features as her brother but lacked his surplus flesh. She was skin and bone and gristle. Her features dominated her head, whereas Stephen's were so swathed in fat you hardly noticed them. I never saw an ounce of fat on Lilian, now or later. I used to think that if she stood naked in front of a bright light, it would shine through her, and her bones would be shadows in a red haze.

She also lacked Stephen's animation. It was not, I sensed, that she was lethargic: rather that she held her energy in check. Today she did not look like a princess at all. It was on this occasion that I began to realize how plastic her appearance was. From some angles, in some lights, she could look beautiful as a child is beautiful – the sort of beauty that for most people is devoid of sexual attraction. More often, she looked dreary: tired, bony-faced, nondescript. Occasionally her face seemed cruel and full of power: she looked like a witch.

Grimalkin, having finished her milk, sat on Lilian's lap and purred. Oh yes, the obvious thought came into my mind: the witch and her familiar. Lilian looked up and saw me. There was a spot of colour in each of her cheeks. Stephen had paused to suck in nicotine and tea; he was, as it were, between paragraphs or sections of his lecture.

'She keeps me warm,' Lilian said softly. 'Like a hot-water bottle.'

'Yes,' I said. 'Yes, of course.'

I was both flattered and embarrassed by her attention. People so rarely bothered to talk to me when Esmond was present. To my relief there was a diversion. The bell on the shop door clanged.

'Oh, God.' Stephen pushed back his chair. 'I am in thrall to commerce.'

He opened the kitchen door. From downstairs came a long and confused sound, a rumbling, clattering, thudding: as if an earthquake had destroyed a mountain of books.

'Oh bugger,' said Mr Sandwell. 'Oh, bigger bogger bugger.'

Nine

In the early days my mother liked the Sandwells, or rather she liked one of them very much and didn't actually dislike the other two. This surprised me greatly. Later I realized that she liked them in the abstract, as it were, and that she liked them for reasons that would have seemed as absurd to the Sandwells themselves as they did to Esmond and me.

'Oh yes, the Sandwells,' she would say if their name came up in the village shop or at a tea party. 'Yes, of course. The poor Sandwells.'

Her tone would imply that she knew far more about them than she intended to divulge, and that this secret knowledge had persuaded her that they should be acknowledged as acquaintances, if only because to ignore them would be uncharitable. In fact her principal reasons for approving of them were: one, that Mr Sandwell had been married to a cousin of the vicar of Ulvercombe; two, that they came from London and spoke with educated voices; three, that they were poorer than we were and could therefore be considered as objects of condescension; and (above all) four, that Stephen treated her as a goddess. Once one had grasped these points, unravelling the rest of her attitude to the Sandwells was relatively easy.

When Esmond and I were at school, however, my mother's benevolence towards the Sandwells seemed positively eerie. Did she not know, for example, that the Sandwells never went to church? That Mr Sandwell was always falling over and saying 'bugger', often in public? That the family lived in conditions of near-squalor? That the butcher and the grocer now refused them credit?

Such information was impossible to avoid if you lived in Kinghampton or its vicinity. It added up to a formidable reputation for culpable eccentricity, which was only partly offset by a vague feeling that the Sandwells and their bookshop lent a certain intellectual distinction to Kinghampton.

My mother pretended to take her cue from Aunt Ada (usually it was the other way round). Her official view was that the Sandwells were more sinned against than sinning, and that it was not for us to cast the first stone, particularly as we all live in glasshouses. She may have been impressed by Aunt Ada's claims that Mr Sandwell had been a senior civil servant in the Home Office before his wife died and his illness set in. But her wholly uncharacteristic tolerance was mainly due to the relentless hyperbole employed by Mr Sandwell's son.

'Ah, what bliss,' Stephen would say if he saw her marching up Kinghampton High Street. 'Our lady of Finisterre.'

'Good morning, Stephen.'

'Good, dear lady? No, now you are here, it can only be the very best of mornings.'

'You silly boy.'

'You must allow me to carry your shopping. In a just world, Mrs Penmarsh, you would never have to carry anything. You would always be attended by a caravan of porters, who would follow at a respectful distance. And possibly camels, too, for that touch of oriental splendour.'

'You mustn't talk such nonsense.'

'But you deserve oriental splendour. That's a thing one can say of very few people indeed.'

'Are you sure you can manage both bags?'

'I wish they were four times as heavy. Now where have you parked your celestial chariot?'

Stephen took care never to keep it up for long. Like chocolate mousse, such extravagant flattery is only palatable in small doses. Crude though the strategy was, it achieved its purpose. Much later I was able to look up the shop's accounts. For the first two years that the Sandwells were in Kinghampton, my mother, whose only reading was the romances she borrowed from the public library, was one of the bookshop's main customers.

'Stephen?' she would say if someone mentioned his name. 'Oh yes, he's surprisingly sensitive when you get to know him.'

Over those two years the shelves in my room began to fill up with modern poetry and books on architecture as a fine art. Even Esmond would order books occasionally: a James Bond novel in hardback; *Lady Chatterley's Lover*; that sort of thing. My mother paid without question the bills the Sandwells sent. She had very little idea what books cost, I imagine, or what we needed to buy for our school work. Also, she must have realized the pleasure they gave me: perhaps she thought of the books as a bribe – or as a drug that would stupefy me and keep me by her side at Finisterre for ever and ever.

Esmond and I almost always met the Sandwells at the shop. Old Mr Sandwell – I think of him as old though when I first met him he was probably in his fifties – never to my knowledge came to Finisterre. My mother might possibly have recognized him if they had passed on the street; I doubt that he would have recognized her.

Lilian came to Finisterre once or twice in the early years but often without my mother realizing it. While I was at school my mother was not interested in a gauche teenage girl whom she felt was not worth the trouble of knowing. Stephen was the only Sandwell who counted.

Sometimes I wondered, purely as an entertaining hypothesis, what she would have said if we had told her what Stephen was like. She would not have believed us; not even, I think, Esmond. She just would not have allowed herself to understand what we said. The stupid have a marvellous capacity for blocking out what they do not wish to hear. This makes them very nearly invulnerable.

One freezing day in January 1960 Stephen and Lilian cycled over to Finisterre. My mother was due to spend the afternoon at the vicarage, but for some reason she was late leaving. She did not know that the Sandwells were coming, and luckily she did not notice their arrival. We intercepted them before they rang the doorbell. Esmond suggested that we went for a walk. By the time we came back to the house my mother should have left.

From Finisterre there were only two possible walks unless you were feeling extremely energetic: either you went up the lane to Ulvercombe village or down the lane to Blackberry Water and the sea. We chose the latter to minimize the risk of meeting my mother or Aunt Ada.

Stephen was even more vigorous than usual; probably he had been gobbling amphetamines. In an open duffel coat he strode down the lane smoking furiously and lecturing us on the merits of the occult sciences.

'Why have none of you read Aleister Crowley?' he demanded. 'Nostradamus? Old Mother Shipton? Good God. If a Martian could see you, he'd wonder if you were educationally subnormal. He'd think there was something fundamentally wrong with you.'

There was no animosity against us personally; his attack was levelled at the vast majority of the human race, dead and alive.

'It is quite incredible. Literally unbelievable. Over thousands of years a body of wisdom has been amassed. Eminently practical knowledge designed to give man whatever he wants. To make him truly the master of the universe. And what does humanity do with it? For three hundred years it does its level best to pretend that this knowledge does not exist. When this fails, as of course it does, humanity tries to ridicule this priceless wisdom. And when this fails, as of course it does, humanity produces piddling little scraps of this and that. Pseudo-science. A pathetic attempt to rival the wisdom of the ancients. The circulation of the blood. Pish. Newtonian physics. Twaddle. Evolution. Claptrap. Relativity. A load of old cobblers. The atom bomb.

Oh my dears – are we lemmings or humans? And now it's the space race, which is potentially the greatest exploration in the history of the cosmos. The two so-called superpowers have reduced it to the level of a playground squabble. Well, really. How childish can people get?'

'When I had bronchitis last winter,' Lilian said, 'they gave me –'

'I know. Antibiotics. Marvellous, I'm sure. Treat the symptom not the cause: the policy of morons. Sophisticated practitioners of the occult sciences have been able to avoid all diseases whatsoever for hundreds if not thousands of years.'

Without warning Stephen stopped. The rest of us clustered round him. Red-nosed, we huddled in our coats. Above us was a bright blue sky. Stephen tossed aside his cigarette. He stuffed his hands in the pockets of his duffel coat and flapped his arms as though trying to ventilate his body.

'What do you want, my dears? What is it you really want? That's the question people never really ask themselves. Or if they ask it, they don't answer it honestly and carefully. I suppose they are scared. Because once you know what you want you can usually get it. People cling to what they know, don't you think? So they cling to their ignorance. They cling to their discontent. They –'

'I want to have money,' Lilian said, 'and live in a nice house and have babies. I don't want to have to work.'

Not only the interruption was unexpected, but also the passion in Lilian's voice. Her attitude reminded me of Esmond's when – in what seemed like another life

– we had to write the autobiographical fictions for Mr Maulet.

Stephen looked at Esmond: 'And you?'

Esmond shrugged. 'I'd like to be rich. Wouldn't everyone?'

Stephen turned to me.

'I'd . . .' Suddenly I realized that only the truth would do. 'I used to think I wanted to be an architect. Now I'd like to be a poet. But I don't think I'm good enough.'

'Pah!' Stephen said. 'You're all the same. You're not seeing the wood for the trees.' He pointed at each of us in turn. 'You want this, and you want that, and you want the other. Can't you see, it all comes down to the same thing. *Power.* If you have power you can have anything and everything. That's what the great thinkers of the past understood.'

'So what do you want?' Esmond said.

Stephen frowned. 'I told you. Power.'

'Power to do what?'

'Power means being able to control people and things. Even oneself. It's the most wonderful thing in the world. It's like a drug. It's the only thing worth having.' Stephen clapped his hands together and danced away from us. 'Come on, children,' he called. 'Where's this beach of yours?'

He started to talk nonsense. He made up limericks, one for each of us. I wondered if this was a diversion; perhaps he felt he had revealed more about himself than he intended, and now he was trying to distract us.

On the beach at Ulvercombe Mouth we found enough dry driftwood to build a small fire. Stephen made us hold hands and dance around it. He had the ability to make the most bizarre behaviour seem perfectly natural – no mean achievement when one is dealing, as he was, with three self-conscious adolescents. Our feet slithered and crunched on the smooth stones. I remember the feel of Lilian's hand in mine. Her bones seemed tiny, like a bird's. This was always part of her attraction for me: she led me to believe that she was even more fragile than myself.

While we danced, Stephen made us all sing 'Ring-a-ring of roses'. We seemed to sing the song a hundred times. Not the whole thing, just the first verse. 'Ring-a-ring of roses, a pocket full of posies. A-tishoo! A-tishoo! We all fall down.'

'Yes, indeed, my children,' Stephen said, suddenly releasing Esmond's and Lilian's hands and clapping his hands together. 'You know what we have been celebrating?' He paused to light a cigarette in the shelter of his coat. The breakers crashed on the shingle. The tide was coming in. Stephen looked up, his eyes bright behind the haze of smoke. 'We were celebrating death. To be precise, the Black Death. The plague. Bring out your dead, and may the Lord have mercy on your souls.'

Esmond had crouched down by the fire. He was trying to light a cigarette of his own with the glowing end of a stick. 'What do you mean? It's just an old nursery rhyme, isn't it?'

'The roses were plague sores,' Stephen said. 'Usually they appeared in rings on your body. You carried posies of special herbs and flowers in your pocket. People believed they helped ward off the plague but they don't seem to have had much effect. Sneezing was another symptom. And then that was it: you fell down. *Dead.*'

'That's horrible,' Lilian said.

'It's God's truth. You fell down and if you still had any family left they would throw your body in the street. On your door they would mark a cross to show the plague was in your house. Then carts would come round and men would collect the corpses and throw them into great plague-pits. Extraordinary places.'

'You mean you can go and see them?' I had a vision of a tree-lined London square in whose centre, instead of a garden, was a great quarry lined with bones and rotting flesh.

'You don't see them, Thomas. You feel them. We know where some plague pits were. If you stand above them you can feel the torment underneath. The un-named, unshriven dead. Those charnel pits are psychic powerhouses. One just has to harness the energy.'

'With the wisdom of the ancients?' Esmond said.

I heard the sarcasm in his voice. If Stephen heard it, he pretended he hadn't.

'Broadly speaking, yes,' he said. 'One can use various techniques.'

'I'm cold,' Lilian announced. 'Can't we go back?'

'Yes, let's.' I stamped my feet, which were in fact perfectly warm.

'This energy, do you mean –' Esmond hesitated. 'Do you get it wherever there are people buried?'

'It depends,' Stephen answered. 'My own feeling is that individual circumstances have to be taken into account.'

'I'm freezing,' Lilian said.

'Churchyards and other cemeteries can be surprisingly disappointing. You see, religious rites, even Christian ones, are not entirely gobbledegook. They can have the effect of earthing spiritual energy.' He giggled. 'In more senses than one. The point is, the energy is dissipated. The funeral service acts rather like a lightning conductor.'

Lilian was moving up the beach towards the gap in the cliffs that led to Blackberry Water. I glanced at Esmond. The wind was blowing the hair back from his face: it looked like a dark halo. He was frowning, apparently absorbed in trying to remove a shred of tobacco from his lips. I followed Lilian.

'Often,' I heard Stephen say behind me, 'one finds a greater residue of psychic current in the places where people have actually died, rather than where they're buried. The plague pits have such a concentration of energy that I wonder whether some of the people thrown into them were still alive. Perfectly possible, wouldn't you say?'

I looked back. Esmond was kicking the embers of the fire apart. He said something I didn't catch to Stephen, who laughed.

'Oh no!' Stephen said, almost braying with amusement. 'Any kind of suffering, whether physical or mental, usually strengthens the effect. Obviously they'd have found the experience rather upsetting, which would have had the effect of increasing the voltage.'

'I wish he wouldn't talk like that,' Lilian said.

'Why does he do it?'

She looked at me. 'Why does anyone do anything? I suppose he likes it.'

We walked on in silence – through the gap in the cliffs, past Blackberry Water and up the lane. I thought of the Christina Rossetti hymn we sang in church: 'Earth stood hard as iron, Water like a stone.' I was panting because we were walking so quickly. The breath dribbled from our mouths like smoke. I noticed that, now it was really cold, our little valley had acquired an echo. Our footsteps scraped and clattered on the frozen mud, and the scrapes and clatters came running after us. I felt large and protective, a novel sensation; the top of Lilian's head was not much higher than my shoulder. She was wearing a dark-blue school raincoat which was a different pattern from those officially sanctioned by Kinghampton High School for Girls. It was too small for her; I glimpsed pink and bony knees and wrists. She also wore three items made of black wool, perhaps knitted by her mother or worn as a sign of mourning for her: a bobble hat, an absurdly long muffler and a pair of gloves with holes in at least two of the fingers.

'I'm so cold,' Lilian said. 'I think my feet will drop off.'

'Tea and toast in the kitchen,' I said. 'Or maybe cake.'

'If your mother's not there.'

'So what if she is?'

Lilian said nothing. I assumed that this was because my bravado was as pathetically unconvincing to her as it was to me. We walked on. Two sets of footsteps joined the echoes behind us, creating more echoes in their turn. Esmond and Stephen had left the beach.

'He hates it down here,' Lilian said, as if to answer a question I had just asked. 'The country, the sea. The people. That bloody shop.'

'It must be a big change. After London, I mean.'

She glanced at me. I thought I read contempt in those pink-rimmed eyes.

'Sorry,' I said.

'You've never known anything different,' she said. 'But to him it's like being buried alive.'

'What about you?'

'It's all right. At least it's peaceful. And some of the history's quite interesting. I like history.'

'So do I.'

'That beach is called Ulvercombe Mouth, isn't it?'

I said it was. It was then that she told me how in 1788 the wreckers had lured an East Indiaman on to the rocks, and how the men from Ulvercombe had clubbed the sailors to death on the beach, and how the shingle had been red and slippery with blood. She described the affair in detail, and in a quiet and unemotional voice. It was almost as though she had been there. By the time she had finished we were almost at the gate to Finisterre.

'I need tea,' Stephen called from behind. 'An ocean of tea.'

My mother had not come back. The padlock was on the garage door, which meant that she must have walked up to the vicarage. We sat in the kitchen. Esmond puffed away – he calculated that it was safe for him to smoke because if my mother commented on the smell we could attribute it to Stephen. I found one of Mrs Jodson's fruitcakes in a tin and put it on the table.

'Just help yourselves,' I said. I put a big knife on the table but I didn't bother with side plates. I wanted to show that I too could be bohemian.

I made the tea. Meanwhile Lilian nibbled cake, and

Esmond and Stephen did most of the talking. They were still on the subject of psychic energy and how you could harness it.

'Look at that light,' Stephen said, pointing at the bulb over the table. 'If someone had seen that two or three hundred years ago, they'd have thought it was witchcraft. Magic. Like something out of a fairy tale.'

Ten or twenty years later, the paranormal and associated subjects became fashionable, especially among the young and the gullible. But in 1960 such ideas were rarely discussed. And if they were, it was generally with mockery. In this as in other things, Stephen was ahead of his time. I know, now, how weak many of his arguments were, how most of the authorities he quoted were little better than charlatans, and how many of his so-called facts were moonshine. But if I heard him now, I think I would still want to believe him. Unlike the vicar, Stephen was a natural preacher; he had the knack of compelling belief irrespective of what he actually said. Unfortunately such beliefs tend to depart with the preacher.

I handed round the tea and again offered the cake to everyone. Esmond and Stephen shook their heads.

'But how do you actually do it?' Esmond said.

'Tap the energy?' Stephen lit another cigarette. 'Difficult to explain. You get as close as you can to the source, make yourself receptive and – well – concentrate. It's a bit like charging a car battery.'

'Could you do it now?'

'What – here?'

Esmond nodded.

'I need something to tune into.' Stephen frowned.

'As I said, churchyards aren't much good. But we could try on our way home if you want.'

'I don't mean Ulvercombe churchyard,' Esmond said. 'I mean *here*.'

'In this house?'

'There's a bedroom upstairs. It's never used. We call it the death room.'

'Really? Who died there?'

'My baby sister.'

Lilian sucked in her breath. 'Stephen –'

'No, it's all right.' Esmond smiled at her. 'It was a long time ago.' He turned back to Stephen. 'Thomas's father died in the same room. That was even more years ago, in the war.' He glanced at me. 'That's right, isn't it?'

I nodded.

'Since then, no one else has slept there. As far as I know, the only exception was my sister. And she died.'

'Is it locked up?' Stephen said.

'No. Aunt Fiona keeps it just as it was. A lot of her husband's clothes are still there. She pretends it's a spare room but no one's ever allowed to sleep in it.'

I was tempted to interrupt with the information that my mother had offered the room to Esmond after his mother's death. But he chose that moment to glance at me again.

'Once a week the room's dusted,' he said. 'And Mrs Jodson changes the sheets.'

'How dreadfully Victorian,' Stephen said. 'I thought the practice had died out in this country.'

'Albert?' I said.

Stephen smiled. 'Quite so. And how do you feel about this proposed experiment?'

'I don't mind.'

'Thomas never knew his father,' Esmond said.

Stephen was still looking at me. 'I was thinking of your mother as much as anyone.'

I didn't know what to say, so I shrugged and tried to look intelligent.

'Of course I may be able to do her a favour,' Stephen went on. 'If the room does contain some sort of psychic energy it's almost certainly a sign of conflict. I may be able to resolve it.'

'Yes,' Esmond said. 'Like a funeral service?'

'Or an exorcism. Though in both those cases the idea is to earth the energy rather than to store it in a reusable form.'

'Is there any more tea?' Lilian asked.

I got up to fetch the teapot and the milk. No one else wanted any more. When I poured the milk from the bottle a few drops landed on the saucer and the table. I think Stephen saw that I was trembling.

'If you'd rather we didn't?' he said.

'No, of course. That's fine.'

'There's nothing to worry about. All we would do is go up to the room, the four of us preferably, and stand there, in a circle, holding hands.'

'Fine,' I said. 'No problem.'

'And then I'll recite something – a formula – silently, if you wish; it doesn't matter. Your presence and Esmond's would be very useful, though. Because you're related to the dead.'

'Thomas doesn't mind,' Esmond said. He grinned at me.

Lilian said. 'Oh God. Let's get it over with.'

The four of us stood up. Esmond and Stephen stubbed out their cigarettes. With typical caution Esmond emptied the ashtray into the Aga and opened a window. We trooped into the hall and up the stairs. Esmond led the way. I was last. The Sandwells looked around them – not obviously; they were too well brought-up for that. Their interest embarrassed me: it was as though they were seeing me without my trousers on.

We reached the landing. The door to my room was wide open and the six bars on the window could be seen. It was quite obviously my room – the bookshelves were laden with my purchases, my pyjamas were on the pillow of the narrow bed, the briefcase I used for school was on the table. The room was full of clear January sunshine.

'I wish I had that view,' Lilian said. 'I could eat it.'

For a moment she stood in the doorway, staring through the bars down the coombe to Blackberry Water and the sea. I looked at her in surprise. I had known that view all my life. It had never occurred to me that it was in any way desirable.

Esmond opened the door of the death room. He drew back so that Stephen could go in first. Stephen stopped on the threshold. For a good thirty seconds he stood there with his back to us. I saw the high bed with its carved headboard and enormous wardrobe. There was a smell of polish and stale air. Then Stephen turned.

'You were right to bring me here,' he said. 'This should have been done years ago.' He waved at the door beside the wardrobe. 'What's through there?'

'It's only a cupboard,' Esmond said. 'It's huge. Almost like a room.'

We crowded into the room. At the end of the bed we formed a circle as we had round the fire on the beach. Once again I was opposite Stephen. Lilian seemed to squeeze my fingers. It was the lightest of pressures; I might have been mistaken. When I glanced at her, she was staring at her feet.

I had expected to feel foolish or even scared but I didn't. If anything I felt apprehensive. There was a noise downstairs. The front door shut with a bang. Suddenly we were no longer a circle.

'Cooee!' my mother called. 'Anyone at home?'

Ten

In our family marriages tend to be short-lived. Two or three years must be the average. In the recent past, only Aunt Imogen's marriage reached double figures, and I doubt if either she or Uncle Arthur saw any cause for celebration in that. My mother wasted very little time in burying my father. It seemed to me that my own marriage was over almost before it began. My daughter Alice carried on the tradition. She left her husband, Esmond told me, after a mere six months.

'A case of nature triumphing over nurture,' I remarked, hoping to earn a smile.

'What?' Esmond said, moving towards the door of my room and eager to be gone: once again I realized that there must be a great deal to do before he drove to Exeter to collect Alice.

'It doesn't matter.'

He nodded and left the nursery, closing the door behind him. I got up and walked to and fro between my chair and the window. I suppose I was trying to walk away from the unpleasantness. But it followed me to and fro like a faithful dog.

I had learned that Alice's husband was called Graham. He was rather older than Alice, which perhaps had been part of his charm for her: at that time she may have needed a father as much as a husband. She had married him the previous March, just two months after the motorway crash in which her foster parents were killed. Graham worked for an oil company and was based in Lagos. Perhaps the ability to whisk her out of England had been another of his attractions.

I felt sorry for Alice, of course I did. She had had a difficult year. But I wished she was not coming to Finisterre. Even if everything was what it seemed, there would be difficulties. Meeting Alice was going to be terribly upsetting for me. No doubt she would want comforting as well as substantial financial support. Perhaps she would want to go on seeing us. I foresaw her becoming a constant financial and emotional drain on my slender resources. She might not object to the changes we had made at Finisterre; she might even be persuaded to agree to Esmond's scheme for altering the terms of the trust; but her cooperation over the house and the trust would not necessarily outweigh the disadvantages which might spring from her visit. Besides, I was not at all sure that I wanted to move abroad. I was used to Finisterre.

And if things were *not* as they seemed, the visit would be even more disturbing. My mind traced the unpleasant consequences that might flow from Alice's arrival at Finisterre. It was like watching a stream running down a beach – the water branches out, it explores channels in the sand, it fills pools, it runs quickly or sluggishly, and often in unexpected directions. And in the end this variety is pointless because all the water comes at last to the sea.

When Esmond first came to Finisterre he thought of it as an anteroom to Heaven. I know this for certain because he told me so, many years later. But an eleven-year-old boy sees things very differently from an eighteen-year-old youth.

We took our A levels in June 1961. Afterwards the school term had a few more weeks to run but no one in our year took this very seriously. Some of us used to cycle to Budstow where Esmond would smoke, drink fizzy beer and ogle the girls on the beach while I worried that someone in authority might report us. Esmond refused to be serious about anything, even the girls. Once, I remember, we were on the beach and two girls were lying on their backs only a few yards away from us.

'Look at those two,' Esmond said loudly. 'Just look at those tits. If either of them stood up, they'd over-balance.'

The girls raised their heads and stared at him. They giggled. We ended up spending the afternoon with them.

It was a curious time. We were both eager to leave school. Yet the future stretched before us like Budstow beach with the tide out on a wet winter Sunday: its emptiness intimidated me. When I tried to discuss it with Esmond he changed the subject. Everyone else in our year at school had their futures arranged: one boy, Bill Jodson, was going to Leeds University; another had been accepted by a bank; a third would help manage his father's farm.

Before supper one evening I tried to raise the subject with my mother. We were in the kitchen. Esmond was mowing the lawn.

'There's no point in talking about the future

now,' she said. 'Not until you've had your A level results.'

'I'd quite like to go to university.'

'That costs money, Thomas. Besides, there are two of you.'

'But there are grants and things.'

'Grants are for people like Bill Jodson.' My mother showed her teeth: to her, the thought of Bill Jodson going to university was a crime against nature. 'It's not so easy for people like us, people who have to depend on investment income.'

She went on in this vein for some time. Her arguments were much the same as those she had used six years earlier, when she'd withdrawn Esmond and me from Bicknor College and announced her intention of sending us to Kinghampton Grammar School rather than Rosington. There simply wasn't enough money – partly because of her generosity in taking in Esmond. This time the arguments were a little more sophisticated, and they included a sweeping condemnation of the fiscal policies of post-war governments. In a coda, she dealt with her subsidiary theme: how unsuited I was, physically, mentally and emotionally, to the rigours of university life.

A mother, she remarked with the awesome confidence that never left her, always knows.

Her response to my question was so swift and comprehensive that I imagine it had been carefully rehearsed. At the time I was overwhelmed. With indecent haste she reduced me to an apologetic jelly. I reddened, I sweated, I squirmed. I apologized for everything – from the inequalities of the British tax system to my temerity in mentioning my foolhardy desire to go to university.

'Don't worry about it, dear,' my mother said, suddenly switching her approach. 'I've got something up my sleeve for you.'

'What do you mean?'

'I won't tell you now. It's not *quite* settled.' She smiled, all sweetness now her point had been gained. 'But I think you'll like it.'

After supper Esmond and I went for our usual walk so Esmond could smoke; in wet weather we used the attics. (I had made a determined effort to learn how to smoke but every time I inhaled I retched.) We leaned on the fence that separated one of the belts of conifers from the field beyond. A blood-red sun was sinking towards the sea. I told him what my mother had said.

'You fool,' he said. 'You should have talked to me first.'

'Sorry.'

'If you wanted to go to university, you should have sorted it all out beforehand and then told her.'

'But she still couldn't afford it.'

'Balls.'

'She said she'd have to give you whatever she gave me. Otherwise it wouldn't be fair.'

'Double balls.'

'I wish I knew what she meant. *Something up her sleeve.*'

'I know,' Esmond said. 'She's going to have you trained as a cook-gardener-chauffeur. Then you'll get a lifetime job at Finisterre. What more could anyone want?'

I flinched from the sarcasm. 'What do you want then?' I mumbled.

He turned his head. He had the cigarette between his lips and the sunset and sea behind him. He looked like an advertisement for something, probably tobacco.

'I've been meaning to tell you.' He paused, and I felt cold. 'But I don't want anyone else to know, all right? Not yet. Especially not your mother.'

I nodded.

'I'm going to London,' he went on. 'Stephen's got a friend who owns a coffee bar. I'll work there.'

'But why?'

I meant why was he leaving me. Why was he planning to go to London by himself? Why hadn't he told me before? He interpreted the question differently.

'Any job will do for a start. Doesn't really matter what it is. I'll sweep floors or wash up – I don't care. The point is, once I'm in London, I can start looking for something else.'

I turned away so that he wouldn't see the tears in my eyes. 'I thought – I sort of assumed – you'd look for something round here.'

'Why?' he said. 'There's nothing to do here, except lick the tourists' arses. And you can only do that for half the year. In six months I'd be dead of boredom.'

'She won't let you go. You're underage.'

The sun brought out the red in Esmond's hair. It was as though there were a bed of glowing coals beneath the hair, not bone. I was frightened.

'She can't stop me. Once I'm in London, she'll never find me. But it won't come to that. Stephen says –'

'Stephen?'

'Yes. He says we'll work on her. All of us, you as well. She might even cough up an allowance if I'm lucky.'

'But she'll want you to stay here.' What I meant, but dared not say, was that I wanted him to stay.

'Maybe. But Stephen says she'll soon realize that half a loaf is better than no bread. I'll be coming here for the odd weekend, maybe, and holidays. Especially if she's giving me an allowance.'

I couldn't speak. Before me was a prospect of misery that I knew would last me for my natural life. The prospect was so terrible that I tried to ignore it by concentrating on a more immediate source of unhappiness: that Esmond had been arranging his future life not with me but with Stephen Sandwell.

Esmond stubbed out the cigarette and flicked the butt into the field. 'Once I'm properly settled – you know, a bit of money coming in, and a decent flat – you can come up and stay with me.'

He paused, looking at me with raised eyebrows: I knew he wanted me to say thank you or show some sign of enthusiasm. I suppose he wanted me to make him feel less guilty. I looked down the field. The sun had touched the water. Between the V-shaped gap in the cliffs I saw a sea of blood.

'If you like, we could share a flat.' He added this a little absently, as if this idea had only just occurred to him and he was urgently trying to work out the implications of his offer. 'How does that sound? You can't spent the rest of your life down here, can you?'

'I'd like to come to London.' I was lying. I wanted to be with Esmond.

'You could go to university there,' he said. 'If that's what you really want.'

Soon after this conversation, and just before the end of term, Mr Sandwell went into a nursing home in Budstow.

'They've given the dear old pater a room on the ground floor,' Stephen said when he ran into Esmond and me at the school Speech Day. 'Jolly thoughtful of them. Means he can't fall downstairs any more.'

It was the nursing home where, nearly six years before, Aunt Imogen had spent the last three months of her life. Perhaps Aunt Ada or even my mother had recommended the establishment to Stephen. I prefer to attribute the choice to fate or destiny, or whatever one cared to call the force that was gradually entwining us with the Sandwells.

Esmond did not comment on the coincidence. He must have recognized the name of the nursing home. I thought it wiser not to bring the subject up. Talking about problems often makes them worse.

I never knew what was wrong with Mr Sandwell, what made him fall down and say bugger so often, what made his speech increasingly slurred, what sent him to the nursing home. I could easily have asked Lilian or even Stephen about their father's illness, but I never liked to. I was afraid they would think me nosy.

'Stephen and I have been putting our heads together,' my mother announced on the first Sunday after the end of term. 'We have an idea.'

My mother had invited Stephen and Lilian to tea –

an unusual move, which took Esmond and me by surprise. It was a fine day and the five of us were on the
lawn at Finisterre. During the sandwiches and the first
cup of tea my mother had interrogated Stephen and
Lilian about their visit to the nursing home that morning. Mr Sandwell, we gathered, was having a wonderful
time.

'I'm quite sure it's the kindest thing for all concerned,'
my mother said.

Then, with the cake and the second cup of tea, she
launched into the real purpose of our meeting. When
she mentioned that she and Stephen had produced an
idea, they exchanged smiles and glances. It is difficult
to give the impression of bowing in a courtly manner
when one is in a deckchair, but Stephen managed it.

'The idea was entirely yours, dear lady. Just as the
gratitude will be entirely mine.'

My mother simpered. 'Shall I, or will you?' she asked
with a playful wave of her teacup.

Esmond, who was slightly behind her, rolled his eyes
at me. I was aware that Lilian, who was sitting a little
withdrawn from the rest of us, was watching attentively
but without involvement, as though our garden were a
theatre in which we were the players and she the audi-
ence. I was ashamed that Lilian was seeing my mother
behave like this.

'You would do it so much better than I,' Stephen
purred.

Suddenly I was poised between horror and hysterical
laughter: I had decided that Stephen and my mother
were going to announce their engagement. My mind,
as so often in moments of stress, shot off to investigate

a minor by-product of the cause of the stress – namely, that after the marriage I should become Lilian's step-nephew.

My mother beamed at us. 'Now that Stephen's father has retired from the business, Stephen needs an assistant to help him in the day-to-day running of the bookshop.'

'Well, I'm damned,' Esmond muttered. His face was sulky. He glanced at Stephen.

My mother's deckchair creaked and swayed as she shifted her weight so that she could look directly at my face. 'And he has very kindly thought of you, Thomas. I need hardly say what an opportunity it is.'

'And you'd be doing me a favour, too,' Stephen said. 'I'm snowed under with work. Dad used to do a lot behind the scenes.'

I was too embarrassed to say anything articulate. I think I spluttered. My mother ignored this.

'Stephen's going to train you, dear. He's even going to pay you a salary. Not much to begin with, of course, but something. Well, what do you say?'

'Thank you,' I said automatically. 'Thank you.'

'I thought you'd be pleased,' my mother said smugly. She added with a really remarkable lack of tact, 'Working in a bookshop is almost like having a proper profession.'

Esmond put down his teacup on the grass. His anger was so obvious to me that I felt it should have concrete form: it should have been something one could reach out and touch like a block of sandstone on the grass. He took out a packet of cigarettes. He put a cigarette between his lips and rolled it into the corner of his mouth. He patted his pockets until he heard the rattle of the matches. My mother heard the noise and glanced at him. He struck a match and lit the cigarette. Their eyes met. My mother looked away.

'Anyone for more tea?' she said.

I doubt if anyone other than myself realized the significance of that moment.

Stephen and Lilian probably thought – if they thought about it at all – that since Esmond had left school he had begun to smoke in front of my mother; in those days there would have been nothing unusual about such an arrangement.

My mother cannot have known what was happening: as I have already made clear, she was a stupid woman governed (though she would never have admitted it) by emotions she could not accurately label. On some barely conscious level she must have realized that Esmond was too old for her to make an effective issue out of his smoking.

Esmond knew more than the others but he must have been partly blinded by his own anger, and in any case he was not the sort of person who went in for self-analysis; he used his intelligence for other purposes.

Even I didn't appreciate the significance at once. I had to think about it for a while: I kept trying different permutations as one does with a chess problem. At last I found the key to the solution. Esmond wasn't angry with my mother but with Stephen. Stephen and my mother had been negotiating behind everyone's back – and Stephen hadn't told Esmond: that was where the offence lay. It was all so obvious. Esmond had got into the habit of trusting Stephen (so much so that I was often jealous). It was Stephen who invited and received confidences; who dispensed cigarettes, whisky and (at least once while we were at school) amphetamines; and who had the obliging friend with a London coffee-bar and a spare room in his house. Poor Esmond had thought that he and Stephen had the special relationship.

'Ho, ho,' I wanted to say. 'Ho, ho. Now you know what it's like.'

Until now Esmond had not realized that Stephen created the illusion that every friendship was a special relationship. He had done it with my mother by treating her like Gloriana. He had done it with Esmond by treating him as an adult. He had even done it with me by finding books for me to read, and talking to me about them as though my opinion were as important as his. Oh yes, I already knew: Stephen was an emotional prostitute, and a very good one. The funny thing was that Esmond had taken so long to realize what Stephen was like. After all, Esmond was an emotional prostitute too.

I have never known a person who prostitutes his or her body for gain. No doubt some are bad at it, more are mediocre and a few are very good at it. The very good ones must be magicians in all but name: they must be capable of casting an enchantment over their clients. A good prostitute must make each and every man who pays to use her body feel that he alone is the exception: that for him the prostitute feels both love and lust; that he arouses passions in her that no one else could ever arouse; that the commercial basis of their transaction is at worst an irrelevance and at best a shared joke.

With magic you can make black seem white, and the fake seem real. Esmond was a magician.

At the end of July 1961, Esmond went to London with my mother's blessing. Her blessing took the form of a tearful farewell, a trunk laden with perfectly laundered shirts and a brand-new made-to-measure suit, plus a promise that three pounds a week would be paid monthly into the bank account which had been opened for the occasion.

'The old bitch feels guilty,' Esmond said to me as we walked up the lane to Ulvercombe on his last evening. 'God bless her.'

'Guilty about what? Not doing more for you?'

'That and other things.'

For the rest of the walk we talked about the possibility of my coming up to London to visit. We went into the saloon bar of The Forley Arms. This was empty as most people drank in the public bar. Esmond ordered for us – he looked older than I though at this point he was still several weeks underage. The landlord poured our whisky ceremoniously, as if he was perfectly aware of the gravity of the occasion. I was uncomfortable because I felt only a precarious sort of adult and because I thought the man was laughing at us.

We took our drinks to the table by the window. Esmond lit the inevitable cigarette. For a moment we sipped in silence. It was still light outside. We could see Aunt Ada trundling a wheelbarrow up the vicarage drive. Everything was normal both here and at Finis-terre, and I couldn't understand it: didn't they realize that this was the end of an era?

'Do you think you'll like the shop?' Esmond said.

'Probably.' I really had no idea. I was comfortable with Lilian, fascinated by Stephen and I liked certain books.

'Your ma will be furious if you chuck it in.'

'And come to London?'

'She'd hate it. But that's not what I mean. She'd also be furious because she'd lose money.'

'But she'd probably *save* money if I moved out. Especially if I got a job in London.'

'No, the point is, she's paying Stephen to take you on. In a manner of speaking.'

I took a mouthful of whisky and it tasted sour. 'Are you sure?'

'I happened to be in the study this morning.' Esmond looked at me, his eyes guileless. 'There was a cheque lying on the blotter. It was made out to the nursing home where old Sandwell is.'

'But – do you think she's paying his bills?'

'What else? It's probably a tax dodge. Otherwise Stephen would have to pay tax on the money your ma's coughing up. It's clever. You've got to hand it to him.'

My glass was empty. Esmond went to the bar to get another round. I looked at my blurred reflection in the polished table and thought, *what a fool I am*. I'd assumed Stephen had taken me on because he thought I would be useful. I had never doubted that. It isn't pleasant to discover that other people think you even more useless than you thought they did, and value you accordingly.

There was laughter at the bar: Esmond and the land-lord had shared some masculine joke like real men do in real pubs. Esmond came back with our glasses and sat down.

'Come on, Rumpy,' he said softly. 'Out with it.'

'I thought . . .' I shrugged and swallowed some whisky. 'Oh hell! What does it matter?' The whisky burned my throat and brought tears to my eyes.

'You needed to know,' Esmond said roughly. 'If you're not careful she and Stephen will walk all over you. God knows what's going to happen when you're on your own.'

'I'll manage.'

'Anyway,' he went on, 'you're forgetting what Stephen's like. I bet he'd have taken you anyway. It's just that he couldn't resist the chance to make a bit of money out of your mother.' He grinned at me. 'Can you blame him?'

Next morning my mother drove us to Exeter. The roads were full of tourists. It was a grey, muggy day, and the car was unbearably stuffy. We arrived early, which led to a protracted session in the station buffet. We drank too many cups of coffee and stared at the clock.

At last the train came. Esmond settled himself in a second-class smoking compartment. My mother des-patched me to buy him a magazine – *Punch*, I think – to read on the journey.

Esmond shooed my mother off the train. He stood at the door, leaning out of the open window. My mother kept talking. She told him to send a postcard from London that very evening, to make sure his sheets weren't damp, and to make a point of drinking at least half a pint of milk a day. Sometimes Esmond looked at me. But my mother would snatch his attention back.

I wanted to scream at her. I wanted her to shut up. I wanted the stupid cow to go away, to leave me to silence, to Esmond and to grief.

Doors slammed. A voice crackled over our heads. Someone whistled. A porter wheeled luggage along the platform. Grey pigeons rose in a flurry of wings. Esmond waved. I think he smiled at me.

The train was moving very slowly. My mother moved with it. The carriages wheezed and clattered along the platform. I was finding it hard to breathe.

'Esmond!' my mother called. 'Remember you must sign on with a doctor tomorrow.'

The train picked up speed. My mother walked faster and faster. She broke into a stumbling run. Her handbag banged against her hip. I had never realized before how ungainly she was. When she ran she rocked from side to side like a squat dinghy on a choppy sea.

'Oh, and Esmond!' she shrieked. 'The cod-liver oil capsules are in the trunk. In the pocket of the tweed jacket.'

The train and the platform became a silvery blur. For an instant I saw clearly my wobbling mother, and Esmond's head and waving arm. I turned away and moved towards the barrier. I wanted to go back to the car and wait for my mother there.

A moment later, I realized that this was impossible. My mother had bought and kept our platform tickets.

I would not be able to leave the platform without showing a ticket. I would not be able to leave without my mother.

Eleven

They forgot to bring me my tea. Four-thirty came and went. I lifted the floorboard for the third time that day. Once again I could hear nothing moving in the sitting room below.

This latest break in routine made me even more restless. All day I had listened to the sounds of surreptitious activity. Bronwen often played pop music when she was doing housework, but there was no music today. I listened to creaks and rustles, to the roar of the Hoover and the clatter of the brush against the dustpan, to footsteps running up and down the stairs.

Just before five o'clock I heard Esmond starting the car. It was his car, one of those big Volvo estates. A few seconds later a cat shot across the lawn and took refuge in our little shrubbery. It was the young tabby, the newcomer to Finisterre.

My room didn't overlook the garage or the drive so I didn't actually see Esmond leave. Part of me wished that he had asked me to go with him to meet Alice at Exeter. But another part was glad that I should have a little longer without her. I am trying to be honest. It is very difficult. One tells lies all the time, even to oneself.

A few minutes after Esmond's departure, Bronwen clumped up the stairs. I sat down in my chair. She flung open my door and stood on the threshold. I looked up from the book I was pretending to read. We stared at each other.

'Well,' she said. 'The room's all ready. Flowers all over the sitting room. I've done as much towards dinner as I can. I've hoovered and polished until I'm totally buggered. Hoo-bloody-ray.'

She marched across the room and slumped on the window-seat. Today she was wearing tight jeans and a maroon sweatshirt, and her hair was tied back with a black velvet ribbon. One of her shoulders was smeared with dust.

I said softly, 'So you've slit the throat of the fatted calf?'

'Don't you start, Rumpy. I get enough of that sort of thing from Esmond.'

'Of what?' I was genuinely interested.

'Of words that say one thing and mean another.'

'One of the definitions of irony.'

She made a rasping sound in the back of her throat. I caught a whiff of her smell – the usual mustiness of her hair, a trace of a metallic perfume and a tang of sweat. A strand of hair had worked itself loose from the ribbon and fallen forward over one eye. She pushed it back behind her ear and she scowled, as though the effort this entailed was another straw added to an already intolerable burden. I had seen her like this once or twice before.

'Sometimes I wish to Christ we were back in London. It's so bloody quiet down here.'

'What do you miss most?'

'People. Shops. Clubs. You name it, really.' She drew her legs on to the window-seat and wrapped her arms around them. 'How do you stand it, year in, year out?'

'I suppose I'm used to it.'

'Esmond says it's all going to be worth it.'

She stared at me, mutely asking for confirmation. I said nothing. I was looking at her hands. She was wearing a wedding band and an engagement ring on the third finger of her left hand. Both rings were gold. The engagement ring had a sapphire set in a ring of tiny diamonds. It had belonged to my mother. I wasn't sure if the wedding band had been hers, too. A woman's rings looked out of place on Bronwen's hands, which were strong and practical, with short nails; her hands never seemed entirely clean.

'This girl,' she said. 'Alice. Funny to think she's your daughter.'

'Yes.'

Bronwen frowned at her hands. 'I hope she fits in.'

'Maybe we shan't see very much of her.'

'Don't kid yourself, Rumpy. She's looking for a family. Otherwise she wouldn't have written.'

'I thought she wanted money.'

'Yes – well, that too.' Bronwen stood up and rubbed her hands down the thighs of her jeans. 'I suppose we all like money. It's human nature, isn't it?'

I shrugged.

'I can't stand here talking all day.' She moved towards the door. 'You and Esmond are first cousins, aren't you?'

'That's right.'

'So what does that make Esmond and Alice?'

'First cousins once removed.'

She frowned. For an instant I thought she was

going to demand an explanation of the degrees of cousinage. She went out of the room and slammed the door behind her.

Bronwen was a big, violent, worried woman. She was not an educated person. I wondered if she knew that one could find a Table of Kindred and Affinity in every *Book of Common Prayer*. Or she could simply have asked me. As far as I knew there was nothing to prevent a man from marrying the daughter of his first cousin; unless of course either of them was already married to someone else.

To the best of my knowledge my mother and Stephen never actually quarrelled. Their relationship changed very gradually over a period of five or six years. For a long time I didn't notice what was happening, and I was better placed than any other outsider to see it. It simply never occurred to me that something might be amiss between them.

My first inkling came as late as June 1963. Stephen and I were both in the shop one morning. He was sitting at the counter sampling a novel and I was shelving a batch of new paperbacks which had just arrived. The shop bell rang. Miss Broadbent-Brown came in. Her eyes flicked past me and fixed on Stephen, who looked up with a smile.

'Miss Broadbent-Brown. What a pleasant surprise.'

'Good morning, Mr Sandwell. I am afraid that Speech Day is looming over us once more.'

She advanced into the shop. I moved in a semi-circular course which took me behind her and into the airless cubbyhole under the stairs. We did most of the paperwork here, and it was shielded from the shop by a curtain similar to the one which concealed the stairs. Miss Broadbent-Brown had never shown any sign of recognizing me as her former victim, and I no longer had any reason to be scared of her. Still, I had not forgotten her. Perhaps you never forget people like that even if you manage to forgive them. Not that I had done that, either.

'The prize-winners have all made their choices,' she announced. 'Here we are.'

Paper rustled. Stephen murmured appreciatively about the wisdom of the choices, which I imagine were made by the Broadbent-Browns; this was certainly the practice when Esmond and I were at school. Stephen had the knack of making the most fatuous comments seem like compliments: 'Yes, a boy who reads Keats at twelve will be reading him for life.' Or, 'Ah! *David Copperfield*. Now that's an interesting choice.'

At Bicknor College they made a fuss of Speech Day. The school was on public display, and the Broadbent-Browns were eager to attract new pupils. There were a great many prizes, all of which were ordered through us. Moreover, we charged an unobtrusive commission for arranging to have the prizes especially bound and stamped with the school's arms. Stephen had also persuaded the Broadbent-Browns to order their text-books through us rather than through the bookshop in Budstow they had used before. The Bicknor College account was worth having.

So Stephen took his time. The approach he used was of one book lover to another. 'I imagine you'd prefer the OUP edition? The Everyman's all very well in its way . . . Yes, I thought you'd want the Chapman: a little more expensive, but most unlikely to date, wouldn't you say?'

In the middle of their discussion the doorbell rang again.

'Dear old Quiller-Couch,' Stephen was saying. 'You're quite right.' His voice changed, losing much of its warmth. 'Good morning, Mrs Penmarsh. Thomas is in the office.' He raised his voice quite unnecessarily. 'Thomas! Your mother's here.'

I tweaked the curtain aside. Miss Broadbent-Brown was studying a catalogue and did not look up. My mother nodded to me. Her incisors gleamed.

'Oh, it's all right,' she said. 'I'll come back later when you're less busy.'

The doorbell pinged. My mother didn't slam the door but she closed it with more firmness than it needed.

'I simply don't agree with those who say we need a new book of English Verse,' Stephen confided to Miss Broadbent-Brown. 'In my view they're in too much of a hurry to bring in the moderns. Like Dr Johnson – was it Johnson? – I believe in waiting for the verdict of posterity.'

This incident, insignificant though it was, made me realize that the relationship between my mother and Stephen had already changed without my noticing it. She had outlived most of her usefulness, and now she ranked noticeably lower than Miss Broadbent-Brown in his scheme of things. By and large I was relieved.

With hindsight I can see that the summer of 1961 must have marked the high tide of their . . . well, what can I call it? It was hardly a friendship or a business connection and certainly not a love affair, though perhaps it had elements of all three.

Stephen had needed money, which my mother gave him; my mother had needed to find me an occupation which would keep me at Finisterre – and Stephen had been happy to oblige. I think my mother recognized that she could not hold Esmond at home for much longer. She was shrewd enough to see that if she made it worth his while he would always come back. Here, too, Stephen made himself useful by arranging a job and accommodation for Esmond. My mother must have hoped that Stephen would help her to monitor Esmond's progress in London.

Her accounts show that she paid Stephen a fee of four hundred pounds in 1961, chiefly in the form of payments to the nursing home. In November 1962 she made a note to the effect that she had agreed to make a further series of payments totalling two hundred pounds. (She kept her word, despite the strains developing between them, perhaps because she was afraid of me losing my job and therefore my reason for staying at Finisterre.) By that time I like to think I was more of a help than a hindrance to Stephen.

'We make a good team,' he said to me more than once. 'Me doing sales and you doing the admin.' Sometimes he would pretend to defer to my superior knowledge in front of a customer. 'Yes, he's published by Faber. But you must ask my colleague. He's our expert on modern poetry.'

When he said things like that I would flush with pleasure. But my pleasure was always marred by the knowledge that Stephen might not mean what he was saying: even I was worth flattering when he had the time and when there was no one more important in our company. I was loyal, obliging and worked all the hours Stephen wanted for a pittance. And it is possible – even in the early days – he had other plans for me. Plans that involved Lilian.

Sometimes I think Stephen Sandwell had plans for everyone. He certainly had plans for Esmond. But Esmond, unlike the rest of us, had plans for Stephen as well. Despite the differences between them they were equal partners.

Esmond was not a good letter-writer. He wrote occasionally to my mother, usually on the back of a postcard: brief, bland notes. He rarely wrote to me, but he used to telephone the bookshop once or twice a month. He tended to ring in the afternoon. Sometimes he wanted to speak to Stephen, but generally he was happy to chat to whichever of us had picked up the phone. In my innocence I worried about what it must be costing him.

I was very lonely without him. For almost eight years he had lived at Finisterre. I had seen him every day. We did almost everything together. He had been better than a brother.

It wasn't so bad when I was working in the shop. The worst parts of my life were evenings, Sundays and holidays. Especially the evenings. They seemed to last for ever. My mother liked to eat supper early. Then we would go to the sitting room. At ten o'clock one of us – we took it in turns – would make the last pot of tea. Then one had to sit and drink at least one cup before it was permissible to make a move towards bed.

We did not have television at Finisterre, not in my mother's lifetime. Our radio was an elderly mains-powered set which lived permanently in the kitchen. Most of the time I did my best to read. A book open on my lap was a legitimate reason not to talk to my mother.

The room was never entirely silent: the clock ticked; pages rustled; knitting needles clicked; the fire hissed and crackled; the wind spat rain at the window. But there was a silence between my mother and me. As the long hours passed, the silence grew deeper and wider: it was as though we were on opposite sides of a crevasse lined with ice and jagged rocks.

Why? Why did I stay in that house? I could have found lodgings in Kinghampton or even gone to London. I can only explain it by saying that my mother had put a spell on me: she had paralysed my will. I suppose it is not so strange. I understand that many predators have the ability to compel their victims to cooperate with them. Esmond once told me that the prison service would be incapable of administering our prisons were it not for the wholehearted cooperation of most of the prisoners.

Everything changed when Esmond came to stay. The house became a home again. His visits were festivals – for my mother as well as for me. Even the weather seemed better when he was back at Finisterre.

In the first few years he came home about once every two months. Often it was just for a weekend. Whether he came in winter or summer, my mother would cook his favourite meal of steak-and-kidney pudding. He brought laughter into our lives, and news of a world that lay beyond Finisterre and Kinghampton. Also he brought alcohol. Often he gave my mother a bottle of sherry or gin when he arrived, and we would all drink this – even my mother, who proved to have a better head for alcohol than I do. He and I would go to The Forley Arms at least once a day.

When you see people every day you rarely notice how they change. Now that Esmond was living in London, I catalogued the differences in him each time he came. His sideburns crept a couple of inches down his cheeks, and he wore his hair brushed up into a quiff. One weekend he appeared with a chunky gold ring on which his initials stood out in relief. My mother thought the ring was vulgar. She gave him another which had belonged to my father.

During one visit I suddenly realized that Esmond's smell had changed. Smells have always been important to me. London had made Esmond smell like a man: sweet and sour, of dust, tobacco and alcohol: alien and a little dangerous. His voice deepened and acquired the resonance that some actors' voices have; the vowels lengthened.

There were other changes. And the one that hurt me most at that time was that Esmond no longer told me everything. He hid more and more secrets from me. This had started before he went to London. I date it from our meeting Stephen, but the process gathered pace after Esmond left Finisterre. He grew vague about what he was doing – I gathered that the job in the coffee bar hadn't lasted long. He talked in an offhand way about freelancing in the entertainment industry and pursuing other business opportunities as and when they arose.

'Flexibility: that's the key,' he used to tell my mother

and me. 'These days, if you want to get on in London, you have to be ready to move.'

He changed his lodgings, too: ten times in the first eighteen months; I know because I remember counting the changes in my address book. My letters were always going astray.

It was clear that Esmond was doing well. His clothes were usually new and fashionable. He brought presents when he came: expensive and short-lived items like out-of-season flowers or handmade, cream-filled chocolates. He had learnt to drive in London, and by the end of 1962 he was motoring down to Ulvercombe. In those days he owned, or at least had the use of, a series of sports cars. On summer visits we would have the hood down and roar through narrow lanes to distant pubs, where Esmond ordered large whiskies and flirted with the comelier barmaids.

On his visits to Finisterre, Esmond usually found time to see Stephen. It used to annoy me that I often had to work when Esmond was staying with us; it seemed such a waste. I never dared say anything to Stephen about it.

On one occasion in the summer of 1963, Esmond drove me into Kinghampton on a Saturday morning. In those days he had a red Triumph sports car – a TR something or other, I think. He drove as if someone were timing us, but I wasn't scared; I knew that Esmond was too good a driver to let us crash. We parked immediately outside the shop.

Esmond looked at the painted board above the window. 'Sandwell and Son,' he read softly. 'Does anyone ever see the old man?'

'I think Lilian goes over about once a week. Or Stephen.'

'No – I mean here. At the shop.'

'I haven't seen him. Not since last year.'

We went inside. Stephen was already hunched over the counter. A few inches away from his elbow was Grimalkin – an apparently headless and legless bundle of dusty black fur. When we came into the shop Stephen waved away the smoke and beamed at us.

'Esmond, my dear, you look blooming. London suits you.'

'I've got something for you. Roger asked me to pass it on.'

Roger was the name of Stephen's friend with the coffee bar. I assumed it was the same man. Esmond took a grey envelope from the inside pocket of his jacket and passed it to Stephen, who pushed it unopened into one of his own pockets. The noise made Grimalkin stir: for an instant she lifted her head and stared at us with eyes the colour of dark whisky. I registered without interest that there was no name on the front of the envelope and also that, though the envelope was small, it was quite bulky, as if it contained several thicknesses of paper.

'Do you and Lilian want to come for a drink this evening?' Esmond asked.

This distracted me. I wasn't sure whether I was included in the invitation.

'Splendid,' Stephen said.

'About eight then? We'll come here, shall we, and go somewhere in town?'

I was relieved: the 'We' must mean Esmond and me.

A moment later, Esmond left. Grimalkin slumbered on.

Stephen sighed. 'The lucky thing,' he said. 'No doubt he's thigh-deep in all those delicious metropolitan vices.'

'Like what?' I said.

'I shan't sully your innocence by telling you, dear boy. You're much too young.'

'I'm older than Esmond.'

'Yes,' Stephen said, making two long syllables out of one. 'So you are. Why don't you go upstairs and see if you can persuade Lilian to make us a pot of coffee? She might listen to you.'

It was not a comfortable morning. Jealousy and curiosity make an unhappy combination. Also it was extremely hot. Stephen and I abandoned our jackets and rolled up our sleeves.

At twelve, Stephen said he would go and have his lunch. During the summer we did not close at lunchtime if we could help it: the casual tourist trade was unpredictable but it could be surprisingly lucrative.

Stephen went slowly upstairs. His footsteps moved about the kitchen. Lilian was out. I heard a click of metal on glass as he opened a bottle of beer. Then silence.

The combination of jealousy and curiosity had formed a sense of grievance. This was also fuelled by the heat of the day and the grudge I felt at having to work while Esmond was staying at Finisterre. Otherwise I can find no explanation for my behaviour.

The shop was empty. I drifted towards the cubbyhole. I intended to look up the publication details of two books which had been ordered during the morning.

Grimalkin was asleep on the seat of the chair, and Stephen's jacket was draped across the back. The top of the grey envelope protruded from one of the side pockets.

Grimalkin opened her eyes. She saw me standing there. Slowly she got to her feet and stretched. I had never liked her, and I knew that the feeling was mutual. To me she always felt like a hostile witness. She jumped off the chair and a moment later I heard the patter of her paws on the stairs.

'It's unfair,' I said under my breath.

I meant it was unfair of Esmond and Stephen to have secrets from me – though they had been so casual about the envelope that perhaps it wasn't a secret, merely something that wasn't worth the trouble of mentioning. But if the latter were the case, I argued to myself, they wouldn't mind my knowing whatever the something was.

Before I knew what was happening, the envelope was in my hand. I squeezed it between thumb and forefinger. It was surely too thick to be a letter. Why hadn't Roger put Stephen's name on the front?

I turned it over. The flap at the back had been gummed down for only part of its length. I pushed a fingertip between the envelope and an ungummed portion of the flap. I exerted hardly any pressure. The gum must have been defective; perhaps the envelope had been kept in a damp place. In any case, the flap sprang up as though of its own volition. Inside was a bundle of five-pound notes, folded once. There was no letter – I checked. Just several hundred pounds in cash.

*

That evening the four of us went for a drink in The Mermaid Hotel, which was Kinghampton's most pretentious pub. Stephen claimed to be particularly attached to the fishing nets and horse brasses.

We sat at our usual table in a corner alcove conveniently placed for access to the bar. Stephen watched the other customers. Esmond watched the barmaid. I watched Lilian.

This was the summer that she left school. In my two years with Stephen I had grown used to her presence; I wasn't shy with her any more. Often she ignored me. Sometimes we talked. There was always something a little desperate about Lilian, as though she alone could see the sands running through the hourglass, as though she had privileged information about a catastrophe that was due to occur when the last grain had dropped into the lower bulb.

I was so used to seeing her around the shop that usually I barely noticed her appearance. That night, however, she had transformed herself into a stranger. She wore high-heeled shoes and make-up, and she had left her glasses at home. She had used the cosmetics to make her eyes look enormous and faintly feline. The eyelashes were caked with mascara. She had darkened the eyebrows, which nature intended to be a mousy colour, and perhaps plucked them too. Her mouth was bright red – the colour of the cheap lollipops they used to sell on the front at Budstow. She had also doused herself with perfume; usually she smelled of coal-tar soap.

I couldn't prevent myself from staring at her. I didn't like what I saw – the changed appearance scared me –

but I couldn't stop looking at it. Lilian had made herself exotic. It was as though she had joined another species.

'Phew,' Stephen said while Lilian was in the lavatory. 'Smells like a cathouse in here.'

I got drunk that evening for the first time in my life. I didn't mean to. Esmond and Stephen were drinking beer with whisky chasers so I had the same. But my stomach couldn't cope with the fizziness and the sheer volume of the beer, so I tended to drink the whisky. Every time I finished my glass someone filled it up for me. I thought they might think it rude if I did not drink. The others smoked continuously and it grew very stuffy. I don't remember much about the conversation.

'Power and money,' Stephen said, or at least I think he did, 'are really different aspects of the same thing. And always remember, my dears: they should be means and never ends.'

When we left the pub at closing time, the fresh air hit me like a slap. Inside, my mind had been reeling while my body functioned with reasonable efficiency. Suddenly the positions were reversed. My head cleared. I staggered against a wall.

'Whoopsy,' Stephen said.

Esmond took my arm. He and Stephen had to walk me back to the car. The four of us moved abreast in a wavering line across the car park. Lilian was walking uncertainly too, but in her case it might have been because she was unaccustomed to her high heels. She tottered along on the other side of Esmond; she clung to his arm, and I had the impression that he was half supporting her.

'We can bed him down at the flat if you want,'

Stephen said. 'Might save you a few problems with the old bag.'

'No,' I tried to mumble. 'No, no, no.'

'He'll have to sleep on the floor,' Lilian said. She didn't sound drunk. 'Or there's Dad's bed, I suppose, but it isn't made up.'

'Esmond will need that,' Stephen pointed out. 'After we've had a nightcap or three.'

'Then Thomas could sleep in the bath,' Lilian said.

'I'm sorry,' I muttered, feeling that I was causing everyone a great deal of trouble. No one seemed to hear me. My stomach heaved.

'Thanks but no thanks,' Esmond said. 'We'd better get back to Finisterre. He'll be OK.'

'Do stay,' Lilian said.

Stephen laughed softly. 'It's no use, my sweet. Esmond's a man of iron resolution. Didn't you know?'

We reached the car. I was lifted into the low-slung passenger seat. It was a warm night and Esmond had the top down.

'Cheery-byes, my loves,' Stephen said.

I was sick on the way home – half in and half out of the car. We were passing through Ulvercombe at the time.

'Don't worry,' Esmond said. 'It happens to us all.'

He drove past Finisterre and down the lane to Blackberry Water. He stopped the car near our picnic place and found a torch in the glove compartment. I heard him get out of the car and open the boot. He came back with a blanket and some wet rags.

He removed the worst of the mess from me and the side of the car. All the time he was doing this he whistled between his teeth – a jaunty little tune called, I think, 'Living Doll'. A breeze was blowing off the sea. Once or twice I shivered.

'There,' he said at last. 'You'll do.'

'I'm sorry.' What amazed me most, and still does, was not the kindness he was capable of but the tenderness.

'Don't be stupid. Get back in the car.'

I lay back in the passenger seat. Esmond tucked the blanket around me. He opened the glove compartment and took out a hip flask.

'Are you in a hurry to get back?' he said.

'No.'

'Good.' He walked round the car and climbed into the driver's seat. He drank from the flask. 'I won't offer you any,' he said. He lit a cigarette and switched off the torch.

The smell of vomit wasn't noticeable because of the smoke, the breeze and the hood being down. I heard the waves combing through the shingle beyond the gap in the cliffs. The only light came from a handful of stars. Neither of us spoke but it was a friendly silence. My stomach was comfortable, and the inside of my head was like a cradle rocking slowly from side to side. I pretended I had blundered into eternity.

'One day, Rumpy,' Esmond said, flicking ash from his cigarette, 'let's have an all-night party here.'

Another event from that summer of 1963 stands out in my memory. One Saturday afternoon my mother drove me to Budstow. She had decided that I needed a new overcoat and a new tweed jacket for the winter.

Budstow in August is not a pleasant place. Still, in

the end we managed to park the car. For as long as I could remember my mother had bought most of my clothes from the gentlemen's outfitters near the church. We spent about half an hour in there. Then my mother suggested I took our purchases back to the car while she did a little more shopping; she would meet me there in twenty minutes.

The streets were so crowded that it was impossible to hurry. I was very hot; my mother believed that even in the warmest weather a man was not fully dressed without a jacket and tie, I decided to buy myself an ice-cream from the shop across the road. I waited on the pavement for a break in the traffic.

A red sports car came down the street. I only caught a glimpse of it because a slow-moving lorry blocked my view; and by the time the lorry had passed, the car had disappeared.

For an instant I was convinced that I had seen Esmond in his Triumph. The man behind the wheel had been wearing a hat and dark glasses. But it could easily have been Esmond.

Then common sense reasserted itself. If Esmond was in Budstow, he would be staying at Finisterre. Besides, I had talked to him on the telephone yesterday, and he had mentioned more than once that he had to go to a garden party in Richmond this afternoon.

I abandoned the idea of having an ice-cream and walked dejectedly back to the car. It is extraordinary how a moment's hope, once dashed, can cause an hour or two's disappointment. I sat in the car like a self-basting chicken in a slow oven for an hour and ten minutes. I tried to read but couldn't concentrate.

My mother eventually returned – she was peeved because she had not been able to find any wool that matched the precise shade required for a cardigan she had nearly finished. She habitually underestimated the amount of wool she needed. Her irritation increased when I reminded her that on our way home I had to call at the bookshop. I needed to pick up a file of overdue accounts; I had promised Stephen I would write reminder letters to our more dilatory customers over the weekend.

'Oh, all right,' she said with a flash of teeth. 'But if you're not out in three minutes, I'm going home without you.'

We drove through heavy traffic to Kinghampton. My mother parked outside the shop, adding to the congestion in Bay Street. I jumped out of the car. To my surprise the blind was down on the glazed panel of the door. I turned the handle. The door was locked.

I glanced over my shoulder at the car. My mother was staring in front of her, apparently oblivious of both me and the hooting of a coach behind her. Luckily I had my key with me, and the door proved to be locked but not bolted. The shop was empty.

'Stephen?' I called. 'It's me.'

I heard movement overhead, then Lilian's footsteps on the stairs. She was wearing her slippers; I recognized the slap-slap they made on the treads. She pushed aside the curtain and peered at me.

The eyes behind the glasses were red-rimmed. As she advanced into the shop I saw that she was carrying a balled-up handkerchief. She walked like someone half-asleep. She stumbled against the corner of a display table.

'What is it?' I said. 'Lilian, what's happened?'

'Go away,' she said. 'I don't want to talk to you. I don't want to talk to anyone.'

'But why's the shop shut? And where's Stephen?'

Her face trembled as though it were trying to dissolve.

I said, more loudly than before, 'Where is he?'

'He's with Daddy.'

'At the nursing home?'

'No, no,' she whispered. 'He's not with Daddy. He can't be. Daddy's dead.'

In the silence Grimalkin stalked through the open door. Holding her tail high and her back arched, she traced a figure of eight around Lilian's legs and miaowed. She was hungry. No one took any notice of her. She miaowed again.

The mind reacts so unpredictably. When Lilian said her father was dead a picture flashed into my mind; part-memory, part-vision. I saw Mr Sandwell falling, feet first, his hands stroking the heads of the invisible dogs which must have been falling beside him. And I heard him speak, too – as clearly as though he were in the shop beside us.

'Oh bugger,' said Mr Sandwell. 'Oh, bigger bogger bugger.'

Twelve

Even if you cut through the back roads, as I knew
Esmond would, it is a good sixty miles from Finisterre
to Exeter. Allowing for delays I reckoned that the round
trip would take at least four hours. He and Alice would
probably arrive at Finisterre between nine and ten.

At six-thirty, Bronwen put her head into my room
and asked me to come downstairs for a drink. She was
dressed for war in a red dress with deep Vs cut fore
and aft.

The fire was lit in the sitting room. It was still light
outside but Bronwen pulled the curtains across the
windows and switched on the table lamps. Her skin
looked better by artificial light – not so much sallow as
smoky. She switched on the television with the sound
turned low and made us both a gin and tonic. I watched
her from the sofa. She sat down in the chair Esmond
used and lit a cigarette. She hardly ever smoked.

'Cheers,' she said, and the pieces of ice tinkled in her
glass as she lifted it to her lips. 'What time do you think
they'll be here?'

'Difficult to know.'

'Why?'

'Well, there might be heavy traffic. Or roadworks.
And trains are often delayed, aren't they?'

'If they're not here by eight-thirty, dinner'll be
spoiled.'

'Oh dear,' I said. 'That would be a pity.'

Bronwen glared at me. By common consent we looked at the television. I strained to hear what the people on the screen were saying. Television came too late into my life for me to be able to ignore a set when it is switched on: it seems a failure of courtesy, like ignoring a person. Heads bobbed up and down in a brightly coloured studio. I think we were watching a news programme, but I cannot be sure. We sipped our drinks.

Had I felt it my place to be frank, I would have told Bronwen that Esmond and Alice might be even later than she feared. Esmond must have had his reasons for going to meet Alice by himself. I suspected that they would stop for a drink on the way back. He would want an opportunity to assess her without Bronwen and me competing for his attention – and indeed for hers. Also, it would give him a chance to charm Alice at the outset. Esmond, it often seemed to me, had learned from Stephen Sandwell the importance of cultivating special relationships.

Esmond's motives might not be wholly selfish. Not necessarily. He might calculate that Alice would be grateful for a chance to get to know her new family by stages, and she might want to question Esmond about me. It was a strange and oddly gratifying sensation for me to know that in Alice's eyes I must be a person of importance.

'We're going to get married soon,' Bronwen said. 'As soon as this business with the house is sorted out.'

'Oh really. How nice.'

'Hasn't Esmond mentioned it?'

'Not in so many words. In fact – well, I thought you might be married already.'

'Common law.'

'I beg your pardon?'

'I'm his common-law wife.' She swallowed the rest of her drink. 'I waited for him, you know. All the time he was inside, that second time. I kept myself for him.'

'I'm sure he was very – ah, very pleased that you did.'

'And it wasn't for want of offers, either. Don't you go thinking that.'

'I shouldn't dream of it.'

'Bloody men,' she said. 'They give you a present and they think they own you.'

She stared at the fire. It had not been lit for long but the kindling was well ablaze. High yellow flames licked the back of the chimney. Bronwen made good fires. I decided that since she was in the mood for confidences I had nothing to lose by asking a question.

'How long was Esmond in prison?'

'Two years, with remission. That judge was a bastard. Anyone could see it was a mistake.'

'Yes,' I said.

'It wasn't as if he'd hurt anyone, either. If anything it was their fault. If they want people to get their VAT right, they should make the tax laws clearer.'

'Yes, it's very complicated.'

'It's bloody ridiculous. There's one law for those who can afford a good accountant, and another law for the rest.'

She inhaled, coughed and flung the rest of the ciga-rette into the fire. Did she, I wondered, actually believe that Esmond had spent two years in prison because he'd made an innocent mistake? Was she alive to the possibility that Esmond's only mistake was getting found out?

'We should have stayed in London,' she said. 'Do you want another one of those?'

'No, thank you.'

'Suit yourself.' Bronwen got up and went to the drinks trolley. 'It wasn't as if we didn't have the openings up there. There were plenty of offers. Esmond's always had a lot of contacts.'

'Then why did you come here?' I asked.

She was concentrating on pouring the gin. She poured some in, frowned and lifted the glass to the level of her eyes. What she saw in it evidently dissatisfied her. She added another half an inch of gin and about the same amount of tonic.

'What was that?' she said.

'Why did you come to Finisterre?'

'Esmond thought it was time for a change.' She turned away to put caps on the bottles. The dark hair masked her face. 'Did we want to spend the rest of our lives in London? Et cetera. And of course you needing help was the thing that really made up his mind.'

'Oh yes,' I said.

'You know Esmond.' She swayed as she walked back to her chair but her eyes were wary. 'He's an old softy at heart. Cheers.'

'Cheers.'

'According to him, families have got to stick together. After all, blood's thicker than water.'

'Yes,' I said. 'That's just what I was thinking.'

*

'Have you ever drunk blood?' Stephen asked us on the day after his father's funeral. August 1963 – thirty-odd years ago. How time flies.

No one answered him.

'It's surprisingly tasty. And you feel it's doing you good, too, like Ovaltine or Bovril.'

It was a Saturday. We were climbing up the cliff path, south of Budstow. The path sloped upwards, steeply in places. To the right was a grassy bank, beyond which – unseen but still unpleasant – was a sense of limitless space. Lilian was in front, head down and hands stuffed into the pockets of her school raincoat. Esmond had come down from London especially for the funeral. Where the path was wide enough, he and Stephen walked together beneath a big umbrella – black fading to green – that had belonged to Mr Sandwell. I followed as closely as I could.

'Bags of vitamins, I expect,' Stephen was saying. 'Not to mention iron and calcium and so forth.'

'Protein?' Esmond said.

'It wouldn't surprise me in the least. It struck me as a meal in itself.'

Although we were in the middle of August, the path was almost deserted because it was pouring with rain. The ground was slippery. My black leather shoes were thick with mud. We couldn't see the sea but we could hear the dull booming of the breakers far below.

There was some consolation in the knowledge that it was terrible weather for the holidaymakers. It had rained all day and for much of yesterday. (It had started raining while we were in church. Everyone got rather wet. Aunt Ada had slipped by the south porch and genuflected in a puddle.) Had the bookshop been open today and yesterday, we would have done a brisk trade.

'Mark you,' Stephen went on, swinging the nylon string-bag he carried in his left hand, 'you can't afford to hang around when you're drinking blood. It coagulates very quickly. And personally I think it tastes nicer when it's still warm from the vein.'

'Hang on,' Esmond said. 'I want to light a cigarette.'

The four of us stopped while Esmond and Stephen lit cigarettes. It took them a moment because of the gusts of rain. Lilian, who was a few yards up the path, walked slowly back. She was hatless, and her hair was soaked. 'Drowned rats' tails,' my mother would have said with quiet pleasure, as though the rain were a fitting punishment for a woman who dared to go outside without a hat. As Lilian passed her brother her bare leg touched the blue string-bag. She jumped sideways as if it had nipped her, and almost slipped on the long wet grass that fringed the path.

'Steady the Buffs,' Stephen said.

She ignored him. Her face was wet. I wondered if tears had mingled with the rain on her skin. She came closer to me. Even her glasses were streaked with water. Again she stumbled. Automatically I put out my hand. She seized it. The tightness of her grip made me grunt with surprise. She let go of me and sniffed. The presence of my hand seemed to have offended her.

'By the left,' Stephen said. 'Quick march.'

He and Esmond set off again. They looked like a deformed and enlarged black beetle: four legs topped by the almost hemispherical umbrella. The bag, an obscene pendant, banged against one of Stephen's thighs.

'The use of blood as a sacrament,' Stephen continued, 'goes right back to the dawn of human culture.'

'Oh God,' Lilian said. She put her hand on my arm and stopped. I turned towards her. Slowly the others moved out of earshot.

'What is it?' I said. 'What's wrong?'

'He wanted to mix the ashes with our blood, and drink it. I said if he tried to do that I'd kill him.'

'Perhaps – perhaps it was a joke.'

'A *joke*?'

'Sorry.'

'Oh, come on. Let's get it over with.'

We walked after the others. I stared at the string-bag. I knew that it contained a small grey pot with a lid. The lid was secured with Sellotape, which was just as well considering the way the pot was bouncing against Stephen's thigh.

The path grew less steep. We climbed in silence. Esmond and Stephen threw away the remains of their cigarettes. We had walked about two miles and all of us were finding it hard going, but at last the ground began to level out. Two hikers, a man and a woman both with bare knees, strode past us in the opposite direction.

'Good afternoon,' they said cheerily, as if they meant it.

We crossed over a stile, beside which was a notice-board announcing that this was Nose Point and it belonged to the National Trust. The umbrella stopped moving.

I had never been here before. We were on a steep-sided, wedge-shaped promontory. Beyond the tip the headland continued in skeletal form: a line of rocky spikes curved like a spine into the heaving water below. On our left I saw – to my surprise – a road with a large lay-by, a bus stop and a shuttered cabin of the sort that sells ice-creams, and buckets and spades. Apart from the four of us, it was a landscape empty of people.

'I didn't realize – we should have come by car.'

'What do you mean, you didn't realize?' Lilian said. 'You don't think all the old farts came the same way we did?'

'Then why did we come by the path?'

Lilian shrugged. 'It was Stephen's idea, not mine.'

The umbrella wheeled round. 'What was my idea?' Stephen asked.

'Walking up by the cliff path,' Lilian said.

'Two reasons. One, the funeral march is conducive to meditation. Gentle but rhythmic physical exercise can help to channel psychic energy. And two, you'll think me sentimental, I'm afraid, but I thought the pater would like it.'

'You don't think he *knows*?' Lilian said.

'What do you think, Lilian?' After a short but uncomfortable pause Stephen returned to me: 'In his younger days, the pater liked to stride for miles across hill and bog. Sometimes he would walk thirty miles in a single day. Can you believe it? I must confess I find it difficult to imagine, but the pleasures of others are always mysterious.'

Stephen looked towards the lay-by. The nursing home had hired a coach for their annual picnic. It must have parked in the lay-by. The staff would have unloaded their inanimate paraphernalia first, perhaps, and then their human cargo. In that company, Mr

Sandwell must have seemed positively youthful. For most of the time he'd still had the use of his legs; and on good days, the matron was reported as saying at the inquest, he was capable of solving some of the clues in *The Times* crossword.

'I didn't like to mention that he usually got the answers wrong,' Stephen had commented when he was describing the inquest to us. 'It would have been unfilial.'

Esmond fumbled for his cigarettes. He took one for himself and held out the packet to Stephen.

'The pater deserved better than a beastly charabanc for his last journey. Don't you agree?'

No one replied. Esmond and Stephen huddled together to light their cigarettes.

'Most of them didn't even come on the headland,' Stephen went on. 'They had their picnic spoon-fed to them in that field. You see? The one behind the lay-by.'

We moved in a group towards the tip of the headland. Lilian was crying openly now, but without sobbing or any other noise.

'But the pater liked to stretch his legs when he could. He always liked the Nose. One of his favourite places.'

The tears ran noiselessly down Lilian's cheeks as though a pair of taps had been turned on behind her eyes. I tried to take her hand – God knows the fools we make of ourselves when we try to be compassionate – but it slid away from mine; she neither looked at me nor changed her course.

Esmond said, so cheerfully that I knew he was feeling dreadfully embarrassed, 'Shouldn't we be doing this at midnight on Hallowe'en to get the maximum benefit?'

'Oh I've already done that sort of thing,' Stephen said, giving the string-bag a little shake. 'Last night, mainly. The pater and I could have done with a little help from Lilian. Unfortunately she was incapacitated, weren't you, dear?'

'Shut up, can't you?'

'Still, we managed quite well, all things considered. What we're doing now is just for auld lang syne.'

Stephen veered to the left, to the south, before we reached the tip of the headland. We entered a shallow depression – it was as though an enormous animal had used his upper incisors to scrape a mouthful from the cliff, thereby removing the top to a depth of five or six feet. In this south-facing hollow, the wind ceased and the sound of the sea was muted. I heard seagulls crying and my own breathing. The springy turf was covered with little stones.

'It was over there,' Lilian said, pointing to a place at the edge of the cliffs.

We walked towards it. You could tell that people had been there recently – there were tyre-marks on the grass, ice-cream wrappers, an old newspaper and an empty packet of cigarettes. Stephen threw away his cigarette and raised his hand. The rest of us stopped. He gave Esmond the umbrella. His face solemn, he glanced at Lilian and me: perhaps he was making sure that he had the attention of his congregation. Then, swinging the string-bag, he walked on the balls of his feet towards the edge of the cliffs.

'Be careful!' Lilian screamed.

He gave no sign that he had heard. He stopped only a foot or two away from the edge and stood there with his head bowed for perhaps thirty seconds. He lifted the bag and took out the grey pot, which he hefted in his right hand, as though estimating its weight. Then he lobbed it clumsily in front of him. It vanished instantly.

The three of us stood there. We said nothing. We didn't move. I tried to make myself believe that this was a sacred moment. Instead I had to repress an urge to giggle. I was aware of a need to empty my bladder. I wished I knew what Lilian really thought about me.

Stephen, his head bowed, turned and walked very slowly towards us. And, as he walked, his podgy little fingers were busy folding the string-bag: into two, into four and finally – at the second try – into eight. Just before he reached us he opened his overcoat. He tucked the neat blue rectangle into an inside pocket over his heart.

That evening, my mother cooked steak-and-kidney pudding in Esmond's honour. She never really mastered suet. Esmond, whose tastes had changed in eight years, failed to find a tactful way of telling her that he would have preferred to eat almost anything else in her limited repertoire.

Before supper, the three of us drank too much sherry in the sitting room. And before that Esmond and I lined our stomachs with whisky in the nursery.

My mother was in a good mood. Other people's deaths excited her – so long as they were not too close for comfort or too distant for interest. Mr Sandwell was ideal. She knew him fairly well but principally at second hand. My mother and Stephen had for a time enjoyed their special relationship. Esmond and I were friends with the younger Sandwells. I was Stephen's colleague. Aunt Ada's husband and the deceased's wife had been cousins. All this gave my mother a pleasant sense of privileged knowledge without the responsibility that usually goes with it.

Over supper she questioned us mercilessly. We told her everything that we could remember about our afternoon. Everything, that is, which we considered fit for her ears. The conversation continued to revolve around Mr Sandwell's death while we washed up. Then Esmond carried the coffee tray into the sitting room. My mother sank into her chair. 'Well,' she said, with deep satisfaction. 'It all sounds quite pagan to me.'

We had eaten earlier than usual. It was still light. The rain had stopped but the sky was heavy with clouds. I could see at the end of our valley the darkening shadow of the sea.

'Switch on the lights, dear,' my mother told me. 'And draw the curtains, would you?'

She poured the coffee and I handed it round. Esmond lit a cigarette. I saw him glance at his watch.

'Casting ashes into the sea,' she went on, just as I was beginning to hope that she would let the subject drop. 'It's not nice.'

'If there's a death on a ship, the bodies are usually put over the side,' Esmond pointed out.

'But this is quite different. A fish might eat some of the ashes. And we might eat it.'

'Or rather him,' Esmond murmured too quietly for my mother to hear.

'I don't think fish like ash,' I said.

'A fish might eat the ash by accident. They just

swim along with their mouths open. Anything might get inside.'

'But the chance of your actually eating some of the ash must be about a million million million to one.' Esmond smiled at her. 'You mustn't worry, Aunt Fiona.'

'But I do worry. We buy a great deal of local fish.'

'The trouble with fish is the bones,' I said. I have never liked fish, and I wanted to change the subject before Esmond made me laugh aloud.

'It's good for you,' my mother said absently. 'And besides, Esmond, there must be theological implications. I can't help thinking that Stephen has been a wee bit inconsiderate, whatever the will said. It's not very fair on the vicar, is it?'

This was just the sort of subject she would enjoy discussing with Aunt Ada. Until now, Aunt Ada had had the unfair advantage of having been to the funeral. My mother's vicarious knowledge of the ash-scattering ceremony would redress the balance.

'Do you think perhaps that Mr Sandwell wasn't in his right mind when he made the will?' Esmond asked.

'Who knows, dear? I know some people called him eccentric. But who are we to judge?'

My mother put aside her knitting and picked up a magazine. She bought a great many women's magazines – chiefly, she said, for the recipes and the knitting patterns. She was wearing her serious expression, the one she wore when she dealt with matters of high moral importance. Esmond shifted in his chair. He glanced at me and rolled his eyes at the ceiling.

'Poor Mr Sandwell,' she said. 'He seemed such a

lonely man, so unhappy. There was a poem in here, I happened to notice it the other day. They have a section called "Poetry To Help Us Through Life". Do you know it? They have some lovely pieces. I read this, and I thought of Mr Sandwell. Free at last. Ah. Here we are.'

She settled her glasses on her nose and licked her lips. She read out in a high, wavering voice the following stanza:

> Stone walls do not a prison make
>   Nor iron bars a cage;
> Minds innocent and quiet take
>   That for an hermitage;
> If I have freedom in my love,
>   And in my soul am free;
> Angels alone, that soar above,
>   Enjoy such liberty.

'Beautiful, isn't it?' she said.

'Yes indeed,' said Esmond. 'It sounds familiar.'

My mother peered at the page. 'It's by someone called Richard Lovelace. I expect that's a pseudonym.'

I bit the inside of my mouth. The pain burst the bubble of laughter. I tasted blood. 'No, Mother,' I said. 'It was his real name. He was a Cavalier poet.'

'Oh.'

'In the seventeenth century,' I added, knowing that it was never wise to overestimate my mother's general knowledge.

She recovered quickly. 'I thought it was too good to be modern. I must show it to Ada.'

'It's a verse from a poem he wrote in prison.' I stumbled as I spoke, not so much from the whisky as from suppressed hysteria. 'I can find you the rest of it if you want.'

'Yes, dear. I should like that.'

No doubt I was being cynical, but I suspected she would think that a whole poem in a book would look more impressive than a single verse in a women's magazine.

'Oh, by the way,' Esmond said in the couldn't-care-less voice he used when he cared a great deal. 'Did you say the ash-scattering was Mr Sandwell's idea? I thought Stephen dreamed it up.'

'Oh no, dear. The vicar made quite sure of that. I believe he actually asked to see chapter and verse, as it were.'

'So he's seen the will? What happens to the shop and everything?'

'Ah.' My mother looked at him. 'Good question. I don't know.'

'It's something that could affect Thomas, isn't it?'

Esmond and my mother nodded; it was as though their heads were synchronized and their thoughts marched together. I was excluded. I felt jealous of the intimacy between them.

My first impression was that Mr Sandwell's death had changed nothing. I felt relieved and disappointed.

That is often the way. You cross (or, more often, are taken or pushed across) what you imagine will be a watershed in your life, and you expect that things on the other side will be quite different from what they were before. At first, however, everything appears the same. This is inevitably something of an anticlimax. Only gradually do you realize that the landscape is no longer made up of the same details, that you and the streams are going downhill not up, and that your relationship to the sun and the mountains has altered. As so often, the problem lies not in the complexity of what we observe but in our simplistic habits of thought: we confuse the line of a watershed with a geometric line, and assume that the watershed exists in only one dimension.

On the Monday morning after the funeral Esmond drove me into Kinghampton; he was on his way back to London. The bad weather had departed with the weekend. Stephen had said nothing to me on Saturday, but I assumed that he would want me to keep the shop running as best I could.

I was nervous – partly because I expected to have to witness other people's grief, and partly because of the prospect of change. We got to Bay Street before nine o'clock. To my surprise, the shop door was already unlocked, and the reversible sign had been turned to OPEN. Stephen sat reading and smoking behind the counter. He wasn't wearing a black armband. Nothing betrayed his bereavement. He looked up as the doorbell pinged.

'Morning, chaps,' he said. 'Thomas, there's a note from Bicknor College. They want a dozen *First Steps in Eating*, all right? Can you do the order this morning?'

'Of course.' Had he asked me to stand on my head I would seriously have considered complying. Ordering elementary Latin exercises presented no difficulty.

'Ritchie,' I murmured, proud to show off my expertise before Esmond. 'And the publisher's Longman, isn't it?'

'Bloody Broadbent-Browns,' Stephen said. 'They always want everything done yesterday.'

I moved towards the cubbyhole.

'Up to town this fine morning?' Stephen said to Esmond. 'Lucky you. Have some coffee before you go.'

'Yes, why not?'

'Thomas – nip upstairs, will you? If Lilian isn't up, can you make us some?'

I went slowly upstairs. I heard the rasp of a match and the murmur of voices in the shop below. Grimalkin was waiting on the landing. She sat upright, her front paws together and her tail curled around her rear, beside the kitchen doorway. She looked at me as I passed her but did not move; I never gave her food or even stroked her, so I did not figure very highly in her scheme of things.

The kitchen was empty. Stephen's coffee cup and his cereal bowl stood on the draining board. The bowl was spotless, so I guessed that Grimalkin had scoured it with her tongue.

The kettle was warm and almost full. I lit the gas and put the kettle back on the ring. It was not worth my returning downstairs, so I leaned against the table. Grimalkin walked in and made a slow circuit of the table in the centre of the room, paying particular attention to the floor around the legs of the chairs and table. Her search was fruitless. As she passed me, I stuck out my tongue at her. Suddenly the cat broke into a run. It was as though she had eyes in her tail – she had seen my childish insult and could not bear to remain in the room with me.

'Coffee,' Lilian said from the doorway. 'Now that's a good idea.'

Her feet were bare and she wore a skimpy dressing-gown which had once been pink, and which was held together by what looked like a man's tie. She stooped and picked up Grimalkin, who purred dementedly. I was glad that Lilian's attention was diverted from me. I assured myself over and over again that she could not have seen me making a face at Grimalkin.

Lilian put down the cat and proceeded to prepare the animal's breakfast. That done, she sat down with Grimalkin gobbling frantically at her feet. The kettle came to the boil. Lilian yawned and stayed where she was.

Until then it had not occurred to me that she would not make the coffee. Those were primitive times. At school, girls learned cookery while boys learned carpentry. After perhaps thirty seconds had passed, it dawned on me that she did not intend to get up. Poor thing, I thought. I ascribed this unnatural behaviour to the mysterious effects of grief; and perhaps, in a way I did not understand at the time, I was right.

'Shall I make the coffee?' I said brightly.

She appeared not to hear me.

I got up. I knew how to make proper coffee in a jug: Stephen had taught me how to do it with an old-maidish attention to detail. But he had taught me on the shared but unstated assumption that I would only have to do it when Lilian was elsewhere or otherwise engaged. I had never done it in front of her. To do so would be to trespass on her field of expertise.

It was a wonder that nothing got broken. My natural clumsiness increased as I felt Lilian's eyes trained on my back. When I used the hand-grinder I spilled coffee grounds all over the draining board. I splashed boiling water on my hand. My memory kept failing me – how many dessert-spoonfuls in the warmed pot? – but fortunately only for a few seconds at a time. The day was already warm and I was soon sweating profusely.

At last the coffee was brewing and the cups were ready on the tray. The strainer was there, and also the milk and sugar which Esmond (braving Stephen's disapproval) insisted on having. I turned round, ready at last to take a modest pride in my achievement. To my mortification, Lilian was to all appearances asleep. She had rested her arms on the table and her head on her arms. At her feet the beastly Grimalkin gnawed at the last of her breakfast.

'Um – you do like the cup with Lone Ranger on, don't you?' I said.

She raised her head and nodded. The cup was not a survival from her childhood but a recent acquisition – that is, it had been bought since the Sandwells had come to Kinghampton.

'Thomas, has he talked to you yet?'

I shook my head. We lived so much in each other's pockets that I knew not only whom she meant but the subject she expected Stephen to raise with me.

'Dad was going to sell the shop.'

'What?'

'I listened to them talking. It was about a month ago. The accountant had been to see Dad at the nursing home.'

'But I thought Stephen did everything.'

'Not everything. Not the big things.'

'But why sell the shop? So Stephen could go to London?'

'You don't understand. Dad said Stephen was cheating everyone. Me. The customers. Him. Everyone. He said he wasn't fit to run a shop.'

I didn't know what to do or say.

'There was something about seeing his solicitor, too.'

'How's the coffee coming along?' Stephen shouted up the stairs. 'I thought we bought the beans ready roasted.'

'Just coming,' I called back. I turned away and poured the coffee. 'What are you saying?' I whispered to Lilian.

'I don't know. That's part of the problem. You know what Dad was like. He tended to get a bit muddled.'

I gave her the Lone Ranger mug. That morning her face was particularly ugly, white and haggard, blotched with pink. She sipped the coffee. Steam misted her glasses.

'I'm sure it'll be all right,' I said.

'Oh, for Christ's sake, Thomas,' she said. 'Just go away, will you?'

For the life of me I couldn't see how I had upset her. I was trying to be as helpful and sympathetic as possible.

I carried the tray carefully downstairs. The voices in the shop stopped murmuring. This had the effect of doubling the sense of injury I felt: Lilian had sent me away, and Stephen and Esmond had secrets they would not share with me. And last night Esmond and my mother had excluded me. I felt very lonely.

'Did I hear Lilian's voice?' Stephen said.

I nodded.

He and Esmond chatted about London while they drank their coffee; I sorted out the Bicknor College order. We had the shop to ourselves; the fine weather kept the customers away.

'Well, I must be off,' Esmond said. 'See you sometime.'

'Why fight it, dear boy? You'll almost certainly be down in four weeks' time. Your visits are getting as reliably regular as the curse in a convent.'

Esmond grinned. I suspect that Stephen's laboured witticisms often bored him, but he never showed any sign of it. He paused in the shop doorway and flashed a smile at me: 'I'll be in touch.'

'I might have left my umbrella in the car,' I said. 'I'd better check.'

'Better safe than sorry,' Stephen said. 'A very good rule in life. It may look sunny, but one should take nothing for granted in this vale of tears.'

He neighed with amusement. I followed Esmond on to the pavement.

'What's up with you?' he said.

I shrugged. 'Was July really the last time you were down here? Four weeks ago?'

'You know that as well as I do.' He reached behind the seat and fished out my umbrella. 'Seems less, does it?'

'I thought I saw you and the car in Budstow on Saturday,' I said, taking the umbrella.

'That's because I *was* there.' He raised his eyebrows: his face filled with gentle mockery. 'You were there too, remember? In the passenger seat, and it was pissing down with rain.'

'No. Not that Saturday. The one before.'

That was the Saturday when Mr Sandwell died.

His face changed. For a moment he looked like an angry stranger. 'You can't have done,' he said. 'Don't be so bloody silly. You know I was in London that weekend.'

'Oh – yes, of course.' I was trembling because of the anger in his voice. 'It's just that the car looked a bit similar, that's all. I only saw it for a moment.'

Esmond lit a cigarette and flicked the match into the gutter. 'There's an awful lot of red Triumphs around. Not to mention other red sports cars. You didn't get a proper look at the driver, I suppose?'

'No. He was wearing a hat and sunglasses.'

'Well, there you are. Have you ever seen me in sunglasses? I don't own any.'

I smiled foolishly at him. Love and loneliness make fools of us all. Esmond patted my arm and climbed into the car. The engine roared. He looked up at me.

'Silly old Rumpy,' he said.

Thirteen

By nine o'clock on the evening of Thursday 3rd October Bronwen was the next best thing to drunk. I calculated that she must have had about six times more gin than I.

We were still in the sitting room and still by ourselves. She sat slumped in Esmond's chair. The red dress was crumpled, and it was spotted here and there with cigarette ash. She looked as though she were spilling out of a wilting poppy.

Bronwen had been doing almost all the talking. Not that there had been a great deal of it. I had the impression that nine-tenths of her conversation was unspoken, though presumably it passed through her mind if not through her lips; the greater part of it was like an iceberg in that its bulk lay beneath the surface. She would be silent for a moment and then come out with something seemingly unrelated to what she had been talking about before. I played a game with myself by trying to reconstruct the submarine connections between one remark and the next.

'Alice?' she said, breaking the latest of the silences between us. 'Did you choose the name?'

I dragged my eyes away from the television screen. 'No. Lilian did. My wife.'

Referring to Lilian as 'my wife' or Alice as 'my daughter' always made me feel self-conscious; I felt I had to explain who they were in relation to me whenever I mentioned their names.

The silence returned. My eyes drifted back to the television.

'The thing I can't bear,' Bronwen said, 'is the waiting. Doing nothing and not knowing. That's horrible, that is.'

It was easy enough to see the connection between Alice and waiting. But after the next interval, Bronwen flummoxed me completely by moving on to beef-burgers and, after another silence, to fire engines and their sirens. A little later, however, she returned to the problem of waiting, albeit from a different direction.

'This is what it's like when the jury's out,' she said. 'You think, they can't be much longer than this. But they are. And all the time you're going over the evidence and twisting it this way and that. And you're thinking about the jurors' faces and their clothes. Over and over again – just in case there's a clue you've missed. Something that tells you how they're thinking. Doesn't do a blind bit of good.'

'Was it like that at Esmond's trial?'

'Eh? I was thinking of someone else's. A friend – a woman.'

'What was she accused of?'

'Manslaughter.' Bronwen fiddled with the cigarette packet. 'She was living with this man, he was West Indian, which didn't help, and they had a fight – the bastard had been messing around with another girl, didn't even try and hide it. Anyway, he started hitting her round the face and she picked up a skewer and poked it at him. It was an accident. Anyone could see that.'

'What happened?'

I meant at the trial. Bronwen misunderstood me.

'It went in his eye. And how was – how was she to know that skewer would go right through into the brain? The bone behind the eye's really thin; did you know that? And it's got holes for the nerves to go through. Apparently you can kill someone by poking your finger into their eye. If you're lucky. If you do it hard enough.'

'*Lucky*?' I said.

'You know what I mean.' She frowned. 'I'll just get some ice.'

She left the room, closing the door behind her. I watched the television, while Bronwen took her time fetching the ice. When she came back, it was obvious that she had tried to tidy herself up, and equally obvious that she had not entirely succeeded. The gin was bringing colour to her face – to the nose, in particular, and to the patches of skin on either side of it. She put down the ice bucket with a clatter and made herself a fresh drink. As she sat down, the clock struck the half hour.

'Can't you say something, Rumpy? Cat got your tongue?'

I smiled. 'Sorry,' I said. And I wondered if she knew how cruel her choice of phrase was. Perhaps not. I was always forgetting how little Bronwen knew.

'Dinner's burned to buggery,' she remarked. 'I don't care. They can eat baked beans on toast.'

'I rather like baked beans,' I said.

'There's a joke, isn't there? About a truck driver driving his rig out of New Orleans. And the punchline's something like "Who needs gas when you got baked beans?"' She frowned at me – I suppose I was looking confused. '*Gas*, Rumpy. That's what the Americans call petrol, get it?' Suddenly she sat up, her face tightening with anxiety. A few drops of gin and tonic slopped over the rim of her glass and on to her dress. 'Oh, shit. Was that the car?'

'No.'

Her eyes focused on me. She looked suspicious, even hostile. 'How come you're so sure?'

'I've lived here all my life. I know what noises sound like. I know this house.'

Her face relaxed. 'All that time in one place.' Bronwen took another cigarette and toyed with it. She glanced sideways at me through her lashes. Like a child who wonders if the adult will intervene if she takes a second slice of cake, she was trying to calculate consequences. 'This thing about the death room,' she said. 'It's all a sort of game, isn't it?'

'It's just a name we had for that bedroom when we were children,' I said. 'It doesn't mean anything.'

'It's the obvious bedroom to put her in,' Bronwen said. 'It's the most comfortable.'

'I expect Alice will be very pleased with it.'

'Nothing will happen, will it?'

I blinked at her. 'I'm sorry?'

'Oh forget it.' She retreated into her mind once more. A few more minutes passed. Then, 'You had a shop in Kinghampton once, didn't you?'

'That's right.'

Alice and the death room must have led to Lilian – an uncomfortable subject – so then Bronwen must have veered away via Lilian's family to the safer topic of Sandwell and Son.

'Where was it then?' she demanded. 'There's no bookshop now, is there?'

I shook my head. 'It was in Bay Street. It's the video library now.'

'Tell me about it,' she said.

I hesitated, gathering my thoughts.

'Tell me about anything, will you?' she said. 'For Christ's sake, Rumpy, just talk to me.'

We never got round to changing the name above the shop window. At first Stephen and I thought it would be tasteless to alter it so soon after his father's death. Then we thought it would entail expense, so perhaps we should leave it until we had a good year. Finally, Stephen decided the original name was actually an asset.

'Two generations make us sound respectable and long established,' he said. 'Let's leave it.'

Then, in the way one does, I forgot all about it. So much so that I didn't bother to change the shop name when at last I was by myself. Sometimes customers or publishers' reps addressed me as 'Mr Sandwell'. I rarely bothered to correct them; in fact I rather enjoyed sheltering behind someone else's name. As the years went by I occasionally wondered if they mistook me for the father or the son.

Mr Sandwell left his estate equally between Stephen and Lilian. The estate consisted principally of the lease on the shop and the flat above, and whatever the business was worth. The lease was due to run out in 1978. The will had been drawn up in 1958. Lilian's share was to be held in trust for her until she was twenty-one. (I sometimes wonder if this might be where my mother got the idea of leaving her estate in trust.) Mr Sandwell obviously envisaged that Stephen would continue to run the shop and provide a home for Lilian until she was settled in life.

About two months after the funeral, Stephen took me to lunch at The Mermaid Hotel. Lilian was left in charge of the shop. We sat at our usual table near the bar, which had recently been redecorated with hardboard anchors and shell-spangled fishing nets. Stephen drank whisky and toyed between cigarettes with a small packet of nuts; I drank orange squash and nibbled a ham sandwich.

'I've been thinking,' Stephen said. 'I think it's about time you had a rise. Say an extra pound a week.'

I reddened, and spluttered my thanks.

'We'll backdate it to the beginning of the month. No, don't thank me. It's no more than you're worth, dear boy.'

He drank a little more; I ate a little more.

'One of my little nightmares,' he went on, 'is that you might get bored. One day you might up sticks and find a more challenging job – in a bigger bookshop, say.'

'No, I'm very happy here. Really.'

'It seems to me,' he said, 'that if I want to be sure of keeping you, it's more than a matter of just paying you more. I've got to give you more to do, not the donkeywork, of course: I mean more responsibilities.'

'I'm fine, honestly.'

'I've got to learn to delegate; that's the long and short of it, old chap. And in point of fact it might work out quite well.'

He looked expectantly at me. I had my mouth full but I made appropriate noises of interest and anticipation.

'I'm thinking of extending the business. Moving into the antiquarian side, that sort of thing. Engravings, too, perhaps.'

I swallowed. 'But where would we put them?' We were cramped enough in the shop as it was. 'And would we find customers down here?'

'You've raised two very good points, Thomas. It's early days, yet, but maybe we shouldn't rule out the possibility of other means of selling.'

'Through a catalogue?'

'Perhaps. Or some private clients actually commission you to find what they want: that's where the real money is, of course, at the upper end of the market. Another possibility would be new and larger premises, or a second set of premises. And in any case we aren't necessarily thinking about Kinghampton. One way or another, we need to be in touch with the right sort of customers.'

'So does that mean London?'

'The world, dear boy, is our oyster. Now let me get you a proper drink so we can celebrate your promotion.'

'I've got a lot to get through this afternoon.'

'Now don't be silly. Anyway, I'm the boss, remember?'

He pushed aside a fishing-net curtain and left me alone for a moment. When he came back he insisted we drink a toast. I didn't want the whisky but I thought Stephen might be cross if I left it untouched. After the toast I said, 'Do you want to start changing things now?'

'We'll come to that. Most businesses fail because they

look only to the immediate future. They lack a grand design. That's what gives one not just a purpose but a yardstick, if you follow me. One can judge anything and everything by the one important criterion of whether or not it fits the grand design. Are you with me so far?'

'I think so.'

'I think our grand design should be a chain of book-shops: new, antiquarian, academic, specialist, second-hand – whatever seems profitable – all trading under the name of Sandwell and Penmarsh. There.' He sat back, smiling. 'That surprised you, didn't it?'

'You mean –'

'Yes, indeed. I'm offering you a partnership. Not immediately, of course, it would be premature; there's no point. But once we have the foundations laid for the grand design, that will be another matter.'

'It's very kind of you,' I said.

'Each of us has his own strengths. I believe them to be complementary.'

I wondered whether all this meant I should have to leave Kinghampton and Finisterre. I felt a positive reluctance to move: it wasn't just my usual fear of the unknown – it was also, I told myself, that I actually liked where I lived. We all have a remarkable capacity for fooling ourselves when it is expedient to do so.

'At present,' Stephen said, 'I think there's a lot to be said for maintaining our Kinghampton outlet.'

'Yes. Oh yes.'

'You're quite right. It makes sound commercial sense to stay here for the moment. The shop gives us a firm base for our operations, doesn't it? It's a solid asset, something to impress the bank, eh?'

'You mean, if we want to extend the overdraft?'

He waved the question away. 'And – don't forget – it gives us a certain standing in the community, too. Also there's the point that any move will inevitably cost money.'

'Does Lilian know?'

He hesitated. 'I'll come to that. To go back to the shop, my feeling is that there's a difference between taking chances and being foolhardy. We need to expand, but we don't want to rush it. Do you agree?'

'I'm sure you're right,' I said. I knew exactly the game he was playing: the old 'special relationship' tactic. But it didn't matter; I was still charmed by the confidential tone of his voice and the way he had of implying that my opinion was the only one he wanted.

'But what happens now?' I asked. 'And what about Lilian?'

'Well – it means one of us going to London and researching the markets, laying the groundwork, making the contacts. Not full time, a day or two a week should be enough. Meanwhile, the other one keeps the business going here. As for Lilian – well, she's at a loose end now, isn't she? She's not a fool even if she did fail her A levels. She might as well do more to help in the shop. Do *your* old job, in a sense.'

I was silent. If Lilian was doing my job, I would be doing Stephen's. I wasn't sure I was capable of that. I could manage the book side, I thought: it was the people who were the problem.

'In fact,' Stephen said, 'it'll seem much the same as now. You're often in charge of the shop, aren't you? I'll only be in town for a day or two each week.'

'Yes,' I said. 'But –'

'Splendid,' Stephen said. 'I knew you'd agree. Let's drink to that.' He held up his glass and beamed at me. 'To Sandwell and Penmarsh, eh? And all who sail in her. May we flourish like a green bay tree.'

My mother was right to be suspicious about the new arrangement but she was suspicious for the wrong reasons. She heard about the grand design not from me but from Stephen. He cycled to Finisterre on the Sunday following our lunch at The Mermaid, and he was waiting for us in the garden when we got back from church.

I was surprised. I soon realized that Stephen and my mother were not. It transpired that he had written to ask if he might call; but neither of them had seen fit to tell me. I imagine that Stephen felt I might not approve of what he proposed to do. His main reason for calling was to discover whether he could wheedle some money from my mother.

'It's a copper-bottomed investment, dear lady. You'd be investing not just in me, or my expertise, or an area of commerce which is due to boom in the next decade. All those things are well worth investing in. But on top of all those, you'd also be investing in Thomas here.'

My mother handled Stephen's application with surprising skill. We were all in the sitting room. Each of us had a very small sherry – the dregs in the bottle which Esmond had brought on his last visit.

'It would be very difficult just now,' she said vaguely. 'But I hope you do very well, of course. I'm sure you will.'

I guessed that she was unwilling to invest in anything

that might take me away from Finisterre, which could happen in the unlikely event that Stephen's more grandiose schemes took the shape he predicted. Also, she distrusted him. On the other hand she probably felt it would be unwise to alienate my employer: if he sacked me or sold the Kinghampton shop I might be foolish enough to look for work away from home. All in all, she must have felt that Stephen had dropped her on to the horns of a dilemma.

'It must be such a comfort for you to know that Thomas will be looking after things here,' she said. 'On all fronts.'

In other words she reminded Stephen that he needed me: to look after the shop, to keep the money coming in, to help keep Lilian occupied. I was a minor but important part of his plans. To replace me would not be impossible, but it would be difficult and time-consuming. Whether by accident or design, my mother stressed this while she was declining to invest in Stephen's proposal.

'He's really quite responsible now,' my mother said. 'Quite grown-up. Aren't you, dear?'

'Oh yes,' Stephen said. 'I know. I've trained him myself, man and boy, Mrs Penmarsh. I certainly appreciate his full worth.'

He glanced at me with a twitch of his eyebrows – to let me know that his ambiguity was not a form of malice but a joke for him and me to share.

'But one thing we could do,' my mother said brightly, 'is help with the storage. Couldn't we, Thomas? I'm sure you'll need a lot of space for all those old books.'

'Oh yes, Mother.'

'There's the loft over the garage for a start. It's quite dry. We use it for apples. You could keep quite a lot of your stock there.'

'I simply can't say how helpful that would be,' Stephen said. 'Thank you so much.'

'What about the attics?' I said.

My mother manufactured an excuse without the slightest hesitation. 'Mr Jodson tells me we need to have some work done in the attics. Indeed, he says it's hardly safe to walk up there. So I'm afraid they're out of the question.'

For several moments the smell of roasting meat had been growing stronger. Our Sunday lunch was in the oven. My mother drained the last of her sherry and hoisted herself out of her chair. Stephen and I leapt to our feet.

'Would you excuse me?' she said.

She lifted an eyebrow. Stephen darted to the door and held it open for her. She moved past him.

'I'll say goodbye now, shall I?' she said. 'Otherwise we'll make you late for lunch. We mustn't be selfish, must we, Thomas?'

She disappeared into the hall. The sound of her footsteps receded. The kitchen door opened and closed. Stephen rubbed the palms of his hands together. He looked delighted, as though she had given him all he asked for, and then a bonus as well.

'Not brains,' he said. 'She does it all by instinct. And you can hardly fault her. Isn't Mother Nature bloody marvellous?'

Then he too was gone.

*

By January 1964 Esmond and Stephen were sharing a flat in Chelsea. In theory it was Esmond's flat, and it had a spare bedroom where Stephen stayed when he was in London. And according to the same theory, Stephen lived in Kinghampton, where he ran his bookshop and looked after his teenage sister. Stephen seemed to believe that the theory corresponded with the reality. He certainly expected Esmond, Lilian and me to act as though this were the case.

Even Esmond was kept at least partly in the dark.

'Stephen?' he said, when he was down at Finisterre for a weekend at the end of that January. 'I haven't seen him for days. Since Tuesday.'

'But he went up to London on Sunday. And he phoned Lilian yesterday to say he'd be back tomorrow.'

Esmond shrugged. 'I thought he was down here.'

'And I thought he was with you.'

It was late on the Friday evening. My mother had at last gone to bed and for the first time that visit he and I were able to have a proper chat. Esmond was sitting on the window-seat in my room with an uncapped bottle of whisky between his legs. He was a little puffy round the eyes and looked as though he needed a good dose of fresh air. His hair was ragged, and at the back it touched his collar. I thought that city life must be wearing him down, that he couldn't even find a moment or two for a visit to the barber's; but I didn't like to say anything because I knew he would think I was fussing.

'You know what Stephen's like,' Esmond said. 'Likes to keep us all guessing. How's business?'

'Ticking over.' I was rather proud of myself. Christmas is usually a good time of year for a bookshop, but

Lilian and I had done almost as well as last year despite Stephen's absence. Things were quieter now. 'Did you know about the antiquarian section?'

'No.' Esmond sounded as if he didn't want to.

'Stephen wants us to convert Mr Sandwell's bedroom into our antiquarian and second-hand department. Lilian and I have been working on that. At present we're trying to sort out stock. It's not for the general public, really.'

'Very ambitious.' He took a pull of the whisky; he wasn't bothering with a glass. 'So the grand design is taking shape?'

'Slowly.'

Two packing cases of books had arrived by carrier. Most of them seemed to be Victorian reprints of popular fiction and cheap pre-war editions of the classics. I had suggested there might not be much demand for these. 'Mere shelf-dressing,' Stephen explained. He said that his real business lay elsewhere. He talked of bidding at auctions and paying calls on potential clients in Mayfair, of signed first editions and gothic-revival typography; he had developed a professional vocabulary of bibliographic jargon, which he deployed as enthusiastically as a boy with a new set of soldiers. He had business cards printed, 'Stephen J. Sandwell, Sandwell and Penmarsh', with addresses in London and Kinghampton – Esmond's flat and our shop. I wondered what would happen when Esmond moved.

'Do you ever get phone calls for Sandwell and Penmarsh?' I asked Esmond.

He shook his head. 'But half the time I'm not there. Do you get them here?'

'No. Well, not yet. It's early days, of course.'

'You really believe that, Rumpy?'

'I don't know. I wish I knew what he was up to.'

Don't worry,' Esmond said. 'I'll look after you.'

My mother often referred to Lilian as 'your assistant' or 'that poor Sandwell girl'. In conversation with others, notably Aunt Ada, she deflated Lilian's importance and correspondingly inflated mine. Stupid though she was, however, my mother never forgot what from her point of view were the two important things about Lilian: that I spent more time with her than with anyone else; and that in two years' time she would own half the business outright. Accordingly my mother asked her to Sunday lunch.

This was in the spring of 1964. Lilian declined, which increased my mother's determination to make her come. Lilian claimed that she had too much to do in the way of housekeeping, washing and so on. My mother discounted this automatically. 'Quite transparent,' she said to me when we were alone. We spent several evenings speculating about the reasons for Lilian's refusal. My mother speculated; I listened.

Was Lilian's reluctance attributable to maidenly reserve? Or was it because she didn't like us? Because she saw enough of me at the shop? Because she hadn't anything to wear? Because she was too lazy to cycle to Finisterre from Kinghampton and back? Because she had a secret boyfriend? Because Stephen had forbidden her to accept?

Finally, in April, my mother swept into the shop one morning and threw out what must have been the third or fourth invitation. Lilian accepted at once, with no reference to her previous refusals.

'Oh,' my mother said, visibly taken aback. 'Oh. How delightful. And what about Stephen? We must include him.'

'As far as I know he'll be up in town over the weekend,' I said. 'He's due back on Monday.'

In the evening of that day, my mother went through her diary. 'Oh bother. I've asked Lilian for the Sunday when Esmond will be here.'

'Oh dear.' I continued reading.

'You didn't mention he was coming did you?'

'To Lilian? No.' I rested the book on my knee. 'But it's in the desk diary at the shop. She might have noticed it there.'

'Of course,' my mother said, her face darkening and the upper lip lifting to reveal the buck teeth. 'She's only coming because he's going to be here. I might have known.'

'I don't think she likes Esmond very much.'

'Don't be absurd. Anyone can see she's chasing him. Perhaps I should put her off.'

'But she'd realize.'

'Not necessarily. One of us could be ill.'

'But if Esmond's –'

'Having Esmond here would be all right even if one of us is ill. He's family.'

'She might not say yes again.'

My mother sniffed and thought. Her face was blank. People often look like that when they are trying to do a complicated sum in their heads.

'Perhaps you're right,' she said at last. 'But on your head be it.'

I have to be honest: Lilian was not a great asset in the shop. She had the intelligence for it, but to work in a bookshop was not what she wanted from life.

Our attitudes to the job were very different. For example, once or twice a year we had a spate of shop-lifting – usually by boys from the grammar school. This made me furious, but I pretended not to see them if this was at all possible. When Lilian saw them, she didn't say anything either – not because she was afraid to, but because her reaction lay somewhere between mild curiosity and complete indifference.

Still, at least she sat behind the counter, took money from customers, gave them their change and put the books they bought in paper bags. She did the job for a smaller wage than anyone else would have accepted. Usually she had Grimalkin on her lap, which kept the wretched animal out of my way. When I was out, she sometimes answered the phone.

If a customer asked her anything, she responded by calling for me. 'Thomas!' she would yell; she could shout surprisingly loudly for someone with such a frail-looking body. Then she would cut herself off again – from the shop, the customer, from me. When I arrived, the customer would have to repeat the query. Lilian wouldn't do it for him. I never liked to ask what happened when I wasn't there.

It wasn't that Lilian was reading under the counter. I should be surprised to learn that she was even thinking in any purposeful way. She was just existing. It was as if only her body resided permanently in this world; her mind was merely an unwilling visitor which slipped back, whenever possible, to the invisible place it came from.

Lilian always had a tendency to disengage herself. My impression is that the condition steadily worsened in the years I knew her. It is only fair to add that the verb 'worsen' may not be the one she would have chosen herself: she was not unhappy.

She had already told us what she wanted on one of her first visits to Finisterre, on that freezing day in January 1960 when we walked down to Blackberry Water and Ulvercombe Mouth; when Stephen made us dance round a fire on the beach and talked about plague pits and tapping the psychic energy of the dead.

'I want to have money and live in a nice house and have babies. I don't want to have to work.'

One could argue that in the end she got her heart's desire or at least a plausible imitation of it. As I mentioned earlier with reference to Aunt Imogen winning the hand of Alfred Chard, getting one's heart's desire does not seem to be an infallible recipe for happiness. In Lilian's case perhaps the process of disengagement had gone too far to be stopped.

Was there a single reason for her disengagement and for her desire to be rich and have babies? I doubt it. Reasons and causes rarely come singly. They come in clusters, tangled together in various stages of growth and decay like an extended family of rats in an overcrowded nest. I shall never know the reason or reasons for certain, any more than I shall know the reasons for

Stephen's pursuit of power, his rejection of emotional ties and his lack of interest in sex.

I suspect, however, that one could construct a working hypothesis to explain what Lilian was and what Lilian became – and that such a hypothesis would have to start from the life and death of Lilian's mother.

No one ever had much to say about Mrs Sandwell. Aunt Ada was uncharacteristically reticent about her husband's cousin. We understood little more than that she was dead and that she had lectured in psychology at one of the colleges of London University.

'Quite eminent in her way, I believe,' Aunt Ada said, unable to resist scoring a point over my mother, who was conscious of her own family's lack of intellectual achievement. 'But I never actually met her.'

Esmond had heard that Mrs Sandwell had died suddenly of 'respiratory failure', and we'd looked this up in the big dictionary in the school library. Eventually we realized that all the phrase told us was that Mrs Sandwell had stopped breathing.

Apart from that, I don't remember feeling curious about Mrs Sandwell's life or death. Stephen and Lilian never mentioned her. If they had, Esmond and I would have felt embarrassed.

Esmond relayed another scrap of information about Mrs Sandwell in the spring of 1964, a piece of gossip he had stumbled across. He told me about it on the day Lilian came to lunch at Finisterre for the first time. I could have tried to confirm it from other sources: the death certificate, for example, or accounts in contemporary newspapers. But I never got round to it. Later on, I could have asked Lilian but embarrassment held me back; besides, if she had wanted me to know, she would have told me. In a way, I suppose, I felt there was no point in looking for confirmation: Lilian was Lilian, and my knowing about her mother wouldn't change that.

We had a dull time that Sunday. Lilian had made an effort with her appearance as she had done once before, that evening in the summer when we went to The Mermaid Hotel and I got drunk for the first time. On this occasion, however, she made a different sort of effort: she was trying to make herself look respectable, not alluring.

Esmond and I had planned to take her out for a quick drink before lunch, but instead she wanted to help; I think she laid the table. During the meal she devoted most of her attention to my mother and to subjects my mother found interesting. I don't mean that she actively directed the conversation. On the contrary, she was obviously shy, if not timid, which was something that did her no harm at all in my mother's eyes.

During the meal my mother was irritable with me and even Esmond; perhaps she found it emotionally awkward to have more than one favourite at a time. As we worked our way through bread-and-butter pudding with custard, she decided to comment on Esmond's hair. It was even longer than it had been on his last visit. The fringe had a tendency to flop forward over his eyes.

'You look like a shaggy dog, dear,' my mother said. 'Don't you think so, Lilian?'

Lilian nodded and smiled.

'I should have sent you to the barber's yesterday.'

'It's fashionable in London, Aunt Fiona,' Esmond said.

'Yes, dear, perhaps it is,' said my mother, whose conviction of her own rightness made her impregnable to rational argument. 'But you're not in London now, are you?'

After lunch and coffee, Lilian and my mother settled down on the sofa in the sitting room. My mother showed her photographs of Esmond and me when we were children. Meanwhile Esmond and I went down to Blackberry Water with the hip flask.

It was a grey and gusty April day. Esmond tried to say something to me in the lane, but the wind snatched his words away. He grinned at me and mouthed the word 'Later'.

The most sheltered place near Blackberry Water was within the 180-degree curve of the lane. We squatted on our haunches and passed the flask between us. It was here we had parked the car on the night I'd got drunk.

'What were you going to say?' I asked.

He passed me the flask. 'I met someone in London who used to know the Sandwells.'

'Oh? When?'

'Ages ago. Before they moved down here.'

He told me about Ricky, the man he had met who was one of Stephen's old friends; they had known each other well at St Pauls, but the friendship had petered out after school. Esmond went into detail, not just about Ricky but about the place where they met, which was a private club in Rupert Street where you went to play poker. He described a particular game: Ricky and he had been among the players and that was how they had met. He became rather technical and, if the truth be told, I grew bored with counter-bluffs and straight flushes. I wanted to hear about the Sandwells, not poker.

'How did he find out you knew Stephen?' I asked.

'Eh? Oh that. He asked where I came from. And when I said Kinghampton, he asked if I knew the Sandwells.'

'We must ask Lilian if she remembers him.'

'I shouldn't.' Esmond paused to light a cigarette, and I had the sensation he was changing mental gear. When he next spoke, his voice sounded amused. 'You want to watch out in that direction, Rumpy.'

'What do you mean?'

'I reckon she fancies herself as the new Mrs Penmarsh.'

'Rubbish.'

'Seriously.'

'Stop it. You're making me feel embarrassed.'

'No point in pretending it's not happening. Not unless you want to end up walking up the aisle with Lilian.'

'But she's not interested in me. If anything she's interested in you. Even my mother thinks so. That time we went to The Mermaid in the summer –'

'I know. When she got herself tarted up. Don't you see? That could have been for you as much as me. Anyway, that was nearly a year ago.'

'She's never said or done anything.'

'Oh yes? She's working in that shop, isn't she?

Stephen was convinced she'd say no, especially for the money he's giving her. She's only doing it to be near you. Anyone can see that.'

I have never been near drowning. But I think I know a little of what it must feel like. The head fills with a great roar. Images cascade through the mind; they tumble over each other in their haste. Panic rises like a tide. Worst of all, perhaps, is the sense of inevitability: you are face to face with your death, and you cannot turn away.

Esmond held out the flask to me. I shook my head. I was trying to shake the fears out of it. I heard myself speaking.

'Why wouldn't she come for a drink then? Why isn't she here now?'

'Come on, Rumpy. You're the easy bit. She's also got to court your mother.'

'I don't want to marry her.'

'Then don't.'

I looked at Esmond. He knew me very well. I think he must have seen the fear in my eyes. He was always so good to me. He understood that I wasn't strong. He touched my arm.

'You don't have to do anything,' he said. 'OK? If there's a problem, just tell me. I'll tell her to piss off.'

'But if my mother likes her – you can't tell *her* to piss off.'

'Why not?'

'The allowance she pays you.'

'Sod that.'

I was silent. Esmond smoked half a cigarette. He was frowning.

'Thank you,' I said.

'You know what you should do?' The savagery in his voice made me flinch. 'Come back to London with me tonight. Just pack a bag and come.'

'I can't do that.'

'No,' he said sadly. 'You can't.'

He flicked the cigarette away and put the flask to his lips.

'I suppose we'd better be getting back,' I said.

'Oh yes. Good lord, it'll be teatime soon. Can't *possibly* be late for tea, can we?'

I was already on my feet. Esmond was still crouching. He took his time capping the flask and finding another cigarette. Perhaps the whisky made him a little clumsy. As he lit the cigarette, the fringe of his hair fell forward. The flame from the match caught it. It ran up individual strands of hair with incredible speed. In an instant, the top of his head was a mass of writhing flames. He dropped both match and cigarette. His face was blank, like a statue's. I flung my arms around his head and held it against my chest. I expected the fire to leap at me. Instead the flames vanished almost as quickly as they had come.

'Jesus,' Esmond said.

For an instant I smelled singed hair. He pulled his head away from me, and stood up, patting his head.

'Thank you,' he said.

I was trembling. 'It looked horrible.'

'Looked worse than it was,' he said. 'Happened to me once before. I was in bed. First fag of the day. Christ, I got out of bed like a rocket.'

'It's hardly noticeable,' I said. That was the strangest

thing about it. The singeing might have been obvious from only a few inches away, but to me it was invisible.

Esmond ran his fingers through his hair, picked up the cigarette, crouched down and lit it.

'Be careful,' I said before I could stop myself.

'It's called playing with fire. Come on. We don't want Lilian to scoff all the scones, do we?'

We walked briskly up the lane with the wind behind us.

'This man you met,' I said. 'Ricky, was it? Didn't Lilian like him?'

'I don't know. Why?'

'You said we shouldn't ask Lilian if she remembered him.'

Esmond looked down at me. 'It's not him personally. I don't think Lilian wants to meet anyone they knew in London.'

'Why ever not?'

'According to Ricky, Lilian's mother killed herself. And Lilian found the body.'

Fourteen

'They've had an accident,' Bronwen said, screwing up her face. She crossed her arms over her breasts and hugged herself: one part of her body trying to comfort another.

I shook my head. Esmond wasn't the sort of person who has accidents.

'Then where are they? Look, it's nearly ten. They should have been here hours ago.'

I looked at the television. I needed distraction. Bronwen's voice went buzz, buzz, buzz, like her wretched chain saw. She stretched out her arm and turned off the set with the remote control. The picture shrank. The screen became grey and blank.

'I think we should phone the police,' she said.

'He wouldn't be pleased.'

'But they might be . . . be in hospital.'

'They've probably just stopped for a drink.'

The clock began to strike ten. Bronwen sat up and smoothed the skirt of her red dress. She took a cigarette but ignored her glass, which still had half an inch of gin in it. She inhaled fiercely and coughed until her eyes filled with tears. But the nicotine seemed to give her strength. She forced her mind back to the consolation of other people's troubles, back to the apparent security of the past.

'The mother – why did she do it?'

'Maybe she was afraid of being left a poor widow,' I said. 'There wasn't much money, and everyone thought Mr Sandwell only had a year or two to live.'

'But she had a job.'

'It didn't pay much. Or perhaps money had nothing to do with it. Perhaps she couldn't face watching him die.'

'You'd think having the children would have stopped her. At the very least you'd think she'd do it when the kids weren't around. I mean, really – letting her daughter find her: that's sick.'

'According to this man Ricky, Mrs Sandwell was severely depressed and almost an alcoholic. And perhaps she'd never been very interested in her children. There's no reason why she should have been. Some women aren't.'

'Quite the little expert, aren't we?'

I remembered a hint from Esmond: a hint I'd interpreted, perhaps wrongly, to mean that Bronwen couldn't have children. As she spoke I heard a car in the lane.

'The cat was there,' I went on. 'It may have been the same one – Grimalkin: I told you about her, remember? Like a witch's familiar? Ricky said he heard it was standing by the bed and licking the blood.'

'What are you trying to do? Make me throw up on the carpet? You really are the –'

'Listen.' I stood up. 'There's a car.'

I swayed; I had to steady myself on the arm of the chair. I wasn't drunk but my legs had temporarily lost most of their strength. I heard the Volvo's engine note on the drive.

'Oh God,' Bronwen moaned. She wiped the back of her hand across her mouth, smudging the lipstick.

The seconds passed. One car door slammed, then the other. I straightened up. Bronwen was on the verge of tears. This evening our roles had almost been reversed. As I stared at her, I seemed to feed on her weakness: my legs regained their ability to carry me.

I walked across the sitting room, opened the door and stepped into the hall. I blinked. *Mine eyes dazzle.* The doors of the other rooms were open, and everywhere lights blazed. I turned my head. I glimpsed fragments of the dining room, the study, the kitchen, the schoolroom and the stairs: all of them bright and lacking depth, like stage sets. Finisterre was ready for inspection. But it wasn't the house I knew. It was a theatrical representation which Esmond had made.

As I walked towards the front door I listened to the voice of common sense. Bronwen must have opened the internal doors and turned on the lights when she'd left the sitting room to fetch more ice. Perhaps she had been making sure that Esmond had not crept back to Finisterre under cover of darkness. I wondered whether she had been upstairs as well, whether she had bothered to close the curtains, whether the sight of lights glowing in every window had worried Esmond.

A key scraped in the lock. The flap of the letterbox lifted.

'Is this door bolted?' Esmond demanded.

'Bronwen must have done it,' I said, breaking into a run. 'Sorry.'

I fumbled at the bolts, which were new and stiff. Bronwen had also turned the deadlocks, put the chain on, and locked the Chubb. I wondered if she had locked the back door and the windows as well. Esmond and Bronwen, like my mother before them, were keen on security. Finisterre was a potential fortress or prison.

I twisted the handle and pulled. The front door opened. I recoiled. A strange woman, Alice, was on the threshold. She saw me and stopped – as though she feared movement would betray her to a waiting predator. Behind her loomed Esmond, flushed and grim-faced. There was no other light outside apart from those streaming from the house. Our nights at Finisterre were very dark.

I muttered, 'So sorry, I – ah – So sorry.'

I had fancied that there was something accusing in those eyes, though Alice had no reason to blame me for anything. But I tend to feel guilty, and often I don't know what I have done so there is no possibility of absolution. That is something else I have to thank my mother for.

I don't know whether Alice heard my apology. I was so flustered that I barely registered anything beyond the fact that she was a tall young woman in jeans and a heavy jacket. Her dark hair was parted in the middle and hung halfway down her neck. I didn't recognize her. I had never even seen a photograph of her. And the last time I'd seen her in the flesh, she was barely six months old.

'Come on, let's get inside,' Esmond said.

He swept Alice into the hall. I smelled cigarettes and whisky on his breath. He was carrying a large blue back-pack with a frame. Alice had a canvas bag slung over her shoulder. Apart from that she seemed to have no other luggage.

'We were worried,' Bronwen said. The red dress rustling, she advanced down the hall towards us.

Esmond propped the backpack against the wall just inside the door. 'I'm sorry we're a bit late – we stopped for a drink.'

I looked slantwise at Alice, and discovered that she was examining me. She was at least four inches taller than I was. In colouring she was not unlike Bronwen, except her skin was creamy where Bronwen's was sallow, and Bronwen's had touches of high colour on the cheeks. Her face was broad across the forehead but tapered almost to a point at the chin: *heart-shaped*. The eyes were small and the cheeks plump. Words like 'beautiful' and 'attractive' are misleading. Old-fashioned words seemed to suit Alice: she was personable and agreeable to look at. There was nothing overtly feminine about her clothes and I didn't think she was wearing any make-up.

'Alice – this is Thomas.'

Automatically I held out my hand. Alice hardly touched it. She was staring so closely at me that I felt uncomfortable. Most women make me uncomfortable in any case. But this prolonged examination was particularly unpleasant.

Esmond took Alice's left elbow and steered her past me. 'And this is Bronwen.'

I looked at Alice. Bronwen said something I didn't catch. Alice shook her head, and her hair moved to and fro but according to a different rhythm from the head's. It was strong hair – thick, and curling forwards at the ends. I thought of the fairy tale in which the princess made a rope from her hair. I should have liked to twist my fingers into Alice's and test its strength. She turned, and I saw that she was blushing. I had forgotten she would be so young. I worked it out: she was twenty-four. A mere child to someone who felt as old as I did.

Alice was saying something about having had a sand-wich on the train and another at the pub. Her voice made the sound you get if you speak with your lips drawn back and your fingers pinching your nostrils. I thought of it as harsh, even ugly. My mother used to call such accents 'colonial', by which she meant white African or Australasian. I couldn't get closer to it than that. Unlike Esmond, I didn't have a good ear for voices. I knew Alice's foster parents had lived abroad but I could not remember where. They were mission-aries; the man, Henry, had been Aunt Ada's cousin, and the woman, whose name I forget, was the daughter of a minor canon. The tendency towards ordination, like left-handedness and Huntington's Chorea, seems to run in families; and when it comes to breeding, like is attracted to like.

Alice glanced from Bronwen to me. I quickly looked away. I stared at the scuffed leather slippers on my feet. I was still slightly pigeon-toed just as I had been as a child.

'Let's have coffee, shall we?' Esmond said.

No one mentioned the dinner in the oven. Esmond and Alice were not hungry; I think he assumed that Bronwen and I would have had the sense to eat without them. As the kitchen door was open, there was a faint charred smell in the hall; in one of her whimsical moods my mother would have made a joke about burnt offerings.

Bronwen went into the kitchen. Alice took off her jacket, turning as she did so to avoid Esmond's attempt to help her. Now that her coat was off I could see that her back was long and straight. There was something primitive about her body, about the way she stood. I could imagine her striding, with a pot of water on her head, around a two-thousand-year-old vase from the Mediterranean. Oh dear. How precious this must sound. But sometimes you have to sound precious if you want to be honest and accurate.

Esmond hung up the jacket and ushered her into the sitting room. She moved gracefully, without fuss. Esmond didn't say a word to me. There was no need. I knew he wanted the three of us to be alone for a few minutes.

Alice said, 'What a lovely room.'

For a moment I saw through her eyes. It was a shock, a pleasant one. As I so rarely saw the sitting room I still thought of it as it had been before Esmond came. In the later years at Finisterre, before Esmond came back with Bronwen in tow, my mother and I spent most of our time in the kitchen, because it was warmer than anywhere else. The sitting room got itself more and more into a mess. It filled up with dust and old newspapers. It was cold and damp, especially after one of the windowpanes was broken by an airgun slug.

Alice and I sat down. She sat on the sofa, which was at right angles to my chair, with her shoulder bag on the floor beside her. We avoided each other's eyes. Alice looked around. She wore the silly smile of someone who is determined to look pleased by what she sees. I couldn't think of anything to say. I put my hands between my legs. The fire and the central heating meant the room was very warm, but my hands were cold. Still, I told myself, there was nothing to worry about. Esmond was there.

Esmond moved about the room. He adjusted the curtains. He threw a couple of logs on the fire. For an instant his eyebrows ran together when he saw the full ashtray and the empty glass on the table by his chair.

'Anyone want a drink?' he said.

My daughter and I spoke in chorus: 'No, thank you.'

'I might have a Scotch.'

Alice looked at me. 'It's difficult, isn't it?'

I wasn't used to directness. 'Yes.'

'I'm sorry. Maybe I shouldn't –'

'This isn't in the book of rules,' Esmond interrupted, quoting himself. 'So we'll just have to make our own rules. The pioneer spirit, eh?'

She looked at him sharply, and her dark hair swayed like a curtain in a draught. But he wasn't mocking her, just trying to jolly her along. Her eyes came back to me. 'Did you mind my writing to you?'

I shook my head. This was not the moment to explain that I hadn't actually seen her letter. My mind was trying to cope with the strange and unsettling idea that this substantial young woman and I were related. I am not sure that I like the idea of having a posterity, of my genes continuing, generation after generation. They say it is a form of immortality. But I have never understood why anyone should want to live for ever. In any

231

case what is the point of such partial and impersonal immortality?

Esmond sat down with his glass. 'Cheers, everybody,' he murmured.

'I read up about it,' Alice said. 'Foster children looking for their real parents. I know there can be problems. For everyone. You must be honest, and tell me if you'd rather I went away.' She tightened her lips and forced herself to squeeze out my name. 'Thomas.'

'Please,' I said. 'Now you're here, you must stay for a while.' I glanced at Esmond, and I thought he gave me a tiny nod.

Her face lightened. 'I hoped you'd say that. Esmond said you would, but I wanted to make sure.' She was so terribly earnest that it hurt me. 'They say you should take nothing for granted.'

'That sounds very sensible.'

I wondered whether we would look like father and daughter to an outsider. Probably not. She was more heavily built; her ears were a different shape from mine, her eyes a different colour; her hair was thick and dark, whereas mine used to be fair and wispy; finally, she was good to look at, which had never been something you could say about me.

'I'm sorry about your marriage,' I said.

'It doesn't matter. It was a mistake. Sort of on the rebound, I suppose. My parents had just been killed.'

Her eyes widened. I guessed she was in two minds about explaining, painfully, laboriously and unnecessarily, that she couldn't help thinking of Henry and Whatever-her-name-was as her real parents.

At that moment, Esmond struck a match. Alice,

who had been looking at me, shifted her weight on the sofa. A tremor ran through her body. The nails on her left hand dug into the palm. I realized then how nervous she was. The scratch of a match on a box can be a vicious sound, particularly if you are not expecting it. This time it made me think of claws: cats' claws, curved and white, ripping through fabric or perhaps skin.

The door opened. Bronwen backed into the room carrying the tray. Esmond leapt up to clear a space on the table.

'It's very kind of you to go to all this trouble,' Alice said to her.

'Milk?' Bronwen said. 'Sugar?'

'Just milk, please.'

Bronwen made the cups and saucers clatter and the spoons tinkle. Not too obviously, not enough to force Esmond to say something. She poured for all of us, and Esmond handed round the cups.

For a few minutes we drank coffee and talked of harmless subjects: the weather in Lagos, the weather in London, the weather at Finisterre; air flights, jet lag and airline meals; the beggars on the streets of London. Most of the conversation was between Esmond and Alice, with Esmond doing the majority of the talking.

'Well, speaking personally,' Bronwen interrupted, 'I'd rather like a brandy. Seeing as we're celebrating. Anyone fancy joining me?'

At that moment, Esmond's face was turned towards mine. As he stood up, he gave me a smile, the sort that invites sympathy. Once again, Alice and I refused a drink. Esmond poured Bronwen a very small brandy.

'More coffee?' he said, picking up the coffee pot.

I was the only person who wanted some. Esmond brought the pot over to me. At that moment I realized that most of his attention was still on Alice, that he was particularly aware of her. A state of heightened sensitivity to one person is often the prelude to sexual attraction. I think that Bronwen noticed or sensed it too, because she cleared her throat and said that she wanted more coffee as well. This distracted Esmond, and he forgot to refill my cup. He changed course towards Bronwen but couldn't resist glancing at Alice. Bronwen saw. Then she too was distracted: she had to drain her cup, which she hadn't touched, before Esmond reached her; and the coffee went down the wrong way so she started to cough.

Esmond wasn't concentrating on what he was doing. Perhaps he spilled a little coffee. In any case, Bronwen temporarily recaptured his wandering attention by making a sound like a cat spitting.

'Could I – ah – use the bathroom?' Alice said. She was looking at me, technically her host.

Esmond said, 'We should have asked you before.' His eyes flicked towards Bronwen. Jealous but still obedient, she stood up.

'Yes, of course,' she said. 'I'll show you where it is.'

'We see very few people,' Esmond went on. 'Our social reflexes are a little rusty.'

At the door Alice glanced back. She looked at me. It's nonsense when people say they can read thoughts in the eyes, faces or expressions of others. If they can do so, it is only because they have first written what they expect to find there.

'It's this way,' Bronwen said.

As Bronwen spoke, Alice's face twitched. Just for the sake of argument, if anyone had asked me to interpret that spasm of Alice's facial muscles, I should have said that it expressed fear. In the fifteen minutes since her arrival, the colour had gradually drained away from her face. Perhaps the room was too hot and stuffy for her; perhaps she was feeling faint. Her skin had become almost transparent. I could see ghostly freckles. I wondered if she really was scared of us, of two middle-aged men and a tipsy woman in a rumpled red dress. I wondered what she knew, what they'd told her.

Alice turned, squared her shoulders like someone determined to face punishment bravely and followed Bronwen from the room. I thought that, though in the flesh they were completely unalike, their physical descriptions would make them sound like sisters. They were the same height; their colouring and their build were similar; their faces were the same shape. Yet to me they seemed as different as chalk from cheese. Or rather as if Bronwen were an inferior copy of Alice.

'I was going to give you some coffee.' Esmond refilled my cup.

'They're very alike, aren't they?'

'Alice and Bronwen? I suppose they are in a way.' Esmond smiled at me. 'But for God's sake don't tell Bronwen.'

He put down the coffee pot and sat down in the wing armchair. The movement threw the back of his head into shadow while leaving his face clearly illuminated. For an instant he looked as if he had dark hair down to his shoulders. Long hair didn't make him look effeminate; his face was too strong for that. But it did make him look like Alice.

By 1966 many males under the age of twenty-five were letting their hair grow, in most cases not much further than their collars. I was never tempted to follow the trend. Even if I had wanted to, I doubt if my mother would have let me. It was different for Esmond.

My mother clucked at his steadily lengthening hair, but he won her over, at least for a time, by being nice to her. 'Esau was a hairy man,' Aunt Ada remarked, not once but many times; she shared with my mother the belief that a joke improves with repetition; and in this case there was certainly a good deal of room for improvement. The two women felt that there could not be much wrong with a young man who opened doors for ladies and took communion at Ulvercombe church. Like many stupid people, they prided themselves on being able to see beyond outward appearances.

One Friday in May 1966, Esmond drove down to Finisterre in a cloud of aftershave, with his hair trimmed well above a crisply ironed collar; and he was wearing not jeans but charcoal trousers and a blazer with brass buttons. I thought this was typical: when everyone else was doing one thing, he would do the opposite. At the sight of him, my mother stopped being a chicken and became a cat: she purred with pleasure. When we were having a drink before supper, she asked why he had smartened himself up.

'It was time for a change.' Esmond grinned at her. 'Of course I really did it just to please you.'

My mother betrayed her pleasure by a little squirm

of her bottom on the sofa. 'You monkey,' she said, in what I can only describe as a roguish fashion. 'Anyway, it makes you look much more grown-up.'

At that time Esmond and I were nearly twenty-three. We didn't care about looking grown-up: we thought we were grown-up, and that we had been for some time.

After supper, we helped my mother with the washing up and sat with her in the sitting room. We drank coffee. My mother grumbled about this and that. She was particularly incensed by the Jodsons. She claimed they were giving themselves airs now that their son Bill, our old schoolfellow at Kinghampton Grammar School, was doing so well as a teacher.

At about ten o'clock, there was a break in my mother's flow. Esmond plunged into the gap and suggested we went out for a drink. I was surprised he had waited so long.

'Yes, why not?' my mother said. 'You boys go and enjoy yourselves.'

'Won't you come with us?' Esmond said, horrifying me. 'Thomas can squeeze in the back.'

'No, no. It's very sweet of you, dear, but you'll have much more fun by yourselves.' In the last year or so she had become increasingly eager to accommodate Esmond in small things.

We fetched our coats and got into the car. I thought we were going to drive to The Forley Arms or even The Mermaid in Kinghampton; I had told Lilian we might pick her up. But instead of turning left towards Ulvercombe, Esmond turned right. He drove slowly down the bumpy lane to Blackberry Water. It was a windless evening, and quite warm. There was still a little light – the soft and ghostly twilight that often succeeds a cloudy day. Esmond switched off the engine and the lights. We freewheeled for the last fifty yards. The tyres crunched and whispered on the stones and damp mud. He let the car drift to a halt.

'How are things with Lilian?' he said.

'Same as ever.'

'Have you done anything yet? Has she?'

'Well, we usually go to the cinema once a week. And sometimes –'

'That's not what I meant, Rumpy. As you know very well.'

'Then the answer's "no". Nothing's happened.'

'Calm down.' He touched me on the shoulder and opened his door. 'Come on, Romeo. Let's go to the beach.'

We walked through the gap in the cliffs and on to the silver shingle. The tide was low and there was no one else about. Esmond took what looked like a large cigarette from his breast pocket. He lit it with a lighter. The cigarette flared up at first, and bits of glowing tobacco fell out of the end. Esmond swore. Soon, however, the cigarette began to burn steadily. The diameter of the orange disc on the end was much wider than an ordinary cigarette's. I moved a step nearer – I was restless; I wanted Esmond to talk to me; I was afraid I had spoiled things by not wanting to talk about Lilian. Just then I caught a whiff of the smoke. It smelled more like a bonfire than tobacco.

'Try it,' Esmond said, holding the cigarette out to me.

'I don't smoke.' As I spoke, I realized what he was offering me. 'What is it, anyway?'

'It's a joint.' He took my hesitation for lack of understanding. 'You know – pot, cannabis, hash.'

For Esmond's sake I tried it. I had heard and read many sinister stories about the ghastly effects that drugs had on people. But I reasoned that Esmond must know what he was doing, and that he wouldn't offer me anything he thought would harm me. Unfortunately the smoke from the joint made me splutter. I felt sick.

'Please,' I said, 'I'd rather not.'

'Don't worry, that's cool,' he said. 'It works for some people and not for others.'

He took the joint back and smoked it slowly. While he smoked he explained that he had been using cannabis off and on for two years. It began when Stephen Sandwell bought some from a couple of sailors in an East End pub. He shared it with Esmond. Now everyone was smoking it.

'It's a seller's market,' Esmond said, his voice thick and amused. 'Demand exceeds supply. If you buy in bulk, or better still buy abroad and import it, you can make a very decent living.' He inhaled, held in the smoke and added softly, 'More than decent, actually.'

'You're doing that?'

'Yes. With Stephen.'

Of course. I felt the old jealousy and tried to ignore it.

Esmond let out the smoke in a rush. 'We wouldn't sell anything that could harm people.'

'But isn't it dangerous?'

'In what way? It's not addictive. It doesn't lead to other drugs. All that stuff you hear about it making you jump out of twelfth-floor windows – that's balls, you know, utter balls.'

'How do you know?'

He waved the joint: it made an angry red snake against the dark sea. 'We've researched this very carefully.'

'I'm sure you have. Sorry, I didn't mean to imply – Look, what I really meant was, isn't it dangerous because of the police?'

For the last few minutes I had been straining my ears for footsteps or engines. I half thought that Sergeant Swift from Kinghampton would rattle down the lane on his bicycle, or the coastguard searchlight would swoop in from the sea.

'There's nothing to worry about,' Esmond said, 'Do you think I'd be doing this down here if there was?'

'But you can't be sure.'

'It's as safe as houses as long as you plan it properly and take a few precautions. Why do you think I'm wearing these clothes? So I don't look like a hippie. That's where all the other dealers go wrong, they want to look cool as well as make money. Well, that's just stupid. Stephen and I agreed on that right from the start. We want to make money – that's the whole point of it. And we're not going to get caught.'

'Have you been . . . selling it for long?'

'About three months. Not full time.'

As he smoked he went on talking. He always liked to talk to me when he was stoned. Looking back, I couldn't distinguish what he told me on this occasion from what he told me later – that is, over the next fourteen months. Sometimes he told me stories I had already heard, and almost always he talked about the same subjects. About buying and selling the cannabis, about the money he made and the famous people he mixed with: rock musicians, actors and photographers: people whom the newspapers had started to call the 'new aristocracy' of 'swinging London'. He talked about the girls – there were always girls in Esmond's London stories, girls who were beautiful, available and grateful; girls who wanted Esmond.

Stephen's name was barely mentioned. Afterwards this struck me as significant. Even at the time I sensed Stephen's presence hovering in the background. He filled the gaps in Esmond's stories. I knew that the planning would have been his, and I guessed that Esmond would be taking most of the risks.

Esmond was boasting. I think the need to boast was one of the reasons why he kept coming back to Finisterre – not only in the 1960s but later, when my mother was dead. It wasn't just a question of money. He knew he could trust me. I was his father confessor. Above all I was his yardstick: he measured himself against me.

I watched and listened to him very carefully the first time he smoked dope in my company. I waited anxiously for deviations from his normal behaviour. In fact the cannabis seemed to have little effect on him. He sounded very relaxed. Once or twice he repeated himself. Everything amused him. I wanted to warn him that the famous people only liked him because he sold them drugs, and that Stephen should not be trusted. I didn't dare, because doing so might imply I thought I was wiser than he was.

'One day soon I'm going to be rich,' Esmond said. 'And I mean really rich. Then I'll stop dealing.' He scraped a shallow hole in the shingle with his shoe and dropped the end of the joint in it. 'Then I'll do exactly what I want. And you can too, of course. There'll be plenty of money for both of us.'

'Thank you,' I said.

We walked slowly back to the car. In the past, I'd never liked to ask too many questions about how Esmond made his money. At different times he had talked vaguely about 'managing a club' or 'doing a bit of freelance selling' to oblige a 'friend in the motor trade' or something he called 'investment broking', which had to do with the 'entertainment industry'. There may have been an element of truth in some of these references. But I think he had been on the fringes of crime for a long time, probably since soon after he went to live in London, and probably with a little help from Stephen Sandwell. This was something he didn't want to boast about. I imagine that Esmond turned his hand to anything that promised a quick profit without too much risk. I even wondered if he had a rich 'friend', male or female – a source of pocket money, expensive clothes and borrowed sports cars.

The cannabis venture was different. This wasn't merely a matter of having a good time and keeping a full wallet. It was more a matter of getting rich. Esmond had started to think of the future. Stephen was responsible for that. Stephen always had a grand design.

'You know why Stephen wants to be rich?' Esmond said when we were back in the car. 'So he can be powerful. A magician. You need money for that.'

'Shouldn't it be the other way round? If you have power you don't need money, or you can get what money brings by other means; or you can make other people give you their money.'

Esmond chuckled in the darkness. 'Stephen likes money. He pretends he doesn't, but he does. He'd sell his soul if he could get a good enough price for it.'

'To the devil?'

'That reminds me. I'd better warn you. Stephen's got plans for Midsummer's Eve. And it's all my fault.'

'I don't understand.'

The lighter clicked. For a second, Esmond's face glowed in the light of the flame.

'You remember I said this would be a great place for a party? We were down here one night, ages ago. I think you'd just puked up.'

'I know.'

'Stephen's thinking of having a special party on Midsummer's Eve, and he was wondering where. I said we'd talked about having one here, at Blackberry Water or even on the beach. He went crazy about the idea.'

'But surely people wouldn't come all the way down from London just for a party?'

'It depends what sort of party it is.' Esmond started the engine. 'Maybe he'll think of somewhere else.'

'What's my mother going to say?'

'I don't think she'll get an invitation.'

Esmond giggled. The giggle went on and on. The sound of it filled the car. It filled my mind. It drowned the engine. The pitch of it climbed higher and higher like a spiral staircase. I wanted to open the door and leap out, to run away from the laughter, to run through the darkness up the lane, to be safe in my bed at Finisterre. But I stayed. I stayed with Esmond.

Fifteen

The death room had changed. When I was a child it had smelled differently from the rest of the house: of polish and old clothes, and air that has been too long in one place. I used to fancy there was a sweet undertow of corruption.

The bedroom was big, but the furniture it contained seemed designed for an even larger one. All the wooden surfaces gleamed, thanks to the weekly ministrations of my mother and Mrs Jodson. The doors, the carved bedhead, the chest of drawers and the great wardrobe were like dark and distorting mirrors which reflected living things as shapeless shadows. There were one or two rugs on the linoleum. If you weren't careful, they would skid like banana skins beneath your feet or try to trip you up. The death room had an echo to it, like a cave. To me it seemed an intensely masculine place because of its associations with my father.

As the years passed, the death room modified itself. My mother became less active and Mrs Jodson lost her enthusiasm for domestic work. In the five years immediately preceding my mother's final and fatal stroke, I doubt if the door was opened more than once a year. There was no reason to do so.

New ingredients changed the character of the smell: it became dank and salty, not unlike drying seaweed. At the same time, the polished wood grew cloudy. A film of moist dust coated all the horizontal surfaces. The wallpaper came adrift near the window. In one corner of the ceiling, damp worked its way down from the attic above. Moths burrowed into the bedding, and there were mice droppings in the big cupboard beside the wardrobe. Nevertheless, if my father had returned to life he would have recognized this as the room where he'd died. The room was dying too, slowly and with a degree of dignity, as a living organism dies of old age. But it was still the same room.

When Esmond and Bronwen came they intervened in this process, as a surgeon intervenes with a knife, and needle and thread. They made the death room look like somewhere else.

'Here we are,' Esmond said to Alice. 'This is the first-class guest bedroom. Only the best will do – eh, Thomas?'

'What lovely flowers,' Alice said; I suspected that she could hardly keep her eyes open.

'Bronwen got them.' He sniffed. 'I can't smell paint, can you?'

'No. Not at all.'

'We finished redecorating about three weeks ago. You're the first person to sleep here.'

To the best of my knowledge, Alice was the first person to sleep in the death room since Esmond's sister, baby Lizzy. Not that Lizzy actually slept; while she lived, she was too busy crying. Almost certainly the last person who literally slept in the room was my father in 1943: according to Bill Jodson, my father had died in his sleep.

Alice was saying nice things about the flowered wall-paper, the bedside lamps and the paintings. I thought the room was dreadful – fussy and feminine.

Esmond put down Alice's backpack on one of the beds. 'Bronwen's got quite a flair for interior decoration,' he said. 'Haven't you, my sweet?'

Bronwen was standing beside me in the doorway. 'Just as well there's someone in this house who has.'

'Now – Thomas is opposite you, and Bronwen and I are further down the landing.' Esmond nodded at a door on the other side of the room. 'Your bathroom's in there. Bit poky, I'm afraid – used to be a cupboard. But everything works.'

Alice said that she was sure that everything would be fine. She was looking not at the room but at the doorway where Bronwen and I were.

'That's your room, is it?' she said to me. 'With all the books.'

I nodded and glanced over my shoulder. My door was open and revealed a section of shelves which stretched from floor to ceiling. The books were double-banked in places, and there were piles on the floor as well.

'Used to be the nursery in the old days,' Esmond said. 'That's why there are bars on the window. And of course they keep old Thomas from escaping, eh?'

He smiled at me, and I smiled back. There we were: cousins and friends, brothers in all but name. I stood back to allow him to come through the door.

'Fancy a nightcap?' he said to me.

'No, I don't think so.'

'I'll take you up on that,' Bronwen said. 'Since you're offering.'

'Right you are.' Esmond turned back to Alice. 'Sleep well. Give us a shout if you need anything.'

We exchanged goodnights. Esmond and Bronwen walked downstairs; Esmond was laughing at something she said. I went into my room. As I closed my door I looked across the landing. Alice's eyes met mine. I thought she was going to say something. She smiled and closed the door.

That night I couldn't sleep. I got into bed and tried to read. I heard Esmond and Bronwen come upstairs, still laughing. I turned out my light. A little later the line of light beneath my door vanished.

As I lay awake, I felt the house settling like an animal for the night. I didn't want to put on the light and look at my watch. The wind strengthened. Once I thought I heard someone moving on the landing. But I must have been mistaken.

Stephen's party was on Midsummer Eve 1966. In the weeks beforehand I thought about it every day with a mixture of excitement and dread. I had a shrewd idea what it would be like. I expected a stream of fast cars bringing glamorous people from London. I expected to see faces I recognized from newspapers and magazines. I expected a clear, moonlit night, with music and dancing and the bonfire stench of joints. I even hoped for flashes of poetic inspiration; and to meet this eventuality I made sure that I had a small notebook and a Biro in my pocket. I feared a confrontation between the partygoers on the one hand and my mother and the police on the other.

I mentioned watersheds earlier: the party was a watershed for everyone who went to it. Stephen was the master of ceremonies. He had recently returned from Morocco with a kaftan purchased in Marrakech. The kaftan was light blue and lavishly decorated with silver embroidery. Stephen was very proud of it. On the day before the party I caught him strutting to and fro in front of the big mirror in his bedroom.

'My party frock, my dear. My sacred robe.'

Esmond and I told my mother that we were going to a party in Kinghampton, and that we would spend the night at the Sandwells' flat; the party might finish late, and we did not want to disturb her when we returned. My mother accepted this meekly.

'Will Lilian be there?' she asked, with an arch glance in my direction.

'I believe she's hoping to come,' Esmond said.

We began the evening in The Mermaid, where Stephen and Esmond lined their stomachs with whisky. Stephen was still dressed in his everyday clothes. He was very excited. Lilian wore a green minidress and her face was plastered with make-up. After three rounds, we returned to the flat above the bookshop. Stephen went to get changed. The rest of us sat in the kitchen. Esmond lit a cigarette and stared at the ceiling. I wished I were at home in bed.

When Stephen came out of the bedroom I noticed that his feet and legs were bare. I do not know for certain but I think that underneath the kaftan he was naked. He was carrying a pigskin briefcase. He put it on the table, opened it and took out a round, brightly painted tin which had once contained chocolate biscuits shaped like animals.

'Our sacrament, my dears. Or rather part of it.'

He levered off the lid. Inside, lying on a bed of grease-proof paper, were four small biscuits with ragged edges. They were thin, close-textured and khaki-coloured – like a piece of dung, flattened by passing feet and dried by the sun.

'Eat up, kiddies,' Stephen said. 'Eat and be merry.'

Esmond smiled. He took a biscuit, sniffed it and began to nibble at the edge.

'What are they?' Lilian said.

'Something to get us in a party mood. Hash cookies.'

I said, 'What exactly will they do?'

Stephen bit into his biscuit. 'The effect is not unlike having a drink or two. It'll just make life a little more fun. A dash of midsummer madness to enliven the summer solstice.'

I looked at Esmond. He had a biscuit in one hand and a cigarette in the other. I thought he nodded at me, confirming what Stephen had just said. Afterwards he said I was mistaken.

I ate the biscuit. It was very dry and tasted unpleasantly earthy. Otherwise there was nothing remarkable about it. I swallowed it, half-chewed, in three mouthfuls. I felt the fragments working their way into my digestive system. I waited. Nothing happened. I was disappointed. I had expected the biscuit to trigger an immediate effect, whether physiological or psychological, in the way that a strong drink will do if swallowed in a gulp; according to Esmond, smoking a joint produced equally swift results. But I felt just as usual, except for a distinct sense of anticlimax. I kept quiet about this in case I was the odd man out. I glanced round the table.

Did the others seem stoned? What outward symptoms should I be looking for? I could not be sure that the anticlimax was due to the biscuit. Perhaps the fault lay in myself: I might have eaten it in the wrong way; or my metabolism might be unhappily unique in that it lacked a component essential to cannabis intoxication.

When Esmond had finished his biscuit, he left the room; I heard him go into the lavatory.

'No point in waiting,' Stephen said.

He fetched four glass tumblers and put them on the table. I assumed we were going to have some whisky before setting off for the beach. Instead he opened the refrigerator and brought out a tarnished silver-plated jug with a lid. It was, like the kaftan, ornate and oriental in appearance. It had probably been made in Sheffield for an Edwardian breakfast table.

'The second part of our sacrament. You've had the body. Now here is the blood.'

With great deliberation Stephen poured into each glass. No one said anything. Stephen's lips moved as if he were engaged in silent prayer. The liquid was not so much red as purple. I hoped it was not alcoholic. The whisky and the biscuit had made me thirsty.

'What is that?' Lilian said.

'I told you. The blood.'

There was an abstract pattern incised on the outside of the tumblers. I saw that Stephen was using this to measure the quantities. He bent down to make sure that the liquid in each glass was level with the horizontal line at the top of the pattern. As he inclined his body, the kaftan gaped at the neck and revealed a white and hairless chest. Around his neck was a piece of household twine on which hung an inverted crucifix. Stephen straightened up and grunted with satisfaction. Solemnly he passed each of us a tumbler.

'Drink, my children,' he said. 'This is my blood.'

At the first sip I realized he had given us Ribena, the blackcurrant drink you dilute with water; I remembered having it as a child. Relief increased my pleasure, and I drank up quickly. I heard the lavatory being flushed. The drink was particularly refreshing after the dryness of the biscuit. I would have liked some more. I looked at Stephen, who had finished. He raised the pot and poured the rest of its contents into his glass.

'The celebrant's perk. But if you would like some more Ribena, you'll find the bottle in the cupboard by the fridge.'

Esmond came back into the room. He saw the four glasses and stopped, his hand resting on the back of his chair.

Stephen looked up with a smile. 'There you are, dear boy. I hope you don't mind. We didn't wait.'

'Is that what I think it is?'

I recognized the anger in Esmond's voice. The consonants were slightly harder than usual; there was a tightness around his mouth. I doubt if his reaction was obvious to the others.

'Yes,' Stephen said. 'A little treat for us. Our midsummer ale. Tonight we shall commune with the infinite. Together we shall open a window on eternity. We shall –'

'You should have told us.'

Lilian licked her lips. 'Was that LSD?'

'Of course it was.' Stephen pointed at her. 'You knew, anyway. Or guessed. Didn't you?'

She said nothing. She looked unblinkingly at him — as cats can do when they want to outface you by sheer willpower.

'I bet you didn't tell Thomas what it was,' Esmond said.

'I'm doing you all a favour,' Stephen said, reaching for Esmond's cigarettes. 'Can't you understand that?'

I had heard of LSD of course, and panic was rising inside me like bile. 'What's going to happen?'

Esmond said, 'I've never had any but I've been with people who have. You'll feel a bit strange.'

'That's an understatement if ever I heard one,' Stephen said. '"If the doors of perception were cleansed everything would appear to man as it is, infinite."'

This raised an echo in my memory. 'William Blake.'

'The point is,' Esmond said, ignoring Stephen, 'it'll last a few hours and then it'll be over. So don't worry. I'll be there.'

'How touching,' Stephen said. 'And will you be joining us, Esmond? Or do you find quotidian reality sufficiently mind-expanding?'

Esmond leaned forward quickly. Stephen recoiled. He thought Esmond was going to hit him. But Esmond picked up the untouched tumbler and swallowed its contents.

'That's my boy,' Stephen said.

'That's the one thing I'm not.'

Stephen smiled at us all. 'What's done is done. And now, my dears — let our revels commence.'

For a few seconds no one moved. Lilian was staring at her hands, which lay like starfish in front of her on the table. She wore green varnish on her long pointed nails. The colour of the varnish just failed to match the colour of her dress.

I looked at Esmond. Slowly his face relaxed.

'You amaze me,' he said to Stephen.

'I amaze me too.'

The two of them stared at each other. Esmond began to laugh. Stephen joined in. Even Lilian and I smiled, though I did not feel like smiling.

'Shall we go to Blackberry Water?' Stephen said.

Esmond spread his hands. 'If you want. If we must.'

Stephen picked up his briefcase and led the way downstairs. Lilian fetched a man's long raincoat from her room and put it on over her dress. She followed Stephen down to the shop.

'Where are all the others?' I asked Esmond on the stairs. 'Will they be waiting for us?'

'There are no others. Only us.'

We went out into Bay Street. It was cold for the time of year, and rain drizzled from an overcast sky. Stephen was prancing on the pavement. Fortunately there was no one around to see him in his party finery. He looked like a great baby in a powder-blue nightdress.

On this visit Esmond was driving a big, navy-blue saloon, not a sports car. The interior smelled of leather and cigars. Stephen sat with Esmond on the bench seat at the front. In the back of the car, Lilian and I kept to our corners with a yard of empty seat between us. Lilian stared at the window beside her. Once we had left behind the streetlights of Kinghampton, there was little for her to see except black glass streaked with dust and rain. I spent most of the journey searching my conscious mind for signs that the drugs were taking effect.

'Stephen?' Lilian said as we were driving through Ulvercombe village. 'What are we going to do about music? I thought you said you'd bring your tape recorder.'

'I meant to, but I left it in London. It doesn't matter.'

'But what about dancing?'

'We shall make our own music, my love, just as our ancestors did.'

We passed the gates of Finisterre, and rolled downhill. Stephen put two cigarettes in his mouth, lit them, and passed one to Esmond.

The car cruised down to Blackberry Water. Esmond stopped. Stephen rolled down his window. I heard the sea. The engine gave off pings and squeaks as it cooled. I felt distressingly normal.

'Damn,' Esmond said. 'I left my watch at home.'

Lilian stirred on the seat beside me. For the first time since we'd left the bookshop she spoke.

'For God's sake, Stephen. When's it going to start happening?'

The long night at Blackberry Water began. Esmond and I built a fire near the gap in the cliffs. With his usual efficiency, he had brought kindling, firelighters and logs in the boot of the car; and we gathered driftwood along the waterline. While we made the preparations, Lilian sat in the car. At one point Esmond went to fetch a half-bottle of whisky from the boot. The errand seemed to take him a long time.

Stephen helped us for a while. Then, fortified by the whisky, he decided to go for a walk in the damp darkness – down to the beach at Ulvercombe Mouth. We heard him cursing the stones that hurt his feet. He must have been very cold. Even I was chilly, and I had on a thick corduroy jacket, a polo-neck jersey and jeans.

Esmond lit the fire. He and I crouched beside it and watched the flames licking up the pile of dry wood. There was no heat, as yet, but it was very beautiful. All the elements are here, I thought, fire and water, earth and air. I wondered if this might be one of those mystical perceptions which were supposedly characteristic of LSD. It did not strike me as particularly profound.

'Is this it?' I said.

'Not yet.'

'But how will I know?'

'Don't worry. You'll know when it happens.'

The wood crackled. Flames danced higher. Esmond smoked at least one cigarette and drank some whisky. I looked at my watch, tilting it to and fro until the firelight lit up the dial. My efforts were a waste of time: the watch had stopped at ten to twelve. *A waste of time.* The wordplay pleased me. I yawned and was doubly disconcerted: yawning seemed such a curious thing to do, and it also struck me as very odd that I had not noticed before just how curious it was.

Esmond threw two more logs on the fire. Sparks shot upwards. We watched them. I wondered why people bothered to buy fireworks when all the beauty was available for the price of a match.

Stephen started to chant. Perhaps 'wail' is a more accurate word. He was somewhere on the beach, perhaps thirty yards away from the fire.

'Hymn number four hundred and three,' Esmond muttered.

There were words, I think, but I could not distinguish them. At times the tune sounded a little like 'Three Blind Mice'. The chant droned on. The flames leapt higher into the air; the wind was trying to drive them away from the sea and up the valley to Finisterre. As I listened it seemed to me that it might not be Stephen singing but the wind itself. I was open to the possibility that it might be the other way round: that the breeze that bent back the flames and ruffled my hair was caused not by an impersonal force like the wind but by a great current of air sweeping from Stephen's mouth. I thought of those old maps on which the winds are represented as plump-cheeked cherubs. Stephen could have modelled for one. In a flash, a further speculation presented itself: that the cartographers of the past were recording what they knew to be the literal truth. The huffing and puffing of Stephen and people like him was the reason why the air moved across the surface of our planet. The speculation was so overwhelmingly plausible that I immediately decided it could be nothing less than the truth. The implications made me gasp.

I wanted to record this astonishing insight. I patted my jacket and felt the outlines of my little notebook. (Incidentally I also made a mental note of the marvellous softness of the corduroy; I had not previously realized how pleasant it was to stroke my jacket.)

My mind was more alive than it had ever been. Each thought, each fragment of a thought, was like a room; and from each room there were thousands of doors, each of which led into another room; and the doors had double-sided hinges so you could open them from either direction.

Beside me, Esmond let out his breath in a rush of air. This reminded me that I had been thinking of the wind. The wind that poured out of Stephen's mouth must be an exceptionally powerful one. I had never been so intimately and inextricably connected with a wind before. It – or, to personalize it, Stephen – had actually got inside my body. I could feel my stomach heaving. The sensation had nothing to do with nausea. Soon the ripples were running from my groin to my shoulders. The image in my mind was one of huge wind-blown waves running beneath the surface of a grey sea. A great pulse regulated these waves as a conductor regulates an orchestra.

I wondered how the wind or Stephen had got inside me. If it had used the obvious orifices, such as the mouth and ears, surely I should have noticed? My knowledge of microbiology was, then as now, sketchy and inaccurate. But I had a notion that our bodies were composed of a three-dimensional web of molecules, and that molecules were extremely small. I concentrated on this idea and soon realized that it was correct: in fact my mind was able to see this extraordinary web and marvel at its delicate complexity. Tiny, almost transparent filaments linked the molecules to their neighbours. Each molecule was imbued with independent life: it breathed in time with the great pulse. I had not realized that 'I' was more accurately 'We' – a plurality of living things. Was it possible that the wind had penetrated my body by wriggling between the molecules and the filaments? Once inside me, it could blow where it wanted. The more I considered this hypothesis, the more likely it seemed.

'Esmond,' I said, 'I've got it. Stephen wriggled between the molecules. It's the only explanation.'

'What?'

'Stephen wriggled between the molecules.'

'It doesn't matter if he did.' Esmond laid his arm on my shoulders. 'It doesn't bloody matter.'

The flames coloured his face and hair. He looked like a lion of the best sort: brave, regal and generous.

'Stephen's a real pig,' Esmond went on. 'Dragging us out here.'

'Yes, yes – you're right.'

When I came to think of it, Stephen's resemblance to a pig was really quite remarkable. Perhaps all of us resembled a particular animal. I tested my theory against particular faces: Lilian was like one of those well-bred but highly strung domestic cats; my mother was an old rabbit; the vicar was plump and monochromatic like a panda.

'The singing's stopped.' Esmond withdrew his arm and lit a cigarette. 'But the trip's started, hasn't it?'

'I didn't think it would be like this.'

'No.'

I yawned, and the yawn went on for ever – outside my head as well as inside it. In my mind it was not so much a yawn as a great wind blowing through the desert at night.

'Esmond,' Stephen called. 'Thomas. Can you bring the whisky?'

We got up. My movements were slow, not because my coordination was seriously impaired but because I had an entirely new range of sensations to examine.

Behind us was the unbearable brightness of the fire.

In front was the car: its windows glowed against a black sky. The rain was soft as fur on my cheek. I put out my tongue and the water refreshed me.

The nearside back door of the car was open. Stephen was leaning against the roof in the angle between the door and the body of the car. His head and shoulders were dark like the sky, but the rest of him was faintly illuminated by the car's interior light. Lilian lay with her feet up on the back seat. She was swatched in the raincoat. Her eyes seemed black, for LSD dilates the pupils, and she was smiling. She looked like a queen.

'Ah. The water of life.' Stephen stretched out his hand for the bottle. He swallowed some whisky and choked. 'Christ's blood,' he said, and it was not clear to me whether the phrase was intended as an expletive or as an attempt to describe the whisky.

'Give it to me,' Lilian said. 'I'm cold.'

She leant forward, her hand outstretched. The raincoat fell away from her. The dress had risen up to her waist. I saw long, bare legs and a scrap of white where the thighs met. She took the bottle and sat back. Unhurriedly she rearranged the raincoat so it covered her once more. It was plain that she had covered herself not for decorum but for warmth.

'Lilian's cold,' Stephen said. 'Can't you get in there and warm her? I can't, I'm busy.'

'Doing what?' Esmond said.

'Haven't you seen? There's blood in Ulvercombe Mouth. Someone's got to do something about it.'

'It was the wreckers,' Lilian said. 'Everyone knows that.'

'The blood's under the shingle,' Stephen said. 'Just

260

streaming down. Tastes salty so it must be blood. Think of it, all that energy going to waste. Have you got a cigarette?'

Esmond lit one with the butt of his own cigarette and passed it to Stephen.

Lilian was shivering. 'The poor sailors. All that blood. Oh God. Oh God.'

'And it was utterly unnecessary,' Stephen said. 'If those sailors had been properly trained, they needn't have come ashore at all. They could have walked on the water. It's not that difficult.'

'Like Christ did, you mean?' I said. 'A sort of levitation?'

'Precisely. There's nothing to it. In India, people are levitating all the time. If they'd wanted to, those sailors could have walked to Wales.'

'It's so cold,' Lilian said. 'Make the blood go away. Please.'

'Righty-ho,' Stephen said. 'In the car, you two. Can't stop now. There's work to do.'

He walked towards the beach. I noticed that he was moving with far more ease and confidence than earlier: perhaps the pain and the cold had numbed his bare feet; or perhaps we were witnessing one of those everyday miracles like walking on the water.

'Amen,' Stephen shouted. 'Ever and ever for. Glory the and. Power the. Kingdom the thine is, I mean, is thine. Er. For. Evil, from us deliver.' His voice was snatched away by the wind.

'Come on,' Lilian said, her voice urgent. 'I'm freezing.'

'You get in the back,' Esmond said to me. 'I'll start the engine and put the heater on.'

I scrambled into the car and shut the door behind me. In normal circumstances I would have held back; but the drug had dissolved most of the social inhibitions that surrounded me like the bars of a cage. I shall never forget that LSD gave me a glimpse of what it is like to be free.

Inside the car was another world. It was out of the wind and much warmer than the world I had left. The shock of finding myself in this snug, enclosed place made me forget all about molecules, blood and the Lord's Prayer. Much later I realized that Esmond did not start the engine and put on the heater: he made this suggestion merely to avoid coming in the back with us.

'Here, Thomas,' Lilian said. 'That's right.'

She must have moved the raincoat for I felt the soft warmth of her skin. The pleasure it gave me was so exquisitely intense it could have been a stab of pain. I tried to jerk my hand away but she gripped my wrist to draw me down beside her. We were lying across the width of the car. Half of me was on top of her, and the rest was poised on the edge of the seat.

It's all right, I told myself, it doesn't matter: I'm tripping, and when you're tripping you can do anything.

She began to giggle. 'Your hands are so cold.'

'So are yours.'

'Let's see whose hands are colder. We'll touch each other's tummies, they're the warmest bits.'

I was laughing now. For a while we tickled and touched and savoured each other's closeness, as children or kittens do. Our limbs tangled themselves together. From the front seat Esmond encouraged the illusion that we were engaged in harmless and normal play by joining in with the occasional joke. He even tickled us once or twice. My sides ached with laughter. I knew that I was in the middle of a miracle – one of far greater significance than mere levitation would have been.

'You've got very pretty hands,' Lilian said. 'I've always thought so. Make them warmer. Put them between my legs – no, silly, not there: higher than that.'

So it went. Part of my consciousness stood aloof from what was happening and marvelled. I am not going to describe every grope and joke, or how our games slowly changed their nature. It amazes me that we managed these contortions in such a confined space. The usual criteria for discomfort were temporarily suspended. I don't know how long it all lasted. I remember stroking an arm, and thinking how incredibly beautiful it was, considered objectively. I wasn't sure whether the arm was mine or Lilian's, and I wasn't interested, either. The important point was the arm's beauty. After a while – minutes? hours? – the important point was not even the arm's beauty but the very fact of its existence.

I should stress that, even at the time, I was well aware that this behaviour was exceptional, and that it was due to the LSD. I remember wishing that some of the effects might be permanent. (In a sense my wish was granted, though not in the way I had expected.) Nor do I want to give the impression that I suddenly became masterful or anything of that sort: I took no liberties until I was invited to do so. I should also record the fact that for much of the time I was terrified. Or, to be more precise, *part* of me was terrified, and deeply apprehensive. I knew that my mind had travelled further than ever before, and I was not sure that I would be able to find my way home. I knew that monsters were waiting to ambush me.

I heard Esmond saying something. I listened not to the words but to the purring roar of his voice.

'What?' Lilian said, and bit the lobe of my left ear.

She and I burst into laughter. While we laughed I heard Esmond speak again, 'I'd better go and see what old Stephen's up to.' There was a click and a rush of cool damp air. The car rocked. The door slammed. Lilian and I were alone. Two's company, I thought with a touch of smugness; I felt sorry for Esmond, and hoped that he did not feel left out. Then Lilian pulled my head towards her and for the first time kissed me on the mouth.

I thought the long night at Blackberry Water would last for ever. Time became elastic: it expanded, never contracted. How else to explain my feeling that I had been trapped in that cage with Lilian for years on end?

Once, when I looked eastwards up the coomb, I thought I saw a faint lightening of the darkness where the horizon must be. Finisterre was there too, but I could not see it. But when I next looked, hours later, the east was no brighter. Another hallucination? Fluid rainbows clung to my fingertips and ran down the line of Lilian's jaw. Small and furry creatures were with us in the car on the edge of my field of vision. I told Lilian about my hallucinating the rainbows and the creatures.

'How do you know there aren't always rainbows? They could be just as real or unreal as not-rainbows. But you don't normally see them.'

She didn't say anything about the creatures. I didn't press her. I thought it possible that they might be her familiars.

I knew that if I were left alone, I would go mad. I would have liked to go and find Esmond but Lilian wanted to stay in the car and talk. I tried not to listen to her. All these years she had been silent. Now the acid made her jabber away. She wanted to tell me about her mother: what she said and did, not how she died. I think Lilian would have talked to anyone. I don't know how long she talked. For hours, perhaps. She went on until she noticed the blood on her raincoat. Then she stopped. Instead she wept. I held her in my arms, and in the end I found myself crying in sympathy. My stomach muscles ached with laughing and crying. I had become colder and colder. I wanted a hot drink. We fell silent. We still had our arms around each other.

'Stephen said it's often like this,' Lilian said. 'You go in giggling and you come out subdued. Oh God.'

I suspected that the effects of the drugs were gradually wearing off. This was a very slow process, so slow that at first I feared I was indulging in wishful thinking. The hallucinations and other sensations continued, but with less force. The tyranny of the here and now diminished, which allowed me occasional glimpses of other times and other places. It seemed increasingly likely that I had reached the outward point of my journey and was now beginning to retrace my steps. My mental processes lacked the febrile quality that had distinguished them a few hours earlier. Now my mind felt calmer and extraordinarily lucid.

'I am I, you are you,' I said to Lilian. 'But we are we, aren't we? We make a third person.'

'God, that's so beautiful,' she remarked.

I was very flattered. While I was searching my mind for any other scraps of enlightenment it might contain, the driver's door opened. Esmond stuck his head into the car. I had forgotten all about him.

'Have you seen Stephen?' he said.

'He went for a swim, didn't he?' Lilian said.

She laughed, and so did I. I sat up. Suddenly I became aware of the world beyond the inside of the car: the cold, salty air and the glowing mound of Esmond's fire.

Esmond was frowning at Lilian. 'He's been gone for ages. At least I think he has.'

'We could try shouting,' I said.

'I have – several times. But he didn't answer. And he must have heard, it's not as if it's a big beach.'

'How do you know he's on the beach?' Lilian asked. 'Ten to one he's on the astral plane, and –' She started to giggle again. '– and as we all know, that's enormous.'

'He might have gone for a walk,' I suggested.

'Yes, that's it,' Lilian said. 'He's walking to Wales. He's walking on the water like Jesus.'

We were in a very awkward position. Esmond, Lilian and I were still drugged – still tripping heavily, as the hippies would have it. It was unlikely that we could sustain a coherent conversation with an outsider on any subject. It was just before dawn on Midsummer Day. I was very thirsty.

'Christ, I'm freezing,' Lilian said.

I gave her my jacket, which she put on under her

raincoat. Esmond thought we had better search the beach together. We stumbled down the shingle, which descended towards the water in terraces like worn stairs. By now the rain had stopped. A grey twilight covered the beach and the sea; it was impossible to distinguish the end of the one from the beginning of the other.

Self-deception was not just easy but inevitable. Lilian screamed; she had seen the oily coils of a serpent slumbering at the foot of the cliffs. I heard footsteps crunching on the stones behind me. The wreckers from Ulvercombe were coming down the beach, and their feet made so much noise you could hear them across a gulf almost two hundred years wide.

'They are alive, you know, all of them,' Esmond whispered. 'We must be very careful.'

He didn't say who 'They' were, and I dared not ask.

The tide was retreating before us. Patches of sodden sand appeared among the shingle. I put my right foot in a pool and soaked my leg up to the knee; I would have fallen if Esmond hadn't seized my arm.

'He said there's blood under the stones,' Lilian whimpered. 'Look, he's right.'

'Stephen!' Esmond called, time and time again. 'Ste-ee-phen!'

The noises of the sea and the night came back to us and mingled with the sound of our own breathing, and our own footsteps. Often I heard voices – Stephen's, and those of seagulls and strangers; and sometimes Esmond said he heard them too.

We came to the edge of the sea. As far as I could see, it was as empty as the beach.

'Told you so,' Lilian said. 'He's walking on the water.'

'Come on,' Esmond said. 'Back to the car.'

We struggled up the beach. I saw a faint red line between the gap in the cliffs. The sun was coming. For a while I relegated Stephen to the army of uneasy thoughts in the back of my mind. For an instant I felt guilty. I reminded myself that we were not in a position to do anything; after all, we were not in our right minds.

This last phrase set me off on a tangent. If we weren't in our right minds, where were we? I reasoned that we must each have at least one wrong mind, and each of us was in it at present. Unless, of course, I was thinking of the wrong 'right' mind: I might be in my left mind, my sinister mind. I realized then that it was all a question of labels; that labelling a thing determined its apparent nature, that beneath each layer of labels was another; that the layers were shaped like a ball or a globe; that I spent my life peeling off the layers in search of the hard core of real meaning; and that if it were possible to remove the last layer, I should find nothing, because there was no centre, hard or otherwise, and the meaning, such as it was, lay in the layers I had already peeled off and discarded.

I felt faint. I had made a discovery which would change the course of history. I wanted to share it with Lilian and Esmond. At last I found the right words – pithy, pregnant and immediately understandable by the meanest intelligence.

'It's like an onion,' I said. But no one was listening.

Esmond deserved all of the credit. When I had returned to my right mind, it frightened me to think what might have happened without him to look after us. We might so easily have freaked out, as the hippies said. But Esmond was too together to let us.

Despite the acid, he retained his grip on the essentials of our grim situation. It was still too dark for us to search properly for Stephen, and in any case we were not in a fit state to look for him or even to summon help. Esmond said, very reasonably, that Stephen had probably gone for a walk along the cliffs or was deep in meditation. He wouldn't thank us for fetching help. There was also the point that in our present condition none of us could afford to attract the attention of the police.

We built up the fire, which took some time, because its beauty distracted us all; but it was necessary, Esmond said, because Stephen would be cold when he came back. Lilian was worried: the fire might draw ships to their doom. I said that only happened at night.

Esmond used my Biro to print a note on a dismantled cigarette packet. 'BACK SOON.' He pinned the rectangle of cardboard to the ground with a pointed stick. We got into the car, all of us huddled together in the front, and drove very slowly back to Kinghampton. It was a marvel that we didn't hit something.

Returning to the Sandwells' flat was like returning to an earlier era of one's life; the place had the inexplicable and unsettling familiarity of a landscape in a recurring dream. We switched on fires. While the kettle was boiling, Lilian went to have a bath. (Later I found that she had got no further than her bedroom: she sat in front of a mirror, still in her green dress and raincoat, and stared open-mouthed at her reflection.) Esmond and I went to look for jerseys in Stephen's room; or rather, that's what Esmond said we were going to do. He was carrying the pigskin briefcase, which he had brought up from the car. It proved to be empty apart from about a dozen stones – small pieces of shingle, each veined with quartz. Esmond emptied them into Stephen's wastepaper basket.

I looked for jerseys. Esmond put his arm up the chimney and brought out a soot-covered japanned box. He opened it, making no attempt to prevent my seeing the contents; Esmond always trusted me. Inside was a bundle of bank notes, a slab of cannabis wrapped in silver foil and several keys, each with a tag.

'Mum's the word – eh, Rumpy?'

'What are the keys for?'

'Left-luggage lockers.'

Esmond searched the rest of the bedroom. He removed a small diary, two big notebooks and a bundle of letters. He packed everything into Stephen's pigskin briefcase.

'Can't be too careful,' Esmond said to me. 'But we'd better not mention it to Lilian, eh? It'd only worry her.'

The closer I came to my right mind, the more my body ached.

At about eight o'clock, Esmond suggested that he and I divide our efforts. I was to stay and look after Lilian. He was going to drive to Ulvercombe, hide the briefcase in the garage at Finisterre and go on to the beach. He would either collect Stephen or, if necessary, look for him. If he saw my mother, he'd say the Sandwells were giving us breakfast, and he had nipped back to collect our razors.

'Are you sure you can manage?' I asked.

'Of course. Why ever not?'

After Esmond had gone, Lilian and I had a bath together: an asexual affair, for we were like tired and fractious children. There was much to admire under the glare of the bathroom light: I examined the water, the sponge, the toothbrushes, the slimy soap and the roll of paper that dangled beside the lavatory. Even at this late stage it struck me as curious that I had not noticed before how beautiful they were.

The bath relaxed us both. Afterwards Lilian went to bed. She asked me to sit beside her and hold her hand.

'Why?' she said after a long silence.

'Why what?'

'Why is it like an onion?'

Sixteen

Esmond wasted no time on the morning after Alice's arrival. He came into the nursery at about half-past eight. He was wearing his red silk dressing-gown and carrying the big tray. I was sitting at the window watching the birds in the garden.

'Good,' he said. 'I hoped you'd be up.'

There were four cups of tea on the tray. I noticed that Esmond had already shaved. He put the tray on my table.

'I've been thinking,' he said, his tone suggesting that he was returning to a subject we had already discussed at some length. 'I think it would be better if you took her the tea.'

'You don't think . . . perhaps Bronwen ought to do it? As another woman, I mean. I don't want to – er, intrude.'

'Rubbish, Rumpy.'

'Why?'

'For a start, you're not really a man – you're her father. Anyway, if anyone's the intruder, she is. She's not going to mind who brings her a cup of tea.'

'Even so, Bronwen's the – er, hostess.'

'I can't trust Bronwen not to pour the tea over her.'

'You're joking.'

'Not entirely. Besides, this is your job. Only you can do it.'

'Take in her tea? Surely not.'

'You know what I mean. Go and ask her how she slept and whether she likes sugar.'

I stood up. Esmond meant that it would be best for everyone if Alice and I were on friendly terms. He gave me a cup and saucer, and patted my shoulder as I passed him. I crossed the landing and tapped on the door. Esmond carried the tray down the landing to the room he shared with Bronwen.

'Who is it?' Alice called.

'Me. Thomas. I've got some tea.'

'Come in.'

She was still in bed – lying on her back, her hair a dark tangle against the white of the pillow, her brown eyes fixed on me, a vertical crease between her eyebrows. Apart from my mother, who didn't count, the only other woman I had seen in bed was Lilian.

'I'm sorry,' I said, trying not to stare. 'I didn't realize, perhaps we should have left you to sleep.'

'No, that's OK. I was awake.'

She sat up slowly; her body was heavy with sleep. She was wearing a thick white nightdress that buttoned up to the neck. There was a maroon woollen shawl on the bed. She draped it round her shoulders.

I put the tea on the bedside table and mumbled the conventional enquires. Yes, she had slept very well. Like the dead, she said. No, she didn't take sugar. Yes, she would be down in thirty minutes, and not to bother about breakfast, thank you, because she rarely had more than a piece of toast or a bowl of cereal. Her legs twitched under the duvet: I guessed she might want to go to the bathroom. I backed out of the room and shut the door.

To my surprise Esmond had come back to my room. He was sitting on the window-seat with his tea and a cigarette.

'Well done, Rumpy. Now – have some tea, and then we'll have a little rehearsal, shall we?'

It was one of those cool, bright autumn mornings when the outside world looks enamelled. We had a lot of them at Finisterre, and I had learned to distrust them. There was always a stiff breeze blowing up from the sea, and within an hour or two – by lunchtime at the latest – the breeze had become a wind, and usually it started to rain.

Esmond knew this as well as I did. During breakfast, however, he asked Alice if she would like to have a look round outside. Esmond had arranged all this before Alice came downstairs; he had decided that Bronwen should stay at home.

'That's right,' Bronwen muttered as I helped her clear the table after breakfast, 'keep the little woman tucked away in the kitchen.'

Esmond herded Alice and me outside. I wanted to find my waterproof jacket, but he gave me no time. Alice was wearing a loose cotton dress and sandals; her legs were bare. Esmond was in shirt-sleeves.

The garden was not at its best. The grass needed cutting. Most of the flowerbeds were a tangle of decaying vegetation. Bronwen hadn't yet tidied up for the winter.

'It's a lovely garden, isn't it?' Alice said. 'Plenty of room to stretch your legs.'

I tried to follow Esmond's instructions. 'A garden

this size means a lot of work. My mother used to have a gardener.'

'Do you spend a lot of time outside in the summer?'

'Not as much as you'd think. It's not very sheltered.'

'See those conifers?' Esmond pointed at the wind-breaks. 'Ugly things. But you can't do without them for half the year. You wouldn't believe the force of the wind.'

'That's why we have to have storm shutters on the windows that face the sea,' I said.

Esmond suggested a stroll down to Blackberry Water and the beach. Once we were outside the garden, the wind obligingly strengthened. By the time we reached Blackberry Water the sun had gone in, and clouds were moving with ominous rapidity across the sky. The stream was trying to run backwards up the valley.

The litterbin needed emptying, and there were empty cans and pieces of broken glass on the ground. Esmond played the good citizen and gathered some of them up.

'People never think, do they? That's the trouble with holidaymakers.'

'Do you get a lot of them down here?' Alice asked.

'In the summer, yes.'

'I'd have thought this was off the beaten track.'

'Don't you believe it. The whole area turns into an enormous holiday camp. The tourists are always coming up and down the lane. Sometimes they park across our drive. Once we had to stop some people putting up their tent in the garden.'

'But it all looks so peaceful.'

'You should try it in high season. You wouldn't believe the noise we get. The bikers are probably the worst. They have races up and down the lane. But every now and then we get teenagers turning up for midnight parties with mobile discos: I'd say they're a close second.'

We walked through the gap in the cliffs to the beach. There were a few streaks of oil on the shingle and the usual litter of man-made rubbish along the waterline.

'Of course it was very different when we were kids,' Esmond said. 'There were far fewer people around, even in the fifties and sixties.'

We stared at the sea. Grey waves slapped against the rocks. It started to spot with rain.

'We'd better get back to the house,' Esmond said. 'Sorry – we should have brought the car.'

'It looked so nice half an hour ago,' Alice said, excusing him.

'Yes, it did, didn't it? But you can never tell.'

We struggled up the lane with the weather behind us. We were damp and shivering by the time we reached Finisterre. Bronwen had coffee waiting in the kitchen.

Alice tried to make conversation with her. She said something about how, as a child, she had envied children who were privileged enough to live by the sea all the year round.

'Christ,' Bronwen said. 'If you only knew how I'm dreading the winter.'

On that morning she looked old and unwell. I noticed the wrinkles in her dry skin and the stiffness of her movements. I suppose the contrast with Alice's youth was responsible for that.

When we were warmer, Esmond suggested that Alice might like to look over the house. We left Bronwen making pastry.

As we went from room to room, I began to realize that this guided tour wasn't easy for Esmond. He was the moving force at Finisterre, yet he was neither the owner nor the life tenant. He had to shelter behind my legal status: it was all 'Thomas-decided-this' and 'Thomas-decided-that'; he allowed the occasional glimpse of himself as a fraternal major-domo-cum-spokesman. He pointed out what we had done, emphasizing the importance of keeping the structure in good repair, and of 'maximizing the asset'.

Alice said less and less. But she attended to what she saw and heard. In the nursery she stood at the window and felt the bars as if testing their strength. She asked if this had always been my room.

'Ever since I was born,' I said. 'Except for a few months when I was a young man.'

There was a silence. I wondered if Alice knew enough to guess the reason for my moving out of the nursery.

'You're forgetting when we redecorated,' Esmond said. 'You slept in the room over the porch for a fortnight.' He smiled at Alice. 'Come and see it. It used to be my room when I was a boy.'

Afterwards we went down to the sitting room. Bronwen was sitting in Esmond's armchair with her knees close together and her body angled away from the vertical; she held a magazine in her hands. There was a smear of flour on her cheek. She looked uncomfortable and out of place.

'Anything we can do towards lunch?' Esmond asked.

'All under control. Should be ready in about twenty minutes.'

'Just time for a drink, eh?'

Alice declined. The rest of us accepted discreet little glasses of dry sherry. I held mine very tightly and wished my nervousness would go away.

'Would this be a good moment?' Esmond asked me. 'Do you want Bronwen and me to go?'

'No. Please stay.'

Esmond waited but I couldn't find the right words. He tried to help me: 'I know you want to have a word with Alice. I thought perhaps you'd rather be alone?'

I shook my head and looked at Alice, at my daughter. 'It's a question of money.' I saw the wariness creep into her face. 'As you know, I – er, the house and everything will eventually come to you . . .'

'Splendid,' Esmond murmured.

'. . . while I have a life interest in the estate. A very reasonable arrangement. But the trouble is . . .' What had Esmond said was the trouble? My mind was blank. 'The trouble is . . .'

Esmond leant forward. 'Would you like me to explain?'

'Please.'

He turned to Alice. 'My aunt – your grandmother – had a very adequate income by the standards of fifty years ago. But nowadays it leaves a lot to be desired. And Finisterre gobbles up money. When your grandmother died no one had done any maintenance for decades. Bronwen and I have actually had to subsidize Thomas to keep this place going, to stop it falling down about our ears. Haven't we, Thomas?'

I nodded.

'Not that we mind that, of course. We're all family. But Thomas thinks that this isn't fair on Bronwen and me. And it's true that sooner or later we'll all have to look to the long term.'

'Yes,' I said. 'It isn't fair.'

'Well, Thomas can't go on as he is, obviously. But there are various options for generating income. He could take paying guests, for example – give them bed and breakfast. Trouble is, that means a lot of work, and the profits aren't wonderful. Quite apart from the inconvenience and unpleasantness of sharing your home with complete strangers.'

He paused for a second to let this last point sink in. I wondered what he had already told Alice about me; he must have had plenty of opportunity last night, when they were driving from Exeter to Finisterre. It must be obvious that I lacked the skills necessary for running a lodging house of any description. I suspected that he had mentioned my breakdown and the various physical ailments. Not in detail, I thought – Esmond understood the value of being vague.

'Naturally we've discussed the other major possibility: leasing the house. In the circumstances, the trustees would probably agree – not much choice, eh? But the chances of getting a long tenancy are very slim indeed. The house could be empty for half the year.'

'And I'd need somewhere to live in any case,' I interrupted, remembering something that Esmond had told me to say. 'That would all cost money, wouldn't it?'

'So, Thomas came up with another idea.' Esmond paused, in case I wanted to continue. I didn't. 'Selling this place,' he went on. 'Not a bad idea. It's a massive capital asset, just rotting away. The tourists may be a pest but at least they inflate the value of the house and land.'

'Yes,' I said, nodding. 'That's a very good point.'

Esmond smiled at me and turned back to Alice. 'The sale of Finisterre would raise a large sum which could be used partly to provide income and partly to buy another, more suitable house. Thomas even wondered about buying abroad – a little money goes a long way. As a long-term investment, residential property performs better than almost anything else.'

'And you can live in it, too,' Bronwen said helpfully, 'while it's appreciating.'

'Quite so.' Esmond turned in his chair so Bronwen was behind him and hence excluded from the conversation. 'So,' he said to Alice, 'there you are. He realizes, of course, that such a move would need the consent of all the interested parties. Apart from Thomas himself, that's you and the trustees. But the trustees aren't going to turn down a sensible proposition if both you and he are in favour.'

Esmond, Bronwen and I stared at Alice; Alice stared at her hands. I looked at the curve of her plump cheek; a chicken, I thought, plucked and ready for roasting. And to my horror I found myself feeling sorry for her.

'I'm sorry,' Esmond said, all charm and contrition. 'I – we didn't mean to spring it on you like this.'

'That's all right.'

'Time isn't on our side. We thought it would be best for everyone if we got straight to the point. Didn't we, Thomas?'

'Yes.'

I knew Esmond wanted me to say something else to support him. I remembered a comment he had made when he was talking to me about the house before breakfast. I decided to reuse it. To me it sounded impressive: it suggested one actually understood something about financial matters if not about the avoidance of cliché and mixed metaphor.

'A wasted asset soon becomes a millstone,' I said.

Alice's fingers pleated her skirt. She looked worried, not impressed. She glanced up from her hands.

'Talking of millstones,' she said to me, 'I'm four months pregnant. I don't want an asset. I want a home.'

After the funeral Lilian told me she was pregnant.

At first I didn't understand what she was saying. We were standing on the lawn at Finisterre, and at first her voice seemed to have nothing to do with me; it was an irrelevance, like the buzzing of a bee. The funeral had affected me deeply – far more than the inquest. To be precise, it disgusted me. I was still fighting the horror of it while Lilian was talking.

Stephen Sandwell's body spent almost three weeks in the water before a storm cast it up on a sandy beach much frequented by holidaymakers. It was found by a family from Birmingham and caused quite a sensation. During his time in the water, Stephen had travelled ten miles south from Ulvercombe Mouth. ('If he was heading for Wales,' Esmond said when he was getting seriously drunk after the inquest, 'he must have taken a wrong turning.') Stephen lost his kaftan, his inverted crucifix, his eyes and a considerable percentage of his flesh and internal organs. They identified him by his teeth.

We had reported him missing early in the evening of the day after the party. During the morning and afternoon we had searched the cliffs and accessible bays within five miles of Ulvercombe Mouth, and found nothing. By that time the three of us were more or less back to our right minds (though the right mind I returned to was, courtesy of the acid, not quite the same as the right mind I had left). We told both my mother and Aunt Ada that we were worried because Stephen had gone for a walk and not returned. Aunt Ada asked Lilian to stay at the vicarage. Lilian kept bursting into tears; we calculated that this would rate as an acceptable reaction to a brother's disappearance.

Esmond and I went to the little police station at Kinghampton and told Sergeant Swift that Stephen Sandwell had vanished. The four of us, Esmond said, had been to The Mermaid the night before, and then gone back to the bookshop. Around midnight Stephen had decided to go out for a walk. Yes, he had done this sort of thing before. Yes, he had had a few drinks but he was a long way from being drunk. He wasn't there when we woke up. We had spent the day searching for him. Might there have been an accident? Frankly, Esmond said, we were worried. Stephen's behaviour had been a little – well – *unusual* in the last few months.

Luck favoured us. The inquest was much less of an ordeal than I'd feared it would be. We had two advantages: the delay in finding the body and the eccentric reputation of Stephen's father. Many people thought this might be the case of like father, like son. As far as I was aware, no one suggested that Stephen's death was anything other than an accident.

Esmond came down for the funeral, which took place a little over a week after the sea regurgitated

Stephen's corpse. I had not seen much of him since the day after the party, though we had had several guarded conversations on the phone. As we were going into the chapel behind Lilian, my mother and Aunt Ada, I asked him if everything was all right.

'Never better,' he said. He was decked out in a new suit and practically prancing with self-satisfaction. 'Why do you ask?'

I said something about Stephen's pigskin brief-case, which Esmond had removed from the garage at Finisterre.

'Oh *that*. Don't worry. It's all taken care of.' He looked down at me. 'By the way, I must tell you something. No need to mention to anyone else, but I'm hoping to buy a flat.'

He smiled and went into the chapel as the organist began to play the opening bars of 'Jerusalem'.

In the crematorium chapel I looked at the coffin. Suddenly I wanted to be sick. I told myself that the undertakers must have made the corpse decent. But Stephen must have been too far gone to be prettified. I thought of the sodden mass of corruption inside the coffin. I wondered whether psychic energy was leaking into the air, whether dying in your wrong mind was different from dying in your right mind, and whether Stephen was observing us and, if so, whether from a celestial, infernal or neutral vantage point. I also wondered exactly how he had died.

'Pregnant,' Lilian said. 'You know – preggers. Up the spout. A bun in the old oven.'

The irritation in her voice distracted me from the

memory of the funeral. An instant later, I realized what she had said. I looked round quickly, worried that someone might be within earshot. We were alone in the garden at Finisterre. My mother had undertaken to provide the principal mourners with a sandwich and a glass of sherry. The others were indoors.

'But, Lilian . . . are you sure?'

'I was due over two and half weeks ago. Yesterday I went to see the doctor. Now I really am sure.'

'What about – ah – you know.'

'Whose is it, you mean?' She spoke so loudly that I looked over my shoulder. It was a warm day, and the sitting-room windows were open. 'Well, there's only one candidate, isn't there? You.'

'You mean – that night at Blackberry Water?' *The night that Stephen died; the night the world shivered.*

'Oh, Thomas! When else could it have been? There haven't been any other times.'

I wished I could discuss this with Esmond. Lilian was looking at me expectantly. She was a different person from the one I had known in the car. In fact, I thought, she was not so much a person as a collection of features. A shapeless black dress below a colourless face and pale gold hair. She wore glasses, but no make-up. The beginnings of a spot in the left-hand corner of her mouth. Irregular teeth. I found none of these features attractive, either singly or in combination.

'What do you want to do?' I said.

'What do people normally do when they have babies?'

'Get married, I suppose.'

'Dear Thomas,' she said. 'I thought you'd never ask.'

*

284

At this crisis in her affairs, Lilian revealed herself as a shrewd tactician. She so often stood aside from what was happening that you tended to forget how swiftly her mind could work, and how determined she could be; an engine does not seem powerful while it is idling in neutral. As soon as she had accepted what she chose to interpret as my proposal, she insisted on our going immediately to the sitting room. Here, standing hand in hand, we broke the news to my mother. (News of the engagement, I mean; Lilian thought it best to save the baby until later.)

'I know this isn't really the right time,' Lilian said, tightening her grip on my hand. 'But in a funny way it is. I know Stephen would have been so happy. He and Thomas had such a lot in common.'

My mother swept Lilian into her arms with an alacrity which surprised me until I had had time to think about it. 'I'm so glad,' she said. 'So very very glad.'

Lilian clung to my mother and wisely held her tongue.

'And I'm glad you've told us now, dear. After all, we are all family, or soon will be.'

The vicar made a short speech about every ending being a new beginning. Aunt Ada wept and tried to embrace everyone. My mother bestowed moist kisses on everyone, especially Lilian. The announcement appealed not only to what my mother conceived her self-interest to be, but also to her streak of sentimentality.

Esmond grinned at me and murmured, while everyone else's attention was on Lilian, 'Ah well, we all have to pay for our pleasures, eh?'

After the first excitement had died down, my mother ran up to her bedroom and came down with an amethyst ring which had belonged to my paternal grandmother;

this, it appeared, was to be Lilian's engagement ring. My mother handed it to me.

'It's been waiting for you for months, dear,' she told Lilian. 'If not for years. A mother always knows.'

They kissed prettily, cheek to cheek, for the third or fourth time. Lilian held out her left hand to me. The women's movements were so assured and fluent that they might have been choreographed and rehearsed. I blundered about, a talentless amateur among professionals.

'There you are, Thomas,' my mother said with the quiet menace of the prompter in the wings. 'You know what to do.'

My fingers fumbled at Lilian's, which were cold despite the warmth of the day. I dropped the ring. Esmond picked it up for me. On my second attempt I managed to slide it on the appropriate finger.

'Beautiful,' my mother said. 'It's almost as if it were made for you. We'll get it sized tomorrow.'

For the rest of the day we gave up all pretence of mourning Stephen and celebrated our engagement instead. Even I was infected by the general jollity. The congratulations made me feel that I must have done something worthwhile. I was still feeling dazed – it is not every day that one learns that one is going to marry one's employer and become a father – and indeed apprehensive; but it was pleasant to be at the centre of attention for once, or at any rate to be sharing it with Lilian. I was glad to discover that my role, though essential, was primarily symbolic. Like a constitutional monarch I assented graciously to a stream of decisions made in my name by other people.

'Now I want you to feel this is your home, dear,' my mother said to Lilian as they were sitting on the sofa with their heads almost touching. 'You needn't be afraid I shall get in the way. I always knew that I should start thinking about moving when Thomas chose his bride. Your needs must come first. It wouldn't be fair to either of you.' She sighed bravely. 'I shall look for a little bungalow in Ulvercombe, perhaps, or even King-hampton. I'm sure it will be wonderful to be closer to the shops.'

Lilian said as little as possible. She dabbed her eyes with a handerchief, smiled or looked concerned at all the correct times, and allowed my mother to pat her hand in moments of deep emotion.

Aunt Ada, meanwhile, was planning the wedding. 'Have you thought about *when*, dear?' she asked.

Lilian gave me one of those rare smiles that made her face beautiful. 'As soon as possible,' she said. She blushed. The two older women cooed, delighted both by her eagerness and by the evidence of maidenly reserve.

The vicar was usually in favour of long engagements. But he recognized that Lilian's case was exceptional. He suggested early in September. The wedding was to be a family affair like Stephen's funeral. We would use Ulvercombe church. The vicar could not take the service: as Lilian's cousin-once-removed, he would be needed to give away the bride. Fortunately Aunt Ada could supply someone else in holy orders from her side of the family – a youngish man, recently ordained and even more recently married; his name was Henry. Esmond would be my best man. Bridesmaids were going to be a problem until Lilian said in her sweet little-girl voice that, if no one minded, she'd much rather not have bridesmaids. She wanted our wedding to be as simple as possible. This sentiment won general approval, if only for the reason that 'simple' meant inexpensive.

After they had all gone, Esmond and I walked down to Blackberry Water because Esmond wanted to smoke a joint in peace.

'Happy?' he said as we were going down the lane.

'I think so.'

'Bloody hell. Don't you know?'

'It's rather complicated.'

'Only if you want it that way. Are you sure you want to go ahead with this?'

'Yes.'

It was a calm evening. When we reached Blackberry Water we went down to the beach. On the way we passed the blackened site of our bonfire. I had not been down here since the morning after Stephen's party. I was surprised to discover that there were no ghosts waiting for me. Perhaps I would avoid them for ever if only I could stay away from my wrong mind.

Esmond lit the joint. We stared out to sea. After a while I told him about the baby. He laughed. He liked the idea of my being a father.

'The only problem is my mother.'

Esmond grunted. 'Does she know that Lilian's in the club?'

'Not yet. I was wondering if we need tell her.'

'I'd wait a bit. You might as well make sure that there really is a baby.'

'But Lilian wouldn't lie about it.'

'Why not? She wouldn't be the first.'

'She's not like that,' I said.

'All right. Assuming there is a baby, then sooner or later your mother will have to know. Because of the dates.'

'Do you think we should tell her before the wedding or afterwards?'

'Afterwards. But don't worry about it – it won't matter. You saw what they were like this afternoon. Practically slobbering over each other.'

Esmond smoked. I sat with my arms around my knees and stared out to sea. It was very peaceful – away from Finisterre, away from the shop, away from Lilian and my mother.

'You'll do very well together,' he said slowly. 'You'll have the bookshop. She'll have a nice house, and maybe the kid. Who knows? Maybe you'll have several kids. It's ideal.'

'You'll come and visit us? Just as before?'

'Of course.' Esmond ground out the joint on a stone and buried the roach in the shingle. 'You know this flat I'm buying? It's off Southampton Row. Quite big – it's got a decent-sized spare bedroom. You can always come and visit me. By yourself, I mean. If you want to get away from them all, you can come and live there.'

Esmond made a good deal of money from Stephen's death. I imagine he was able to take over not only Stephen's share of their stock of drugs, but also his share of the profits. Only Esmond knew what was in those left-luggage lockers. He had some sort of official standing, too: after the inquest, Lilian asked him to sort out everything in London for her – Stephen's possessions and his business affairs.

Esmond now had sole control of the network of buyers and sellers that he and Stephen had set up. I think he was relieved to be independent. He cannot have found it easy to work in Stephen's shadow.

At Lilian's request, Esmond and I cleared out Stephen's bedroom in the flat above the shop. I dipped into one of his journals and was astonished to find out how juvenile his wooing of Satan and his quest for paranormal powers seemed. Surely he could not have believed this nonsense?

In the end we burned all his private papers, most of them unread: unread because we feared they would be boring, not because we respected Stephen's privacy. I put his books – a catholic collection from Chaucer and Plato to Dr Leary and *The Tibetan Book of the Dead* – into our second-hand stock at the shop. We gave his clothes to a woman who was organizing a jumble sale for the Girl Guides. There was, as Esmond said, no point in being sentimental.

We wound up the grand design. This was not difficult. In its final form the grand design amounted to little more than a suitcase full of seventeenth- and eighteenth-century books, mostly of a devotional nature, none of them worth more than a few shillings. There were also some booksellers' catalogues and nearly five hundred cards on which was engraved 'Stephen Sandwell, Sandwell & Penmarsh, Rare & Antiquarian Booksellers, London & Kinghampton.'

I missed Stephen only at the shop. He had always

been available, if only after a delay and at the other end of a telephone. Even before his death had been confirmed, Lilian made it quite clear that the business was now my responsibility alone. She owned it, I ran it; she left all the decisions to me. She refused even to help behind the counter.

'Sorry, I'm busy,' she'd say. Or, 'I don't feel very well.' What with the pregnancy and the preparations for the wedding, she had an ample supply of excuses. In a while I stopped asking her and she didn't have to make any excuses at all. It would be facile to attribute her aversion to having any other career than that of a wife and mother to the life and death of the late Mrs Sandwell; facile, but perhaps not entirely inaccurate. In any event, she divorced herself from both the shop and the flat above it from the day after Stephen's disappearance. Lilian remained at the vicarage in Ulvercombe until the wedding.

So, in a very short space of time and with surprisingly little effort on our part, Stephen disappeared. Each of us encases ourself in a protective shell, a combination of prison and fortress. Esmond and I broke up Stephen's shell and dispersed the pieces. In a sense, it was almost as though he had never lived.

I spent my last weeks as a bachelor in a daze. This was partly because I had even less control over events than usual, and partly because the acid trip had left me with the feeling that nothing really mattered in comparison with the terrifying dramas in my mind. My experiences that night had revealed the arbitrary nature of the assumptions on which I based my life. Many of the assumptions were so deeply buried that I had not previously known that they were there. Now I saw them clearly for the first time, and saw them for what they were: a sort of magic, an attempt at self-enchantment.

As the wedding day approached, I had a number of flashbacks to the time when the magic had failed. These happened without warning when I was between sleeping and waking. My pulse began to race. Sometimes the grain in the wood of my bedside table liquefied and formed itself into the faces of grotesques. I would shut my eyes only to find that the faces were under my lids. The other creatures, the ones that lived deep within my wrong mind, stayed out of sight; but I sensed that they were stretching their furry legs and ruffling their feathers.

Worst of all, Stephen was there, hiding in my wrong mind like the Phantom in the bowels of the Opera; I heard him giggle, and I knew that he was still alive and waiting to feed on my energy.

Despite these distractions, I guessed that my mother had something up her sleeve. For days before the wedding she went around the house smiling to herself and gnawing her lower lip. She made unexplained visits to Kinghampton. I knew better than to ask her outright. I hoped she might be visiting estate agents and looking at bungalows.

Lilian and I were to be married on Saturday the 11th September. On the Friday evening Esmond arrived in a Rolls-Royce he had hired or borrowed for the occasion. In the boot was a morning suit from Moss Bros, a case of Roederer and an ounce of a superior hashish known as Nepalese Temple Balls. By this stage my mother was so excited that when she thought no one could hear her she squeaked to herself. 'Eee-Eee-Eee-Eee-Eee-Eee . . .'

For supper we sat in the dining room and ate ham-and-beetroot sandwiches and drank a bottle of Esmond's champagne. My mother had two glasses and behaved in a manner she might well have described to herself as 'vivacious'. This involved playful remarks about Esmond's unmarried status and the exhumation of jokes remembered since her adolescence, which had usually mislaid their punchlines along the way. Finally, and with much girlish hesitation, she brought herself to the point.

'I think this is a good moment to have a family conference,' she said. 'Don't you, boys?'

'Yes,' Esmond said, as obliging as ever, though the hash had made his eyes bloodshot and thickened his voice. 'I suppose it is.'

I wondered if he remembered that she had convened another 'family conference' on the day that his mother died.

'I've just made my will,' she said. 'I should have done it years ago. But now with Thomas getting married . . .' She seized my hand, which I had incautiously left on the table, and gave it a painful squeeze. 'As you know, I think of you both as my sons. And I know –' Here she looked languishingly at Esmond '– that Thomas thinks of you as his brother. You, too, Esmond, may soon be a married man with a family to support. So, when I'm gone, I've decided that my estate will be divided equally between you both.'

Yes, she really did speak in that sentimental and

pompous way. My theory is that she cribbed a lot of it from whichever romantic novel she was reading at the time. She was acting the part of the matriarch in some family saga: a woman of substance making far-sighted provision for the next generation.

Esmond and I looked at each other. My mother was waiting. The trouble with such speeches is that they require replies in a similar vein.

'Thank you,' Esmond said. He cleared his throat. 'It's really very good of you.'

I tried to thank her. I was grateful that she was treating Esmond as my brother. I didn't mind his having half of my mother's estate. But when I opened my mouth, all that came out was a giggle. It didn't sound like one of my giggles. It sounded like one of Stephen's.

Seventeen

'Oh, really?' Esmond said when Alice told us about the baby. 'Well, that *is* a surprise. Tell me, is your husband the father?'

'I don't think it matters who the father is.' Alice's cheeks filled with colour. 'The point is, I'm its mother. It's mine.'

'I don't think anyone's trying to take it away from you.'

'I think lunch is ready,' Bronwen said. 'Shall we eat?'

She couldn't keep her eyes from straying over Alice's figure. The pregnancy didn't show. Nor did Lilian's for the first five months, not unless you saw her naked.

We ate in the kitchen – chicken pie, I remember, followed by apple crumble. The sky darkened. As we began to eat, a squall hit the house. The frantic tapping of the raindrops made us all jump.

'They said we're going to have gales over the weekend,' Bronwen said. 'But you know what weather forecasters are like. They always look on the black side, don't they, so no one can blame them like they did when we had that big gale – when was it? Late eighties?'

Bronwen chattered about the weather. Alice and I said very little. Esmond glowered at his plate for most of the first course. Suddenly he interrupted Bronwen in mid-sentence.

'Ah, nursery food,' he said. 'How appropriate.'

I wished he wouldn't be so unpleasant. The one thing I can't abide is unpleasantness. I like the atmosphere to be easy and unstrained. I don't like it when people shout at each other. I don't like it when you can glimpse the hatred in half-averted eyes, and hear it in whispering voices. Unpleasantness unsettles me.

'Let me give you some more pie,' he said to Alice.

'No thanks. I'm full.' Alice spoke not to Esmond but to Bronwen. 'Not that it isn't wonderful: real English cooking – that's something I've missed.'

'You sure?' Esmond mimed surprise. 'After all, these days you're eating for two.'

Alice lost her smile. 'In that case we're both full.'

'Oh, Thomas,' Esmond said. 'You said you wanted me to look through the accounts.'

'Yes.' I had said nothing of the sort.

'How about after lunch?'

'Yes. Fine. Right.'

'Good,' he said. 'That's settled then.'

He looked directly at Alice. He was trying to persuade her that the words meant more than they said. Squabbling over Finisterre, I realized, meant squabbling over me.

Esmond dragged me off to the study immediately after the meal. He sat me down at my mother's desk. He paced up and down in front of the window. I had not seen him so agitated since just after Lilian's death.

'You don't owe her anything,' he said. 'You mustn't let her just walk into your life like this.'

He lit a cigarette and began to talk about the past, about the times he had helped me and protected me from my mother and the rest of the world. I didn't like to mention the fact that for over twenty years he had hardly spared me a thought. There was enough un-pleasantness in the house already.

'I told you right at the start,' he said. 'That woman's just out for what she can get.'

There was a knock. For a second Esmond stared balefully at me. Then he darted across the room and flung open the door. Bronwen was outside with a tray of coffee.

'I thought you might like –'

'Where is she?'

'Alice? In the kitchen. She's helping clear up.'

Esmond grunted, implying that his worst suspicions were confirmed. He took the tray, nodded curtly at Bronwen and shut the door in her face. He turned back to me.

'You see? Now she's trying to get into Bronwen's good books. Devious little bitch.'

He went on in this vein for almost half an hour. Anger made him ramble, and he repeated himself several times. I sipped my coffee and waited. Esmond circled round the point he wanted to make. I wished there were some way of stopping him.

'She's just trying it on,' he said for the third time. 'You've got to make it quite clear that there's absolutely no question of her living here while you're alive.'

'But she won't let us sell,' I said.

'So it looks like stalemate.'

'But what if she objects to the changes we've made? Or to ones we make in the future?'

'Whose side are you on? Have you forgotten what I've done for you?'

'I could never forget. It's only that there's no point

in upsetting her, is there? Not if she could make things difficult.'

Esmond walked up and down, up and down. Suddenly he stopped and turned to me. He had the window behind him so his face was in shadow.

'Whatever happens, Alice is going to make things difficult.' He was talking very quietly now, almost whispering. 'Unless of course she dies.'

Alice was a little more oblique in her approach. By teatime she had developed a consuming interest in her 'real' family. She asked me to show her the family photographs. We were in the sitting room with Esmond as our chaperon; Bronwen was chopping kindling outside.

Alice and I sat side by side on the sofa with the albums on a long, low table in front of us. Esmond couldn't resist joining in as we leafed through our past. There were generations of dead Chards and Bradleys; there were snaps of Aunt Ada and the vicar, Esmond and me as children, youths and young men; there were snapshots, studio portraits and school photographs from Bicknor College and Kinghampton Grammar School. Alice studied them. I think for a moment or two she lost track of her purpose and started to look for her own face or, failing that, for a feature or two she held in common with her forebears.

'Who was the baby?' she asked, pointing at a photograph of myself and Esmond on a rug in the garden with baby Lizzy lying on her back between us.

'My sister,' Esmond said. 'She died.'

'Oh. I'm sorry.'

Alice stared at the baby in the photograph. The

telephone rang. Esmond went to answer it. At the door he glanced at me, as if to say, 'Watch yourself when I'm gone.'

'There are none of my mother, are there?' Alice said. 'Or of me, come to that.'

'No. My mother weeded them out.'

'Out of sight and out of mind?'

'She thought it would be better.' This sounded callous, so I added, 'At the time I wasn't very well.'

After a pause, Alice went on, 'It must have been wonderful to grow up in a house like this. I spent most of my childhood being dragged round Africa.'

'In the service of God?'

'It certainly wasn't in the service of Mammon.'

'Did they send you back here to school?'

She shook her head. 'Henry thought boarding schools were bad for the health. So my education came in scraps, here and there. I'm very good on the exports of Brazil and the books of the Old Testament. But I haven't got anything that qualifies me to earn a living.'

There was another silence. Alice picked up another album and leafed through it.

'Look,' I said. 'That's my parents on their wedding day.'

She examined the photograph. 'You don't look much like your father.'

Nor did she. I said, 'Perhaps that's a good thing. He reminds me of Dr Crippen.'

She giggled. 'It was him who bought the house?'

'Oh yes.'

'So the money came from his side of the family?'

I nodded. Was she reminding me that it was Penmarsh

money, not Chard or Bradley money? By blood, Esmond had no claim to a share of my mother's estate. I wondered if Esmond had implied otherwise. Alice wriggled beside me. She was very earnest, and her youth made her lovely. I thought she must be telling herself that the welfare of her unborn child was at stake, and that this gave her a mandate to be ruthless.

Esmond came into the room. Alice and I looked up: no doubt it seemed to him that we had been sharing a guilty secret.

'Talking of photographs,' he said, 'have you got any of your parents, Alice? Of Henry and Doris, I mean. Interesting to see what Henry turned into. We only met him the once, didn't we, Thomas? That was at your wedding.'

I was worn out. After supper I decided to go to bed early. My departure took them all by surprise.

When I came out of the bathroom, Bronwen intercepted me on the landing and herded me into the nursery. Her breasts actually nudged me. She kicked the door shut behind her.

'You've got to do something, Rumpy,' she whispered.

'I'm sorry?'

'He's going to go round the bend if this goes on.'

'If what goes on?'

'Stop pissing about, will you? She's an obstinate little cow, your daughter. It's all her fault.'

'I am sure we'll smooth things over,' I said. 'Seeing her again was bound to be a bit difficult for everyone.'

'It won't stop being difficult until you kick her out. You can do it; it's still your house while you're alive.

Don't you see? If you don't get her out, someone's going to do her a mischief.'

'Oh, surely not.'

'You know what Esmond's like when he gets angry,' she said. 'You should know better than anyone.'

She came very close to me. I smelled onion on her breath and the musty perfume of her body. A breast grazed my arm. She took the lobe of my left ear between her finger and thumb.

'What are you doing? Let go.'

'You'd better do something,' she said, squeezing the lobe. 'I'm telling you: I won't be responsible.'

She squeezed a little harder. I yelped. With a grunt of exasperation, she released the lobe and pushed me on to the bed. I fell awkwardly, banging the knuckles of my left hand on the headboard.

'Remember,' she said. 'Esmond's done everything for you. Ever since you were kids. Do you think you'd still be here without him? Christ, you'd be in a loony bin by now.'

I stared at her. Bronwen was fighting for Esmond as Alice was fighting for the foetus in her belly. I rubbed my bruised knuckles and wished they would all leave me in peace. In my head was a humming that rose jerkily in pitch. Higher and higher, louder and louder: like the humming of a string being tightened on a guitar or a violin, tightened until the string breaks or the neck of the instrument snaps.

'Right then,' Bronwen said. 'Have you got the message now? You owe him. And this is where you start paying him back.'

*

When we got back from Torquay, Lilian was about three months pregnant. Our honeymoon had been a chaste and sedate time because she hadn't wanted to upset things 'down there'.

On our first evening at Finisterre, Lilian said, 'We're going to have a baby.' It was fascinating to watch my mother's face. It took her about five seconds to reach the obvious conclusion.

'When?' she said grimly.

On the whole, she took the news surprisingly well, partly because Lilian implied that a secret engagement had preceded the fornication. Love, my mother remarked, had found a way. Boys would be boys; girls, she implied, had very little to do with it. Young passion had burst into bud and borne fruit. We had been very naughty, of course, and she wasn't in any way condoning our conduct; she wasn't one of those who agreed with the modern relaxation of morals. She shuddered to think what Aunt Ada and the vicar would say. Still, at least Cousin Henry had joined us together in the sight of Heaven. Better late than never. She for one remembered that piece in the Bible about not casting the first stone. Judge not – was it? – that ye be not judged. Something to that effect. Had we decided on a name for the baby yet?

There was a price to be paid for this complaisance. My mother was sure that she, Lilian, wouldn't mind if she, my mother, pointed out that she, Lilian, was not only totally inexperienced as a mother but also totally unprepared to run a substantial house like Finisterre. Housekeeping was a skilled job which required a long period of training. Furthermore, Lilian could hardly be expected to shoulder this heavy load of domestic responsibility while pregnant with her first child. We had to think of the health of the little one in her tummy.

'It's not like the old days,' my mother said in her fruitiest voice, 'when one could afford staff.'

'No,' Lilian agreed. 'One has to do it all oneself.'

The only sensible solution, I gathered, was for my mother to stay at Finisterre and unobtrusively help Lilian with her new burdens. There were many lessons for Lilian to learn – for example, how to get the best from the Jodsons; which Kinghampton butcher to patronize; why one should on no account light the study fire when the wind was from the east; and how to make the meat puddings which Esmond adored. My mother also advanced an army of subsidiary arguments: from the ill-advisability of leaving Lilian alone during the day to the fact that neither Lilian nor I could drive.

'Don't let the old hag get away with it,' Esmond said when I told him the news on the phone. 'You'll never get rid of her.'

'Well, perhaps Lilian does need help.'

'She won't need help for the rest of her life, will she? The rest of your mother's life.'

'She said she'd only stay until we had settled down with the baby.'

'Balls.'

'But what can we do?'

'Move into the flat over the shop. Then Lilian would be near the shops and the doctor, and you could keep an eye on her during the day. Your mother won't stay at Finisterre by herself.'

'I did suggest that to Lilian. But she wasn't very enthusiastic.'

'You should insist.'

'It's too late,' I said. 'My mother seems to have found us a tenant. It's not as if we don't need the extra money.' The truth was that Lilian wanted to live at Finisterre: as far as she was concerned there was nothing more to be discussed. 'I tried to tell her what it'll be like. She just won't believe me.'

A match scraped at the other end of the phone; somewhere in London a flame flared. 'Don't say I didn't warn you,' Esmond said.

Our marriage led to a number of changes at the house. When we came back from our honeymoon, I discovered that my clothes had been moved out of the nursery. My mother had decided to put Lilian and me in what had been the spare room. We had twin beds, each with a shiny salmon-pink eiderdown. My mother remained in the bedroom which was to be hers until she died. When Esmond came to stay he would sleep in his old room over the porch. The death room, of course, was empty.

The prospective tenant for the flat above the shop was a new teacher at the Girls' High School; she wanted to move in at once, for term had already started. My mother and Aunt Ada had seen to everything while we were away. The lease was prepared. All Lilian had to do was sign it.

The teacher was a silent and self-contained creature who spent more time in the lavatory than anyone I have ever known. Though she never knew it, she played a small but significant part in what was to happen in May 1967. She turned out to be one of those people who can't bear cats. Lilian had toyed with the possibility of leaving Grimalkin to police the shop. Our tenant's ailurophobia made this impossible.

So Grimalkin came to live at Finisterre. By that time she was elderly and set in her ways, many of which were unpleasant. She outraged my mother and sickened me by bringing dead and dying creatures into the kitchen. Grimalkin gave the impression that she liked no one very much, even Lilian. But she tolerated Lilian because Lilian was prepared to spend hours stroking her in a way she enjoyed.

During the autumn evenings, I packed up my books and carried them downstairs to the little room we used to call the schoolroom. I left them in their cardboard boxes – a brown mound which leaned against the wall and almost reached the ceiling. In the spring Esmond was going to help me build shelves for them.

Gradually Lilian transformed the nursery. As the weeks went by, she disengaged her attention from the rest of Finisterre; she left the management of the house entirely to my mother, who was delighted. On some days Lilian, my wife, hardly said a word to me. Her face grew thinner and more like a witch's as her body grew fatter. If she needed help during the day she asked one of the Jodsons; I was usually at the shop. At night she often went to bed soon after supper, so I spent many evenings alone with my mother in the sitting room. When I went upstairs, Lilian was almost always asleep. Sometimes she was still asleep when I got up in the morning, and still asleep when I cycled off to work.

The nursery was wallpapered, painted and carpeted from wall to wall. Furniture arrived from Kinghampton and Budstow. The cupboard and the chest of drawers filled up with immaculately folded nappies and minute vests. In December Lilian made up the Moses basket, where the baby would sleep for the first few weeks of its life, and placed the basket in the cot, so our child would become accustomed to the bars from the very start of its life. There was also a low armchair in the nursery – the only piece of furniture Lilian brought from the flat. It stood between the cot and the window. She would sit there doing nothing, her long hands folded on her lap. Grimalkin sat on the window-seat and bided her time.

Looking back, I realize how tranquil those few months were. The three of us had stumbled upon an equilibrium – just as Esmond, Bronwen and I were to do over twenty years later. At the time, none of us noticed.

'I don't know how you can bear it,' Esmond said when he came down at Christmas.

Alice Elizabeth Penmarsh was born on the 26th March 1967. I had nothing to do with it: I was at the shop when Lilian went into labour, and my mother drove her into Kinghampton; I was at the shop when the baby was born, and my mother was at Finisterre.

So Alice was born among strangers. Lilian chose her names. The baby wasn't called Fiona or even Mary, which was my mother's second name. My mother was coldly furious. She took the omission as a deliberate slight.

'When I think of what I've done for them,' I overheard her telling Aunt Ada. 'It makes me feel quite ill.'

Her emotions could easily have swung the other way, had Lilian been more diplomatic. My mother was a stupid woman with strong passions: given the slightest encouragement she would have doted on her grandchild. But Lilian's love was a jealous love.

My mother's attitude had one immediate and surprising effect. While Lilian was in hospital, I made a habit of visiting her after work. One evening I arrived to find Aunt Ada in the visitor's chair. It was a colourful sight. The ward was full of flowers, and Aunt Ada was wearing a dress that would have afforded her excellent camouflage in a herbaceous border. Lilian was sitting up in bed with Alice sleeping in her arms.

'So we'll pencil in the 14th June, shall we?' Aunt Ada was saying. 'Oh hello, Thomas. We're talking about the christening.'

I touched Lilian's cheek with my lips. She did not appear to notice. Not normally a religious person, she was taking the arrangements for Alice's christening very seriously.

'We'll have to sort out godparents,' Lilian said. 'It's so important to make the right choice.'

'We'll get Esmond to be the godfather, shall we?' I suggested.

'Well, perhaps.' Lilian frowned. She turned to Aunt Ada. 'In fact I was wondering if you'd like to be one of the godmothers.'

'Oh my dear, I'd love to.' Aunt Ada's face reddened. 'The poor little mite,' she murmured; I wasn't sure whether she was referring to Alice or Lilian. 'I've got a little surprise for you.'

She opened her handbag and took out an envelope, which she handed to Lilian. Lilian, much of whose attention was on the baby in her arms, opened the flap of the envelope and pulled out a cheque. She blinked, and looked more closely at the piece of paper in her hand.

'But you can't,' she said. 'Really, it's –'

'Yes, I can, dear. I had a little legacy last year. It's not as if we've been blessed ourselves.'

'But it's such a lot.'

'I want you to put it towards Alice's education. After all –' Aunt Ada glanced at me, and through me at the invisible presence of my embittered mother '– she may need all the help she can get.'

Lilian, still cradling her baby, leaned forward and stretched out an arm towards Aunt Ada. The two women embraced awkwardly. A tear trickled down Aunt Ada's fat, wrinkled cheek.

The cheque slipped from Lilian's fingers and fluttered to the floor. I picked it up. It was made out to Lilian and was for the sum of one thousand pounds.

Alice was two weeks old when she and her mother came back to Finisterre. For the first time she lay in the Moses basket within the cot in the nursery. She cried and cried. The breast would quiet her sometimes, and so would sleep, but neither for long.

I did not take to her, perhaps because I was rarely allowed near her. She was on an unbelievably small scale, with a purple face of great ugliness and a wrinkled skin that hung baggily on her body; she was like an apoplectic homunculus which had lost too much weight in too short a time. Lilian treated her as though she were infinitely delicate – far too fragile to be trusted to my clumsy hands or my mother's brutal ones. Even Grimalkin was banned from the nursery; Lilian was prepared to use force to keep her out. I suppose that for her the cat had been a surrogate child, something to care for, but now the real child filled the role to overflowing.

Alice, I gathered, was like no other baby. Lilian said as much a hundred times, an assessment necessarily based on faith, not rational comparison. To me Alice seemed a mass of physical needs and a source of foul smells. I could not help holding her responsible for the increasingly unpleasant atmosphere at Finisterre.

In those days Lilian was in a trance: her entire being was concentrated on the baby. Physically she was at a low ebb, because it had been a difficult birth, and because she wasn't having enough sleep. She insisted on feeding Alice herself, though the midwife had advised against it.

'She's mine,' Lilian said. 'Anyway she likes it.'

When Lilian came back from hospital, I offered to help with Alice. I could have rocked her to sleep. I could have brought her to Lilian in the night. I might have learned how to change nappies. Who knows, I might even have enjoyed it. But Lilian refused almost angrily even to entertain the idea. She wanted the baby all to herself.

'I think I shall go mad,' my mother said on Alice's third day back at Finisterre. 'I cannot abide a whingeing child.'

We were alone in the sitting room on a Sunday

afternoon in the middle of April. I was trying to read. My mother had a Mills & Boon romance on her lap but she preferred to spend the time grumbling. Lilian was upstairs in the nursery, trying ineffectually to quieten Alice.

'In my experience,' my mother continued, 'it is rarely the child's fault. The mother is almost always to blame.'

'I'm sure things will settle down soon,' I said.

'I wish I could believe that, Thomas. I really do.'

Ghosts hovered between us: was my mother thinking of Aunt Imogen and baby Lizzy, as I was? I thought of that Christmas almost thirteen years before, the time full of wonders, at the end of which Esmond came to live with us at Finisterre. *For ever and ever.* It seemed to me that we were trapped in our own folly, doomed to repeat ourselves until death set us free.

The door, already ajar, opened a little more. I looked up, full of fear. It was only Grimalkin, not her mistress. Alice's thin wails continued above our heads. The cat prowled across the carpet to the hearthrug, swished her tail in the air, sat down and licked her private parts. As usual she ignored us completely.

'Do you know what she asked me to do this morning?' my mother said. 'She wanted me to feed that wretched animal. All because the baby needed changing. It wouldn't have harmed Alice to wait for another minute or two. In fact it would probably have done her good.'

Grimalkin stopped licking herself and stared at my mother. She yawned, revealing the pink cave of her mouth, and applied her tongue to her pudenda with renewed vigour.

'Every child has to learn that it's not the centre of the universe. In my experience the sooner it learns the lesson, the better for all concerned.' My mother glanced upwards towards the nursery on the other side of the ceiling. Her teeth gleamed. 'Some people,' she added, 'never seem to learn the lesson at all.'

We sat in silence for a moment. The baby cried more loudly and with a dreary and penetrating persistence. Lilian's footsteps moved to and fro above our heads.

My mother said, 'Tuh!' She lobbed her library book on to the hearthrug. It hit Grimalkin on the shoulder. The cat squawked and fell on her side. Her legs splayed; in an instant she became graceless and ridiculous. Claws flashed out and dug into the dark blue rug. She laid back her ears along her skull and spat. A cat on the verge of panic is not a pretty sight. For a fraction of a second she looked not at my mother but at me. Then she bolted out of the door.

'Ah,' my mother said. 'I've dropped my library book.'

'Oh. Yes, so you have.'

To this day I have no idea if she meant me to be deceived. Did she really believe I hadn't seen her throwing the book at the cat? She beamed at me, her good humour temporarily restored.

'Well, Thomas? Would you mind picking up the book for me?'

At four o'clock on that Sunday my mother made a pot of tea. I took a cup up to Lilian, who was sitting in the low chair with Alice in her arms. The baby was asleep and breathing heavily. After all the crying, its skin was almost puce, its face was like a lizard's, and its scraps of black hair were damp and matted. Lilian looked at me with a mixture of anger and urgency in her face. I wasn't wanted. I was a potential danger because I might wake the baby. I tried to put down Lilian's tea as quietly as possible but the spoon tinkled in the saucer.

My wife said, 'Tuh!' Just as my mother had done, only less loudly.

'Lilian,' I whispered. 'There's something I wanted to ask you. The shop's going through a bit of a bad patch. I'm afraid we're going to have to extend the overdraft soon. Perhaps by a couple of hundred pounds.'

Lilian was rocking the baby very gently to and fro while staring into its face. She gave no sign that she had heard me.

'Of course I could ask Mother instead, but I'd rather not. You know how it is. She's being a bit awkward.'

I paused. I didn't want to ask the bank manager either. I always felt he despised me, both as a businessman and as a person. Besides, I was frightened that he would say no, which would make my interview with him even more unpleasant than usual. I waited, but Lilian said nothing.

'So I wondered, perhaps, if we might borrow two hundred pounds of Alice's money from –'

'No.' Lilian looked up. 'That money's for Alice. Do you understand? For no one but Alice.'

'But Lilian,' I whispered, 'it would only be until . . .'

I saw Lilian's face and stopped. She was staring over my shoulder, and she looked furious. I turned. The door was open. Grimalkin had slipped into the nursery, and it was all my fault.

With her eyes, Lilian damned me for my stupidity

and ordered me to get the cat and myself out of the room. But Grimalkin didn't want to go. She hid under the bed where she hissed and scratched at my attempts to reach her. I yelled as her claws cut through the soft skin under the wrist. Alice woke and began to cry.

'Now look what you've done,' Lilian said. 'Hush now, dearest. Mummy's here.'

I pulled Grimalkin out by the scruff of her neck and threw her on to the landing. I looked back at Lilian. She was already absorbed in the baby. I left the nursery and shut the door very quietly behind me. Grimalkin was on the stairs. The intolerable unfairness of my situation crystallized into hatred for the loathsome animal in front of me.

'You watch it,' I said to the cat, and my voice sounded as though it belonged to a cruel and coarse stranger. 'You just bloody watch it.'

I realized how empty the threat was. So did Grimalkin. She didn't move. She stared at me. She seemed to be mocking me, laughing at my impotence. I heard the humming in my mind.

'You wait. I'll show you.'

So, you see, it was all the cat's fault. I went into Esmond's bedroom. It was still a boy's room, filled with a boy's possessions. I opened the door of the little wardrobe. Inside, on the floor at the back, was a tall cardboard box. It contained a couple of tennis rackets in need of restringing, a walking stick, sections of tent pole and Esmond's air rifle.

I took out the gun. Its weight surprised me; so did its shabbiness and the coldness of the metal. I remembered the air rifle as it had been in its heyday, when

Esmond cleaned it with love and oil after every time he used it. I tried to wipe off the dust with my handkerchief. My hands trembled with anger. Soon the handkerchief was filthy. Afterwards, the stock rewarded me with a dull sheen. It was speckled with minute drops of paint; the wood was scarred and notched; and in some places the varnish had been rubbed away. The sights were caked with grime.

Would the gun still shoot? I remembered how Esmond used to pull a long, stiff lever in front of the trigger guard to build up the compressed air: he would pull the lever towards him and then back again until it clicked into place parallel with the barrel of the gun. The mechanism was very stiff but it appeared to work, though I did not pull the lever back to its full extent because I recalled Esmond saying that one should never shoot the gun when it was empty.

There was another, much smaller lever behind the rear sight. I moved this through ninety degrees, which rotated the cylinder holding the lead pellet. This looked hopeful: the cylinder moved easily, the chamber was free from dirt, and it gleamed with oil.

All I needed now was some slugs. I searched the box, the cupboard and the rest of the room without success. As I searched, my anger slowly receded. I felt hot and stupid. The anger hadn't gone for ever: it had merely withdrawn to await a better opportunity. Tomorrow, I promised myself, I would buy myself some slugs in Kinghampton.

For want of an airgun pellet . . . If I had managed to find a slug on that Sunday afternoon, Lilian might still be alive. I find that thought very unsettling.

That night, at suppertime, Lilian and my mother had their first open quarrel. Ostensibly it was about the cat. In reality they were fighting to establish which of them was mistress of their little world and its inhabitants. I wouldn't have minded so much if they'd left me out of it. They shouldn't have tried to drag me in. They should have left me in peace.

Soon it seemed they were quarrelling every evening. Each woman nagged me about the other. It got so bad that I feared going home. As often as I could, I made excuses to stay late at the shop. When Alice cried at night, cold fingers squeezed my stomach, and I prayed that she would stop.

'It's your fault,' my mother hissed when she met me on the landing one night. 'It's all your fault, Thomas.'

Lilian would get me alone in our bedroom. 'Can't you have a word with her? I think she's getting senile. I know the signs. This is how Dad began.'

'She's your wife, Thomas,' my mother whispered. 'It's your baby. Why don't you do something?'

'You've got to be firm with her,' Lilian said, crossing her arms beneath her great, milk-rich breasts. 'Otherwise she's just going to get worse and worse and worse.'

The humming often filled my head. When I closed my eyes at night I saw the wires shimmering in the darkness. The wires tightened, gleaming like knives, and the humming rose in pitch. I knew wires were dangerous. Cheese wires cut. Barbed wire keeps you in or keeps you out. Live wires electrocute. Garrottes strangle.

Nevertheless, even at this stage everything might have been all right. Left to ourselves, Lilian and my mother might have reached stalemate; out of sheer exhaustion they might have stumbled into a compromise. But we weren't left to ourselves.

On the afternoon of Thursday the 11th May, about a month after the first open quarrel, Esmond phoned me at the shop.

'I think I might come down tomorrow,' he said without bothering with the usual preliminaries.

'Oh, I thought you were coming the weekend after next.'

'It won't cause any problems, will it?'

'The only thing is, Mother's having dinner at the vicarage on Saturday. I'm not sure she can get out of it.'

'All the better, as far as I'm concerned.'

'But she'll be delighted, I'm sure.' My mother saw Esmond as a potential ally in her war against Lilian.

There was a silence at the other end of the line.

'Esmond? Are you OK?'

'Yes. Of course I am. See you tomorrow.'

He put the phone down. The change of plan wasn't surprising in itself – Esmond's movements were often erratic, owing to the exigencies of 'business'. But his manner had been uncharacteristically brusque. Usually when he phoned, we would chat for a moment or two; he would ask how I was, and lately he had taken to enquiring about the baby.

On Friday evening I shut up the shop and cycled back to Finisterre. The weekend was a pleasant prospect before me. However, I was surprised and a little hurt to see a car already in our drive – a green Morris Minor, an unusually modest choice for Esmond. I went inside. He was having tea with my mother in the kitchen; Lilian was upstairs with Alice. Everything seemed relaxed and normal: the room was thick with cigarette smoke, Esmond was smiling, and my mother was talking.

Esmond gave me a nod, which reassured me; I was beginning to wonder if I had somehow offended him. I fetched myself some tea. I watched him while my mother talked. I thought his face looked thinner than it had been.

My mother finished her tea and said she would do something about supper. 'It'll have to be scratch meal, you naughty boy. You really should have given us more warning.'

'I'm sorry.' Esmond said. 'Shall I nip into town and get us some fish and chips?'

'Don't be silly,' she said, laughing. 'Now off you go.'

'Can't I help?'

'You'll only be in my way.' The mistress of her kitchen, she bustled round the table towards the Aga. 'Why don't you get a breath of fresh air? You both look as if you need it.'

It was a fine evening. Esmond went upstairs to fetch a ready-rolled joint. A moment later we wandered into the garden. We walked down the lawn to the fence nearest the sea; here the conifers shielded us from the windows of the house. Esmond scraped a match against the heel of his elastic-sided boot. I stared at the sea and the sinking sun.

'Something's wrong,' I said.

'Does anyone know I'm here?'

'Aunt Ada perhaps. My mother didn't go into King-hampton today but she might have gone into the village. The Jodsons are on holiday.'

'Would Lilian have told anyone?'

'I doubt it. She hardly goes anywhere at present. Doesn't talk much, either. Why?'

'Oh, just I'd rather not advertise the fact I'm down here. That's why I drove straight here rather than picking you up at the shop.'

This relieved me: I was afraid I had offended him; in the past, Esmond had always given me a lift home if he had been able to reach Kinghampton before I left the shop.

After a pause, Esmond went on, 'I don't know if you've seen it in the papers – there's been a lot of trouble lately. The police are hassling everyone.'

'Oh God, have you been arrested?'

'It's not that bad. But it will be if I don't get hold of fifteen hundred quid by the end of next week. In fact it'll be worse.'

Faintness hit me. I clung to the top rail of the fence and stared at my knuckles. Esmond sucked on the joint and held his breath. My head cleared. I tried to calculate what I could do to help.

'I could manage about fifty, probably, even sixty –'

'I've been bloody unlucky. I'd just taken delivery of a consignment, you see. The biggest yet. But I hadn't actually paid for most of it. Special favour, they gave me credit. It's almost unheard of. But I had customers lined up and everything. I could have shifted the lot in three days.'

'What went wrong? Don't they want it any more?'

'Oh they want it all right. But I haven't got it. The cops have. I had most of it stashed in this chick's flat in Ladbroke Grove. And she went and got herself busted.'

'Won't she tell them it's yours?'

'She would if she knew. But she doesn't. Don't worry, they can't connect me with the acid. Not yet. They might suspect something but they can't prove it.'

'I thought you only sold cannabis.'

'Had to change with the times.' He was talking jerkily as though he were a little short of breath. 'Supply and demand. Anyway, it doesn't matter – except the legal penalties for dealing acid are even worse than for dealing dope. The point is, unless I come up with one thousand five hundred pounds in cash, my main suppliers are going to get very pissed off.'

'Couldn't you explain – ask if you can pay in instalments?'

'On the never-never?' He snorted. 'These people are professionals. They're into all sorts of things besides dealing. They've got their reputation to consider.'

He stared at the joint, which was only half-smoked. He flung it down and ground it into the bare earth with his heel.

'They're going to crucify me twice over,' he said. 'First they'll send the heavies in, and they'll tread me into the carpet. Then they'll pass the word to one of the coppers on their payroll. All they need do is connect me with that acid. They could do that with a fingerprint.'

'If you give me time I could probably raise two hundred. I could try to increase our overdraft again.'

'Thanks. But it's too little too late.'

'Have you still got some of the acid? You said the police got most of it.'

'A little.'

'Couldn't you sell that?'

'Given time, yes. But it wouldn't help. Not so's you'd notice. I'd make eighty or ninety quid at best. Even with your two hundred, it's not much more than a drop in the ocean. And who would I flog acid to round here? I just haven't got the contacts.'

'You mean you've got it with you?'

'I wasn't going to leave it for the pigs, was I?' Esmond took out his cigarettes. 'Besides, it's worth good money.'

'Where is it?'

'In the death room.' He must have sensed my shock. 'Safest place in the house. It's in the wardrobe.' He lit the cigarette. 'It's only for a day or two.'

'Esmond – Aunt Ada gave Lilian a thousand when Alice was born.'

His face lightened. 'Did she now?'

'She put it in the bank. But it's for Alice's education.'

'This would only be a short-time loan,' Esmond said. 'I'd pay her interest.'

'I don't think she'd lend it to anyone.'

'You're sure about that?' he said.

'Yes. It's for Alice, you see.'

Neither of us spoke for a moment. Esmond jingled the change in his pocket. We were both thinking of the obvious person, my mother.

'The old bag could do it, you know,' he said softly. 'She'd hardly notice. She wouldn't even have to sell any shares. She's got that much and more in her deposit account.'

I didn't ask him how he knew.

'It'd only be temporary. Give me a month or two and I can flog the flat; I'll have more than enough to pay her back.'

'What would you tell her?'

'A defaulting partner? Something like that. She wouldn't miss the money, would she? Not for a few weeks. It'd be as safe as houses.'

We shared another silence. I followed a different train of thought to the end of the line.

'Anyway,' I said slowly, 'it's all going to come to us sooner or later. Isn't it?'

Esmond planned to ask my mother after supper. He worked on her during the evening. He had three helpings of shepherd's pie. After supper, he manoeuvred my mother into putting her feet up in the sitting room while we washed up and made the coffee. He listened with apparent admiration to an involved anecdote about my mother getting the better of a recalcitrant saleswoman in the chemist's at Kinghampton.

Lilian had gone to bed immediately after the meal. While my mother was in full flow, I murmured goodnight, slipped out of the room and went upstairs. There was no light underneath our door. I peeped into the nursery. A night light burned on the chest of drawers. Alice lay very still in her cot; she no longer slept in the Moses basket. The room was silent.

I cannot explain the moment of panic I felt. I was suddenly convinced that Alice had stopped breathing. My mother might have tiptoed upstairs while Esmond and I were in the kitchen and Lilian was having her bath. Or death might even have come naturally.

At that time Alice was, at most, an inconvenience to me, and her death should not have seemed so desperately undesirable. But biology makes fools of us all. I crouched by the cot. I listened but heard nothing. I touched her. The tiny body under the blanket didn't move. I felt a soft-skinned arm, almost as thin as a cat's leg. I gave it a little pinch.

Alice wailed – a thin sound that lasted perhaps two seconds. Her arm twitched. I realized I was sweating with relief or fear, or a mixture of both. I waited in suspense. To my relief, she made no other noise and Lilian did not come flying out of our bedroom with a dressing-gown trailing behind her.

I left the nursery and went into Esmond's room. I didn't turn on the light. Leaving the door ajar, I sat on the bed and waited. A line of light from the landing sliced across the room and touched one end of the mantelpiece. Metal gleamed: I had remembered to buy a tin of pellets for the air rifle. I tried to make my mind go blank and silent.

Downstairs a door closed. My mother's footsteps tramped down the hall to the kitchen. A moment later she came upstairs. She went into the nursery for a moment, and then into her room. I slipped on to the landing and ran down the stairs.

Esmond was still in the sitting room. He was in the big armchair with his legs drawn up on the seat. He had a tumbler of whisky in his hand. The bottle was on the table beside him.

'Get a glass,' he said; and his tone of voice made it clear we were not celebrating a victory but drowning our sorrows. 'It's not a good time for me, dear,' he went on in a whispered parody of my mother's voice; he even lifted his upper lip to show the teeth. 'In fact I was going to suggest that as you were doing so well, you might not need the allowance any more.'

'What will you do?' I asked as I uncapped the bottle.

Esmond said, 'I don't think she believed me. I told her all about my embezzling partner. And you know what? She wanted to see documents, wouldn't take my word for it, oh no. Then she said maybe her solicitor could help, so why didn't I make an appointment to see him? Oh yes, and had I been to the police? Oh, *Jesus*.'

'Can't you hide or something? Or even go abroad?'

'You don't understand, Rumpy. These people know where I live in London, they know who my friends are. They'll trace this address in five minutes once they start looking. And afterwards they'll pass what's left of me to the pigs.'

'If only my mother would be sensible.'

'She's not likely to start at her time of life, is she? I'll just have to think of something else. Like join the Foreign Legion.'

'If only one could wave a magic wand and make her disappear,' I said. 'If only she wasn't here.'

Eighteen

The cats at Finisterre were buried among the bushes that divided the lawn from our little drive. My mother used to refer to this part of the garden as the 'shrubbery', which was something of an overstatement: there were two viburnums, a laurel, a dead rhododendron and a young fir tree that had strayed from one of the windbreaks.

Fortunately the soil was friable, and the roots were neither large nor entangled with their neighbours. It was easy to scoop out small, shallow graves. Time did the rest. I marked the graves with stones from the beach. I was particular about the stones: I chose ones which were striped with quartz and as nearly ovoid as possible. Only when the series was well established did it occur to me that these stones were very similar to the ones which Esmond and I had found in Stephen Sandwell's briefcase.

By the time the adult Alice came to Finisterre there were eleven stones in the shrubbery. I had made my last addition to the collection the previous January. A ginger-and-white kitten, I remember, quite young.

I nearly made it a round dozen. I am talking about kills, of course, not hits. This was in June – just after Esmond and Bronwen had moved into Finisterre but before they'd started their programme of renovations. It was a clear, mild night with a moon which was almost full. The others were in their bedroom, occupied with each other. I didn't want to think about that so I decided to try my luck with the gun.

My window was open at the bottom. I had my light out and I was kneeling on the floor with my elbows on the window-seat and the air rifle poking between the two central bars. The gun was loaded and ready to fire. A night shot was always more of a challenge. Far from making it easier, the moon gave a treacherous, en-chanted light, which created shadows where there were none and made distances difficult to judge.

I stayed there, hardly moving, for almost twenty minutes. Patience is everything. Suddenly my old enemy appeared on the lawn – the black-and-white tom with the torn ear. I recognized him even by moonlight. He was strong and agile but for a cat unusually graceless. One of his rear legs dragged behind the other; I am pretty sure that this was as a result of my winging him in the autumn of 1988.

The butt of the rifle was snug against my shoulder. I sighted down the barrel. The cat paused, cocking his head to listen. I couldn't believe my luck.

To my horror I heard a door slam and footsteps on the landing. My concentration was broken. The barrel twitched, and the sights wavered in and out of align-ment. Desperately I squeezed the trigger. The nursery door opened. The overhead light snapped on. I turned, blinking. I didn't even bother to look for the cat. I knew that the shot had gone wide.

'Jesus, Rumpy! What are you doing?' Esmond swayed in the doorway, and I smelled the whisky on his breath from four yards away. He was naked except for a towel round his waist. 'Is that thing a gun?'

'Er – yes. It's your air rifle, actually.'

'Give it here.' Hand outstretched he came towards me. 'Come on. That bloody thing's dangerous.'

A habit of obedience can be very hard to break. I gave him the gun. He asked for the slugs and I gave him those too.

'What were you shooting?'

'Cats. Just cats.'

'Do that often, do you?'

'It depends.'

'Oh God. You realize that if –' He broke off, frowning. 'How long have you been doing it?'

'Since you went away. Off and on.'

'I've come back now. You can stop. OK?'

I nodded.

'Do you actually hit them?'

'Quite often,' I said. I was proud of my marksmanship.

'And kill them?'

'Yes, of course. Sometimes.'

'What do you do with the bodies?'

'They're in the shrubbery,' I said. 'What was it you wanted?'

'Eh? Aspirin or something. Otherwise I'm going to have a headache in the morning.' He hesitated. 'Look – about the dead ones – are you just leaving them there, on the ground?'

'Oh no. *In* the ground. There's nothing to worry about, Esmond.'

The cats were in various stages of decomposition. Just before my mother died I had dug up Grimalkin to see what was left. I dug twice as deep as usual. I found no animal traces whatsoever. I fancied the soil was a little discoloured but that may have been imagination. We see what we expect to see.

Did this mean, I wondered, that Lilian had disintegrated as well? I wasn't sure. The greater bulk of a human body and the coffin surrounding it must retard the processes of putrefaction.

I am losing the thread again. When you have more than one thread to deal with, they get tangled together, and sometimes it is difficult to tell them apart. I only mentioned my cats because of my talk with Alice in the shrubbery. It was a case of one thing leading to another.

First things first, however. Alice ran off to the shrubbery after her conversation with Esmond just after breakfast on Saturday morning. Saturday the 5th October – it was her second full day at Finisterre.

Everyone came down to breakfast with good intentions. We smiled at each other and enquired how we had slept. When in doubt one tends to talk about the weather: in our case we discussed how the rain had stopped and the wind decreased overnight, and how this situation was unlikely to last; Alice said it was fresh and mild outside now, though the sky was grey; Bronwen told us what the weather forecast had told her; and Esmond said that he was going to put up the storm shutters tonight because there was no point in taking chances. Then we ran out of weather and had an awkward silence instead.

It was clear that the other three had decided that open hostility was not necessarily the best way of dealing with the difference of opinion that had arisen on the previous day. Alice was looking fresh and rested despite yester-day's troubles. She was dressed in jeans, trainers and a light blue jersey. Her casual appearance contrasted with Bronwen's: the latter was wearing more make-up and smarter clothes than usual. Esmond had pink pouches under his eyes and ate nothing except half a slice of dry toast, but he seemed relaxed; he exerted himself to be agreeable.

'I found a couple of letters from Henry to Thomas's mother,' he said to Alice. 'I wondered if you'd like to see them.'

'Do you mean now?'

'No time like the present. Let's take our coffee into the sitting room and I'll show you them.'

What letters? I had never seen any from Henry. There must have been several around the time of Alice's adoption, but my mother hadn't kept them. I noticed in passing that one of Esmond's barriers was down: he was no longer pretending to Alice that he was merely a sort of major-domo at Finisterre. He made not even a token attempt to consult me. I nibbled my toast and watched him as he arranged two coffee cups on a tray; he took no more notice of me than he would have done of a fly on the wall or Grimalkin by the fire.

No – *not* Grimalkin. Why did I think of her at that point? Grimalkin was long since dead. She belonged to another time. She lay on the sitting-room hearthrug, her legs outstretched, her belly facing the empty fire-place, her flanks rising and falling. In my dreams I sometimes held the muzzle of the air gun an inch above the furry triangle of her ear. She opened her eyes as I pulled the trigger.

Esmond and Alice left the kitchen. Bronwen started to load the dishwasher. I muttered something about fetching my glasses and slipped out of the room. I don't think she noticed my departure. The sitting-room door was already closed. I ran upstairs and into the nursery.

No need to worry about visitors: I would hear Bronwen coming, and the others were in the sitting room. I didn't even bother to put a book on the floor. In a few seconds I was on my hands and knees beside the chair. I rolled back the triangle of carpet, prised up the floorboard and poked my head in the gap between the joists.

I heard Alice, but unlike Bronwen she spoke too softly for the words to be audible.

'No, nothing like that,' Esmond said. 'We got off on the wrong foot yesterday. My fault. I wanted to say I was sorry.'

Alice said something else.

'I'm sure we can. If only for poor Thomas. There's something else I should have told you . . .'

Then Esmond, too, lowered his voice. The pair of them talked for several minutes. It was infuriating. I caught stray words, including my name and Bronwen's, but nothing that enabled me to make sense of what was being said. Nothing, that is, apart from the tones of the voices.

Esmond started off being persuasive. Gradually the voices sharpened and hardened, and the pace speeded up. It was like a game of tennis where the players begin lethargically but slowly warm to their work as the competitive instinct is aroused from its sleep.

'No, I will not!' Alice said, suddenly loud, clear and very angry.

'Can't you see it makes sense?'

'It makes no sense at all, not to me. You're crazy. I wouldn't touch you if you were the last man alive.'

Esmond lowered his voice again. This time I thought I heard an undercurrent of menace. Alice made a monosyllabic reply to this and to the next few remarks he made.

'Think about it,' Esmond said. 'Think hard. After all, these days you've got to do your thinking for two.'

The door shut with the next best thing to a bang. I pushed the board back over the hole, straightened the carpet and pulled myself up. I stood there, panting slightly and gripping the back of the armchair. My left knee hurt and I had a dizzy spell. I don't know how long it lasted. Seconds? Minutes? My mind swayed and nausea slopped from side to side. Esmond and Alice were bent on making things more and more unpleasant. I wasn't sure I could bear it.

I remembered to find my glasses before I went downstairs. The doors to the study and the kitchen were shut. I went into the sitting room, which was empty; but through the window I caught a glimpse of Alice walking across the lawn in the direction of the drive.

Panic held me: suppose she were leaving? I had hardly articulated the thought before the objections crowded into my mind. If leaving, she would have packed her belongings, put on her coat, and said goodbye; she would have phoned for a taxi if she hadn't wanted Esmond to drive her.

Unless, a little voice whispered, *Esmond had frightened*

her so badly that she could think of nothing but the need to get away.

I darted into the hall and slipped outside by the front door. I was in such a hurry that I didn't bother to get my coat, though there was quite a nip in the air. I shut the door behind me as quietly as I could. I knew that Esmond would be coming to look for me. If he had failed with Alice, he would want to make sure of me. He would have assumed I was still in the kitchen. I had very little time to spare. Bronwen might be as hungry for information as I was, but she would not be able to delay him for long.

The grass was heavy with dew. My feet felt the cold as soon as I stepped on the lawn. Looking down, I saw that I was still wearing my slippers. A dampness seeped after the cold. I could not afford the time to go back and change into outdoor shoes.

I glimpsed a flash of blue among the dark green leaves of the viburnums, but dared not call out in case Esmond or Bronwen heard. I walked quickly towards the shrubbery. As I drew near, Alice took a step backwards towards the drive. I thought she was going to run away. The idea of someone fleeing from me made me smile. I beckoned frantically. To my relief she stopped: she did not move towards me but at least she stayed where she was. I darted round the nearer viburnum. I knew that here in the shelter of the bushes we should both be out of sight from the house. Alice looked down at me. She swallowed.

'What do you want?' she said, her voice much rougher than usual. 'Has he sent you?'

'No. Are you all right?'

'What do you think?'

'What happened?'

'There's no point in talking about it.'

'He frightened you,' I said.

She turned away.

'I've known Esmond most of my life. See those stones on the ground? The ones with the stripes?'

Alice glanced down, then at me. 'Well?'

'They mark the graves of cats.'

'So what?'

'You don't understand,' I said. 'He shoots them with an air gun. He keeps the air gun locked in the cupboard in the study. The big one on the left of the fireplace.'

With my foot I pushed aside the stone that marked the grave of our latest acquisition, the ginger-and-white kitten which had been there no more than nine or ten months.

'Look, I'll show you.'

The loose soil slid up to one side. I glimpsed something white, probably the skull, before the soil slid back again.

'For Christ's sake,' Alice said. 'He said he's going to kill the baby too. My heir, you see, the heir of my body.'

What a curious way to describe a foetus. I heard Esmond calling from the lawn.

'Thomas! Thomas, where are you? Have you seen Alice?'

'I don't know what to do,' Alice said. 'I don't know how seriously to take him.'

'You should never underrate Esmond.'

'But he's nothing,' she said. 'He's got no claim on us, and nor has Bronwen. All we need do is tell them to go. This is our house. If they won't go, we call the police.'

'You make it sound so simple. But think of the cats.'

'What?'

'Perhaps you're being too reasonable about this. None of us is reasonable, not really. Especially not Esmond.'

'Yes, maybe.' But she shrugged, and I guessed that in her heart of hearts she believed everyone was capable of being rational if only he made the effort; Alice wasn't much more than a child in many ways. She went on, 'In the end I suppose it's up to you.'

'Thomas?' Bronwen shouted. She sounded further away than Esmond, probably she had been sent to look for us in the upper part of the garden on the landward side of the house. 'Alice? Would you like another coffee?'

Alice looked at me, her eyebrows raised. 'Well? What do you say?'

First, second and third thoughts jostled through my mind. *For God's sake make up your mind, Rumpy. It's not that difficult.* Leaves rustled and I smelled fresh tobacco. Esmond strolled round the viburnum. He looked tall, handsome and distinguished; he was immaculate in blazer, grey flannels and gleaming black shoes.

'There you are, my dears. Now what shall we do with ourselves today?'

Despair has a curious and often unpredictable effect on people. I always felt that Esmond was psychologically capable of killing someone – albeit with regret, and only if he felt that circumstances left him no choice.

I remembered what he had done to Miss Broadbent-Brown when we were boys at Bicknor College: in a way such lingering mental torture was far worse than killing her would have been. And consider this: for many people, selling LSD is an occupation only an amoral person could choose.

All those deaths. I wish I could make them go away. Not forgetting Stephen Sandwell and his poor father, Aunt Imogen and my mother. Oh yes, and baby Lizzy too.

Not that all this proves anything. Proof is such a cold and rational thing. It has nothing to do with living people, has it? Besides, I don't want to prove anything, because that would only cause yet more unpleasantness. People would get hurt. I could never willingly hurt anyone. I could never willingly hurt my dear Esmond.

Esmond thought I had betrayed him on the evening of Saturday the 13th May 1967. He must have believed I had tried to kill two birds with one stone. *Kill*? But it was an accident. No one disputed that.

The whole day had been most unpleasant. I awoke with a hangover from the whisky Esmond had given me the night before. I was the last down to breakfast. No one took any notice of me as I came into the kitchen. Lilian and my mother, whom I had expected to suspend public hostilities during Esmond's visit, were absorbed in being nasty to each other. I slid into my chair.

'I wish you wouldn't leave that bucket of dirty nappies in the bathroom, dear,' my mother was saying. 'It's not very nice, is it? And of course so unhygienic.'

'But there's nowhere else to put them,' Lilian said, staring at her plate.

'Why not in the nursery? So much more convenient for everyone.'

'But it wouldn't be good for Alice. They've got very little defence against infection at this age.'

My mother tittered. 'But the bucket has a lid.'

'Even so, one couldn't be sure.' Lilian looked up. 'I know – I could put it in the other bedroom. The one we never use.'

'No, dear. I don't think that would be suitable at all.' My mother showed her teeth for a second, and then launched a surprise attack from another quarter. 'While I remember – was that your milk saucepan I found on the draining-board last night?'

'I'm afraid I didn't have time to wash it. Alice started crying.'

As Lilian was speaking, Alice began to cry once more. Lilian pushed back her chair and almost ran from the room.

'When isn't she crying?' my mother asked of no one in particular. 'It's wind, of course. It does help if one winds babies after one has fed them. Still, one can't expect old heads on young shoulders, can one?'

I tried to finish my toast; the crumbs clung to my throat and after a couple of mouthfuls I gave up the attempt. The others drank tea. The crying stopped. As if this were a signal she had been waiting for, my mother let out her breath and cocked her head.

'So. I'm going into town this morning. What have you boys got planned for today?'

Esmond and I looked at each other. He shrugged.

'Now what about those books in the schoolroom,' my mother suggested. 'Weren't you two going to build some shelves? Why don't you start measuring up or whatever you need to do.' She paused. 'And don't worry about the cost. I'll pay for the wood and everything else you need.'

She sat back, waiting for gratitude. Esmond concentrated on folding his napkin.

'Thank you, Mother,' I said.

'By the way,' she continued, looking at Esmond, 'I have to go out to dinner this evening. Did Thomas tell you? I promised Aunt Ada I'd help with the archdeacon. He's new, and his wife's said to be rather a trial. But I'll leave a casserole in the oven.'

'Oh good,' I said. My mother's casserole used to be Esmond's second favourite dish.

After breakfast, Esmond and I went into the schoolroom with a tape measure. Esmond sat smoking in the one armchair while I tried to measure the wall we proposed to line with shelves. We heard my mother banging around the house. In a while she put her head into the room.

'Do you want anything from Kinghampton, boys?'

'No, thanks,' I said. 'We're still planning.'

'I shouldn't be too long. I'm just going to have my hair done.'

She glanced at Esmond and went away. A moment later we heard her starting the car.

'At bloody last,' Esmond said. He threw his cigarette into the empty fireplace and stood up. 'I want to have a word with Lilian.'

'If it's about the money, I shouldn't bother. She

wouldn't let me use it for the business. And I only needed a few hundred.'

'This is different. This is an emergency.'

I shook my head. 'You don't know her.'

'If you don't ask, you don't get. Come on, Rumpy.'

'But there's nothing I can do.'

'Yes there is. I want you to go in first in case she's feeding Alice or something. Then leave us alone.'

In the event we met Lilian in the hall. It seemed that Alice was asleep and Lilian wanted some tea. Esmond gave me a wink and followed her into the kitchen. Despite everything he had to cope with, there was a jauntiness about him, a gallantry: like Robin Hood, he refused to be cowed.

I went on upstairs. I didn't want them to feel I might be eavesdropping. On the landing I had an idea. I opened the door of the death room. The stale smell of my dead father swept over me. Breathing through my mouth, I went in – automatically on tiptoe; I am not sure whom I did not want to hear me. The wardrobe was on the wall on the left, with the door to the big built-in cupboard beside it.

The wardrobe door had its key still in the lock. When I twisted the handle, the door swung open. I jumped back; as I did so a furtive little man darted to the side; and as I gasped I solved the mystery. No mystery at all, just a long mirror on the back of the door.

My father's jackets and suits packed the wardrobe like a frozen file of soldiers. My mother had draped them with sheets and old dressing-gowns to keep off the dust. I searched the sides, floor and top of the wardrobe. I even looked behind it. With no success. If

Esmond had told me the truth, which I had no reason to doubt, he must have hidden the acid among my father's clothes.

I went rapidly through all the pockets, not a pleasant job, but failed to find the drugs. I made myself try again, paying particular attention to the linings. I was sweating, the dust made me cough and I hated the grime that coated my fingers. As I was exploring a sports jacket, the back of my hand brushed against the tails of the evening coat beside it. My knuckles nudged something hard on the other side of the material. I felt the outline of a small rectangular tin with something softer above it. I had not realized that a tail coat could have a pocket in the tails.

Inside the pocket was a plain brown paper bag containing several dozen little tablets. They were lying loose like the sweets we used to buy by weight from Atkinsons. I took out one tablet and placed it on the palm of my hand. It was extraordinary that this small orange disc had such power to change a person's life; the cause bore no obvious relationship to the effect.

Oh Jesus. Someone was running up the stairs. I pushed the bag back into the pocket and shut the wardrobe door. I edged towards the open door of the room. Lilian appeared on the landing. Her face was white and her eyes were wide behind her glasses.

'What is it?' I said.

She ignored me and went into the nursery. I came out of the death room, shut the door very quietly and tiptoed towards the head of the stairs.

'Thomas,' Lilian whispered behind me.

I turned. She beckoned me into the nursery. I tried

to think up an innocent reason for my being in the death room.

'She's all right, thank God,' she said, nodding towards the cot. 'For a moment I thought he might have done something. Or *you* might have. But you wouldn't, would you?'

'What are you talking about?'

'Esmond, of course,' she hissed, still whispering because Alice was asleep. 'He's mad. He tried to make me lend him Alice's money. And when I wouldn't, he threatened to harm her. So what's going on?'

'I'm sorry, I don't understand.' My hands clenched inside my pockets.

'Don't be stupid.' Lilian glared at me. 'He tells you everything. It's something to do with drugs, isn't it?'

'Well – in a way, I suppose. Yes.'

She poked a long white forefinger into my chest. 'Alice is your child, too. So you're going to tell me. Why does he need all that money?'

The fingernail was like the tip of a knife. Lilian had summoned her strength from the dark place inside her. I tried to justify the surrender I knew was inevitable. What did it matter if I told her? She already knew about the dealing. And if she knew the truth she might realize how badly Esmond needed her help. I explained about the acid the police had seized and about the criminals who wanted to make an example of Esmond *pour encourager les autres*.

'Well, that's his problem, isn't it?' Lilian said. 'Anyway, it's about time he settled down and did something sensible with his life. That's why I don't want him to be Alice's godfather.'

The change of subject confused me. In a sense, however, the choice of godparents was only another aspect of the same subject – Alice's well-being – which had obsessed Lilian in so many forms long before our daughter's birth.

'I know you want Esmond. But I just won't let him after this. He's not fit for it. I'm going to ask Henry instead.'

'All right,' I said, yielding a small point in the hope of gaining a larger. 'I suppose a clergyman would be very suitable, and it would please Aunt Ada. But what about lending Esmond the money? He'd pay you back as soon as he's sold his flat.'

'No. You should have heard him, Thomas. He was threatening us. Not you – Alice and me.'

'I'm sure . . . I'm sure he didn't mean to. What did he say?'

She shrugged. 'He didn't put it in so many words. He's not stupid. He made nasty little hints instead.'

'Obviously he's a bit upset at present. Fifteen hundred pounds is a lot of money.'

'He told me it was a thousand.'

'I expect he didn't want to bother you with all the details.'

'And how's he going to get the rest of the money? Sell some more drugs?'

'Well, among other things, yes.'

'He's got some at Finisterre?'

'Ah – yes.'

'He swore he didn't have anything here. I don't want that stuff anywhere near my baby.'

I couldn't understand her concern. I was tempted to

remind her of the circumstances in which Alice had been conceived. Our child was an acid baby.

'It's all right,' I said. 'There's nothing to worry about. He put them in the death room. They're in the wardrobe.'

'Keep your voice down, can't you? Listen, Thomas, I don't like him in this house. He means trouble.'

'Oh no, surely not. Anyway, this is his home.'

Alice had begun to wriggle. Three seconds later she began to cry.

'Now look what you've done.'

'Sorry,' I said.

'It's incredible, she can sense I'm upset,' Lilian muttered. 'You'd better go.'

I backed out of the nursery and shut the door. I heard the key turning in the lock and knew that I was excluded. I knew, too, that Esmond would be waiting for me downstairs. I took my hands out of my pockets and unclenched them. I looked at the orange tablet glowing like an angry spot on the palm of my left hand.

When I went down, Esmond was back in the school-room armchair.

'Did she tell you?' he asked.

I nodded. 'I'm sorry. I tried to make her change her mind.'

'The bitch,' he said softly.

'What will you do?'

'I've nearly run out of options.' He got up. 'At least I can trust you, eh? That's something.'

'Of course you can.'

'Come and keep watch.'

For an instant we looked at each other. Every now

and then a friendship reaches a point where the roads could easily divide; we had just passed such a point and we were still together. Esmond smiled at me, and we went upstairs to my mother's bedroom. He found her jewellery roll in a drawer of the dressing table.

'I think she put most of her stuff in the bank,' I said. 'She's getting worried about burglars.'

'Jesus, there's nothing left worth taking.'

But Esmond pocketed a few rings. Then we went downstairs and into the study. He sat down at the desk and began to pull open the drawers.

'Sooner or later she'll notice the rings,' I said. 'Next week, next month.'

'Maybe I won't have to use them. It's a risk I have to take.'

He continued rummaging through the drawers; he took nothing out except an unused cheque book and an envelope containing last month's bank statement. My mother would have the current cheque book in her handbag.

'There used to be a folder of share certificates and things like that. And the passbooks for the deposit accounts. And a big gold watch with a chain.'

'My father's,' I said. 'Perhaps she put them all in the bank.'

'Oh, Christ.' Esmond glanced at the bank statement and then at me. I had never seen such despair on his face. He put his elbows on the desk and his head between his hands.

'Couldn't you forge a cheque? You could practise her signature first.'

He did not look up. 'Maybe.'

'You could take a couple of cheques from the back of the new cheque book. How much is in the account?'

'About three hundred. But the bank might query a large cheque, especially if it put her in the red.'

'Well, every little bit helps, doesn't it?'

'Oh Christ, Rumpy! Don't you see? It'll be pointing a finger at me.' Nevertheless, he tore out three cheques and stuffed them in his pocket. 'Come on,' he said. 'I can't stand this place. What we need is liquid inspiration.'

We had lunch at a pub in a village further down the coast. Esmond found the liquid in abundance, if not the inspiration. The saloon bar was almost empty; the pub was the sort of place that only came alive for three months in the summer. We didn't talk much. There was nothing to say.

We left when the landlord made us go. We got into the car. Esmond stared at the sea. The day was full of unexpected gusts of wind, more like March than May. As we sat there, it started to rain.

'Can't you sell the car?' I said.

'I'll probably have to. But I won't get what it's worth. I don't have a logbook for it. Shit, shit, shit!'

Esmond started the engine and drove noisily out of the car park. On the way home the Morris Minor wandered across the road. Several times I clutched my seat and closed my eyes.

'I'm going to go abroad,' Esmond said. 'It's the best chance. I'll raise as much money as I can, take what's left of the acid and go.'

I blinked at him. 'When?'

'I'll leave Finisterre tomorrow and England on

Monday or Tuesday. I can't go sooner – I need to get to a bank, and a pawnbroker's and a jeweller's. Oh, and sell the car. Thank God I brought my passport. Light me a fag, will you?'

I reached for his jacket, which was on the seat behind us, and found a packet of Senior Service and some matches. 'Did you know this is your last one?' I asked, but he didn't reply. I passed him the cigarette. 'Where will you go?'

'Ireland, maybe, for a start. Or France. I'd like to go to the States but you need money for that.'

We drove on. My eyes filled with tears.

'Anywhere but here,' Esmond said. And he glanced at my face, sending a wave of alcohol towards me. 'But one day, it'll all blow over. You'll see.'

A moment later we reached Ulvercombe. During the last few miles the rain had become steadily heavier. The car dawdled past the church and The Forley Arms. Esmond stopped outside Atkinsons and staggered into the shop to buy some cigarettes. He left the car in the middle of the road. Nothing much wider than a motorbike could have got past us.

I peered in both directions to see if anything was coming. This sort of situation always makes me very uncomfortable; it is so unpleasant when people get cross. It was thoughtless of Esmond – I was going to feel anxious whether or not a car needed to pass ours. I stared through the windscreen, past the red rectangle of the telephone box which marked the edge of the village. Beyond it lay Finisterre and Blackberry Water, Ulvercombe Mouth and the sea. There was a pram outside the phone box, a purple one.

The door opened and Esmond climbed into the car.

'See that pram?' I said. 'I think it's Alice's.'

'Really?'

'Should we offer them a lift?'

'I've nothing against Alice. It's just the company she keeps.' He sang in a loud, tuneless voice the first verse of 'Mary had a little lamb'.

'Lilian's going to get soaked if she walks back in this weather.'

'Let her.' Esmond started the engine. 'That's her problem, not mine. Anyway, we haven't got room for the pram.'

At a quarter to seven that evening my mother swept into the sitting room. She stood just inside the door and waited for compliments. She was permed and bathed, dressed and perfumed. The dress was new, bought in honour of the archdeacon and his wife.

'You look nice,' I said at last.

Esmond said nothing; Lilian was in the nursery with Alice.

'I promised I'd go early and help. Poor Ada finds occasions like this very heavy going.'

'I hope you have a nice time.'

'I'm just going to help Ada, dear. I don't imagine it will be fun. Now – the casserole will be ready in about an hour. There should be more than enough for the three of you. All you need do is boil the potatoes and lay the table. The potatoes are already peeled. They're in the big saucepan with the wooden knob. Have you got that, dear?'

'Yes, Mother.'

In the event only two of us sat down to the casserole, which was full of stringy slabs of beef and pale, mushy objects that had once been root vegetables. Esmond muttered 'Jesus wept' when he saw it. We ate mainly potatoes and gravy, washing them down with whisky and water. There was spotted dick for pudding but at Esmond's suggestion I wrapped most of it in an old newspaper.

Lilian wisely abstained from the food my mother had prepared. While we were eating, she made herself a boiled egg and some toast. While the egg was boiling she laid a tray.

'I hope you're not going upstairs for my sake,' Esmond said.

She glanced at him, her face catlike and scornful, and said to me, 'I want to keep an eye on Alice.'

'Is there something wrong with her?' I asked.

'She got dreadfully cold when we went out this afternoon. I think she might be going down with something.'

'Shall I bring you up a drink afterwards?'

She asked for a mug of cocoa made with milk. Esmond said something about mobile milk bars, which she also ignored.

'I think I might sleep in the nursery tonight,' Lilian said as she picked up her tray. 'Just in case Alice needs me. The bed's made up.'

I shut the door behind her.

'She's scared,' Esmond said, and he smiled.

After we had finished eating, I put the milk on for the cocoa and took the spotted dick out to the dustbin. When I came back Esmond was standing over the Aga with a cigarette drooping from his mouth.

'As near as damnit boiled over,' he said. 'Where've you been?'

'Sorry. I dropped it, you see, and I had to . . .'

'Dropped what?'

'The spotted dick. And I –'

'Oh never mind.'

I made the cocoa in the Lone Ranger mug and took it up to Lilian. I washed up while the coffee was brewing. After that nothing much happened for over an hour. Esmond and I sat in the sitting room. He smoked a joint – the first time he had done it in there. I had rarely felt so unhappy; sorrow and worry made me ill. We didn't talk about the future. Esmond didn't want to talk about anything. He sat there, smoking and staring at his hands, as if brooding over his fingers offered a possible solution.

Suddenly he looked up. 'I'm going to brush up my skills as a forger.'

'Can I help?'

He shook his head and stood up with the joint still smouldering in his hand. There were two vertical lines between his eyebrows.

'I'll do it in my room. Just to be on the safe side.'

On his way to the door, he stumbled against the arm of the sofa.

'Are you sure it wouldn't be better to leave it till the morning? Till you're fresher?'

He swung round. 'Don't preach at me, Rumpy!' he roared. 'I'm not in the mood.'

He stormed out of the room. I didn't move. His anger paralysed me. Esmond was never, ever angry with me. I heard him on the stairs and I heard the slam of his bedroom door. It's nothing personal, I told myself; he doesn't mean it; it's just that he's a little upset; he doesn't realize how hard I'm trying to help.

I curled up in the chair and hugged my knees. I must have stayed there for at least ten minutes. For most of that time I managed to keep my mind out of focus, which blurred the outlines of the misery I felt. Suddenly it occurred to me that Esmond might need me, that he would think I was sulking. Why was I wasting time that I might be able to spend with him?

I went quietly up the stairs. All the bedroom doors were shut. The house was so silent I might have been alone in it. Now I was here, I lacked the courage to disturb Esmond. I went into the room that I shared with Lilian. I left the door open and sat on my bed. I tried to read but my eyes kept drifting from the page to the landing. I could see the head of the stairs and the door to the death room. Once I thought I heard someone whimpering: a sexless and ageless sound, so faint that it might have been the wind.

Then a door opened. There were footsteps on the landing and Lilian appeared in the doorway of our room. Her hair was a tangle, as though she had run her fingers through it, this way and that way, time and time again. I waited for her to speak. She opened her mouth, shut it and opened it again. All the time she frowned at me, not with displeasure but with surprise, as though she had expected to see someone else sitting on my bed.

'Lilian? Are you OK?'

Her eyes were black and gleaming like drops of wet ink. 'It's happening again,' she said. 'Stephen said it might.'

'Stephen's dead.'

'What's that got to do with it? He had a word for it. A flash – a flash . . .'

I stood up, slowly so as not to alarm her.

'He said it could happen at any time. Oh God, I wish it would stop.'

Her eyes slid down from my face, down my body, down my legs. The carpet seemed to become an object of fascination for her. It was not a nice carpet – brown and green flowers repeated themselves with dreary regularity across a pink background. Her mouth opened again. It made an O of wonder.

'Lilian? Lilian?'

She appeared not to hear me, but transferred her attention to the chair. 'Did you know that wood moves?'

'No.'

'Perhaps it's just the wood they use for furniture.' Her nails raked up her thigh – once, twice, three times. 'Yes, I'm worried about something,' she added. 'But I can't remember what.'

'Is Alice OK?' I said.

'Alice?' Her voice rose from a near-whisper to a near-scream. '*Alice*? What's wrong with her?'

She turned and blundered out of the room. I followed. On the landing she stopped so suddenly that I cannoned into her. Grimalkin was sitting at the head of the stairs. And Esmond was standing in the doorway of the nursery with one hand holding the door and the other resting on the jamb. The room behind him was dark and silent. He smiled at us.

'Oh there you are,' he said, still smiling. 'I thought I heard Alice crying. What's up?'

'Lilian says she's having an acid flashback. Is that what you call it?'

The house was quiet. Even the wind had dropped. I thought Lilian had stopped breathing. Esmond smiled and smiled. His face was alive with amusement.

'Let's go into the death room,' he said. 'We don't want to wake the baby, do we?'

Nineteen

The wires were singing.

Esmond decided that we should show Alice some of our celebrated coastline and introduce her to a few of our picturesque villages. On our way back to Finisterre, we would stop in Kinghampton and have lunch at The Mermaid Hotel. When he announced this decision, the four of us were in the sitting room; we were drinking cups of coffee and pretending to one another that everything between us was pleasant and easy.

'Not a very nice day for a drive, darling,' Bronwen remarked. 'And it's going to get worse.'

'That's the point,' Esmond said. 'We want to show Alice what this part of the world is really like. It has its own beauty – eh, Thomas? But it's nothing like the postcards, and it's not what the tourists see. This is a savage place.'

'*Savage*?' Alice said. She didn't want to look at Esmond, I noticed, not since their conversation after breakfast.

'It's a wreckers' coast. They used to set up false lights to lure the merchant ships on to the rocks.' He reached for his cigarettes, and added with relish: 'Kegs of brandy and blood on the beach. There were a lot of wrecks at Ulvercombe Mouth.'

Alice glanced at me, as if for confirmation. I nodded.

'As a matter of fact,' Esmond went on, 'your mother

knew a good deal about the wreckers. Didn't she, Thomas? Haven't you still got some of Lilian's books?'

'Possibly. But not in my room. There might be some in one of the tea chests.'

'Thomas has at least a dozen tea chests full of books,' Esmond said to Alice. 'They're in one of the attics. I'm surprised the floor can cope. It's a total waste of space.'

While Esmond talked, Bronwen's eyes roved between our faces, lingering on Esmond's. I think she suspected something had happened. Love can make fools of people; it can also make them extraordinarily acute.

Fifteen minutes later we wrapped ourselves in coats and trooped out to the garage.

'I'll just reverse her out,' Esmond said.

The garage was small and the Volvo was big. Esmond squeezed between the off-side of the car and the wall. The rest of us watched. I noticed one or two damp patches on the concrete floor between the near-side and the opposite wall. The dampness struck me as curious – Esmond had laid the concrete floor himself, and it appeared to give him great pleasure. 'Dry as a bone now,' he had said only a few days ago. 'Amazing what a bit of concrete will do.' In that case, perhaps the damp marks were in fact partly dried-out footprints left by someone who had visited the garage earlier in the morning.

The starter motor whirred. The engine didn't fire. Esmond tried again, without success. The battery sounded strong enough to my inexpert ears. He tried three more times and then got out of the car.

'Sorry about this,' he said. 'It's probably the damp. You might as well go back inside while I take a look.'

The rest of us trailed back into the house. Bronwen said she would do some vegetables for supper, or possibly for lunch if the car wouldn't start; Alice offered to help her, and they both disappeared into the kitchen.

On impulse I pushed open the study door. The room was calm and quiet. It smelled of polish and tobacco. Apart from the telephone and an ashtray, the desk top was clear. I looked at the cupboard on the left of the fireplace. It was about four feet high and it filled the width of the alcove. It was as old as Finisterre itself.

We do so much on impulse. And as we do, we divide ourselves into two people: the one who does the unexpected; and the one who watches, puzzled and often worried.

Leaving the door wide open, I went round the desk and tugged at the handle of the second drawer down on the right. The drawer moved silently towards me. It still contained the bunch of keys. They were all little keys – belonging to boxes, drawers and cupboards. Some of them still had the yellowing labels attached to them with rotting pieces of string. One label said *Study Cupboard* in my mother's writing.

The house was silent. I heard the faint whine of the Volvo's starter motor as I unlocked the cupboard door. The air rifle was on the top shelf. There were no slugs with it, or at least none that I could see, but that didn't matter. I didn't touch the gun. I closed the cupboard door but did not relock it, and returned the keys to the desk.

The hall felt like a sanctuary: when I reached it, the two parts of me, the observer and the observed, slid back together. I went into the sitting room and picked up one of Bronwen's magazines. I stared at the cover: a woman with bright red lips and two rows of white, preternaturally regular teeth. The front door slammed and I heard Esmond's footsteps striding down the hall. He came into the sitting room.

'Well, it's not damp that's the problem,' he said. 'I think the fault's in the fuel system.'

'Can you mend it?'

'I'd have to take the bloody thing apart to find out.' He held up his hands, palms outwards; they were streaked with oil. 'I'm going to get someone else to do it. Life's too short.'

'So we'll just have to stay here?'

'Yes. We'll have to entertain ourselves. We could play cards or something.' He bent down, and I smelled oil and tobacco and felt his breath on my ear. 'And you'll always play by the house rules, won't you, Rumpy? As I said, life's too short.'

He smiled at me and went away. The wires sang a little higher.

By lunchtime the wind was rattling the windows.

'It's going to be a bad one,' Esmond said. 'Wreckers' weather, eh? Not very pleasant.'

Afterwards I went upstairs to the nursery. I shut the door, rolled back the carpet and lifted the floorboard. I didn't want to listen, not this time. I pushed up the sleeve of my jersey and put my hand into one of the spaces between the rafters. My fingers touched a cold, round tin which I pulled out. The tin was coated with dust. As always, its weight took me by surprise.

When the room was tidy again, I sat down and cleaned the tin with a paper handkerchief. As I rubbed, the familiar blue lid emerged, with its drawing of a wasp in the middle. '500 ELEY WASP': 500 stings, and – potentially, in an ideal world – 500 cats prematurely deceased. I opened the tin and stirred the soft, silvery lead pellets with my forefinger. This had been my reserve supply. When Esmond confiscated the gun, he had also taken the tin of slugs I had been using; he might have hidden them or he might have thrown them away. But he hadn't asked if I had any more slugs. So I hadn't told him.

There was a knock on my door. I stood up, almost spilling the pellets. I tucked the tin between the arm and the seat of my chair.

'Come in.'

Alice came in; I was expecting it to be her, because neither Esmond nor Bronwen would have knocked.

'Thomas,' she said, 'You haven't seen my key, have you?'

'What key?'

'The one for my bedroom door. It was there last night.'

'You can try mine if you want.'

She looked down at the lock. 'It's not there either.'

I stood up and we went on to the landing. The keys had gone from all the doors on the first floor.

'That's odd,' I said. 'Were they there yesterday?'

'Mine was.'

I led the way back to the nursery. Alice sat down in my armchair. She folded her hands across her stomach.

'If one of us mentioned it to Esmond,' I said slowly, 'it might seem as if . . .'

Alice cut me off with a wave of her hand. 'Yes, I know.'

'Perhaps you could wedge a chair?'

'Am I making too much of this? I know pregnant women are meant to have strange fancies . . .' She pushed back her hair with her fingers. 'But this is ridiculous.'

'I don't know,' I said. 'I just don't know.'

'But you've known him all your life. You must have some idea what he's like.'

I stood by the window and looked down on the garden. The bushes in the shrubbery swayed in the wind, there were dead leaves on the grass and grey clouds streamed up from a grey sea. I felt that circumstances were battering me and harrying me, pushing me into unknown territory. This was my window, my house, my garden.

'He's been in prison,' I said. 'I think Bronwen has, too.'

'What for?'

'If I'm right she killed a boyfriend in a fit of jealousy. Poked a skewer in his eye. It was probably manslaughter.'

'Oh God.' Alice's hands clung together. 'And Esmond? What did he do?'

'He was involved in a big VAT fraud. That was about ten years ago. And they got him in the sixties for selling LSD and for theft – he'd stolen some things from my mother. That was when she decided he wasn't fit to be a member of the family. Sounds very Victorian, doesn't it?'

'Sounds perfectly natural to me,' Alice said.

'I think it hurt him terribly. This was his home, and she used to treat him as a son. He had expectations, as they say. In fact at one time she liked him better than me.'

'Was he ever physically violent? That's the important thing. Have you known him hurt people as well as cats?'

I shrugged. I looked at the garden, not Alice. 'He never hurt me.'

'But he hurt other people?' Alice said, goading me onwards. 'Are you implying that?'

'Sometimes. There was a boy at school, I remember. But it wasn't sadism, or anything like that. I shouldn't like you to get that idea. Esmond always has a good reason for whatever he does.'

'*Good*?' Alice snorted. 'Good for him, you mean.'

'That's what most people mean when they say they've got good reason to do something.'

'Something he said to me this morning made me wonder if he's ever had good reason to kill people.'

I said nothing.

'Well?' she prompted.

'It's true that people have died,' I said slowly. 'His sister, for example. Baby Lizzy. He wouldn't have been asked to live here if she'd been alive. My mother hated babies.'

'So what happened to his sister?'

'She was very young. They'd probably call it cot death nowadays. I saw the coffin. It was tiny. Like a toy.'

'I'm sorry.' She must have sensed my distress. 'Look, why don't you sit down?'

I huddled on the window-seat. Bronwen came round the side of the house. She was carrying a huge basket

357

of logs. I thought how strong and muscular her arms must be. She did not look up at my window.

'There've been other times. Other people.' I looked at Alice. 'Or perhaps there were – I don't know. How could I? Let's not talk about it. Please don't ask me to. It won't do any good to you or me. Anyway, there was never any proof.'

'My mother?' she said, her voice breathless. 'Is that what you mean? What did he do to my mother?'

Esmond put his arms round Lilian. That's what he did when she started to scream. When he touched her, she stopped screaming. Her pupils were so dilated that the eyes looked black. She became rigid, like a waxwork or a mannequin. He manoeuvred her into the death room.

'Now, it's all right,' he said to her. 'Don't panic. Just follow the instructions.'

I spoke without thinking. 'And all manner of things shall be well.'

Alice began to cry in the darkened nursery. Lilian groaned and tried to wrench herself out of Esmond's arms.

'Don't worry,' Esmond whispered to her. 'Thomas will look after Alice. After all, he's her daddy.'

'No, let me go to her,' Lilian said.

'Soon. Be patient.'

Her glasses fell off. Esmond trod on them by accident as he pushed her into the death room.

'Bring me her handbag,' he said to me. 'Then do something about that bloody baby.'

'But Esmond –'

As I spoke I heard Lilian saying, 'What? *Blood*? My baby's bleeding?'

Ignoring her, Esmond lowered his voice and said: 'She won't change her mind afterwards. Because she'll know that if she does, this might happen again. And again.'

'That's not what I meant.'

'Stop my baby bleeding!' Lilian screamed. 'Give her to me!'

One of her hands appeared on the edge of the door. Esmond swore. The clawlike nails scrabbled on the painted wood. She shouted the words 'blood' and 'baby' over and over again. I watched the blood beneath the skin retreating as her grip tightened.

'You stupid girl,' Esmond said.

He peeled the fingers back. Her voice was hoarse by now. The stress had stripped away its genteel modulations, revealing the ugliness and the shrillness beneath. Then the hand had gone, and so had Esmond. The door slammed. I saw scratch marks on the wood: I was sure I did; but when I looked for them later, they had gone.

'*Blood*,' I heard, but the word was made almost tolerable by the wooden barrier between it and me. '*Baby*.'

In the meantime, Alice's wails had acquired the penetrating see-saw quality one associates with the emergency services. I closed the nursery door to lessen the volume and ran into the bedroom I shared with Lilian. Her handbag was missing from its usual place on the dressing table.

I searched for it with growing desperation – by the

bed, in the wardrobe, on the chair. At length I went back to the nursery and switched on the light. The wails were deafening. I saw the bag at once, on the table at the end of the cot.

I saw Grimalkin too: she was crouching under the table and presumably savouring the joys of being in a forbidden place. We were both trespassers in this room but she looked at me with disdain as though I were the only intruder. I spat at her.

'Just you wait,' I said. 'You foul creature. You sodding succubus.'

The wires sang and my head ached. I snatched the bag. My movement dislodged the Lone Ranger mug, which was beside the bag on the table. The mug fell to the floor but did not break. The baby cried.

Shaking with anger, I crossed the landing. The death-room door was closed. I tapped on it. A moment later, Esmond took the handbag from me. I couldn't see Lilian but I heard her sobbing.

'For Christ's sake get Alice downstairs,' Esmond murmured. 'Somewhere Lilian can't hear her.'

'No!' Lilian shouted suddenly in that strange new voice of hers. And I don't think she was talking to me or Esmond. 'Don't put her there, you fool. There's blood on the stones, can't you see?'

Esmond sighed and closed the door. In the nursery Grimalkin was still beside the cot. This time we ignored each other. Alice lay on her back, covered by a mound of blankets. Her face was red. Her eyes were screwed shut. She was still screaming. I had not believed so small a body could contain so much anger.

'Hush,' I said softly. 'Please hush.'

Alice appeared not to hear me. I leant over the cot and touched her gingerly on the shoulder. It had no effect. I hooked my hands under her armpits and yanked her up. I miscalculated the necessary force because I assumed that she would be much heavier than in fact she was. She shot up, her head swinging first backwards then forwards. The crying stopped, probably from surprise. I held her against my shoulder, as I had seen Lilian do, and patted her back.

Two things happened simultaneously: Alice belched, and from her bottom came a rumble. I noticed that below the waist she was very wet. She started to cry once more.

'*No*,' Lilian shouted from the death room. '*No, no, no.*' The words were evenly spaced like blows from a hammer.

I carried Alice down the stairs. I didn't know what to do. Everything was so unpleasant I could have wept. The wires sang, quietly at first, like the dull booming sound the sea sometimes makes; but with each step the singing rose in pitch. Despite the distractions, I remembered what Esmond wanted me to do: to get Alice out of Lilian's earshot. I guessed that he would persuade Lilian to write him a cheque for the thousand pounds, in return for which she would be reunited with Alice. But if Lilian could actually hear Alice crying, she would not be able to concentrate on anything else. Not in her state of mind. In her wrong mind.

The kitchen was at the opposite end of the house from the death room. Also it would be warm. I remembered my mother saying that you had to keep babies warm. I marched down the hall with Alice shrieking in my ear and Lilian shouting overhead. I was wondering how one changed a nappy.

Suddenly the shrieks and shouts stopped. For a second the house was silent. Then the silence was split in two by a long, jagged ring on the doorbell.

In my head the wires sang higher and higher. I don't know how long I stood staring down the hall at the front door. Alice was a moist, warm bundle on my shoulder. The bell rang once more. Esmond appeared at the head of the stairs.

'You'll have to answer it,' he whispered. 'Lilian's out, got it? You're babysitting.'

He ducked out of sight. Still carrying Alice, I walked slowly towards the door. As I reached it the bell rang for the third time. I put the Yale on the latch and opened the door.

Outside it wasn't quite dark. The dull grey twilight outlined four shadowy people. There was no sign of a car. The visitors, all strangers, moved towards the door, into the light that spilled out from the hall. Before I could say anything they pushed past me, two on each side, into the house.

'Mr Penmarsh, is it?' said one of them, a tall man in a leather car-coat. He smelled of dead animals and whisky. 'Mr Thomas Penmarsh?'

There were two other men, younger than the first, and both with drooping moustaches like South American revolutionaries. The fourth member of the party was a woman in her forties. She sported a moustache too, but it was less luxuriant than her colleagues'.

'We're police officers, sir.'

The tall man said a name – his own? It sounded like

'Heaven' or 'Hebburn'. And he thrust a sheet of paper in front of me. I couldn't read it because he was talking to me, and Alice began to cry again.

'Upstairs,' Heaven-or-Hebburn said.

I was finding it hard to breath. The woman, who in profile had a face resembling a cleaver, prised Alice away from me. Alice cried more desperately than ever. I walked up the stairs with the tall man on my left and one of the moustaches on my right; the others remained in the hall. The tall man was telling me something but I couldn't hear the words because of Alice's wailing and the singing wires. I wanted Esmond to come and help me but he was no longer there. I heard a mysterious pounding in the distance, like hysterical tom-toms from the depths of the jungle.

The nursery was in darkness, and its door slightly ajar; I had left the light on and the door wide open.

'Is that a pair of glasses?' the moustache asked, pointing at the broken glass and twisted wire on the landing floor.

I nodded.

'Later.' Heaven-or-Hebburn opened the death-room door. 'We'll start with the wardrobe and that bloody racket.'

In the death room someone was drumming on wood. Where was Esmond? Alice cried. It was the cleaver-woman's fault.

'Open that cupboard,' snapped the tall man.

I looked blankly at him. The moustache stepped forward and pulled back the bolt. The door burst open.

'*Jesus*,' one of them said, and whistled.

The two men moved forward; I moved back.

Between their heavy shoulders I saw the opening of the cupboard, dark like an animal's lair. And there was the animal itself: white-faced and whimpering, it crouched on all-fours, with long and stick-like limbs, the black eyes gleaming behind a matted fringe of hair. Lilian, my wife. Now the wires were so taut I could hardly hear their singing.

Alice shrieked with rage, as though the cleaver-woman had stuck a pin in her. Lilian charged out of the cupboard. She slipped between the men. The younger one tried to stop her. She slashed him across the cheek with her nails. He yelled and threw up his arm. She darted past me and through the door. The two men followed, pushing me before them on to the landing like a piece of driftwood on a wave.

As we moved, I saw Grimalkin streaking across the landing from the nursery. The cat was fleeing from Esmond, I thought, so Esmond was in the nursery. Or was the familiar running after her mistress? Grimalkin and Lilian converged on the head of the stairs. Alice cried, and her voice beckoned Lilian like a siren's.

Grimalkin reached the stairs a second before Lilian. Their collision had the dreamlike inevitability that slapstick shares with tragedy. Grimalkin wound her furry body around Lilian's right ankle. The cat squealed.

Lilian stumbled. And then she was no longer a mother going to her baby. She was no longer human, no longer a witch or a wife, no longer even a distressed animal trapped in her wrong mind. Instead she was a falling doll, turning in the air, a toy acrobat.

The back of Lilian's head hit one of the treads with a snap. I didn't see the impact of bone on wood. But I heard the snap, and I heard it again every time I pulled the trigger of the air gun.

I looked down from the head of the stairs. Lilian lay face-up, half on the stairs and half in the hall. Her body twitched once as though a charge of electricity had passed through it. After that she was still.

The big man in the leather coat pushed me aside and ran down the stairs. Alice cried in the cleaver-woman's arms. Beside me the younger man had two streaks of blood on his cheek.

'Cover her face,' I whispered.

Suddenly I saw that Esmond was standing on the other side of the scratched man, but a little behind him. I was relieved to see him, yet also worried for his sake. *Run*, I wanted to say, *run while you can*.

The man in the leather coat glanced up from the body. 'There's Chard,' he said. 'Get him.'

'You little Judas,' Esmond said, ignoring the hand on his arm, the other people and the talking and the shouting and the screaming. He and I might have been alone in the house.

He should have trusted me. Lilian was his Judas.

'Cover her face,' I said. And I turned away from Lilian, from Alice, from Esmond.

Twenty

I looked at Alice, who sat head bowed in my armchair, and I hoped she would not start crying. A door closed on the landing. Two pairs of footsteps went down the stairs. Esmond and Bronwen had come up to their bedroom about twenty minutes earlier for one of their afternoon naps; and now they were leaving.

'The police said they'd had an anonymous tip-off,' I went on. 'And their colleagues in London had already asked them to keep an eye on Esmond. So the local drug squad decided to make a bust. Those people knew just what they were doing. They went straight to the wardrobe, straight to my father's tail coat. The only recognizable fingerprints were Esmond's. And when they searched him, they found the cheques and rings as well.'

'Did they ever find out who phoned them?'

'A woman with an educated voice. That's what they said.'

'*Lilian.*' Alice hesitated. 'My mother. I mustn't forget to call her that, must I? After all, she did it for my sake.'

'It was never actually proved to be Lilian. On the other hand, who else could it have been?'

Alice said nothing. It occurred to me that I did not find her silences uncomfortable, another point in her favour. She made it easier for me by not showing her face.

'The judge made out that Esmond was morally responsible for Lilian's death. That's what my mother told me. You see, Lilian wasn't having a flashback. They found traces of LSD in what was left of her cocoa. So the prosecution argued that Esmond had given it to her without her knowing, that he deliberately set out to terrorize her into giving him a loan. His defence was that she must have stolen the acid, and that in any case she and her brother had introduced him to drugs in the first place.'

'Turned him on,' as Esmond used to say. What an absurd phrase. It made us sound like light-switches.

'Esmond said she was having a bad trip, and he was just trying to help her. He blamed the drug squad for Lilian's death. Said they'd frightened her. That didn't go down very well.'

'Your mother told you all this? But didn't you know? Weren't you a witness at the trial?'

'I wasn't at the trial. The police questioned me beforehand, and I did my best. But at the time I was hardly alive. They made me like a zombie.'

In the daytime, Librium and Valium and (when things were very bad, and the wires sang) Largactil; and in the long, comatose nights Seconal and Sodium Amytal. Even after I came out of hospital, there were still tablets and capsules: there were red ones and blue ones, and white ones and yellow ones, an entire armoury of mental analgesics. My mother was my devoted armourer.

'But I don't understand,' Alice said. 'Even if Esmond had spiked the cocoa, he couldn't have been sure my mother would have been in a fit state to write him a cheque.'

'But she would have been in the morning.'

'In the morning she could have gone to the police or someone.'

'And said what? She couldn't have proved anything. Even if they found traces of LSD, she might have taken it herself.' I paused. 'I think Esmond must have thought of all this. Sooner or later, Lilian would have written him that cheque. Because otherwise he'd have slipped her another dose when she wasn't looking. He might even have threatened to give you one.'

'You can't be sure . . .'

'No. Because Lilian's dead. Only Esmond knows what he said to her in there. Only Esmond knows what he planned to do.'

Alice looked at me. Her eyes were bright. 'I can't believe it. I can't believe anyone could be so cruel.'

'You have to,' I said. 'For your sake you must. For your baby's sake.'

She looked away. 'What happened to you?'

'After a while they said I could go back to work. That helped a little. And my mother and the pills made it seem that neither of the others had ever existed, not as you and I exist. I began to feel that Lilian and Esmond were not quite real. That it had always been just the two of us.'

'And what about me?'

'My mother and Aunt Ada saw to that. To you, I mean. I know they gave me something to sign. My mother said she couldn't cope with a baby, and nor could I. This was just before she died. She said it seemed like the hand of providence, that Henry and Doris couldn't have children, and that they wanted you. And

Henry was a sort of relation. It was a question of trying to do what was best for you, and indeed for everyone else.'

I paused, waiting for Alice to speak; waiting, I suppose, for a form of absolution. None came.

'I'm sorry,' I said. 'Do you mind?'

'Why should I mind? And what would it matter if I did? What use would it be?'

'What will you do?'

Alice raised her head. 'I have to think of the baby. Like my mother did.'

'I understand.'

'I'd better leave.'

'But I want this to be your home,' I said. 'Yours and the baby's.'

'So do I, but not with Esmond around. He's made it quite clear, hasn't he? It's him or me.'

Alice stood up. She walked slowly across the nursery. She was a big, long-legged girl – a fine physical specimen, as was Esmond. She towered over me on the window-seat.

'Why don't you just tell them to go?' she murmured.

'Because it wouldn't be that simple,' I said. 'Don't you see, with Esmond it never is.'

'You mean he wouldn't go? Then we'd phone the police.'

'He would be back. Next week, next month, next year. This is a lonely house. There are no neighbours. He would be angry, too.'

'But we can't let him get away with it.'

'In my limited experience, you can get away with quite a lot,' I said, looking at my hands. 'So long as you're ready to be a little bit more ruthless than the next person.'

She sighed. 'I have to think of the baby,' she repeated. 'I'm going to phone for a taxi.'

'You're leaving now?'

'It's best. And on Monday I'm going to see a lawyer. Why don't you come with me?'

'Oh, I couldn't do that.'

'Why not? It would be so much better if we acted together.'

I looked out of the rain-streaked window at the twilight world beyond. The afternoon was almost over. We must have been up here for hours. I wondered what Esmond would be thinking and what he had been doing with Bronwen in their bedroom. Night was coming, and I was afraid.

'Why not?' she demanded again.

Because it would not be pleasant. Because Finisterre was my home. Because this business was private and I did not want outsiders poking their noses in it. Because it would be foolish to jump out of the frying pan into the fire. Because of second thoughts and third thoughts.

'It's such a big step,' I said. 'I'd have to think about it.'

Her mouth tightened. Then she said, 'Is it OK if I use the phone in the study? Will you come with me?'

On the landing she hesitated only for an instant before moving towards the head of the stairs. My daughter had courage. We were halfway down when Esmond came out of the kitchen; he was laughing at something that Bronwen was saying behind him. As he closed the door, he looked up and saw us. The laughter stopped.

'Careful,' he said, switching on the light.

'What?' I said. 'Why?'

'Bronwen nearly tripped this morning.' He smiled up at us. 'Could have been quite a nasty fall.'

Trip, I thought. *Fall*. 'Why did she trip?'

'I don't know. You know what she's like first thing – barely half-awake. But we'd better check the stair carpet isn't coming loose again.'

I looked back. The carpet was at least twenty years old. I remember Mr Jodson tacking it in place and grumbling because the new carpet was too wide to be retained by the stair rods we had used before. But to my knowledge it had never come loose.

'Better safe than sorry, eh?' Esmond said. 'Particularly in your delicate condition.'

Alice went down the rest of the flight with her hand on the rail. 'I'd like to use the phone.'

'Be our guest.' Esmond glanced at me and smiled. 'Or rather Thomas's guest if we're going to get technical about it.'

'I want a taxi to take me to Exeter this evening.'

'Eh?' Esmond looked flabbergasted: that is to say, he looked like a person miming astonishment and sorrow; his reaction was almost insultingly out of scale with its cause. 'But why on earth do you want to leave today? We hoped you'd be staying over the weekend at least.'

'I need to get back. I . . . I have someone to meet. I forgot.'

'That's a pity – isn't it, Thomas? Just as we were all getting to know each other.'

'I'm sorry.'

'Can't be helped.' Esmond stood aside to let her pass. 'But you'll be back, won't you?'

'I hope so,' Alice said. 'I really do.'

'Next time you mustn't leave it so long.' He followed her down the hall and opened the study door for her. 'I haven't called a local taxi-service for years. Thomas, your mother must have used taxis after she got rid of the car. Was there a particular firm?'

'Ah – I'm not sure.' I turned on the light. 'I think there was someone in Kinghampton.'

Esmond came into the room and picked up the Yellow Pages, which were kept with the other directories on the top of the cupboard. 'Let me see. Finbury, James? Micron Mini-Cabs? R.T. Taxis?'

'It was Mr Finbury,' I said. 'My mother liked him because he hated trade unions.' And he also hated Roman Catholics, civil servants, sex before marriage, tourists and foreigners of any description, especially those with black skins.

Alice picked up the phone. 'What's the number?'

'Nine-eight-three –'

'The phone's dead,' she said.

Rain rattled on the window. I looked up, startled, and saw my own face, pale and distorted, staring at me. The glass was a dark mirror; night had come prematurely.

'Let me try.'

Esmond took the handset from her. Their hands touched, and she jerked hers away.

'Dead as a doornail,' he said. 'The line must be down. It's this damned storm.'

'How long will it take to repair?'

'I don't know. I don't even know where the fault is.

For all we know, the whole village is cut off. Let's hope so, eh? If that's the case they'll probably sort it out sooner than they will if it's just us.'

'What about the car?' Alice said. 'Can you take me into Kinghampton? Would you mind?'

'Of course I wouldn't mind. But it's broken down, if you remember.'

'I thought you were going to phone someone.'

'The garage said they'd send someone today. But he hasn't come yet. I imagine they're up to their necks in emergency call-outs. I was just about to give them another ring when you came downstairs.'

'Could you mend the car yourself?' I asked.

'I could try. In the morning. If this rain goes on, we won't be able to get up the lane even if I could mend the car.'

'Why not?' Alice moved round the desk to stand near me.

'Bronwen was listening to the local radio station. There's been a lot of flooding already. In this sort of weather, you're better off under a roof. Is your meeting that urgent?' There was only concern in his voice, not a hint of mockery.

Alice nodded.

'Look, when is it?' Esmond asked. 'If it's in the afternoon you may still be OK.'

'Yes. Here's hoping.'

'What can't be cured must be endured.' He grinned at us. 'That's what the old bags used to say, didn't they? I'm just going to put up the storm shutters. There's no point in leaving it any longer. Bronwen's got some tea on the go if you're interested.'

He left the room. I heard the kitchen door opening and closing.

'The old bags?' Alice whispered as she went into the hall.

'My mother and Aunt Ada.'

'Sometimes I feel so stupid,' she said. 'I could be imagining the whole thing.'

'You didn't imagine what Esmond said to you this morning.'

'No. But I might have interpreted it wrongly. I might have –'

The kitchen door opened.

'Tea, anyone?' Bronwen said. There was something hatefully sleek about her, like a well-fed cat.

Alice wanted to go upstairs for a moment. I sat down at the kitchen table. Bronwen poured tea for us and took the chair opposite mine. We were alone – hanging the storm shutters on the seaward windows was a time-consuming job.

'The wind's worse,' she said with satisfaction. 'We could get trees down by the morning. What's this about Alice going?'

'I think she feels a bit uncomfortable,' I said. 'And she's got a meeting tomorrow afternoon.'

'Business meeting, is it?'

She didn't trouble to conceal her disbelief, any more than my mother had done when Aunt Imogen had attempted to explain her husband's absences.

'I'm not sure,' I said.

'And why's she uncomfortable here?' Bronwen reached for Esmond's cigarettes, which were on the table. 'Is the service not what she's accustomed to?'

She slotted a cigarette between her lips and struck a match.

'You'd better ask Esmond.'

Seconds slipped by. I drank some tea. I heard a lavatory flushing upstairs. The flame crept towards Bronwen's finger and thumb. She blew it out just in time, and dropped the blackened and twisted match on the scrubbed pine table.

'What do you mean, *ask Esmond?*' Her hand shot out and pinioned my wrist to the table.

'I didn't mean to say anything. Just forget it. Please.'

Her fingers tightened. They were rough-skinned and ingrained with tiny flecks of dirt; a gardener's fingers are never entirely clean. I tried to pull my hand away. Tears filled my eyes.

'Come on. Spit it out!'

'He told her – that you and he – aren't properly married.'

She hit me on the cheek lightly with the back of her other hand. She still had the cigarette in her mouth, and when she spoke it made her mouth lopsided, as though she had suffered a stroke.

'You're a liar,' she mumbled. 'Know what your problem is, Rumpy? You're jealous.'

I bowed my head. 'But I'm only telling you what Alice told me. That's why she ran into the garden this morning. Surely you must have noticed that something was wrong?'

The fire went out of her. I think she was remembering the events of the morning and reinterpreting them. She let go of my wrist.

'Well . . .' she said. 'I think . . . Hang on.'

She struck a second match, lit the cigarette and dropped both used matches one by one into the ashtray. She inhaled twice and tried prematurely to tap ash from the end of the cigarette. Her inability to remove any ash seemed to disturb her. She scraped the glowing end of the cigarette against the lip of the ashtray until at last she got rid of a few flakes like grey dandruff. This success appeared to give her inspiration.

'Well, maybe he did say something like that. Nothing to get excited about, is it? It's a common-law marriage, no one's saying any different.' Her voice had become as gentle and persuasive as nature would allow, which was only to be expected because she was trying very hard to convince one or both of us of the truth of what she was saying. 'Maybe it just slipped out when they were talking about something else. Like Alice's marriage, for instance. If she really was married.'

'When she ran outside, she was running away.'

'From Esmond? Oh, bullshit.'

The hall door opened. Alice came in.

'Why don't you ask her?' I went on. 'Ask her why she was running away. Ask her exactly what Esmond had in mind. Ask her what he did as well as what he said.'

'Well?' Bronwen said. 'You heard. What's it all about? Has my husband been making a pass at you?'

Alice coloured. She said nothing.

Bronwen pushed back her chair and stood up. 'Come on, I've got a right to know, haven't I?'

'I'm sorry,' Alice said. 'It was nothing to do with me, I promise. I – I left something upstairs.'

She turned and stumbled out of the room.

'I'm sorry too,' I said, wishing this hideously un-pleasant business was over. 'But you see now why she wants to go.'

'Maybe she's a liar too,' Bronwen whispered.

There were footsteps marching down the hall. Some-one was whistling 'Tom Tom, the piper's son'. I finished my tea and stood up.

'Here's Esmond,' I said. 'Why don't you ask him?'

'This house is a prison,' Alice whispered.

As she was speaking the lights went out. It was after supper and she was alone with me in the nursery; our excuse was that we were searching for an anthology of sea verse that had once belonged to her mother.

A sudden darkness frightens me. It is as if someone has cast a spell to make me blind. Alice's hand touched my arm. I shied away, though I knew the touch could only come from her. We were crouching in front of one of the bookcases.

'Now what?' she said, still whispering.

'I don't know.'

'Don't laugh but I'm frightened. Have you got a torch? Candles?'

'Not in here. In the kitchen.'

'Matches, even?'

'Sorry.'

She found my hand and gripped it. 'I hate the dark-ness,' she said. 'It's like a prison.'

'This is a prison anyway. You were right.'

The outer doors were locked, deadlocked and bolted. There were shutters on some windows and locks on almost all; on my window there were bars. Esmond had the keys. Even if one could get outside the house, the gale itself was another form of prison. Esmond had said that he could barely walk upright outside, that there was a torrent gushing down the lane and that at least two of the trees on the windbreak had come down. And of course the car had broken down – according to Esmond.

'I wonder if the phone's working now,' Alice said. 'Oh, God. I keep telling myself how stupid it is to feel scared.'

'Listen,' I whispered urgently. 'You know Esmond's air gun in the cupboard in the study? Before supper, I found some pellets for it. I put them in the cupboard with the gun.'

'So what?' Fear made her sound petulant. 'Are you trying to make a fool of me?'

'You could always have the gun in your room tonight. It might make you feel more comfortable.'

'What good would that do? It's just a toy.'

'You'd be surprised.'

'Anyway, I don't think I –'

The lights came on. Alice and I blinked at each other. She snatched her hand away from my sleeve and stood up. I felt foolish, as one does when the lights come on; the private fears that flourish in darkness seem pathetic when divorced from their natural habitat.

In the distance, a door slammed. In the kitchen, perhaps, or the sitting room – somewhere downstairs. If you slammed one of the interior doors at Finisterre the whole house vibrated.

'Just piss off, will you?' Bronwen screamed. 'You double-crossing bastard! You two-timing shit!'

I heard Esmond's footsteps on the stairs. Alice

picked out a book and pretended to be examining it. A moment later Esmond lumbered into the nursery. He was breathing hard and his face was more flushed than usual. In his left hand was a big torch. Tight-lipped, he stood in the doorway and looked from Alice to me.

'I want a word with you,' he said.

'One or both?' Alice said.

'Just Thomas. So if you don't mind?'

He held the door open and raised his eyebrows at Alice. She glanced anxiously at me and moved slowly out of the room. I wondered whether the anxiety was on my behalf or hers. Esmond shut the door behind her. He stared round the room. His eyes returned to me: they slid down from my head to my feet. There was no kindness in his face.

'What is it?' My mouth was dry, and I ran out of breath before I had finished the sentence.

He said nothing. But his eyes returned to my face. He had been drinking heavily that evening but I don't think he was drunk yet, though it had already affected his movements. He walked to the fireplace and stood the torch on the mantelpiece.

'All for one,' he said slowly. 'One for all. Christ, that's a joke, isn't it?'

'Oh – is it?'

'You should know.' He came towards me and lowered his head until our faces were no more than six inches apart. 'Tell me now. What possessed you to tell Bronwen?'

'What about?'

'Don't mess about.'

'About what you said to Alice?'

379

He nodded, and his whole body swayed to and fro, to and fro. His eyes were bloodshot. I heard footsteps on the stairs.

'Isn't that Bronwen coming up?' I asked.

'Don't try and change the subject. Look at me. Why did you tell her about Alice?'

'She wormed it out of me, I suppose.'

'Oh yes. Bronwen's good at worming.' He prodded me in the chest with his forefinger. 'And good with worms, eh?'

'But I hardly told her anything. I –'

'And how do you know what I said to Alice in the first place? Listening at the door?'

'No, of course not. Alice told me in the garden.'

As I was talking, I heard a thud from the landing. Esmond appeared not to notice.

'You're getting very friendly with your daughter, aren't you?' he said. 'So she came to cry on Daddy's shoulder. How touching. Blood is thicker than water. How bloody sick-making. Where will this end, eh?'

'It wasn't like that. All she did was give me an idea of what you'd suggested.'

'Do you know what I think?' Esmond seized my shoulders and swung me round so that I had my back to the window. 'This is all your fault. If I thought you were capable of it, I'd say you were deliberately trying to sabotage everything.'

'Please, Esmond, I'd never –'

He cut me off by placing his right hand on my chest with the thumb and forefinger curving round the front of my neck. For an instant he said nothing. The wires hummed as though they were swaying in a great wind.

I heard another noise from the landing – a scraping sound, as though someone was dragging a heavy object across the floor.

'But let's assume you are capable. Just for the hell of it, eh? If you were, I'd wonder why you were trying to screw things up, wouldn't I?' Still talking, he pushed me slowly backwards. 'It's never wise to underestimate little Thomas, is it? Quite a lot of people have done that in the past. And look where it got them, one way or another.'

'Esmond, I promise –'

'I don't want your promises.'

From the landing came the sound of breaking glass. He let go of my neck, strode across the nursery and opened the door.

'Oh, *Christ.*'

I followed him to the doorway and peered over his shoulder at the landing. Esmond's clothes and shoes had been scattered in a ragged arc across the floor. I saw a hairbrush, a razor, a tube of toothpaste and a whisky bottle lying on its side. The light glinted on a heap of broken glass beside a large blue suitcase, open and upside down.

The door of the death room was open a few inches; I thought I glimpsed movement in the crack. Then I was distracted by Bronwen, who suddenly appeared in the doorway of the room she shared with Esmond. She flung half a dozen fat paperbacks on to the heap.

'I don't want your crap in my bedroom,' she said.

'It's my bedroom, too.'

'No, it's not, ducky. Haven't you got that yet? It's Thomas's while he's alive, and then it's Alice's.'

'So what are you going to do? Spend the rest of your life in there?'

'Don't be stupid. Tomorrow I'm going back to London.'

Esmond moved towards her. 'Look, I know you're upset.'

'Oh you've noticed, have you?'

'And I understand why. But can't we talk about it?'

He held out his hand. She recoiled.

'If you ever touch me again,' she said, 'I'll kill you.'

She shut the door in his face. A second later, I heard a click as Alice closed her door.

'Ah shit,' Esmond said. He turned back to me, and his face was full of hatred. 'This is all your fault.'

'Do you think she means it?'

'About killing me? Don't be stupid. She'll come round in time. But it's no thanks to you, is it?'

I retreated to the nursery. He followed me. Once inside he shut the door and slowly advanced towards me. Step for step, I moved backwards.

I knew that I must do nothing to anger him further. With Esmond, meekness was often the best policy. *The meek shall inherit the earth.* I remember Aunt Ada telling us so in Sunday School; once a year, she devoted a session to the Beatitudes. On this occasion, Esmond asked her if that meant the strong would inherit the rest of the universe; if so, he implied, he would happily forgo his claim to the earth. But as we age, our desires shrink. Esmond no longer wanted the rest of the universe. He was as earthbound as the rest of us.

'When I think of all I've done for you, it makes me want to puke,' he said. 'Really – I feel physically sick.

Half this is mine, you know. Half of everything. Your mother promised. And you owe it to me.'

'Yes, I know,' I said. 'But I had nothing to do with her changing her will. I told you. I think she must have known that what's mine would be yours.'

The back of my legs hit the window-seat. I sat down unexpectedly.

'Oh, I believe that.' Esmond took my chin and forced me to look at him. 'Up to a point, that is. But now you've met Alice and everything's changed. Well, that's what you think. But you're wrong.'

'What are you trying to do to her?'

'What do you mean?'

'Taking the keys away. And there were wet footprints in the garage this morning. Did you do something to the engine so it wouldn't start? And the phone . . .'

He waved his free hand. 'All right. You don't have to go on.'

'And the electricity?'

'You can put that one down to providence, like the gale.'

'You're trying to frighten her, aren't you? To stop her being awkward. Just like you did with Lilian.'

'I didn't give Lilian the acid, though, did I?' he said. 'I thought it was just a flashback until they sprung it on me at the trial.'

'She – she might have taken it herself.'

'Crap. And you know it. You gave it to her, didn't you?'

'I did it for you,' I said. 'I was trying to be helpful.'

'Were you being helpful before? When Lizzy died? Because Lizzy dying meant I'd stay at Finisterre?'

I said nothing.

'I didn't see you do it,' he said. 'I heard you going into the death room. I didn't realize what was happening until afterwards. You put a pillow over her head, didn't you?'

The wires whined, much more harshly than before: they made what was almost a buzzing noise, not unlike the sound of Bronwen's chain saw. My head ached and ached. If only, I thought, if only I knew a spell to make everything pleasant again.

'And I didn't tell anyone that you spiked Lilian's cocoa,' Esmond continued. 'All for one and one for all. Ain't I the little gentleman? Not that it would have helped me much. After all, I couldn't have proved it. But the main reason I kept quiet, then and before, was because I reckoned you'd done it for me.'

'I did. I did. I did.'

'But naturally I was fooling myself. In the end, you did it for you. You do everything for you, don't you, Rumpy?'

'It's not true.'

'You wanted me with you as you want to live in this house. You're a sort of parasite, eh? The house and I are your host organism.'

He let go of my chin and lit a cigarette. He moved restlessly around the nursery. I stayed on the window-seat.

'And now,' he said softly, 'it's almost as if you've changed your mind. You still want Finisterre. But you're not so sure about me. You don't want us to sell the house. And Bronwen does get in the way, doesn't she? Maybe it would be nicer to live with Alice, eh? More comfortable for you.'

'No – really – you're imagining –'

'I hope so. Loyalties take years to build. Did you know that? And you can't tear them down in a couple of days, can you, not without leaving a scar.'

He paused; I nodded.

'So it's still you and me, Rumpy, it's still all for one and one for all?'

'Of course it is,' I said. 'It always will be.'

'If you had to choose between me and living in this house, which would you choose?'

'You,' I said. 'Every time. I promise.'

'Then prove it.'

'What do you want me to do?'

'Just listen and let me tell your fortune,' Esmond said. 'You can cross my palm with silver afterwards. Somehow you're going to persuade Alice to agree to our selling this white elephant. Even more importantly, you're going to persuade her to bugger off out of our lives. Am I making sense?'

'Yes, of course. But how?'

'You'll find a way.'

'I'll try my best. Perhaps in time . . .'

'And if by any chance you fail to persuade her, there's always other ways of achieving the same end. Aren't there?'

'I don't know what you mean.'

'Try harder. You're the one with the imagination.'

He stubbed out his cigarette and picked up his torch from the mantelpiece. As he walked towards the door, the wires sang higher and higher, and this time the scraping sound they made reminded me of courting cats. In my mind I saw Grimalkin lying on the dark blue hearthrug in the sitting room. She looked almost undamaged from above but my mother had had to throw away the rug. If a pellet goes right through its target, the entry hole tends to be small and neat, but the exit hole is large and irregular.

Esmond paused in the doorway, and his voice whispered across the nursery to me on the window-seat. 'Oh, and one other thing, Rumpy, and this is quite apart from the rights and wrongs of what you owe me. Don't forget that you need me. You need me to look after you.'

It was the last thing he said to me. As he finished speaking, the lights flickered and went out again.

Twenty-One

The screams woke me, just as they had done before.

I lay with my eyes closed in the borderland between waking and sleeping. The wires were no longer singing but I felt sad and confused. Nothing could ever be the same again. I knew that without knowing why. For a few seconds the years vanished, and I was a child wrenched out of a deep sleep. I heard Aunt Imogen screaming and sobbing at the same time. Once again I realized for the first and worst time you can never go back.

I opened my eyes and saw light on the other side of the barred window. This was not the middle of the night but the morning of Sunday the 6th October. Alice, not baby Lizzy, should be in the death room. I sat up, dislodging the quilt, and reached for my dressing-gown. I had not drawn the curtains last night. Outside the window there were patches of blue sky and white, wispy clouds. The gale had blown itself away.

Meanwhile the screams continued. They were dreadfully unpleasant. I looked for my slippers under the bed. There was a tap on my door and it opened a few inches.

Alice poked her head through the gap. 'It's Bronwen,' she said; the screams were so loud that she had to raise her voice. 'I think you'd better come.'

I put my feet into my slippers and stood up. 'Where is she?'

'Downstairs.'

All the bedroom doors were open. I glanced into the little room over the porch. Esmond's belongings lay in a heap on the floor. The bed was made. I padded after Alice across the landing.

She was wearing her white nightdress, its thick cotton much creased. Her hair was unbrushed, and parts of it stood up in tufts. She looked warm and had a sweet and sour smell, as people often do when they waken from a long sleep. On the stairs she remembered to hold on to the rail and not to hurry.

Bronwen was in the hall near the door to the sitting room. She was crouching, her arms round her knees, and leaning against the wall. She wore a red towelling dressing-gown and, I think, nothing else. She had been sick. When she saw us approaching she stopped screaming. But she panted, greedy for air, and rocked gently to and fro. Her mouth hung open. Her lips glistened with spittle. She looked at us with huge, puzzled eyes.

'What's happened?' Alice said. 'What's wrong?'

I went past them. The sitting-room door was ajar. I pushed it wide open.

'That's what's wrong,' I said.

From the doorway you could see the big armchair Esmond liked to use. He sprawled in it: his back curved; knees apart; round-shouldered; chin resting on chest; and hands palm-upwards on his thighs. His body was slightly askew in the chair and he looked most uncomfortable: it was as if he had tried to get to his feet, failed and fallen back. He was still dressed in the clothes he had worn yesterday – the dapper blazer and the grey flannel trousers so suitable for lunch in the restaurant of The Mermaid Hotel. Now there was ash on the blazer and a dark stain on the crotch of the trousers.

The only light in the room came from the standard lamp behind the chair. The windows were still shuttered and curtained.

I moved very slowly towards him. It seemed important to move quietly, making as little disturbance as possible, as a well-disposed unbeliever does in a strange church.

'Is he – is he all right?' Alice said behind me.

We ask so many questions whose answers we already know. She followed me into the room. Bronwen stayed where she was, sucking in the air.

What should I do, I thought, to seem normal? How do people act?

Beside the armchair was a table on which stood a bottle, almost empty, and a glass which still had a little whisky in it. There was also the torch, an ashtray, a packet of cigarettes and a box of matches. There were three butts in the ashtray. The grey remnant of an almost-complete cigarette was attached to one of the filters. The only other item on the table was a small round tin with a blue lid, on which was a line drawing of a wasp.

The air in the sitting room was stuffy. The smell of yesterday's cigarettes was familiar, but not the underlying whiff of a lavatory in need of cleaning.

'Look, there's a gun,' Alice whispered.

The BSA air gun lay with its barrel between Esmond's legs and its butt resting on the carpet. The woodwork looked as if it had been polished, and even the metal had a dull sheen.

'I suppose we shouldn't touch anything,' she said.

I knelt down by the chair. I touched one of Esmond's hands. 'Feel it,' I said. 'It's cold as ice. Colder.' Then at last I looked into his face. It was like one of those faces in dreams: when, for example, you see your mother from behind – and then your mother turns and stares through you, and she has the face of a hostile stranger.

Esmond's mouth was open. So were the eyes. From a small puncture in the right-hand eyeball there oozed a greasy trail of blood mingled with a straw-coloured liquid, the aqueous humour from the chamber of the eye. The trail ran like a long and solitary tear down his cheek and neck until it disappeared beneath his collar. The red and yellow streaks had set on the skin, as wax or soap sets when it cools.

Alice touched the hand. I heard her swallow twice. 'He's freezing,' she said. 'He must have been like this for hours. Is it the air rifle you told me about?'

'Yes. You didn't take it last night?'

'Of course not.'

'I wish you had.'

'What do you mean?'

I stood up and moved away from the body. My legs trembled. I had to sit down on the sofa. Esmond had gone away again, and this time he had left me for ever. Such finality was difficult to grasp. In my mind I tried to catch this absolute fact and it danced away from me like a butterfly. Esmond wasn't in London or in jail. This absence was different from all the others. He didn't exist any more.

'What do you mean?' Alice said again, and I knew that it was important to answer her.

Lizzy and Lilian, my mother and now Esmond: you would think it would get easier to cope with people dying, not harder. Perhaps it only seemed harder to cope because it was Esmond who was dead. Esmond was always special; he always had to do things differently from everyone else.

I turned my head towards the door. Bronwen was leaning against the jamb. Alice sat down beside me on the sofa and took my hand.

'If you had taken the gun,' I said to her, 'Esmond wouldn't have been able to find it in the cupboard.'

'But how was I to know?' she said defensively, though I had accused her of nothing.

'Esmond wouldn't kill himself,' Bronwen said. '*Never*.'

'Wouldn't he?' I said.

'Why should he?'

'I suppose he hadn't much left to live for. In a way we'd each of us rejected him. Also,' I nodded at the whisky – 'he was probably very drunk.'

'He isn't the type,' Bronwen said.

'Wasn't,' Alice whispered.

I let go of her hand and rubbed my eyes. 'Then it must have been an accident.'

'Christ, can't we stop him looking at us?' Bronwen said.

'We could cover his face,' I said. 'Or go into another room.'

Neither of the women moved.

Bronwen went on, 'He wouldn't load a gun, point it at his eye and pull the trigger. People don't do that sort of thing by accident. Esmond may have been drunk but he wasn't stupid.'

'Then what do you think happened?' Alice said.

'One of you ... He was sleeping in the chair. He didn't have a chance. He – he –' Bronwen began to gasp. She beat the air with her hands. It was as though there were an invisible creature at her throat.

'Can we get you some water?' Alice asked.

'No. One of you came in and pointed that – that thing in his eye.'

'But why, Bronwen? Why should Thomas or I want to kill him?'

'Because you were scared of him. The pair of you. You were scared of what he'd do.'

'This is England, not the Wild West. Anyway, why should we?'

'Thomas owed him. That's what Esmond always said.'

'If anything, it was the other way round. You and Esmond are Thomas's guests. So am I, for that matter.'

'You're twisting everything.'

'Let's face it,' Alice said gently, 'the only person who had reason to kill Esmond was you. Thomas and I both heard what you said to him last night.'

'Bitch.'

'Bronwen, I'm not saying you did kill him. Of course you didn't.'

'A crime of passion?' I murmured. 'That's how they'd see it – in the circumstances.'

'We'd better find out if the phone's working,' Alice said, standing up. 'We need to get a doctor. And the police, I suppose.'

But she didn't move to the door. She was waiting. So was I.

'Oh Christ.' Bronwen shivered. 'God knows what was going on in his mind. He was very upset. The poor bastard.' The tears dribbled down her cheeks. 'Maybe he just couldn't handle it. I just don't know. I don't know anything. I suppose he must have killed himself.'

'Yes,' I said. 'Definitely suicide. Poor Esmond.'

Bronwen sat down on the floor. She put her head in her hands.

I got up and followed Alice into the study. The cupboard doors were open. Alice stood by the desk and glanced expectantly at me. I picked up the phone. I heard the dialling tone. The digits fluttered before my eyes. I felt very cold. The cold was making me shiver. I cannot think properly when I am cold.

'Would you like me to do it?' Alice said.

'Please. Would you mind?'

'Don't worry. Leave it to me.' She took the handset away from me. 'Why don't you sit down? You've had a shock.'

I sat behind the desk. Alice tapped out a number. As she waited for someone to answer the phone, she smiled at me and stroked the palm of her hand down her belly. Her upper lip rose, exposing her front teeth and giving her a fleeting resemblance to my mother and Aunt Imogen. But you can never go back, can you?

If you enjoyed *The Barred Window* look out for:

The Raven on the Water

Andrew Taylor

Back in 1964, in the wild and overgrown garden of a Somerset vicarage, Peter Redburn and his best friend Richard had spent a golden summer holiday playing out their special game – a private world of secret rituals and oaths of loyalty.

But the boys' peace was suddenly threatened when an unwelcome new playmate introduced sinister elements of a mystical religion into their innocent game. Then, one terrible night, the childish dreamworld turned into a nightmare . . .

'Like Hitchcock, Taylor pitches extreme and gothic events within a hair's breadth of normality' *The Times Literary Supplement*

(Available from Penguin at £6.99)

READ ON FOR A TASTER . . .

One

She knew what she wanted to do was wrong.

Not really wrong. Not a sin. Not the sort of thing she would have to confess to Father Molland at St Clement's on Wednesday afternoon. After Mr Coleby's visit, she needed the relief it would give her.

John had asked her not to go up to the loft. But he hadn't forbidden her.

'Please, Lucasta,' he'd said. 'Just for me.'

'I'm not an invalid.'

'Yes, I know, dearest. But it's a heavy ladder, and you'd have to lug it all the way upstairs.'

'I'd be very careful.'

'You might slip off the stepladder. Lifting the hatch is rather tricky even for me.' He ran his finger down the nape of her neck. 'And then you'd have to haul yourself into the loft. Once you get there, it's a minefield. It hasn't even got a proper floor. You could trap a foot between the joists or something.'

'But it's such a mess,' she said. 'I'd like to sort things out before baby arrives.'

He knelt down beside her chair. His face was only inches away from hers. His concern warmed her.

'The nesting instinct?' he said. 'But seriously – if you had an accident when I was at school, you might lie there for hours. It's not as if people are popping in and out of the house all day.'

No, this was their home; they didn't want strangers to disturb them at 29 Champney Road. That was the way it would always be. For ever and ever. Amen.

All right, dear John didn't like her going up to the loft, especially when he was out of the house. She would never disobey him; she had promised. But he hadn't actually made it an order. In any case, when they had talked about it, the circumstances had been different. At the time she had had Peter in her tummy and a fall could have had serious consequences for both herself and the unborn baby.

John was very late this evening. It had been dark for hours. In term time he worked all the hours God gave. The school didn't appreciate his dedication. She wished he would come home. She wished he had been here when that unpleasant Mr Coleby had called. Dealing with people like Mr Coleby was a man's job. John would have known exactly what to say to him.

Mr Coleby was clever. He always came when John was at school. She had been expecting Hubert Molland with the parish magazine, which was why she had answered the door.

Mr Coleby was standing right on the step. His big brown car was parked beneath the streetlamp on the road. As she opened the door, he leaned forwards. She stepped back. Too late, she realized her mistake. He was in the house. Flecks of rain sparkled on the shoulders of his navy-blue overcoat.

Mr Coleby had a loud Fen voice with broad vowels that grated on her ears. She was afraid that he would wake Peter if she talked to him in the hall. She retreated to the sitting room. He followed. He was a big man with a square red face. The room was small and so was she; Mr Coleby was out of scale. He took up too much space, like a baby cuckoo in someone else's nest.

'Well, Mrs Redburn,' he said. 'I wondered if you'd reconsidered your position.'

She shook her head. She sat down to conceal the fact that she was trembling.

Mr Coleby sighed. 'It would be nice to get something settled by Christmas.'

Lucasta stared at the pile of library books on the table. 'There's nothing to settle.'

'Now, be reasonable.'

'Your reasons,' she said. 'Not mine.'

'You won't get a better offer.'

'Sorry. Not interested.'

He moved to the bay window, parted the curtains and looked out on Champney Road.

'It's a funny area, isn't it?' he said. 'I reckon you'd be happier somewhere like Locksley Gardens or Ivanhoe Drive.'

'I'm quite happy here, thank you,' Lucasta said.

However, she understood what he meant. Hubert Molland had said as much the other day. Champney Road was on the east side of Plumford. Here were the factories, the council estates and – just a few yards beyond the Redburns' back garden – the railway. Most of John's colleagues lived to the west of the town centre in a suburb where the professional classes clustered in a grid of tree-lined streets with names taken from the works of Sir Walter Scott.

'Not much of a house, either. Don't you find it dark?

A bit depressing? Needs a lot of work done to it. Anyone can see that.'

She shrugged. Money was tight, especially since Peter's arrival. She didn't think the house was dark. True, it faced north, but you got used to that. Number 29 was their home.

'You're quite isolated, too. Not even a telephone.' Mr Coleby peered into the darkness on either side of the streetlamp. 'Big hedge in front – needs a trim, that does. A blank wall the height of a house on your right. Can't say I'd like to live next to a bakery. And on the other side you've got all those trees on the strip of wasteland. My wasteland now. You must find it quite worrying.' He turned, slowly, and stared at her. 'Seeing as you're on your own for so much of the time.'

The little room filled with menace. It hung like a haze and obscured the outlines of the furniture. Mr Coleby was a huge shadow. His face dissolved. Only his eyes were as crisply defined as before: cold, clear and blue.

If only John were here. Lucasta touched her breast. It was full of milk. The knowledge steadied her. Peter was still feeding from her, and would continue to do so for months. She had to be strong.

The haze cleared.

'I'm afraid you're wasting your time, Mr Coleby.'

'Am I?' He raised his eyebrows. 'Why don't you have another little think about it? It's a big decision – I know that. You've got to look at all the angles.'

'The decision's already –'

'Like, for example, what happens if you have an accident when you're alone in the house? Or if there's a fire in the night? Or if some of the local yobbos come round in search of beer money or a bit of fun?'

Deliver me from evil, she thought. For Thine is the kingdom, the power and the glory.

'You're threatening me.'

'Me?' He chuckled. 'That's a good one. Just trying to help, Mrs Redburn, that's all. You know me. Anyway, I mustn't keep you. Don't bother – I can find my own way out. I'll be in touch.'

Mr Coleby's footsteps echoed in the uncarpeted hall. She hoped that they wouldn't wake Peter. She heard him open and close the front door. The latch on the front gate clicked. She went to the window. A moment later the big brown car pulled away from the kerb.

Lucasta went into the hall. She was tempted to bolt the door. But if she did that John wouldn't be able to let himself in with his key. She never used the bolts when John was out. *Hurry home, John.*

She listened at the bottom of the stairs. All was quiet, which was a blessing. Peter had only just begun to go through the night without demanding a feed. Unbroken nights were such a luxury. In the evenings she and John had time to be together.

Gradually the trembling stopped. She tiptoed upstairs and listened outside the door of Peter's room. She didn't dare go in: he was such a light sleeper, and he seemed to know by instinct when his mother was in the same room. She glanced upwards, at the hatch that led to the loft. The temptation was so strong it made her feel breathless.

John wouldn't mind if she went into the loft. He would understand. She would tell him about Mr

Coleby's visit and her going to the loft as soon as he came in.

She crept downstairs, through the kitchen and out into the little back garden. It was much darker on this side of the house. Behind the garden were several acres of rough pasture, which Mr Coleby had bought at the same time as he bought the strip of wasteland that linked the pasture to Champney Road. The railway ran in a cutting along the far boundary of the fields. You couldn't see the trains but you could hear them.

The stepladder was strapped to the outside wall beneath the kitchen window. John had built a little shelter for it; he was so clever with his hands. She undid the straps and carried the ladder into the house. Mindful of what John had said, she stopped to rest – once in the hall, twice on the stairs and once on the landing.

She set up the ladder beneath the hatch. Practice had made perfect: she hardly made a sound. Peter slept on.

Rung by rung, she crept up the ladder. Two-thirds of the way up, she paused to get her breath back before lifting the heavy hatch and sliding it away from the opening. A shower of gritty dust pattered on her face. Try as she might, it was impossible to keep the loft as clean as she would have liked. She climbed higher and at last managed the difficult transition from the top of the ladder to the edge of the hatch frame. She glanced down at the landing and the dizziness swept up to meet her.

'Serves you right, my girl,' she whispered. 'You know you've got no head for heights.'

Lucasta reached through the darkness for the light switch. The loft sprang to life. She sighed with relief.

The loft ran the length of the house from front to back, and it was lit by two unshaded forty-watt bulbs. Down the centre was a narrow gangway; she had placed boards across the joists to make movement easier. On either side of the gangway were neat piles of trunks, cases, cardboard boxes and tea chests – even a bed, propped on its side and wrapped in polythene. Everything was as she had left it. Everything was in apple-pie order.

For a moment she stood listening. Peter was still asleep. She walked slowly down the gangway, her eyes lingering on the treasures she passed. She paused twice. First she lifted the lid of a trunk plastered with the labels of railway companies. The smell of mothballs rose to greet her. She stroked the lapel of one of John's old suits, a Prince of Wales check that he had bought before they even met. She shut the trunk and moved on to a large cardboard box. She eased off the lid. Inside, buried in acid-free tissue paper, was her wedding dress. She closed her eyes and let her fingers burrow through the tissue paper until she felt the lace of the collar.

One day, God willing, she and John might have a daughter; one day their daughter would want to get married. Carefully she replaced the tissue paper and the lid of the box.

Her excitement grew steadily higher. On the left, near the end of the gangway, was a blue suitcase resting on top of a tea chest. John kept the photographs here. Before their marriage he had made quite a hobby of photography. Some photographs were in albums, others in envelopes and folders, and everything was neatly labelled. John was a scientist by training and inclination;

he had a passion for order. It was one of the many characteristics they shared.

She stared at the contents. Spoiled for choice, she thought, like a kid in a sweetshop. She glanced at the framed print of John at the Salpertons' wedding, which was lying on top. John had been best man; he looked so beautiful in morning dress, far more handsome than the groom.

Tonight, because of Mr Coleby's visit and because John was so late, she deserved a treat. She would compare the snaps they'd taken of Peter on the lawn in the summer with the photographs of John as a baby. She delighted in finding resemblances between father and son.

'My two men,' she crooned.

She lifted out the Salperton photograph. Underneath was a team photograph – a schoolboy cricket eleven with John the second from the right in the back row. As she lifted it out, she realized that the backing was beginning to come away from the heavy cream cardboard of the mount. Perhaps the loft was too damp to store photographs. She would have to mention it to John. She examined the edge of the mount. All it needed was a little glue. She would do it this evening. John would be pleased.

The edge of a sheet of paper between the mount and the backing caught her eye. She widened the gap and tried to see what it was. Not the print itself – that was further inside the mount. She gripped the edge of the paper between thumb and forefinger and gently pulled it out.

It was a letter written in blue ink. The handwriting

was small and upright. Lucasta knew instinctively that it belonged to a woman. There was neither date nor address.

Johnny, The doctor agrees, so there's no doubt any longer ...

She read to the end. A mistake – it must be a mistake or a forgery.

Pain stabbed at her chest, twisting like a barbed snake. Lucasta screamed. The pain retreated. The snake was biding its time.

She stumbled down the gangway to the hatch. Sobbing for breath, she lowered herself on to the ladder. For once in her life she left the loft with the lights on and the hatch open. The letter slipped from her hand and fluttered to the landing floor.

John, how could you?

Lucasta pushed open the door of Peter's room and went in. She wanted, more than anything she had ever wanted in her life, to pick up her baby and cuddle him: to feel his warmth, to feel his need for her.

'Peter – wake up. It's Mummy.'

But the cot had gone. In its place was a narrow bed, stripped to its horsehair mattress.

'*My baby –*'

As she screamed, Lucasta remembered that she had lost even Peter. As she remembered, the barbed snake slashed across her breast. The pain radiated across her chest and pierced her neck. The snake wrapped its coils around her. She could no longer breathe.

She fell – first to her knees, then forwards on to her hands. The snake squeezed.

The dim light from the landing shone on her hands, the hands of a woman with breasts full of milk for her baby, with a husband working late at school. They were the last thing that Lucasta Redburn saw. The last thing she felt, apart from the pain, was surprise.

She recognized her wedding ring but nothing else.

The finger joints were inflamed with rheumatoid arthritis. The nails needed trimming. Wrinkles and brown spots disfigured the skin. The hands belonged to a stranger.

ANDREW TAYLOR

A STAIN ON THE SILENCE

You can run from a guilty conscience, but you can't hide . . .

James wasn't much more than a child when he had an affair with Lily. And now, twenty-four years later, Lily confesses to James that their affair led to a daughter, Kate.

And Kate desperately needs her father's help: she's wanted for murder.

But there is no room for murder in James's life. He has a wife, a good job, a nice house in the country . . .

As Kate comes crashing into his world, so she lights the fuse under his ordered life. Because James has also been keeping a secret – a very dark and deadly one . . .

A Stain on the Silence **is an unputdownable psychological thriller that will keep you guessing till the very last page.**

'Told at a cracking pace . . . a very readable, fast-moving thriller'
Spectator

He just wanted a decent book to read …

Not too much to ask, is it? It was in 1935 when Allen Lane, Managing Director of Bodley Head Publishers, stood on a platform at Exeter railway station looking for something good to read on his journey back to London. His choice was limited to popular magazines and poor-quality paperbacks – the same choice faced every day by the vast majority of readers, few of whom could afford hardbacks. Lane's disappointment and subsequent anger at the range of books generally available led him to found a company – and change the world.

'We believed in the existence in this country of a vast reading public for intelligent books at a low price, and staked everything on it'
Sir Allen Lane, 1902–1970, founder of Penguin Books

The quality paperback had arrived – and not just in bookshops. Lane was adamant that his Penguins should appear in chain stores and tobacconists, and should cost no more than a packet of cigarettes.

Reading habits (and cigarette prices) have changed since 1935, but Penguin still believes in publishing the best books for everybody to enjoy. We still believe that good design costs no more than bad design, and we still believe that quality books published passionately and responsibly make the world a better place.

So wherever you see the little bird – whether it's on a piece of prize-winning literary fiction or a celebrity autobiography, political tour de force or historical masterpiece, a serial-killer thriller, reference book, world classic or a piece of pure escapism – you can bet that it represents the very best that the genre has to offer.

Whatever you like to read – trust Penguin.